DREAM FANTASY

Playa Martiánez was a beautiful beach and many people sunned themselves, but it was not as crowded as the other beaches had been.

"Black sand just fascinates me," Caitlin said softly. They had left their clothes in the car and lolled on the beach, with Marty in black swim trunks, his virile, tanned body on display.

Caitlin had selected several swimsuits, but the one she wore was a favorite. She took off her white eyelet smock to reveal a cream-colored top and skirt, both fashioned of alternating petals of watermelon pink and cream. The skimpy top and short skirt made Marty whistle lustily, and a number of male heads turned.

Sitting on the warm, black sand, she took a big bottle of oil from the beach bag and spread it on Marty's body, going to the flesh between his ribs where he was especially sensitive. Washboard abs. Biceps that wouldn't wait. Pectoral muscles that were to die for, she reflected. As the wild juices flowed through her body, she thought: *There ought to be a law*.

"Watch it, woman," he growled. "I don't believe in public ravishing. Or can a man ravish his own wife?"

Caitlin laughed. "You know damn well he can and you better not."

"I'd tell any judge you were asking for it. Okay, love, turn the bottle over to me and I'll do *my* thing."

DREAMS OF ECSTASY

FRANCINE
CRAFT

BET Publications, LLC
http://www.bet.com
http://www.arabesquebooks.com

ARABESQUE BOOKS are published by

BET Publications, LLC
c/o BET BOOKS
One BET Plaza
1900 W Place NE
Washington, DC 20018-1211

All Kensington Titles, Imprints, and Distributed Lines are available at special quantity discounts for bulk purchases for sales promotions, premiums, fund-raising, and educational or institutional use. Special book excerpts or customized printings can also be created to fit specific needs. For details, write or phone the office of the Kensington special sales manager: Kensington Publishing Corp., 850 Third Avenue, New York, NY 10022, attn: Special Sales Department, Phone: 1-800-221-2647.

First Printing: May 2005
10 9 8 7 6 5 4 3 2 1

Printed in the United States of America

To my editor, Demetria Lucas, who is right on the button with everything that adds to readers' enjoyment.

To Dorothy W., a wonderfully savvy lady whose love of life and people shines through everything she does.

Acknowledgments

I always thank June M. Bennett, Charles K. Kanno, and Vivian Fitz Roy for their superb and heartfelt help. You're the best!

Chapter 1

That mid-afternoon in late September, Caitlin Costner stood at her floor-to-ceiling office windows in the art gallery she owned and operated. The September sun filtering through warmed her and she hugged herself, smiling as she thought of her friend, Marty Steele, coming into D.C. the next day to stay a while.

She hadn't let herself realize how lonely she was until she reflected on him. Old friends were like wine, she thought now, better as the relationship aged. She and Marty had so much in common. Her life lay in remembering her beloved dead husband and little boy, and Marty's pain was a feckless and beautiful wife who had betrayed him, broken his heart, then left. They had always been able to help each other.

She smiled again. Tomorrow morning she'd meet Marty at the airport. It felt so good to anticipate his arrival.

Her art gallery was thriving. The Tuskegee Eagles exhibit was a big hit, and the gallery clocked more visitors than ever. Rena, her associate and best friend, came in.

"You look . . ." Rena hesitated for a moment, "well, happier than usual, as if you know something good is going to happen. You're still meeting Marty Steele tomorrow morning?"

"Oh yes. He always gives my spirits a lift."

Rena chuckled. "Hmmm. He's really making a name for himself in the art world. Photos of his paintings make me drool. He's unattached now, and God knows you are. I like the possibilities."

Caitlin shook her head, looking at her best friend with deep affection. She couldn't help noticing the slightly swollen belly that said Rena was two-and-a-half months pregnant. The sharp ache in her heart made her wince.

"The two of you would make a great couple," Rena said gently. "When he was here last year, I thought you were growing closer; then you got cold feet and sent him away."

Caitlin looked at her levelly. "My life is set in comfortable emotional concrete now and I'm happier than I show. Marty and I will always be the best of friends, but anything more . . ."

Rena touched her face. "Somehow I don't think he feels the same. I watched him looking at you when he was here last year, and his were a wannabe lover's eyes."

Caitlin's breath caught. "You've got a vivid imagination. You're so in love with your hubby that you see love everywhere."

Rena stuck to her guns. "I trust my instincts, girlfriend, implicitly."

In D.C., at Eighteenth and K Streets Northwest, Marty Steele leaned forward and stared out the taxi window. The area was an architectural mix of the new and the old. His whole body thrummed with anticipation as he thought of Caitlin. Last summer when he'd been here, she had been the very good friend she'd always been, gently fending off his advances. Lord, she was sweet, but she was closed to any world that didn't hold Sylvan Costner, her late husband, and her son. They were gone, but she couldn't seem to accept that.

Marty sighed and shook his head. He wished he were a magician and could pull her love out of some magical hat. He half closed his eyes. This time he was going to lay loving siege to her rigid defenses. He knew well the depths of her love, knew how giving she could be. He smiled wryly. Yeah, he knew by having watched her with Sylvan and her son. And he, Marty, had been the beggar on the outside, having to make himself content with the beautiful Bianca. He swore now that this time was going to be different. He was enlisting his belief in God and all his angels to make it so.

In front of the gallery, he tipped the driver generously and got out, carrying an overnight bag. His luggage would be sent to Caitlin's house tonight. He thought it would be nice if she put him up for a few days. She'd said on the phone yesterday that she had a surprise for him, and he wondered about it.

Starting up the short flight of steps to the gallery, he found he couldn't stop the grin that tugged at his mouth. His heart drummed as he went inside, past the receptionist who greeted him warmly. Caitlin's secretary, Nelda, was coming out of her cubbyhole of an office. An attractive woman in her early twenties, she smiled brightly, dimpling her cocoa-tan cheeks.

"Mr. Steele, what a pleasant surprise. I'll tell Mrs. Costner you're here."

Marty smiled. "Let me surprise her."

Nelda laughed. "Of course." She loved romance, and heaven knows Mrs. Costner needed some romance in her life. And this fine dude would fulfill any woman's fantasy.

Caitlin had remained standing at the windows after Rena went out. She felt pensive, quieter than when Rena left her, but tomorrow would be different. Maybe she didn't love him, but Marty was always *fun*. He made her laugh and she was grateful. Then she was deep in thought as she heard the door open softly. She didn't turn around because she was expecting Rena to come back. Gasping a bit, she felt strong, masculine fingers cover her eyes. For a moment, she stood still, inhaling a delightful musky and expensive men's cologne.

She laughed and patted the fingers over her eyes. "Who is this?"

"Well, I plan to be your Excedrin number-one headache for a while," the rich baritone voice drawled as he removed his hands from her face.

Caitlin turned and flung her arms around Marty Steele. "You rascal! You weren't supposed to get in until tomorrow, and I was to meet your plane."

Her old friend's arms went around her in a tender, gentle embrace.

"Cait, Cait," he murmured. "It's so good to see you again. We've got a whole lot to talk about."

It felt wonderful to have him hold her like this. His big hands gently squeezed her shoulders. "I came early because it's your wedding anniversary and I didn't want you to be alone again."

She touched his face. "You were always so thoughtful, sending flowers, calling me every year, even when Bianca didn't want you to."

"I knew you first. Bianca got used to it, and it wasn't as if she didn't have her own way to go . . ."

Caitlin glanced at him, at the bitterness that filmed his handsome features. His marriage had been as filled with hell as hers had been filled with heaven. Now both those liaisons were in the sorrowful past.

"I'm sorry," she said softly, "for both of us. You're going to be here a while, you said, and I've got the townhouse ready for you."

"Thank you. I arranged to have my luggage sent to your house because I wasn't sure where you'd put me." Wryly, he mocked his disappointment that he wouldn't be at her house, closer to her.

"That's fine. You'll love your house. The upper floors are so sunny and I had a loft built. I want to always rent to artists only. They appreciate things like that."

"You'd better believe it. I want to take you to dinner tonight. Somewhere quiet, homey."

She shook her head. "I need to stay in. I had a solitary dinner planned, and I'd love to have you to share it, but thanks for the invitation. Marty, I'm so glad you're here. Let's sit down."

"I can't just now. I'm too keyed up from the trip, from looking forward to seeing you again."

"Me too." He looked at her in a certain new way she couldn't decipher. Had he always been this magnetic, this handsome? she wondered. At six foot two, the smoothly rippling muscles under his black silk Armani suit did him full justice and the black silk turtleneck sweater flattered his rough, coal-black hair.

Marty's face was red tinged and leathery, and his heavy, silken, black eyebrows helped to define the black-olive eyes that missed nothing. People of other races often mistook him for another race, but his slightly flared nose and a sense of close kinship immediately let African Americans know he was "one of ours." She had seen him so seldom in the past few years.

He paced restlessly. "Lord, you're thirty-three and I'm thirty-five. Where have the years gone?"

"I wish I knew."

"Your gallery seems to be flourishing."

"We're doing well, but there's been trouble."

He looked at her sharply. "Oh?"

"One of Sylvan's paintings was stolen recently. It was kept in the vault and was outside to be photographed for a *Post* article. We've never had anything stolen before, never needed guards, but I've recently hired a young female ex-cop."

Marty stood frowning. "Was it a special painting?"

"Yes. *Wild Storm at Sea.*"

He whistled. "The thief's got taste. That was one of Sylvan's best."

"It was one of my favorites, too," she said quietly, "if not my favorite."

"The cops are running it down?"

"They've been really good with this. I understand a couple of other galleries have been hit." She paused. "You're staring at me."

"I always did. Does it bother you?"

"No. It's just that when a man grows used to a woman as beautiful as Bianca, doesn't it spoil him for other women?"

Marty drew her to a navy leather sofa and they sat close to each other. "You never really believed in your own beauty, Cait. No, you're certainly not perfect, but with my artist's eye I see everything in you I value." His long fingers caressed her cheek as she sat very still. "Silken skin the color of darkest honey, healthy earth-brown hair, golden-brown eyes under sooty eyelashes that're sinfully long in an oval face.

"Your body, Cait, is one I would never tire of painting. Lush lines, too many curves for some, but not for me. Breasts that could pillow my head forever, swell with my hands cupped around them. And your hips and legs were fashioned by a master. I've never done it before, but I'm going to paint you, and soon."

Caitlin drew in a sharp breath. *He shouldn't be talking like this*, she fretted. This was her old friend, her *very* old friend. And yet this man before her was almost a stranger—an exciting stranger.

She changed the subject. "Did you eat on the plane? There's a Starbucks near here. Do you still drink lots of coffee?"

He nodded. "Yeah, and the health writers are beginning to say it could be good for me. A recent study found a lower incidence of diabetes in heavy coffee drinkers."

"Interesting. I haven't heard or read that, but then I've been very busy."

"Too busy, I suspect. As for food, I did eat a decent meal on the plane. Spanish airlines serve good food, so I don't need anything else right now. You shouldn't be working today, so be good to yourself. Rena can take over."

Caitlin smiled impishly and rolled her eyes. "She can and you're taking me over."

His face was grave, intense. "I don't mean to take you over, as much as I'd like to. You're a sleeping beauty, my dear, and I'd like to be the one who wakes you up to life again."

His words and his hypnotic voice were getting to her. It had been so long since she'd felt desire swell in her like this and she swallowed hard. She wasn't ready for deep feelings for any man who wasn't Sylvan. She had dedicated her life to Sylvan and her tiny son, now dead, and it had been enough.

"You're right," she said suddenly. "I'll turn things over to Rena and take you to your place. I'm sure you're tired. I think you'll like it."

They walked out into the large gallery, with its stark white walls and patches of coral, black, and aquamarine. Rena came to them and hugged Marty. Rena laughed. "Hey, you're looking a little worse for wear, but gorgeous as usual. If you ever decide to play around . . ."

Marty laughed uproariously. The very dark chocolate, exquisitely beautiful Rena and he always flirted. Now she was two-and-a-half months pregnant and beginning to show.

He grinned, pointedly looking at her abdomen. "But what on earth are we gonna do about hubby? As I remember, he's pretty big and plenty possessive. And congratulations, Rena. You'll make a great mother."

Caitlin's breath shallowed. Already it had begun to be rough being with Rena as she expanded with her child. Caitlin bit her lip. She had had a son once and a man who filled her life. Now her life was comprised of her work, a few good friends, and memories. But she felt her *memories* of Sylvan and Sylvan Junior were more satisfying than a *life* with someone else.

Costner Art Gallery was in the Adams-Morgan area of D.C. One of the most multicultural areas in the city, its charm was legendary. The houses were mostly old, mostly brick, and well built. The cream-colored stucco townhouse Marty would occupy was only ten blocks from the art gallery and four blocks from Caitlin's own red brick house.

As they walked along, Marty looked around him. "I always liked Adams-Morgan when I visited here. This is where I hung out, you remember? It's quite a place, a bit like Paris."

"I like it, but it's changing. Gangs are getting a toehold here."

They were on the sidewalk of an avenue and the median strip was planted with small shrubbery that flourished in late September. Marty took her hand as they prepared to cross the street.

"It's such a magnificent day," Caitlin said. "I could pass the afternoon just ambling along in this warm sunlight."

"I'll do just that with you if you ask me nicely."

Caitlin laughed. "I want to show you your digs, then we'll think about it."

They prepared to cross the street. Then, like a surreal action, a big, black car with tinted windows headed straight for Caitlin. Marty's big hands swiftly pulled her back.

"*What the hell*?" he raged as he held her close. "What's going on here?"

For a long moment Caitlin couldn't speak. Her heart raced painfully, with drumbeats resounding through her body. "Oh my God," she whimpered.

He held her fast as her knees threatened to give way under her. Her throat was dust dry and her body shook with chills.

"I'll tell you about it," she managed to say.

He still held her close. "You told me when I last called that you had witnessed a gang shooting and might have to testify. Could this have something to do with that?"

Her voice was taut with resolution. "Probably. They're not going to frighten me."

"Maybe they should," he said grimly.

"No. I live in this neighborhood and I love it. The gangs aren't going to drive me out. I'm so glad you're here."

"So am I, and I'm gonna take care of you."

Pressed against him, she wanted to stay in his arms and feel the way she hadn't felt for so long a time.

Without wanting to, she gloried in every inch of his splendid body, hard and virile against her own softness. Then she came to herself, thinking someone had almost run her down, and here she could think of nothing save Marty's arms around her, holding her so tightly she couldn't breathe. She was grateful for the safety he offered, but terrified of the new danger she felt with the gangs and now with him.

Marty felt hot tears fill his eyes as he continued to hold her close. "Are you sure you're all right?" His voice was sharp with anxiety.

Her voice trembled with emotion. "Yes, thanks to you. I'm glad you were with me."

"That was deliberate, Cait. We're going to the nearest police station."

"Yes, they need to know about this. Don't be too concerned, Marty. There's been talk about a growing drug problem in this neighborhood, complete with turf wars. I know there's drag racing. It's probably some stupid kids on drugs and having a joyride."

"It's mid-afternoon," Marty scoffed. "Doesn't that kind of activity begin later?"

"I've heard them racing as early as this." She expelled a harsh breath. "You can't hold me forever, Marty. Don't worry so much. I'll first try calling the police. In this neighborhood we work with them and they'll take a telephone report and send someone out if we're lucky."

"This needs to be handled as quickly as possible, Cait."

"And it will," she said, wriggling out of his arms.

Strong sunlight beat down on them as they crossed the street and went into the white stucco townhouse with the dark blue tiled roof.

Chapter 2

Marty turned to Caitlin in the cool, white living room. "You seem so calm, so collected," he said gently, "but I know you, my girl. You've got to be really shaken up by what just happened."

Caitlin's heart beat faster at the tender concern in his voice. "Don't worry so. Gangs have just made plans to move into the neighborhood and we're going to hand them the surprise of their low-life lives."

"Be careful. Those guys can play rough. A lot of them feel they don't have much to live for."

Caitlin laughed shortly. "Have you ever known me to back down from a worthwhile fight?"

He placed a hand on the side of her shoulder. "I don't want you hurt. You're my best friend, precious to me, and I intend to keep you close, protect you. I want to talk with the police about what's going on."

"And I'll introduce you to a detective who's very involved." She stopped suddenly, all too aware of his black-olive eyes narrowed on her. "Well, what do you think of your new digs? Of course if we keep standing here, you can't give me a good answer."

He shrugged. "I think you know my tastes. If the rest of the place is like what I see from here, I'm captivated. Can't wait to get to work. How's *your* painting coming along?"

"My painting," she echoed him. "I'm afraid it's getting short shrift."

"Why?"

She found it hard talking with him when his eyes tenderly watched her like this. A small chill of fear went through her. His big, muscular body radiated heat like a still summer day. She was a reserved, cool woman with deep fires. "I'm afraid I'm busy with the gallery," she said slowly.

His big hands took her shoulders. "You're too good an artist to neglect your painting, and I don't think you've ever realized how good you are. Your flower paintings rival Georgia O'Keeffe's in her younger days."

"Thank you," she said formally, pleased. "My best efforts always went to supporting Sylvan. He was the genius of our family."

"I know," he said slowly, "but you've got your own genius to nurture. I want to help you do that."

She smiled then. "You're generous. I've read all the comments in the art publications. The critics have worshipped you since you've been in Europe, and even before you left the U.S., critics sang your praises loud and long. What was it they dubbed you? Ah yes, the "Soul Master." And you deserve it all."

Marty drank in his friend's warmth, the face that held a deep humanity that went past surface beauty. He found himself getting lost in the depths of those golden-brown eyes and the thickly fringed black lashes. He ran his tongue over dry lips. "You're leaning away. This isn't about me; it's about you. I don't want to crowd you, but I want to get to know you even better."

They stood near the door and she felt he had backed

her against a wall and held her his willing prisoner. She told herself: *Be straight with him from the beginning.* So she told him, "Sylvan will always be my life, Marty, even though he's dead. I've dedicated my life to him and to my dead child."

He pressed her shoulders hard. "You're wrong, you know. Life is for the living. You could have another love, another child, other children."

Heresy, her heart cried; she wanted no other life. She drew a deep breath. "You know," she said slowly, "he died five years ago. He wanted his paintings held for five years before I begin to release his genius to the world. I've worked hard, Marty, to make his dreams come true. Will you help me? I feel selfish asking it. I know you've got your own work, but I'll appreciate any help you can give me."

He smiled a bit. "Of course I will. We once called ourselves 'The Four Musketeers.' You and Sylvan, your twin, Caleb, and I. We prided ourselves on being among Pratt's finest, and we were going to have it all." His smile deepened. "I had a crush on you, wanted you for my girl, but Adonis Sylvan put an end to all that. You two married just after you graduated and you never looked at another man . . ."

For a moment she couldn't get her breath and she felt the sting of acid tears behind her eyelids as she continued in a shaky voice. "Then our son was born and no two people were ever happier." She was silent a long moment. "But it ended on an upstate New York road when a tractor trailer plowed into the back of Sylvan's car and he and Caleb were killed instantly."

He took her in his arms, held her against the remembered pain. "I'm so sorry," he said, taking a fresh handkerchief from his pants pocket and blotting her tears.

"I know you are. You helped me so much. You were always there for me. I had Sylvan's son, Sylvan Junior, and my love for him was truly fierce, but I grieved Sylvan so hard I couldn't properly care for my baby. He had a strep throat, caught pneumonia and died so quickly I couldn't believe it." Her voice went still. "My baby needed me and I failed him. How can I ever forgive myself?" Talking about it hurt, but it soothed her too.

He shook her lightly. "Don't do this to yourself, Cait," he said gently. "Great love like the love you had for Sylvan sometimes carries its own price. You were shattered and you did the best you could."

"No, I should have done much more for my son. I was his mother. He was so little, so helpless . . ."

"You can have other children. Stop punishing yourself."

"And can I have another Sylvan? Marty, let me tell you, some people are damned to love only once in their lives. You read about them, hear about them every day. Some die when a mate dies. I intended to keep living for my child. Did you ever truly know how much I wanted to die when Sylvan Junior died?"

"Yes, I knew."

"And you did everything to help me, but I couldn't feel you, couldn't feel anything. Finally, you gave me the courage to go on with my memories. Did you also know that?"

"I'm glad. Now I want you to go further and come out of your shell. Today is your wedding anniversary. I want you to get dressed or not get dressed, as you will. There's a Spanish restaurant I visited several times the last time I was here. It's dark, quiet, has wonderful food and a great wine list. I know you said you wanted to stay in, but let me dominate you a bit here. You need to be waited on."

"Oh Marty, I . . ." she began, but suddenly the idea

appealed to her. "Okay, let's do it." She knew the place he mentioned well and liked the strolling violinists who performed in the evening, liked the ambience of the place.

They walked over the rest of the first and second floors and he complimented her taste in decor.

"I stocked the kitchen with items I thought you wanted and I'll go shopping with you for other things," she told him.

"Hey," he said, grinning, "one day I'll fix you my Puerto rabbit stew with its special sauce."

"Good. I'll look forward to that. A Puerto de la Cruz delicacy."

"You'd better believe it. One day you've got to go to Puerto. Sylvan always loved it when we lived there summers when we were students. You were always too busy to go."

She thought a moment. "Speaking of Puerto, Bianca's leaving really tore you up. I wanted you to come here so I could help you the way you helped me. Has time done any good at all? It doesn't always."

He rubbed his nose with his forefinger. "It's been two years and yes, I'm better. Betrayal is a dirty business, Cait. It's a knife in your heart that never seems to stop twisting. But I find the knife has slowed since I've seen you."

"You haven't been here a day."

"I was dreaming on the way over and in the limousine coming from the airport. Then I saw you, and I've been with you for two hours now and it helps more than I would have believed. Count yourself a miracle worker."

She touched his ruddy face, laughed. "You always look like you've got a sunburn. Such healthy skin. You're a throwback."

"Yeah, to an Indian grandfather—Shoshone tribe—and a renegade white grandfather who wanted to marry his Black love on the other side. It all came out in me."

"You're a handsome, sexy man who's getting the world at his feet, and you deserve it. Do you know how valuable you are? I'm so glad you're my friend."

He raised his eyebrows. "If I don't know my own worth, we go well together. *You* certainly never have known yours. Sylvan covered you, kept you for himself. You were so completely wrapped up in him, you never came to know who you really are. I want to help you develop into the woman you were meant to be."

Fear began in Caitlin's tense body and she heard his words, fought them. "My life is pretty much set," she said as her voice went hoarse with stress. "Don't try to change it, Marty. I'm as happy as I have any right to be the way I am."

His eyes held hers. "You have every right to be completely happy, Cait. You've got to give yourself a chance. Give *me* a chance."

On impulse he hugged her tightly and thrills went through him like small rockets. His loins were fierce with wanting her, but he didn't crave conquering just her body, but knowing her heart and her soul. She was so soft, so tender. Her five-eight-and-a-half-inch body fit well against him and he felt sick with needing to stroke her, comfort her. A mocking voice in his head said he wanted to possess her warmth, know her in every possible way. But he could, he would, wait.

"You're still on the rebound; friend," she told him. "We've always been close since college. We had an incredibly good time, all wild and carefree. You offered me compassion then and you offer it now, and I'm grateful. I'm sorrier than you know at how much Bianca hurt you. You loved her so much and she's so beautiful."

Caitlin reflected that Bianca's grandmother had been

a brown baby, the offspring of Black American G.I.'s and European women. Those bloodlines had come together to make a woman whose beauty was breathtaking.

After a moment, he said, "Thank you. Bianca has beautiful physical features. I've painted her many times and never been satisfied with my work. Finally, I understood why. Bianca has no soul. She has sensations, but she doesn't truly feel. You *thrum*, Cait, with deep, deep feelings. You're a hot-blooded, passionate, sexual, sensual woman."

He stopped then before he could tell her how much he wanted her and frighten her away.

Beginning to relax more than she wanted to, caught by the hypnotic cadence of Marty's voice, Cait patted his arm lightly.

"You're in great shape," she teased him, seeking to change his somber mood. "Let's go and see your loft."

Once upstairs, they passed a bedroom with the door open. The colors were dark and light blue with tomato red and yellow touches. "Right away, I'm more attracted to this room," he said. "I'll sleep well here."

"But you haven't seen the others."

"I get stuck on some things I see and don't need to see others." His look said he was talking about more than bedrooms. He closed his eyes against an onslaught of fantasies of her naked beneath him. His voice got hoarse as he told her, "Let's move on, Cookie." That had always been his pet name for her. Sylvan had had no pet names for her.

On the third floor, Marty reflected that the loft was perfect for painting. Several easels had been set up and painting paraphernalia lined the stark, white room. Brilliant prisms of light were everywhere. "You seem to know just what I need," he said.

"For painting, yes," she murmured. "Remember how well I know you."

"I can arrange it so you know me even better."

She sighed. "Marty, you've coming from bone-deep hurt just as I'm coming from a hurt that will never end. Listen to what I tell you. We can both save ourselves so much heartache this way."

"You're asking me not to crowd you."

"Yes. I know myself and my life isn't too bad the way I'm living it. In a short while I begin to really work on Sylvan's exhibit, and I'll be far happier, feel even closer to him."

"You *want* another child, Cait," he said bluntly, "the same way I want a child. I watched you looking at Rena's belly, totally dreaming. You don't have to be in love to bear the child you want."

Waves of anguish rose in Caitlin's breast. "Please don't talk like this. You've always comforted me. You were a rock when Sylvan and my son died, so please keep being that way."

Trembling, she thought, dear God, he had stripped her senses bare, revealing all the terrible hunger for a baby she had known for so long. And she wondered what was going to be the end of this.

Chapter 3

Later, Caitlin moved about thoughtfully through her home. She had hidden it well from Marty, but she was still shaken thinking about the near-accident that afternoon. She was convinced it was no accident. Some sixth sense had had her on guard before the black car had gunned for her. The Latino El Marico group and the African American A-M Crewe had banded in a devil's pact to take over that section of the city. And Caitlin was one of the ones most highly profiled in newspapers and on TV. This community meant to fight back. Articles and photos of her had appeared in the daily papers.

In the middle of her living room, she stood thinking. She and Sgt. Jim Draper of the Third District police station were working on a plan to involve the disenchanted and violent young men, take them into the life of their community. Would it work? She wasn't sure, but they had to do something. She liked her neighborhood and wanted to stay there.

Then her mouth turned upward into a wide smile as she reflected on her coming date with Marty. She half giggled. It wasn't a date, just a dinner with an old, old

... and neck were ... Bianca," she said softly, ... I can." Besides, as fond as she was of Marty, he would always be a friend, nothing more. No man would ever be more than a friend to her again.

A large, lighted self-portrait of Sylvan was mounted in a living room alcove. His dark skin in the painting glowed with life and desire. Oh yes, Sylvan had been full of desire, she thought now. That quality in him had informed their life. He had done himself full justice in that painting and it was one of her dearest possessions. His splendid body was made for life, not to lie mangled on a highway. Nearby sat a smaller painting of their son, so like his father. She stood back with her heart filling, hurting. She had become used to this mixture of pleasure and pain inextricably interwoven in her breast.

Pulling herself sharply out of her reverie, she realized she felt guilty about Marty and the delicious feelings of pure life he aroused in her. Well, he needed her help in getting over Bianca's betrayal, even after being divorced for two years. When he had visited the year before, he hadn't wanted to talk about it. She had watched him down too much liquor, start smoking again, drive his rental car aggressively, and swear at the slightest incident.

That had not been a happy time. Now he looked much better, was calmer, more at peace. Still . . .

In her bedroom, she took off her clothes, did a series of calisthenics, turned back the covers, and lay naked on the bed. The fifty-gallon aquarium in the living room alcove filled that section of her house with pleasant white noise and she was soon napping with a smile on her face.

* * *

Marty picked her up at her house promptly at eight.

"Wow!" Marty exclaimed. "You are one sharp cookie—the chocolate chip–laced kind you make that I'm so crazy about."

"Flatterer. You ought to set up a charm course, my friend."

Marty took her hand, kissed it, then kissed the other one. Her heart beat too fast at his closeness and she shuttered her eyes.

"It's always easy to find words to compliment you, Cait. There are so many things about you, and you neglect them all."

Caitlin chuckled. "You're going to make me fall in love with myself, and I'm not that great."

"You *are*, you know. Will you call a taxi before I change my mind and insist on staying in with you? I love that dress that shows off your shoulders and throat, and the side slits in your skirt showing off legs that set my blood racing."

Caitlin looked at him obliquely. "You're one fresh hombre," she said, "but thank you, I think. We're not taking a taxi. It's just four brightly lit blocks and the orange-hat patrol is out in full force on Wednesday nights. I understand we've got a full moon and I want to look at it. Indulge me."

"For you, anything at any time," he said huskily. "No mention of anywhere."

Caitlin laughed. "My friend, the honey-tongued Martin Edward Steele, artist extraordinaire and ladies' man, par excellence. Let me get my wrap and we'll go."

"Umm, I was going to suggest that you cover up. No point in flashing a jewel like you before hungry thugs, or for that matter, upright citizens."

She got a black, close-fitting taffeta coat from the hall closet and he helped her put it on.

Once outside, they stood on her front steps and studied the full moon and the gorgeous galaxy of stars that Caitlin found so beautiful she hurt. Sylvan had been a stargazer.

"You know," Marty said as they walked along, "it's when I see things like this that I thank God I'm an artist." He pointed at a shooting star. "And when I see a woman like you, I'm even happier to be an artist."

"Remember when we were students we often sat up all night to watch stars out on Long Island, with the river rushing by?"

"Yeah. You don't forget things like that. The Atlantic Ocean around Puerto de la Cruz is fabulous. I've got to take you there."

"I'd like to go sometime."

"Soon."

"Maybe. I'll think about it. Lord, I hate to go in, as much as I'm looking forward to a good dinner."

He took her hand, laced his fingers through hers. "We don't have to go in. There's a park right over there and a big, burly cop nearby. We could ask him to stay and we could star- and moon-gaze."

"I'd like that, but my stomach is demanding its due and it gets growly and rowdy when I don't feed it."

A quicksilver moment went through Marty as he listened to laughter come into her voice. He intended to see that she laughed more, began to live again, damn it. She surely deserved that—and more.

In the cozy restaurant, the lights were low and the decor soothing. The maitre d' came to them swiftly. "Ah, Señora Costner. It's always wonderful to see you."

Caitlin acknowledged his greeting and introduced him to Marty. "He'll be eating here from time to time. Please take good care of him."

"It will be my special pleasure and he will get the best we have to offer." The smile of the maitre d' was wide and warm. "You always like the strolling violins," he told Caitlin, "and they come on shortly. This weekend we have the best of the flamenco dancers. They are visiting this city and agreed to perform here."

"I'll be sure to come by," Caitlin said quickly.

Seated at the table covered with snowy damask, Caitlin drew a deep breath. Fat, dark aquamarine candles enclosed in glass lent a romantic air. A waiter came and took their orders, then in a few moments brought them bread sticks and sparkling water.

"Your eyes are star bright," Marty told her. "That's always a good sign."

"Yours are star bright too. We're always so happy to see each other."

"Men's eyes don't get star bright."

Caitlin threw back her head, laughing. "You see life your way; I'll see it mine."

His leg brushed hers and a renegade shiver ran the length of her body.

"Sorry," he said.

"Sorry for—?"

"Okay, I'm *not* sorry. Maybe I was acting out a fantasy."

"You're full of fantasies. We both are. It's part of being an artist."

"Yeah. Caitlin, about that car nearly hitting you this afternoon . . ."

"Shhh. We're not going to talk about unpleasant things. I meant to call Sergeant Draper, but I overslept taking my nap, and he was off duty when I woke up. I'll be sure to talk with him first thing tomorrow morning."

He frowned and his expression got serious. "Please don't play heroine. Assume the worst scenario. These days anything can happen and usually does. Call me when the sergeant comes to talk. I want to be in on this."

"I surely will. What are your plans for the next few days?"

He pondered her question for a few moments. "Well, maybe tomorrow, but no later than Friday, I'm going up to New York to see Jayson. There are new galleries opening and he wants to introduce me to the owners. I plan to work my butt off in the next few years." His mouth had set in a fairly grim line.

At the mention of Jayson's name, Caitlin grew thoughtful. He was a wealthy art dealer she and Marty had known since their college days. Jayson Giles was forty-five years old, distinguished looking, and a sharp dresser.

Marty knew very well that Jayson wanted Caitlin and he was jealous.

Caitlin smiled. "I'll check on your house while you're in New York and I'll bring you an orchid plant I saw at my florist's. Do you still like orchids?"

"More and more. The orchid mania is exploding. People are going to prison for stealing rare varieties in other countries and sneaking them into the U.S."

"Uh-huh, in this country too. I like orchids, so I keep up with the news about them."

His tongue flicked lightly over his bottom lip. "Speaking of Jayson, is he still hitting on you?"

Caitlin sputtered, "I wouldn't say he *hits* on me. Jayson's a gentleman. He's like you, fond of women."

"And like me, some women far more than others. I noticed him with you last year when I was here and I've noticed him long before. I'm always reminded of a lion on the prowl when I see him around you. Does he come down often?"

Caitlin raised her eyebrows. "Often enough, and by the way, male lions don't prowl. The female does the kill and brings home the bacon, and Papa Lion just lazes about and takes care of Mama Lion desirewise."

Marty laughed. "Sweet life. Humans could take a page from that book."

Caitlin pursed her lips. "Oh, you like the idea of that, do you?"

His leg brushed hers again as their eyes caught and held.

He shook his head. "Sorry, babe. I've got restless legs tonight. My body's talking to me—and you. Hell, my restless leg touching yours once is understandable, but *twice* in the span of just a little while— I *am* sorry, Cait. I never want to drive you away. I respect you too much for fun and games. And I was never more serious."

"It's all *right*, Marty. We're both nervous. We need each other and we want our friendship to last, so we'll make it work. How long will you be in New York?"

"You're damn right, we'll make it work. You're my last straw. After you, I'm drowning." He hadn't answered her question.

"We can't let that happen. How long will you be gone?"

"I'm not certain. Maybe only a day, but Jayson and I have a lot to talk about. Probably a couple of days."

"I know you're sorry your folks are away," she said.

"I sure am, but I'm happy to know they're busy loving the Canary Islands."

"I'm sure it was hard for you to leave."

He thought a moment, expelled a harsh sigh. "Not anymore. I think I can find everything I want here. Does my sister call?"

"You bet. Dosha, Caleb, and I should have been triplets instead of Dosha and Damien being twins."

"You're almost as close to my family as I am. They love you, you know."

"And I love them. I'll never forget how they took me and Caleb in when our parents were killed in that plane crash. We were eighteen; Caleb and I felt like helpless children. Your parents were, are wonderful."

"Well, they'll all be back in two weeks. Let's go to Minden and tell them how great we think they are."

"Deal. I'll look forward to that. While you're in New York, I'll check on everything at your house. Do you want me to get you an animal? Fish? Birds?"

He shook his head. "I'm going to be too busy to do them justice right now. Fleeing Europe, a lot of ideas've flooded my brain, and I've got to begin painting. We have a few minutes before the food comes. Would you like to dance?"

The dance floor held a few couples and the slow and sensuous Latin American music surrounded them as she slipped into his arms. The steady pressure of his body jolted her, set small fires along her nerve endings. He held her too close, she thought, but she didn't hold herself away from him. Did he guess what he did to her? She hurriedly glanced at him and found him studying her. The scent of his expressive men's cologne filled her nostrils. He was one of the most compelling, appealing men she had ever known. If her life hadn't been hotwired to Sylvan, she might have chosen him. Now it was out of the question. They were forever locked in friendship—with nothing more to come.

"You move like a professional dancer," he told her because he had to talk to her. Her jasmine scent aroused him. Her warm, soft body was filling his arms, his body, his heart and soul with liquid fire that licked his loins and threatened to ignite.

She suddenly became acutely aware of the hard bulge near her center and it nearly undid her. *Whoa girl!* she cautioned herself. *It's only natural that being without a man so long, you'd feel this way. You and Marty can handle this. Will handle this.*

"I could dance with you all night," he said softly against her ear.

"So could I, but our dinner is being served. Shall we eat?"

Dinner was superb. They began with gazpacho, then roast rack of lamb, couscous, asparagus tips, and baby corn. A salad of several greens and ripe, fresh garden vegetables tantalized the tongue, and the sharp vinaigrette awakened their taste buds.

"We have excellent strawberry flan," the waiter told them. "Also blackberry and blueberry."

Caitlin and Marty looked at each other, remembering their favorite Spanish restaurant on Long Island and the blackberry flan they often ate there in late summer and early fall.

They both asked each other at once, "Blackberry?" and nodded "Yes."

"You have made an ideal choice," the waiter said and went away.

"I can see this restaurant is going to be a favorite of mine," Marty said.

"It does bring back memories."

Marty sighed. "Memories are fine; they sometimes sustain us, but we *cannot* live in them. Those days are gone . . ."

A few angry tears stood in her eyes. "For me, they'll *never* be gone. I remember my husband as clearly as if he were here with us, and my little boy."

Looking at her steadily, Marty said, "I don't mean to be cruel, but Sylvan isn't here with you or me. He and Sylvan Junior never will be with us again. I think you need to accept that, bury your dead, and move on."

Caitlin was shocked to find herself shaking with anger so fierce she wanted to strike him, but she forced herself to calmness, soothed the prickling of her skin.

"Let it rest," she said softly. "Don't keep trying to stop me from feeling the way I feel. I told you, some loves last a lifetime. I'm sorry you haven't known that kind."

And looking at her, Marty thought it wasn't the time to say, "But I *am* knowing that kind of love. It's too soon to tell concretely, but I feel that kind of love for you—and it's been going on nearly as long as I've known you."

Chapter 4

In her gallery office two mornings later, Caitlin reflected that she felt better than she had in many moons. She swivelled around in her tan leather executive chair to face the windows and clasped her arms behind her head. It was so good to have Marty in town, to think he'd be here for a while. A light tap sounded on her door and Rena came in.

"Someone's still happy." Rena dimpled as she looked at Caitlin carefully. "Yesterday, I thought you'd touch the sky; that hasn't changed. Marty's good for you."

"He's like a part of me," Caitlin said. "We go so far back."

"Umm, I've talked about that with you *and* him. Are you aware how much he cares for you?"

Caitlin drew a shallow breath. "We care for each other; we always have. Nobody was tighter than we were, The Four Musketeers, Rena. Nobody."

"I, ah, don't think we're talking about the same thing really. I'll be blunt. I noticed when he was here last year and I'm seeing it now, Marty's in love with you, Cait. Are you in love with him?"

Caitlin shook her head slowly. "You know I'm not. As I told Marty, I live with and love my memories. You weren't lucky enough to know Sylvan, but if you had, you'd understand. Some people really are irreplaceable."

Rena bit her lip and began to say something, but Caitlin cut her off. "How's our baby coming along?"

Rena smiled widely. "Calm, peaceful journey so far. This baby has to be a girl. My little boy was surely a hellion when I was carrying him. I'll be getting another sonogram soon, and later, I guess, I'll let the doctor tell us whether it's a boy or a girl."

Caitlin felt it coming and tried to ward it off—the sick feeling of longing for a baby in her womb. This time it came too swiftly to fight down. Sylvan Junior had moved lustily inside her, as if he couldn't wait to be born.

Rena's eyes were warm, compassionate. "It could be so different, Cait. Sometimes we have to settle for less than we want. Listen, Sergeant Draper said he needed to talk with us. He went out for a cup of Starbucks. I've had my share for the morning. He asked if you'd like a cup and I said I thought you would."

"Thanks, I can use it."

Caitlin's buzzer sounded and her secretary announced Sergeant Draper. The stocky, dark brown man came in, handed Caitlin the coffee. "Rena said you could probably use this," he said.

"Thank you. Please have a seat, and have a Krispy Kreme, or one of your choice."

Sergeant Draper rolled his eyes. "Now this is like turning the henhouse over to a fox. You don't know my appetite for doughnuts, lady."

He came back and they sat in a nest of chairs. Caitlin laughed. "Indulge yourself. You lead a dangerous life."

Drinking the coffee, munching on his chocolate

doughnut, Sergeant Draper reflected, "It's coming to be true now. This gang stuff is wearing me down, but at least we're trying to do something constructive about these young men. Mrs. Costner, I came by to say I've been transferred off the gang detail."

"Oh?" Caitlin said, frowning.

"Yeah, but you'll be seeing more of me. I'm heading the investigation of your break-in and the theft of your husband's painting. A rookie and I will be snooping around. Your husband was building a name for himself when he died. You told the cops who came around that the stolen painting was very valuable. I imagine it had great sentimental value too."

Caitlin nodded. "It was one of his best. I have to get it back." She slid her shallow center desk drawer open and showed him a photograph of the painting.

He studied it and whistled low. "Gorgeous! We'll sure do what we can to recover it. As soon as possible, I'll need to talk with you and all your employees further."

"There aren't many," Caitlin said. "You know Rena, and there's Luther, our general caretaker, who's been with me from the beginning. We have commercial cleaning people who come in at six P.M. I have a friend," she began and her throat almost closed with nervousness.

After a minute Sergeant Draper queried, "Yes, a friend?"

"A very good artist friend is here for a while. And, oh yes, a few months back I hired an ex-policewoman, Rita Glass, as night security."

Sergeant Draper nodded. "That's part of our investigation. Have you ever been hit before?"

"No. Never." She knocked lightly on the small wood table by her desk.

"I, ah, know Ms. Glass." His eyes narrowed. "She's a friend of mine, and she's crazy about working here."

"She's on the ball," Rena said, laughing. "I wouldn't want to be a thief on her beat."

Caitlin wondered why Sergeant Draper's face flushed. He was recently divorced, she knew from talking to him. He'd said he was lonely. Had he found a friend to help him make it through his nights? She certainly hoped so, because he was a good man, a good cop.

"How long has your gallery been open?" Sergeant Draper asked.

"A little over four years. I had dreamed of this all through college, grad school, and further training." She ran her tongue over her dry bottom lip. "Then my husband and my baby died. This is home, so I came back to do something to keep myself from going mad. You could say we were a nearly instant success. I was lucky enough to get Rena, and the rest has been a piece of cake."

Sergeant Draper looked somber. "I'm sorry about your loss and I've said it before. You work so hard, but you've always looked to me like you've got a dream in your mind. I've envied you that. Maybe soon I'll have the same."

Caitlin leaned over, patted his hand. "I'm sure you will. You've got so much going for you."

Rena nodded in agreement, and Caitlin wondered if his hope for a better future had anything to do with Rita Glass.

They talked a while longer as Sergeant Draper ate two more doughnuts. "I'm a hungry man," he said. Wryly, Caitlin thought he was hungrier for more than doughnuts.

The rest of the morning passed swiftly. This was the beginning of the Twentieth and Twenty-first Century Landed Black Eagles exhibit, depicting the life of the famous Tuskegee Institute World War II pilots. An entire room was devoted to these men; so few were left. And it saddened her that they'd had to fight a common enemy as well as their own country. At least it was far different now.

Luther, the caretaker, came to her, pushing his wide-angled broom on the polished floor, his smile beatific.

"Ms. Costner. How you be?"

"I'm okay, I guess. And you?"

"As well as can be expected. Not complaining. That don't help."

"Good information. You seem happy."

"Now, I was gonna say the same about you, ma'am."

She studied the short, beefy, beige-skinned man of nearly fifty, with his glistening bald head and curly brown locks in back. Luther had been a handsome man, and he still carried himself like one. He continued, "I reckon I am. I reckon I might as well be."

"Well, you're doing a good job and I appreciate your help."

"Thank you, ma'am. I appreciate you telling me. Gonna move on now."

As he walked away, pushing his broom, Caitlin thought about her employee. He never missed a day's work and he was more intelligent than his speech indicated. He had an ex-wife and six grown kids scattered over the country. She knew a lot about her employees.

Standing in an alcove, Caitlin rolled her head in circles, feeling more relaxed. She would stop by her florist's a few blocks away and pick up a gorgeous white cattleya orchid plant for Marty.

She could imagine him in New York, unmindful of the stares he drew from women as he strode along. Yes, she was glad Marty was here in D.C., but it was plain there were going to be problems. They'd just have to work them through.

* * *

At Marty's back door an hour later, a big lavender orchid plant in her arms, Caitlan glanced around the backyard, deciding on just where to have the commercial gardener put in another evergreen. She loved this town house almost as much as she loved her own house. And it was perfect for Marty, which gladdened her heart.

Letting herself in, she closed the door softly, set the orchid plant down on the kitchen table, and went into the living room and up the carpeted stairs. Lost in thought, she frowned and her heart thumped as she thought she heard water running. Then there was silence. Recently, in Montgomery County, a woman who lived alone had come home to find a strange man in her shower.

She stood in the hallway near the bathroom door. Well, had she heard it? Or hadn't she? She wasn't a fearful woman, but the newly forming drug gangs had everybody on edge.

Then she was in sweet shock as Marty came out the bathroom, naked and powerful. For a long moment they stared at each other as turbulent feelings rose in her breast, and heat swept her body like no energy she had ever felt before. She couldn't speak, and she swallowed the lump in her throat that seemed as big as a small egg. Hot honey dripped through her veins, and she was going under, spinning wildly.

Marty looked at his friend, said, "Cait? What's wrong?"

She couldn't answer. He wanted to save her embarrassment, but he couldn't leave her looking as if she would faint. He needed to get a towel from the bathroom to cover his loins, but she needed him here before she fell.

"I thought you were gone," she said thickly, stinging tears of frustration coming into her eyes. God, he was so beautiful. Michelangelo's *David* had nothing on him. Even half blinded with warm tears, she knew that.

"You're upset and embarrassed," he said, "and I don't blame you. Here, let me help you to a chair."

She flung out her arms, then drew herself close. "No, please. I'll be all right." But she stood there, unable to move.

"We're artists, Cait, both of us," he said gently. "We're well-used to the naked human body. I want you to let me help you to a chair and I'll get something on. But I've got to help you first."

She let him lead her into his bedroom and to a chair. His touch was easy and respectful, but it was driving her crazy.

Once she was seated on a padded chair in his bedroom, he stepped back into the hallway, then to the bathroom, and quickly came back out in his pajama bottoms and a robe. He raised his eyebrows and shook his head as he came back to his bedroom. *We're in the same boat, Cait,* he thought. *Even imagining your body is torture for me.*

As he came back in, she told him, "I came by to bring you the orchid plant I promised. I thought you were in New York . . ."

"First, are you all right? I'm going to get you an aspirin and a cup of black coffee to settle your nerves."

"No. I'll sit here a few minutes and I'll leave. I thought you—"

"Were in New York," he finished for her. "I got a call from the buddy who was piloting the plane. The weather's going to turn bad and they're not certain just when. We're delaying until Monday. I tried to call you, but you didn't answer your cell phone. I left a message on your answering service. I would have called just after my shower."

She would explain later that she had cut her cell phone off during her talk with Sergeant Draper and forgotten to turn it back on.

Marty drew a quick breath, all too aware of his betraying bulge. Desire was a wild horse in his loins, but he had to be strong, as she had to be strong.

"I'm sorry," she said.

"For what? Being human? Being blessed with passion, with sensuality? I'm going to quickly put on some clothes, then I'll get you some coffee."

She felt better then, more in control. "Okay," she murmured. "And thank you."

He wanted to touch her so badly he hurt, but he knew he shouldn't just then.

"Thank *you*," he said gravely, "for bringing deep desire and magic back into my life."

He turned and went into the walk-in closet and came out in a few minutes in a white T-shirt and black trousers. "Feel better now?" he asked.

"I do." But the better she felt, the more her renegade eyes insisted on going over Marty's body, uncovering him, glorying in the splendor of him.

In the kitchen, Marty found a bottle of aspirin he had left out the night before, heated and poured a mug full of fresh black coffee, got a cloth napkin, and took everything back to Caitlin. Feelings were crowding him that he couldn't remember having felt before. He wanted to take care of this woman, go deep into her body, make children with her, and love her and those children forever.

Cait breathed more easily, but she still didn't trust herself to stand. "Thank you," she said quietly as he handed her the mug.

"It's hot now. Be careful. Take very light sips."

She did just that, cooling the hot liquid on her tongue. This was her third cup of coffee. Relaxing a bit, she thought ruefully that she'd need about six more this day, where she usually drank no more than two.

"You're a very nice man," she said softly. "You deserve someone you can have."

He got up and dragged another chair over to her, sat down facing her. "Maybe I'm the way you say you are, more content with living a wondrous dream than a so-so reality."

She didn't respond to that, said only, "I've got to go back to the gallery. There's a lot going on this Sunday, and I've got to help prepare for it."

"After a while you can go back. I want you to lie down and rest for a few minutes. A big, burly clown frightened you half to death."

She had to say it. "You're beautiful, Marty, all the way through. I wish I were free for someone like you, but I'm not. I wasn't frightened. I was quivering inside and out, uncertain whether I could hold fast. Now I know I can. I feel so good about that."

After a little time passed, she lay on his bed while he sat on a chair watching over her. When she got up, he stood and came to her.

"How do you feel?"

"Much better. I'm okay now. I'm a big girl and I can take care of myself, but thank you."

He smiled then. "Thank you again for the gorgeous orchid plant and for coming over. I apologize for surprising you."

"You couldn't know." She patted his shoulder and looked at his concerned face. Wistfully she thought she'd like to spend the rest of the day there, with him.

Chapter 5

The following Sunday night, Marty walked around his loft, appreciating the fact that Caitlin had taken such pains with decor he liked. At Pratt The Four Musketeers had had great lofts they decorated themselves. This was going to be a perfect place to paint, he thought. Caitlin's reaction to his nude body was still on his mind, and he narrowed his eyes, clasped his hands behind his back. She was attracted to him, or maybe it was just her attraction to a healthy male body. That would be natural.

Damn it, she was wasting her life, and she was too vital, too beautiful to do that. As that thought arced across his mind, felt less frustrated. Reaching into his pocket for his cell phone, he dialed Caitlin's number. No answer. Had she turned off her phone again? His phone call had been the beginning of the scenario that had seemed to shake her so. Should he crowd her? He wasn't sure. No, let her get her bearings, but he would keep subtly surrounding her with his love.

He looked around the room at the easels she had set up, the array of paint cans and brushes. Picking up a sable-tipped brush, he ran the soft bristles over his fingers. Cait's hair was soft, alive. He'd call again later.

He picked up his phone on the first ring to Jayson Giles's deep voice.

" 'Lo, Marty. How's the world treating you?"

Marty laughed shortly. "Contrary to the usual remark, I *am* complaining."

"Caitlin giving you a hard time?"

"Not really." He'd be damned if he was going to tell Jayson his problems, cspccially regarding Caitlin.

"I'm sorry you didn't get up here this weekend. We had everything going on. There's this new, small gallery in the Village. I tell you, the woman who runs it is a live wire and she drooled when I mentioned you. She lived a short while in Puerto a few years back. Loved it. Name's Amelia Waring."

Marty reflected a moment. "I don't remember meeting her. I was traveling a lot."

Jayson laughed. "You were well tied up with the gorgeous Bianca then, trying to make a kid. What happened to that dream?"

"It's not a subject I can talk about," Marty told him evenly.

"I can understand that. Ah, Marty, I'm going to be upfront about this. I'm caring more and more about Cait, and I think she's warming to me. I've been in D.C. pretty often lately. Cait's a prize package."

"She's a woman, Jayson, not a package, and she's the best there is."

"Touchy, touchy. Listen, lad. I'm older than the two of you. At forty-five, I'm feeling my age. I decided long ago that Cait's the one I want to go all the way into my sunset years with. Wish me luck."

"I'm afraid I can't do that."

"Why?"

"Because *I'm* in love with Cait." He hadn't intended to say it.

"Whoa! I know from the grapevine that Bianca hurt you big time. Her cousin, Cedric, is a friend. You know him—"

"All too well."

"So you're coming in from heartbreak and you've got to still be bleeding. I can give Cait the world, Marty, everything she needs."

"Funny. That's the way *I* feel."

Jayson was silent a long moment. "Well then, the die is cast. We're both gentlemen, and we'll just have to emotionally slug it out for the fair lady's hand. You're coming up tomorrow?"

"Yes."

"To stay a few days?"

"I'll need to be back by Thursday night."

"Have you seen much of Caitlin?"

"Quite a bit." Why was he lying? He'd seen her several times, but then he'd only been here five days. He wanted to be with her constantly.

"I see. I've got a lot of people lined up for you to talk with. You've done great work, Marty, and your name is hot. Let's take advantage of it."

"We'll see. I've gotta go now."

"Sure. See you tomorrow."

After he hung up, Marty found he no longer felt like painting. Jayson's mention of Caitlin had knocked that into a cocked hat. Hell, he hadn't just mentioned Caitlin, he'd slavered over her like a teenager. Marty laughed aloud as his anger rose. Jayson Giles was a formidable rival, Marty thought, but he wouldn't make a good father. Too involved with himself. Sometimes men changed when they had kids, but somehow he didn't think Jayson would. That thought warmed him.

The Four Musketeers had known Jayson since their college days, but he and Marty only had a cordial acquaintance. Jayson was one of the best art dealers in the country and the two men admired each other's talent. Jayson had driven many sweet deals for him, but *any* move was expendable where Caitlin was concerned, he thought.

Marty went to a chest of drawers and took a carved brown pipe from the top drawer. It had never been filled with tobacco since he'd had it, but his father had once owned that pipe when Marty was a child. That had been before smoking had been proved dangerous. Now, the empty pipe gave him the solace of memory as he put it between his teeth.

After a few desultory attempts to draw, he went to bed early without even trying to paint. He usually mapped out his paintings in his mind before doing his sketches. Now he tossed on the dark blue sheets, palpably feeling Caitlin's soft, curved body beside him. No, he didn't want to torture himself. In a few minutes, he'd get up and open the windows. Just then, his body felt drugged. The phone on his night table rang and he answered it.

"Marty?" Her voice was so hushed, so sweet.

"Yes, Cait. I'm here."

"You sound like I woke you up. If I did, I'm sorry.

"You didn't wake me up. I was thinking about you."

"Oh. Don't do too much of that. I'm a lost cause. Listen I'm just calling to wish you a safe and profitable trip. The New York art scene has so many glamorous women. They'll eat you alive."

"I like your teeth better."

Caitlin laughed in spite of herself. "You're a wonderful nut. Have a good trip, Marty. I've got to get to bed early. Hard day ahead."

She hung up, and for a few seconds he held the humming line open until the operator's cheerful voice told him to hang up.

He turned off the night-light and tossed, but he soon drifted to sleep. Caitlin's fantasy presence enveloped him immediately. She was a goddess and she came to him without hesitation, without coyness. They sat beside a crystal stream in a densely wooded forest. It was summer and magnolias in full bloom lent their perfume, which blended with the incredible fragrance of a yellow-flowered catalpa tree. He lay back on a sandy patch while she tickled his face with blossoms from the catalpa.

"I love you," she said softly, kissing his face.

"And I love you."

How did they come to be naked so swiftly? he wondered, but they were and each delighted in the flesh of the other. In the *spirit* of the other.

He felt immobilized with rapture at her presence, but his loins were girding for action when she whispered, "I want your baby. Please put your baby inside me."

Her words were heated, riveting, and he responded with a surge of joy so profound he was astonished. Her breasts were swollen, the brown nipples pebbled. Cool moonlight lighted them, lured them on, but the night was hot the way their bodies were hot.

He laughed merrily as he told her. "I'm going to give you the baby we both want. Sweetheart . . ."

Groggily he realized the phone was ringing again. *Cait?* he questioned as he picked up.

It was Jayson reminding him to bring a certain sketch he had done of a couple under a Drago tree in Puerto de la Cruz.

"So much for dreams," he muttered as he none too gently put the phone back into its cradle.

* * *

Cait went to open her windows for the night and looked at the waning moon. She couldn't stop wondering what Marty was doing and she didn't want him to be on her mind so much. She glanced down at her soft, light blue cotton shift. She had far prettier nightgowns, but they were part and parcel of a sensual, sexual life she would never know again. Then she reminded herself that she did know that life, *still* knew that life through fantasy. She dreamed often of Sylvan and it soothed her, satisfied her. She could feel a dream of him in her mind now.

Getting into bed, she switched on the remote for the CD player and the strains of "Evergreen" softly filled the room. That song represented her and Sylvan's love forever. Ever, evergreen.

She sat up, took a glass of warm chocolate milk from the nightstand, and sipped it slowly, licking her lips afterward. Her cream-colored Egyptian cotton sheets seemed unusually silky that night, inviting. Sylvan used to tease her about her sensuality, her sense of touch. She cut the bed lamp off, snuggled down, and was asleep immediately.

Masculine hands roved her body with wanton tenderness as she gasped with delight. Baby's breath flowers lay in bunches nearby and she was laughing because she was making another baby with Sylvan. Her flesh and her spirit knew fulfillment then. This was her destiny. There were those in this world who would never know rapture the way she felt it now and sorrow lay in her heart for them because this was life's core. *We sprang from this act of procreation*, she thought.

She smiled then because what was it a wag had said? If God made anything better, he kept it for himself. Oh, this was life and this was loving, deep and profound, going back to the very beginning of the world.

Her partner's big hands cupped her hips, then her buttocks, feverishly went to her female center and stroked the soft hairs, felt the buttery flesh. He rained kisses over her half-fainting body and she became acutely aware of his beautiful shaft that sent wildfire racing in her veins.

That instrument was familiar. It filled her with hot honey, with passion and love like nothing else on earth. And as the feelings grew, she saw him with her heart and soul as well as her eyes.

She stiffened then because the man with her was not Sylvan, but Marty. Confusion began in her brain for a moment and she tried to stop the powerful feelings, but it was useless. Marty was placing a baby in her womb and the joy in her heart and soul was like nothing she had known before.

She sat up abruptly, rubbing sleep from her eyes. Such an ecstatic dream—and with the wrong man. Marty was her *friend*. She didn't want him as a lover. *Oh*, her memory mocked her, *could heavenly thrills fill you when you were with the wrong man*? Of course, she scoffed, and decided firmly that no one was in control of thoughts and dreams. But she was firmly in control of what she would let happen between Marty Steele and her.

Chapter 6

"Dosha!"

"The last time I looked, I still was. How are you, sweetie?"

Caitlin was on the phone with her friend Dosha Steele, Marty's sister. Dosha was one of a pair of fraternal twins.

"Better when I can see you. When do you folks get back?"

"Next Thursday, and we want you and Marty to come over pronto."

"I don't know about Marty, but I'll be there."

The conversation took place the day after Caitlin had dreamed of Marty, and she blushed, remembering it.

"How is the family and where are you calling from?" Caitlin asked.

"Everybody's fine and I'm calling from the front of the Tlide Valero outside Puerto. Yesterday we all went shopping and you'll get your share of the booty. Cait, we've had a wonderful time."

"I'm glad, but I want you back."

"And I'll be there soon. Next year, why don't you and I make the trek? You've been to Italy, loved it because of the art treasures. Wouldn't you like to go back?"

"You know I would. I'll consider that suggestion strongly."

"Great. Listen, I met a nice man, Christian Montero. His father's Spanish, his grandmother is a brown baby. He hit it off with the family—and me."

"Oh?" Caitlin laughed. "You mean he even passed muster with brother Adam?"

"Even. Sometimes Adam gets on my last nerve with his I'm-a-cop-and-I-know-the-whole-score attitude. One of these days I'm going to fall in love with someone he detests and marry him."

"Ah, Adam. What's Damien up to?"

"My twin is busy ogling every shapely señorita he sees. Damien, the musician. Damien, the lover."

"Ummm. And I'm sure your parents are enjoying themselves."

"Don't they always? Those two long ago took out a patent on enjoying life. Everybody sent love when I said I was calling you. When you see Marty . . ." Her voice went somber. "I've talked with Marty several times as I have with you. He seems cheerful enough, but how is he really, Cait? My brother's life has been shattered and yes, I know he's been divorced nearly two years, but he takes things hard. I could strangle Bianca for what she did to him."

Cait thought a long moment. "From what I know about Marty—and that's a lot—I'd say he's still suffering and covering it well."

"Marty wants children. He was striding mountaintops when he and Bianca first married. Fathering a child was all he talked about."

"You're right about that."

"Which brings me to ask how *you're* doing. Cait, is there anyone new in your life—other than Jayson Giles?"

Caitlin chuckled. "Why do you put it that way? Jayson could prove to be enough."

"I guess I just don't see him as your type."

"Why not? He's handsome, suave, rich . . ."

"And you're being flippant. Are you aware that Marty cares so much for you?"

Cait hesitated before she spoke. "Yes, I'm aware, and I care a lot for him. You know we go back forever."

"You might want to hook up with him to see how it works. We get pleasant surprises in this life sometimes."

Caitlin felt her body warm as she thought about coming upon Marty in his hallway and getting so turned on at his magnificent naked body. She thought about the long, wonderful dream she'd had of him and felt a small fire in her nether regions. Her body wasn't cooperating with her mind very well since he'd come to visit, she thought with mild irritation.

"Are you there, Cait?"

"I'm here. I was just thinking."

"Drive up together when we come back, and come after the gallery closes on a Sunday. Let Rena take over Tuesday and Wednesday, and spend three lazy weekdays. Look, love, Mom's beckoning to me, so I've got to go. I'll be talking with you again soon." She made a kissing noise and hung up.

Caitlin leaned forward, somber now. Marty would be back that night. She wouldn't see him again just yet. She glanced at the wall clock. Noon. She felt hungry, craving a chicken teriyaki sub sandwich with thin sliced tomatoes, lettuce, and drizzled with feta cheese and tomato sauce on a big wheat roll. She felt so alive, a bit skittish, and yet happier than she'd been in some time.

Talking to Dosha always gave her a lift. The whole Steele family did.

Caitlin's twin, Caleb, and she were the only children her parents had and they had been closer than close. At Pratt he studied theater art and became a set designer. He and Sylvan were friends. Lord, life was so perfect then.

In college, Marty had begun taking her home occasionally with him when Sylvan traveled in his wanderlust.

Then in her first year of college her loving parents died in an air crash, and Marty and his family had comforted her and Caleb in ways Sylvan had been too impatient to do—he'd been too busy building his life.

She sat thinking she had to check on Marty's house on the way home. He admitted that he was a klutz with flowers, so she had said she'd look after his plants and the orchid collection she had begun for him. Ella, the middle-aged woman who took care of her house and his, handled the really basic care. Caitlin's face got hot; she'd be on guard against having him come out of his bathroom.

She frowned. Seeing Marty naked went far deeper than just the one incident. She *knew* this man, had known him for so long. He had watched over her, taken care of her when Sylvan and Junior died. She had cried night after agonizing night in his arms and he had comforted her, had made her eat when she'd wanted to starve. Had furiously stopped her from drinking too much.

She had begun to go on blind walks about the Village after Sylvan Junior died, wanting some stroke of fate to take her from this world. One night he had followed her, found her and raged, "Sylvan would hate your acting this way, Cait."

On the rain-misted April street, she had cried brokenly, "I have nothing to live for. Let me die!"

He had taken her into a small, nearly empty restaurant and ordered a pot of hot black coffee. "I can't let you do this to yourself. I'm going to take you home with us to stay at least a short while." He and Bianca had been married a year then—beautiful Bianca.

She had cried harder. "You and Bianca are happy, planning a baby. She won't like having me there. Just let me—"

"No. Damn it, *no*!" he'd thundered.

So she'd gone home with him and Bianca had tolerated her, been as kind as she knew how to be. And after several weeks she'd stabilized and gone to live in a small house her church maintained for at-risk children. And miraculously, helping them, she'd been able to begin to heal.

"You're the best there is, Cait," he'd told her one night. "You've got talent you don't seem to realize you have and God intends that you use it. There *can* be another love for you, another child." Hot tears stung her eyes now. Bless Marty. He was still saying that. But she knew there would be no other love, no other child. Yet, her body tore up when she thought it, tore up with fiercely wanting, with a *need* to swell and bear. It was natural, normal—and it hurt like hell.

"Cait?"

Caitlin looked up quickly, batting back the last remnant of tears.

"What's wrong?" Rita Glass, her lone security officer, was standing there. "Your door was open. I knocked, but you didn't hear me. Can I help?"

Caitlin smiled sadly. "It's all right, Rita. I get morbid sometimes."

"Now that I can understand. If there's anything I can do . . ."

"Thank you. I'll be all right. Do you need to talk? Sit down."

Rita lowered her thin form into a chair by Caitlin's desk. "As a matter of fact I do." She nervously smoothed her light brown hair back from her silken yellow-rose face. "You hired me because your husband's prize painting was stolen, and I've enjoyed being here. I needed the job and I've been doing a few extra things." She stopped, frowning.

"I just came by on a whim to check this morning. As you know, I'm usually here from ten P.M. to six A.M. Police are guarding the stores nearby more heavily most of the other hours, but I'm getting ahead of myself. I just found a lock that someone tried to jimmy."

"Oh?"

"Yes. I've never seen anything suspicious in the three months I've been here. A gallery this size can't afford the most effective security. I talked with a gallery owner over in Alexandria who suggested a new kind of vault that's said to be very good, and not prohibitively expensive. He's promised me all the data and he'll talk with you if you're interested."

Caitlin sat up straight. "I'm *very* interested. I'll call him and set up an appointment if you'll give me his number."

Reaching into the desk, Caitlin found a Post-it slip and wrote the number down.

"You look happy," Caitlin said.

Rita's forefinger traced her chin. "I guess I am, but I'm bothered too."

"Would you like to talk about it?"

Rita paused a long moment and closed her eyes. "You've been so helpful since I've been here. You know I knew Jim Draper from when I worked at Third District Police. We were seeing each other after he and his wife split up. Look, I don't want you to think I was the cause of that breakup because I wasn't. He told me they'd been growing apart a long time. She was neglecting his children, driving him to get ahead, railing that he had no ambition. Jim's a laid-back guy. He has some ambition, but not the kind she wanted him to have. His aim was to be the best *father* he knew how to be, not chief of police. He wants to marry me, Cait."

"And you're sick with guilt."

"Yes. I love him so, and I think he loves me and I think we can be happy."

"How's his ex-wife taking this?"

Rita shrugged, sighed. "That's the major reason I left the station house. She threatened to drag my name through the mud, do all kinds of crazy things like passing out flyers saying what a—well, I don't have to tell you the names she called me." Rita laughed harshly. "It's not like her own life is so squeaky clean. Jim felt she was having an affair, at least once."

Caitlin smiled. "Nothing makes us as holy as having slipped along the way."

"Yeah. I guess I slipped too with Jim, so I can't talk."

Caitlin reached over and patted her hand. "You *can* talk, you know. You're not trying to destroy someone."

"Thank you. Jim's coming by to speak with you today."

"I always enjoy talking with him. You've got yourself a nice man, Rita. Build your relationship house and live in it happily."

"Thank you. I love his three kids, but she does everything to turn them against me."

"In time that'll change."

Rita nodded. "Jim's said we'll move away if we have to."

"That may be wise, but don't run if you don't have to."

Caitlin looked up abruptly as Marty's tall form loomed in the doorway. "Look," he said, grinning as he held up a shiny small red bag. "I'll go visit with Rena and come back when you're through talking."

Caitlin felt a rush of pure adrenaline fill her body, and sunlike heat wash over her. For a brief moment, she shuttered her eyes.

Rita got up. "We're finished." She glanced from Marty to Caitlin. "Thank you so much."

"Any time. I'll call and ask about that vault." She introduced Rita to Marty.

Rita left, closing the door behind her.

Caitlin looked at Marty with a smile tugging at her mouth. "You weren't due back until tonight."

"I got lonesome for D.C. and sick of Jayson. We got some business handled, but there wasn't nearly as much going on as he seemed to think."

"Oh? I thought you two were such good friends."

"Hardly." It was on the tip of his tongue to make a remark about Jayson's many compliments about her, but he wasn't going to further Jayson's cause. He pulled a medium-sized dark blue shiny box from the red bag, saying, "Open it."

As he handed her the box, her fingers touched his and a shiver of delight raced along his spine. Her face was a study in wanting, as was his own and neither could hide it.

Marty looked at her, smiling. "You and I are deeply drawn to each other," he told her.

"It happens," she answered softly. "We've known each other so long, and we're good friends."

"I'd like to take it further. Open your package." He wasn't going to take it further because he thought he knew what her answer would be.

"I love presents, getting them and even more, giving them. Did you meet any interesting women in New York? I'll bet they sang you some siren songs."

"No groupies. My mind was back here. I wouldn't have noticed."

She glanced at him sharply and didn't comment.

Package opened, Caitlin gasped at the beauty of a pendant. A ball the size of half a robin's egg of exquisitely blended colors in crystal on a gold herringbone chain. Holding it up caused sunlight to dance from the bauble. She glanced at the small gold and black tag, but she would have recognized the craftsmanship.

"Lladro," she said softly. "How did you know I love his work?"

"Don't you know by now I can read your mind?" He laughed then. "I asked Dosha and we settled on something like this."

"Thank you so much. I love it."

"I like being kissed when I please someone."

She wasn't going to run from him emotionally. Besides, she needed their friendship back on the even keel where they'd always held it. She got up and went around the desk and began to kiss him lightly on his cheek. He pulled her trembling body to him and held her loosely, kissing her gently on her soft, warm lips. "You can break my bank with Lladro trinkets any time for a kiss like that."

She looked at him steadily. "Thank you for not pushing it, Marty. We need each other. Let's not mess it up."

"I can't promise what I can't deliver," he said tersely.

She had drawn away, but his heart still beat hard from the closeness.

"Have you eaten?" she asked. "That sound you hear isn't low thunder, it's my stomach demanding its lunch."

"I deliberately didn't eat on the plane because I want to take you to lunch. Can you check out for a little while and let me take you someplace nice?"

She hesitated. "I haven't got a lot of time, but we could go to a nearby Subway shop if you're willing. Give me a few minutes to sign some letters for my secretary to mail and freshen up."

"Sure."

"Why don't you sit down? I'm certain you didn't get much sleep in New York."

"I got enough."

He walked over to a wall near Caitlin and stood looking at a watercolor of lush, exquisitely rendered brown-edged magnolia blossoms. She called it *Faded Magnolias*. It was glorious, he thought. O'Keeffe had nothing on Caitlin. He had always told her this, but she had chosen to concentrate on her plans for an art gallery, subsuming her own work to Sylvan's. Her eyes had always been starry when she'd told him again and again, "I've fallen in love with a genius and I've made it my mission to nurture him and his incredible talent."

"But what about you?" he'd always protested hotly. "Your work certainly shows plenty of genius. You love nature as much as Sylvan does. You've got even more heart and soul. You owe it to yourself to develop your own God-given talent.

She had kissed him hard on the cheek then. "I have a genius lover I'll marry soon *and* a genius friend, you. That's enough for one circle of friends."

Now Caitlin smiled. "You've always liked that painting. I did it so quickly and Sylvan was critical. He said my lines were imperfect, the lights and shadows weren't all they should be. It lifted me when you liked it so much. Marty, you've lifted my spirits so many times."

"I'm glad I did because this is one of the best small paintings I've seen. I paint *people* because that's where my best talents lie, but I love nature."

She raised her shoulders, then let them slump. Marty was such a dear man and she hoped he'd find a love to replace Bianca. In his dark brown summer trousers with a natural-colored linen jacket and a cream-colored shirt, he was eye candy and he didn't seem to have a clue that he was.

Marty did his own study of her. Dressed in pale blue handkerchief linen with a lined, fitted skirt that showed off her small waistline and wide hips and caressed the fairly heavy, well-rounded buttocks, she was his Venus. The pin-tucked bodice of the dress was cut low and displayed cleavage that made his mouth water. Her tan strap sandals flattered her very good long legs with their flared calves.

"You say you're not beautiful," he said huskily, "but I'm an artist and I know beauty when I see it."

"I'm an artist too," she said pertly, pleased at the compliment, and she complimented him back. "My own personal friend—not Michelangelo's but *My David*."

Marty threw back his head, laughing. "I'm ready when you are. *David* indeed. You're out of your mind."

A feeling swept over her, a reckless feeling almost foreign to her and she spoke before she'd realized what she'd say. "Don't forget I've seen you *and* the statue. I'd say it compares favorably."

Marty stiffened a bit against the heat that took his loins. Teasing her, he said, "Why, you're shocking me, Cait. I didn't think you'd *let* yourself remember."

A bit shaken at her own brio, she told herself that he had been savaged by a woman and she, Caitlin, wanted to help him heal, as he had long ago helped her to heal.

"Let's go, woman," he said. "That sunlight is fierce out there and I want my share of it."

As they walked along, they passed a small park. Marty turned to her.

"Let's sit down a bit. I want to tell you something."

He took her hand and began. "In Puerto I became a part of a well-respected organization that tries to make the world a better place to live in."

"Oh? Is it for the U.S. government?"

He shook his head slowly. "It's bigger than that. One day I'll be able to let you know the whole story."

He sighed then and she asked him, "Is it dangerous?"

He hesitated before he nodded. "It *can* be dangerous, but I haven't been exposed to much danger. That could change at any time."

They were silent for a long moment, then he squeezed her hand. "We're getting closer and I always want to be honest with you. My part is to furnish information about the art world."

"Sounds exciting."

"Sometimes it is." His voice got fierce. "You know I'd never involve you in anything that would hurt you."

She pressed his hand. "You've always protected me and I'm grateful."

"I want to do so much more for you."

His eyes on her made her vulnerable; her defenses began to give way.

So Marty had a secret life. She found she wanted to know all about that life. She looked away for a moment at an ebullient group of small boys shooting marbles on the sidewalk.

When her gaze returned to him, she was shocked at the passion that lay between them. She said nothing, but she plainly heard him say he loved her.

Chapter 7

The first late Sunday afternoon that the Steeles were back, Caitlin and Marty drove to their place out in Minden, Maryland, to visit. As they rounded the bend in Marty's leased burgundy Mercedes-Benz, she felt the lift she always felt when she saw the large white stone house that predated the Civil War. Painted a sparkling white, there were blue shutters and massive evergreens. The Steeles owned five hundred acres of prime land that had been in their family for generations. It was six P.M. and the sun hung low in the late September sky. A black wrought-iron fence surrounded the property and extensive woodlands lay behind and on both sides of the house.

"It's so beautiful," Caitlin murmured.

"And always here. Look at that old bay."

The Chesapeake Bay was less than a mile away and long ago trees had been cut to afford a clear view.

Marty looked at her closely. "Tonight we'll come back outside and watch the moon. It's waning now, but it still gives a good show. Later, let me bring you back when it's full." He chuckled. "Hell, *bring* you back. You belong here as much as I do."

She reached over as they pulled past the cattle-guard entrance and under the carport. "You're such a doll."

He cut the engine. "Men aren't dolls."

"*You* are."

Inside, Dosha had hovered near the windows and she came flying out when she saw the car stop. She stood at Caitlin's side of the car, thrumming with excitement as she opened the door. "Hurry and get out. I need a hug bad. I've missed you."

Caitlin got out and the two women caught each other in a close embrace.

"You look wonderful," Caitlin said. "If a European trip is going to make you this happy, I'm going soon."

Marty had gotten out and walked around to the two women. "See here, you aren't the only one who needs hugs," he said to Dosha. "Where's mine from you?"

He took the shapely Dosha into his arms and hugged her tightly, feeling love for his sibling flood him. He looked approvingly at his pretty, thirty-two-year-old sister with her long, earth-brown kinky-curly hair and smooth allspice-colored skin.

Dosha patted his face. "You're both looking prosperous and well. I'd say you're good for each other."

"I'd second that," Marty said.

Caitlin blushed, remembering all the times Marty had bailed her out emotionally.

Mel and Rispa Steele came out and hugged Caitlin and Marty fervently.

"Oh," Rispa kept saying to Caitlin, "we're so glad to see you again. I'm going to insist you come often." She turned to Marty. "We never saw enough of her, son. We were driven to going into D.C. to see *her*."

"You needed to get into town, and I didn't want to wear out my welcome," Caitlin protested.

Rispa's heart-shaped face glowed. "As if you ever could." The black- and silver-haired, tall, slender Rispa, at sixty, looked fifty, and moved with the grace of a dancer. Her very dark chocolate-colored skin was little lined and fresh with love and tender care.

"Well now, Marty," Mel spoke up. "Now that you're back, we plan to see a lot of you both." He hugged Caitlin again. "I still say you'd make us a great daughter-in-law."

Marty laughed easily. "Don't push her, Dad. She scares easily."

Rispa looked at Caitlin. "Don't be scared at all, honey-bunch. I raised all three of my boys to be good husbands. Luck sometimes just isn't on their sides." She was sad for a moment; then looking at her tall, red-skinned, white-haired husband, she felt no sadness ever lasted in her heart very long. She and Mel were still fit and still thrilled each other's very souls.

"Hey, where's twin and Adam?" Marty asked.

"Well," Dosha said, "Adam hasn't come back from town yet with Rick, and Damien doesn't know you're here. He's out back being a pigeon fancier. He played his violin all afternoon. Now he needs something different."

Marty grinned. "Hell, he's thirty-two. Time he was out chasing women, settling down."

"Ummm, he chases women too," Dosha said, laughing, "but he doesn't seem to be settling down. He chases women maybe too much, but I can't criticize. People marry much later now, so don't start on me, bro. I've got time."

"Just remember your biological clock."

Dosha glanced at Caitlin, feeling Marty's remark would have hurt her. He was a very sensitive man and she realized he had made the remark deliberately. He loved Caitlin and her heart hurt for him. Bianca had proved a devil in his life, had nearly destroyed him.

Mel stood rubbing his hands together, looking over his wife, his brood, and their beloved guest. Then he amended that; Caitlin was a daughter, not a guest.

"It's about time," a mellifluous baritone voice said as Damien came around the house and greeted them. He hugged Marty fiercely, then caught Caitlin in a fond embrace, kissing her soft cheek. "I thought I heard happy voices. Caitlin, you're a peach and you smell like no other perfume I've ever known." He breathed deeply, grinning mischievously.

Marty gave him a mock glare. "Twin, you're a player. It's jasmine you smell, and watch your step. I wouldn't want to challenge my own brother to a duel."

Caitlin looked at him and drew a sharp, swift breath. He spoke as if they were lovers, and she tried to be annoyed, but her feelings went far deeper.

"Properly warned and threatened," Damien said. Damien strongly resembled his twin Dosha, but his earth-brown hair was curlier. He and Dosha were so close. He lived in Nashville, wrote country music, and owned a record-publishing company there. They were a highly attractive family, and he was no different.

"When are Adam and Ricky due back?" Marty asked.

"Jim said they'd be back about now," Mel said. "Ricky wants to see you two. He's talked of little else for days. But he's been hungering for a new video game, and Adam's buying it for him."

Caitlin and Marty went with the others to the huge country kitchen where food in all stages of preparation lay on countertops and butcher blocks. Done in varying shades of yellow, it was a cheerful, homey place where most of the family meals were cooked and eaten.

Rispa bustled about, in her element. Mel came up to her, kissed her brow. "My woman wears well, don't you think?"

Caitlin smiled. "I only hope I can do the same."

"You will," Marty assured her. "You're both made of good stuff."

"You're no slouch yourself, Mel," Caitlin said. The seventy-four-year-old beamed at the compliment.

"I find I'm holding up," he said, glancing at his wife, "with a lot of support."

The front door slammed and a rich-timbred male voice called, "Hey gang, don't eat all the food before we get there!" No sooner said than a tall, chocolate-colored man and a wiry tan boy of thirteen burst through the swinging door.

"Adam!" Caitlin cried and went to him to be caught in a bear hug.

"Ah Cait," he said heartily. "You're just who I needed to see. I told my sib if he didn't bring you, he needn't come either."

The boy, Ricky, squeezed between them. "Hey Cait, I picked you some flowers before I left. They're in my room, but I want a big hug first."

"Thank you, sweetie." Caitlin smoothed the boy's coarse, black hair and hugged him tightly. The supple bones felt good and the old, familiar heartache that came with any child she encountered began. She couldn't stop herself from hugging him again.

Marty came to them. "Hey guy," he told Ricky, "you're beginning to court a little early, aren't you? But then you came by it honestly. Your pop was married at nineteen. We're lucky he kept on for his degree."

Adam looked wistful then. "Don't knock it," he said evenly. "You took your time . . ." He stopped short, shrugging.

Marty looked down for a minute. "Touché," he said quietly.

"I'm sorry, Marty," Adam told his brother. "I didn't mean to be unkind. Losing Kitty hurts even after all this time." He looked at his son. And my kid's a constant, welcome reminder."

"It's okay," Marty said, glancing at Caitlin with all the love he felt as his family smiled.

"Hey, I'm gonna wash up and bring down your flowers," Ricky said as he fairly flew from the room.

Caitlin finished shredding iceberg and romaine lettuce, and cut up chunks of fresh tomatoes, green and red peppers, and Vidalia onions, while the others each finished making a dish.

In a very short time, they sat at a big round oak table covered by cream linen on the large, screened-in back porch. Southern catfish dinners were a specialty with this family.

"This is a po'-man's dinner," Rispa said. "Now tomorrow, we're pulling out all the stops. We've only got one special thing tonight."

"And that is?" Marty inquired.

Rispa looked at Caitlin, smiling. "All the chocolate chip lace cookies you dare eat, and Cait always says you'd better make one enough."

Caitlin's chocolate chip lace cookies originated in a mistake she made when she and Dosha were making regular chocolate chip cookies. She had poured extra melted butter into the final mix and had begun to throw the whole batch out.

"No," Dosha had protested. "Let's bake them and see how they taste."

And the cookies had proved a sensation. Thinner than the regular cookies, and far richer, they were delicate morsels indeed.

Seated beside Caitlin, Marty patted her hand. "I'm

going to risk a second one. I can only die once. Now you all know why I call Cait 'Cookie'."

"Likely comparison," Mel said. "It figures. You two make a fine couple."

Marty raised his eyebrows. "Except we're not a couple—yet."

Caitlin's heart lurched as her eyes met his and held. None of the others at the table missed the electricity between the two.

Ricky's big vase of white and yellow and bronze mums sat near Caitlin and she touched them from time to time. "You've got taste, young man," she told the boy.

Marty laughed. "Sure he has. He's got a crush on you. He couldn't have better taste."

Mel Steele looked at his oldest son. "Marty, *all* the Steele men have the best taste in women." He narrowed his eyes. "And we go after what we want. We don't often fail."

"I don't wonder," Caitlin said quietly. "You're a magnificent bunch."

"And you, honeybunch," Rispa chimed in to Caitlin, "no daughter could be more precious to us than you are."

"Thank you." Caitlin's voice caught.

The simple meal was superb and Caitlin thought she had never tasted more delicious food. The succulent catfish from their large pond in back was coated with coarse yellow cornmeal and bread crumbs, then deep-fried in olive oil. Low-fat macaroni covered with extra-sharp cheddar cheese and thick skim milk, corn on the cob and corn pudding, and tender green peas with carrots and small pearl onions were seasoned to perfection. The baked cinnamon yams were scrumptious. Cornbread-cake muffins dripped with butter mixed with olive oil. There was delicious iced tea or hot tea, lemonade made with Splenda, the new sugar substitute, and milk for Ricky.

It was a happy gathering, with gospel music playing on the CD player in the background. "The Singing Steeles," Caitlin murmured. "I've always loved your and their music, Mel."

The strains of "Go Down, Moses" filled the air with both Ashley and Whit Steele's gorgeous voices. They were two of the children from Mel's first marriage to Lillian. Annice, a noted psychologist, was another.

"I feel soothed all the way through when I listen to your music," Caitlin told Mel. "Soothed and lifted. No wonder you're a favorite."

Mel was silent a long moment, remembering. "I was happy then," he said. "I'm happy now. My oldest son, Frank, followed in my footsteps. He's better than I ever was."

"No," Rispa told him. "No one sang better than you," she said as Mel flashed her a big smile.

Rispa pressed her husband's hand, saying to Caitlin, "His first wife, Lillian, sang with him and Frank. I worshipped them from afar. I fell in love with him from the beginning. No, we didn't become lovers then, but I was there when Lillian left him. I kept praying that God would make him mine and draw me closer to him. Finally, God answered my prayers."

Mel looked at his wife, grinning. "It wasn't like that, baby. I had to work to get you to marry me."

Rispa threw back her head, laughing. "You know the song, sweetheart. 'A boy chases a girl until she catches him.' "

Mel tapped his foot. "Now don't make me kiss you with one of my savage kisses before all these people."

Caitlin nodded. "Watching you two always makes me know the wonderful place Marty comes from."

"Our firstborn," Rispa said tenderly, favoring her son with a deeply maternal look that he vividly responded to.

"On to the cookies!" Ricky yelled.

Adam put his hands over his ears. "Boy, you've surely got the Steele lungs."

"Told ya. I'm gonna be a singer like the Singing Steeles, like Grampa and Uncle Whit." Then he looked sheepish. "Sorry, Dad, I know I get loud sometimes."

"Ha," Mel said. "You should have heard your dad as a boy. He was loud city." He glanced at his daughter. "Why're you so quiet, love? You haven't said a word all evening."

Dosha blushed. "My mind keeps going back to Puerto de la Cruz. Oh, I was glad enough to come back and see Caitlin and Marty, but I . . ."

"You miss seeing and talking with Christian," Rispa said firmly. "I think you two got closer than you realize. He's called twice, and we're only back a few days."

"Oh Mom, you're the matchmaker of the century."

Mel twitted her. "Then why're you looking so flushed and happy when your mama mentions that young man's name? It's time you thought about getting married, girl. Lord, we've got four children, and not a married one in the bunch. I'm beginning to feel we failed as parents." Mel's wide smile said he felt no such thing; give them time and they'd all come in winning. Even Adam would love again.

The chocolate chip lace cookies were the sensation they always were, and Ricky took over serving them. "Next time, Gramma's letting me make them," he said. The huge cookies with semisweet chocolate chunks and pecans melted in their mouths. Ricky served them on Rispa's best cutwork china dessert plates. He also served the coffee.

Rispa grinned happily. "You see," she announced to the table, "he's already in training to make a good husband."

"Ah, gramma," the boy protested.

"You're a Steele, son," Mel said.

Dosha put her elbows on the table. "I'm remembering when you entered the ten-thousand-dollar special flour bakeoff, Cait."

"Those were the days," Caitlin said. "That was one stressful time. My mom taught me to bake the basic chocolate chip cookies, but I made a mistake one day and put a second supply of melted butter in the bowl. And lo and behold, the cookies were much thinner, chewier, looked lacy, and were . . ."

"Delicious!" Dosha finished. "You won second prize and you deserved first prize."

"Yeah," Marty said, remembering. "That money kept us, The Four Musketeers, in grits and watermelon for a long time. You ought to market them, Cait."

"Too much trouble. Besides, I don't get the thrill I get from running my art gallery."

Rispa looked thoughtful. "Speaking of galleries and paintings, your watercolor of magnolias from our tree in the backyard gives me deep pleasure every time I think about it. It's exquisite. Your painting, Marty's. I feel so blessed to have you in our lives."

"Then it's yours," Caitlin said quickly.

"Oh no, we couldn't. It's a small masterpiece." Rispa looked pleased.

"It's yours. No arguments."

Mel and Rispa thanked her fervently.

"You've got quite a heart, Cait," Adam said fondly.

Damien grinned. "She's a Steele, so sure, she's got heart."

Ricky looked at her soberly. "You gonna be a Steele, Cait?"

Marty reached over and smoothed Ricky's hair. "She already is, my boy." But his eyes on Caitlin held more anxiety than he knew.

"Yeah," Mel said. "You could do worse than old Marty here, girl. You'd . . ."

"Dad," Marty said gently. "You're pushing it."

"Okay. Okay, but I raised four great lovers and I'm proud."

Caitlin thought each time she went there she felt the pull of roots. She had been under the Steeles' wings for so long and she loved them as they loved her. But she loved her past life with Sylvan and Sylvan Junior more. People couldn't help what they felt. Still, looking at Ricky hurt. Sylvan Junior would not have been as old as Ricky, but he would have been as precious.

"How's police work, Adam?" Caitlin asked.

"Everything I ever thought it would be. Lieutenant now. Captain, commander, chief tomorrow. Lord, Caitlin, I still love it. A good, highly placed cop interested in the community I serve is all I ever wanted to be. I'm taking courses at the University of Maryland in criminal justice for my master's. Later, I may pick up a law degree, but I'll stay in police work."

Ricky looked at his father as Adam talked, his face lighted with love.

In the big music room were wall-to-wall photos of the Singing Steeles and gospel greats like Mahalia Jackson, the Clara Ward Singers, and the old greats Vernon Barnett, the Fisk Jubilee Singers, and Mississippi's world-famous Utica Jubilee Singers, who had sung in a command performance for England's queen. It was such a beautiful room, hushed and hallowed, done in rich cream and blue.

Mel sat at the old grand piano and the others picked up guitars and tambourines. Mel's second family had never performed in public, but they often sang at home.

Now they sat on cushions on the floor and on sofas, getting the beat of the glorious music depicting a long struggle that had ended in triumph.

"Wade In the Water" was the first spiritual they sang. Mel's mellifluous voice rose above the rest as he led them.

Wade in the water,
Wade in the water, children.
Wade in the water.
God's gonna trouble the water.

Finishing, they were silent for a long moment before they sang "My Lord, What a Morning." And Mel's voice was special as he mournfully sang, "when the stars began to fall."

Surrounded by love, Caitlin felt her heart expand. She became aware then that a certain gladness had crept into her heart and now lingered there.

Chapter 8

It was late when the Steeles and Caitlin piled into the large backyard swimming pool. Ricky had gone to bed, protesting, "You never let kids have any fun. It's a weekend."

Caitlin had taken him in her arms. "Growing boys need rest. Don't you want to grow into a big, strong man like your dad and grandpa and uncles?"

The boy had seemed a little mollified then and had meekly gone to bed.

Marty looked long and hard at Caitlin in her ivory and coral two-piece bathing suit and nervously ran his tongue over his bottom lip at her slender top and lusciously rounded hips. *Lordy lord*, he thought, grinning to himself. The woman had it all going on.

Damien slapped Marty on the back. "How about a four-man race the way we used to do it? Hey, Dad!"

Mel shook his head. "Your mom and I are going to take it easy."

Like three much younger turks, the three brothers lined up after the others had gotten out of the water.

Dosha raised her eyebrows. "You guys will never grow up."

"Sure we will," Adam said, laughing, "when we're a hundred and five." And with explosive laughter, the three stretched out for a six-lap race. Marty was the tallest, the strongest of the three and he easily led for the first two laps. He felt exhilarated as he saw Caitlin sitting in a cabana chair watching him. In the competitive spirit of men since ancient times, he needed to win to impress his chosen mate.

Afterward, Caitlin was never sure why she did it, but when Marty caught her eye, she threw him a kiss, then fretted. *That isn't like me*, she thought. *I shouldn't give him ideas, but friends kiss friends and it was only a little kiss*. Then she sat on the cabana chair with mild shock as she felt Marty's lips on her in a very deep kiss. Her lips parted as if he were with her.

And, feeling that same fantasy kiss, Marty swam like an Olympic swimmer. Three laps. Four. Five. Hell, he wasn't swimming, he thought, he was riding the crest of the waves.

As the brothers, Dosha, Mel, and Rispa congratulated Marty, Damien grumbled, "I could win, too, if I had a goddess egging me on."

Marty laughed uproariously, tingling with Caitlin's presence. "Get started," he said to Damien. "They're out there."

Dosha shook her head. "Oh, please don't push him. He's got more women than he knows what to do with. I'm not sure but my twin is turning into a player."

"*Has* turned," Adam twitted.

"You two make me miss my own twin," Caitlin said softly.

Dosha looked from Marty to Caitlin. "I know you miss him. Twins in both families. If you two were married, you'd more than likely have twins."

Caitlin felt her breath almost stop. They were really pushing it tonight and she felt her emotional moorings begin to slip. But she had a dedicated life and it would remain that way. Still, it felt so good to be surrounded by love and caring. She looked at Dosha, smiling. "Why don't *you* get married, girlfriend? Rispa says she and Mel raise good husbands. I'm sure that goes for wives too."

Dosha blushed, red tinging her brown skin. "It does occur to me sometimes."

"Tell you what, Mama," Mel said to Rispa. "I'm betting at least three of our brood are married within three years."

Rispa shook her head. "Sometimes I wonder. Okay, sweetie, I'll take the bet. Five hundred wager? That's all I need to rejuvenate all my flower beds."

"You're *on*."

"Gambling away our future, huh?" Adam scoffed. "And I thought you loved us."

"Adore all four of you," Rispa said pertly, "but I crave the patter of more little feet. You're supposed to pass our tender care along."

"I tried," Marty said, meaning to be flippant, but pain unintentionally cracked his voice. Recovering quickly, he told them, "I'm going upstairs to get my other digital camera. Hold everything."

Dosha went in for a solitary swim as Mel, Adam, and Damien talked nearby. Rispa came to where Caitlin sat and sprawled on a mat beside her. "Love your bathing suit, sweetheart. Marty hasn't taken his eyes off you. You're such a princess, Cait. Are you happy?"

Caitlin had to ponder the question before she said, "Thank you, and I think so. Being with this family makes me more happy."

"Then why not link with us?"

"I *am* linked to all of you," Caitlin replied evasively.

"You know what I mean—Marty. Listen, love, life isn't perfect. I know how you and Sylvan worshipped each other. You shared the type of great love Mel and I have now, but we've always worked hard on our marriage." She paused and drew a deep breath. "Mel adored his first wife, Lillian, the mother of his eldest children whom I love dearly and who love me.

"Early on when money was tight, Mel did a stint in the Merchant Marines and was away a lot. Lillian fell in love with another man and divorced Mel. He was so *bitter*, Cait. I had known him before through mutual friends. I loved him from the start . . ." She looked at Caitlin. "The way my son loves you now. My love finally won him over and we were married. He still loves her, you know, perhaps more than he loves me. She's been dead three years and I encourage him to go to the cemetery in D.C. and put flowers on her grave. Her new marriage didn't last. She had no more children."

Caitlin placed her hand over Rispa's. "You're a wonderful woman," she said.

Damien stood at the edge of the pool watching the others when Marty came back with his camera. "There's a question I've been meaning to ask you," he said to Marty. "It often really means something when a man calls a woman a pet name. I know it does with me. You mentioned it at dinner. You call Cait 'Cookie.' Why?"

Marty grinned slyly. "Because she *tastes* like one of her chocolate chips."

Damien threw back his head, laughing. "Well, you're a Steele. I'm sure you've raided the cookie jar."

Marty shook his head, smiling. "So far, it only goes to barely tasting. Remember I was very close to both Sylvan and Cait. He died five years ago and she doesn't't think she'll ever get over him. Her heart as well as her soul is a shrine for him, her baby and their love."

"He's dead, bro. Shrines can be cold comfort."

"Trouble is, Cait doesn't feel that way."

"Does she know how much you love her? Have you told her in no uncertain terms? Or just hinted at your feelings?"

Marty smiled sadly. "Cait has always needed space. Sylvan was away a lot, painting, so she had that space. He was cultivating the Atlantic Ocean and he often went down to Atlantic City. You know he was obsessed with big bodies of water. He was often compared to Burn, the famous seascape painter."

"I know who Burn is. A friend owns one of his paintings. Broke his bank. I'll take *your* paintings any time." He clapped Marty on the back. "*Paintings of the soul*. Isn't that what they say and write about you?"

"Critics are kind."

"And perceptive."

They didn't go in until long after midnight. In her cozy room next to Marty's, Caitlin undressed and slipped into a rose-colored, lace-trimmed tricot shortie gown and a matching short robe. A knock sounded and she went to the door.

Marty stood there holding a small tray with a glass of chocolate milk and a chocolate chip cookie. He couldn't resist saying, "I wanted to bring a cookie to Cookie." He grinned, thinking of Damien and their conversation.

"How thoughtful. Thank you." She was so conscious of her naked body under the nightwear, but Marty was even more conscious. He felt a fever begin in his groin and a familiar hardening he usually knew around her. His flesh was hard, he thought, but Lord, his heart was softer than down, where she was concerned. She affected his soul as much as anything.

"Would you like to come in?" she inquired gently, masking heat that began in her brain and spiralled swiftly to her toes.

She was so close to him as she stood holding the small tray of milk and the cookie. She wanted, needed to move away, but she couldn't.

"If I came in," he told her, his eyes narrowing, "I'd get on my knees and beg you to let me spend the night—and if I had my way, we wouldn't be sleeping." He stopped then at the wondrous expression on her face. He saw a yearning that made his heart turn over. What he *said* was different from what she plainly saw. "I've decided to stop crowding you. I'll be your friend, Cait, as long as you let me be. But just know that if you ever want to come to me . . ."

They stood looking into each other's eyes. She could have wept with frustration at the raw passion slamming through her body. A spirit child in her womb cried to be born.

"Just know one other thing," he told her. "When you let me make love to you, *if* you take pity and let me make love to you, it'll be something to change both our lives. I won't press you again, but I have to keep telling you about my love and I *do* love you. You need to know that."

"Marty," she said sadly, "next to Sylvan and my little son, you're my heart and I love you too, but not the way you want me to."

She wanted to ask him to go, but she couldn't. This whole night she had been enraptured with his presence. She walked over, put the tray on the night table, and came back to him.

He intended only to kiss her brow, but his lips fell to one corner of her lips and he lightly flicked that tender place with his tongue. She drew a deep, shuddering breath and came closer. In the open doorway he began to kiss her feverishly, hurting with desire.

He stopped abruptly, and it seemed to him the hardest thing he had ever done. "I'm not going to take advantage of your need," he said, "or of our both wanting a child. I love you, Cait. No matter what happens, always remember that."

He left then and she stood for long moments before she closed the door. She sat on the edge of the bed and drank the milk, then slowly ate the cookie. After opening the windows, she got into bed and to her surprise fell asleep immediately.

With the warm night breeze caressing her, she dreamed of Sylvan and her son. They were here, the three of them, with the Steeles. The baby lay in a bassinet. Sylvan and the Steeles and she swam a long time. Then Sylvan kissed her lightly on the lips and said, "I have to take Junior and go now."

She protested, but he climbed out of the pool, took the baby and left, never looking back. Stunned and hurt, she cried, "No! Don't leave me!" But Sylvan faded in her dream as he had faded from her life.

Then it was Marty who took her in his arms and held her, saying, "I'm here, Cait. I am here for you."

She woke up gasping for breath and her heart hurt the way she had hurt when Sylvan and Sylvan Junior had died. Sitting up, then lying back on three big pillows, she drew up her knees and watched the stars. And she thought of Marty in the next room. The stone walls were thick, so she could hear nothing, but her imagination held full sway. She and Marty were in the doorway of her room and he kissed her again, lifting her spirit and every cell of her. Involuntarily, she touched her flat stomach, which fought to swell and bear fruit.

Chapter 9

Caitlin and Marty were on the Baltimore-Washington Parkway headed for D.C. when her cell phone buzzed. She answered and Rita Glass breathlessly asked where she was. When she gave her location, Rita asked, "Can you come to the gallery before going home?"

Caitlin felt the start of alarm. "What happened?"

"Something weird, Cait. When I checked out this morning at 6:00, someone had left a large package that looked like a wrapped painting at the front door. I thought about package bombs . . . Oh lord, you name it, I thought it, and I called Jim, who was on early duty. He brought a bomb squad guy and they checked out the package. No ticking. Wrong shape. They opened it and it *was* a painting, and get this. It was the same painting that was stolen a bit back."

"*Wild Storm at Sea*?" Caitlin asked excitedly.

"The same beautiful painting. What do you make of it?"

"That's wonderful news. We'll be there as quickly as we can. Have you had any time off?"

"No, and that's okay. I knew you'd want me to look

into this as best I could. Jim got me food, stayed around some. I can always catch up. Jim said he'd be back around ten-thirty."

Caitlin looked at her watch, which registered ten A.M. They had stayed with the Steeles for a heavy country breakfast of sausage, bacon, ham, eggs, and grits.

She cut the phone off and put it back into her tote bag, told Marty what had happened. He whistled. "What the hell's going on?"

"We'll find out soon enough."

They reached the gallery an hour later. The place was abuzz and Sergeant Draper was there. Rena came up to Caitlin, hugged her, and said, "It's wonderful news, yes, but what's the explanation?"

"I haven't the foggiest, but we'll find out, I hope. Where did you put the painting?"

"In your office, and I locked the door."

Jim Draper walked up. "Good news for once," he said heartily. "Only thing is, we're going to have to take the painting in. Stolen property . . ."

Caitlin looked at him sharply. "We've got a small vault here where it would be safe. Have you got anything like that?"

Marty had been silent, observing. "Couldn't you make special arrangements?" he asked Sergeant Draper. "That's a very valuable painting."

Jim nodded. "I know. I was in on the investigation when it was stolen. We thought one of the kids in my former gang group was responsible. I could speak with my lieutenant. He's pretty flexible, but there are rules." Sergeant Draper stood, stroking his chin with his thumb. "And when him we catch this guy—*if* we catch him—we'll need to follow all the rules so some misguided defense lawyer won't be able to find loopholes."

"Yeah," Marty said.

All the employees had been told about the returned

painting and excitement ran high. Caitlin gave Marty her keys and he opened her office door. Switching on the fluorescent light, Caitlin's eyes immediately went to the painting that had been set on a table near a window. The blinds had been lowered. Marty pressed the sides of her shoulders in his big hands.

They both looked at Sylvan's masterpiece and salty tears came to Caitlin's eyes as she breathed her late husband's name.

Gently Marty turned her to face him. "I'm glad the painting's back in your hands," he said. "Crying will help you."

Now she felt warm, cared for. She leaned into him. "Thank you for what you do for me. Do you know how much I thank you?"

He didn't mean to say it because he had decided to hold back, give her space, but it came, unbidden. "I love you, and don't let that frighten you. I won't take it further for now."

His words eased her heart, made her relax a bit. Now it seemed *she* was the one who wanted him, *needed* him. Marty was a rock, had always been a rock. *Her* rock. And what did she give him but trouble?

"I wish it could be different," she said wistfully. "You're one of the finest men I've ever known."

"Thank you. I'll always be there for you, like I've told you before." He smiled sadly then. "Right now, you're my mission in life, as Sylvan is yours."

"That's unfair to you. You need someone to take Bianca's place."

"In due time."

Leaning forward, she kissed his cheek, saying softly, "Precious, precious Marty. My best friend."

Feelings she didn't understand flooded her. His big, muscular body pressed in on her softer one as mild, pleasant electrical energy flowed through and around them. His very light men's cologne filled her nostrils, but Marty also smelled of the woods he was so fond of, smelled of earthy things. Her mind held him at bay; her body clamored for him. And on some very deep level, he understood this and waited patiently.

They walked over to the table and stood looking at the fabulous painting. There were lights and shadows reflecting a master's touch. Blended colors so rich, so deep they mesmerized.

"He would have been famous," she said. "Already he was so well known, so well regarded." She clenched her fingers. "Why couldn't it have been different?"

"So many questions," he said sadly. "And sometimes no answers at all."

The painting looked, she thought, as if it had all the answers. In this painting, you felt this raging storm, became one with it because this was a human storm as well as a storm at sea. Every heartache, every bitter tear, every torn-up wail of desolation lay on that canvas, put there, stroke by genius-laden stroke, by a master who had not lived long enough to weather many storms.

"If only he could have lasted," she said slowly. "Sylvan used to say, 'If anything happens to me, Marty will help you. You have your twin, of course, and you two are bound in ways the rest of us can only imagine. Marty is stable, solid, the way the rest of us only aspire to be. Lean on him, Cait, if you need to. He'll never let you down.' " She had never told Marty this. Could she tell him now? She decided against it. She didn't want to give him false hopes.

Instead she said, "Oh Marty, I'm so pleased about the painting. I'm going to call Dosha and give her the good news."

Dosha taught music at D.C.'s Ellington School for the Arts. She had taken a few extra days' leave for the vacation with her family, but she was in full swing now. Caitlin flexed her shoulders. She'd call her during the noon hour.

Glancing at Marty, she saw that his face radiated a beatific smile.

"Why are you smiling so?" she asked him.

"My mind went back to the weekend. You fit in with us so well, Cait. You belong with us, with—" He stopped then.

"With *you*?" she questioned gently. "It's okay, Marty. You don't have to say it. I'm really sorry."

"We can't help where our hearts take us," he said staunchly.

She pressed slender fingers to the side of his face. "Thank you for being so understanding. One day you'll find someone."

He said nothing, but his every heartbeat murmured, "I already have, love. I already have."

The rest of the morning was taken up with talking to Sergeant Draper and his lieutenant, who decided that the painting could be kept in the gallery vault. The lieutenant shook his head. "This is one unusual case. If I were a mystery writer, I could probably do a book around this idea."

Rita and Jim exchanged glances filled with longing. When would they be together as a married team? Rita wondered. In the hallway, Luther Moore came up to Caitlin and Marty. "I heard the news and boy, this is a great turn," he said.

"You bet it is," Caitlin responded. She liked Luther, who was nearly fifty but didn't look or act a day over forty. He worked hard, was always there, and took his job seriously. He handled the gallery caretaking chores by himself mostly, but supervised the commercial heavy-duty cleaners who came weekly.

"Anything you need me for," he told Caitlin, "I'm here."

Caitlin smiled at him. "Thanks, Luther." He insisted that everyone call him by his first name, even children. "No need in growing up," he often said. "Life's more fun if you stay a child. I'm always reminded of the boy in the IBM ad who looked up at a beautiful blue sky and said, 'That sky is so beautiful, it makes me want to bite my toes.' " And he always cackled when he said it.

He didn't quote the boy in the ad now, but Caitlin smiled, remembering. Gorgeous blue skies made her want to bite her toes too. She guessed that's why Luther took such pride in his work. Basically he was an artist, the way so many people were.

A sense of peace filled Caitlin as she walked along the polished gallery floors with Marty. Her gallery always excited her the minute she stepped in the door. Local artists exhibited there and loved the gallery, but she was gaining more and more widely known talents. A few Romare Bearden collages. Lou Stovall silk screens. Paris scenes done by Lois Mailou Jones. They were all so gifted, they blessed the world they lived or had lived in.

Rena came to her with a small, brown wren of a woman. A Latina. She introduced her as Maria Vasquez and Caitlin recognized the name. She had quite a following in the Latino community and wanted to be more multicultural.

"Buenas dias, señorita," the woman said. "It is such a great thing you do, showing local artists, other cultures. Rena tells me you like my paintings."

"I love your paintings," Caitlin said. "You're especially fond of flowers, as I am."

"Ah," the woman said, "you are right, but I've seen *your* paintings and my watercolors are not in the class with yours because yours are—" She groped for a word.

"Inspired?" Marty suggested after a moment.

The woman's merry laughter pealed. "Yes, inspired. You are amazing."

"I keep telling her," Marty said.

"And so do I," Rena chimed in.

Caitlin smiled broadly at the compliments. She knew her colors were like Lois Mailou Jones's and Alma Thomas's, both renowned African American artists, but Marty most often compared her to the venerated Georgia O'Keeffe. High praise indeed and it bothered her. She had moved in Sylvan's shadow from the beginning of their relationship at seventeen, when the four of them had become The Four Musketeers. Sylvan had been an Olympian god and she had always been his handmaiden. "You seem perfectly content to reflect me and my passions," he'd often said, "and I think that's why I love you so. I have *your* energy as well as my own. Don't change, Cait." Then he'd said fiercely as he pulled her to him, "Don't *ever* change."

And she hadn't. Five years after his death she hadn't changed. She felt it was something to be proud of. In life she had belonged to him and to Sylvan Junior. In death he was still her dream.

Caitlin smiled as an absolutely beautiful young black girl of eighteen came toward them. Her skin was burnished black and her swanlike neck could have served as a model for a Modigliani painting. "Lisa!" Caitlin said and the girl and the woman embraced.

"I brought you a painting," the girl said.

Caitlin hugged her again. "Tell her, Marty, that I don't flatter her. They say *you* see and paint the soul, so you'd know." She introduced them.

"I have to agree with her," Marty said. "You are beautiful and you have presence. Do you model?"

The girl shook her head. "No. I, too, like to capture the soul." She turned to Caitlin. "I wanted you to know that I got the scholarship to Pratt, thanks to you. I love you for the way you've helped me and I'm going to do you proud."

"I know you will," Caitlin told her. "I want you to keep in close touch, you hear? I'll be sending you care packages." Lisa was poor, one of eight children in an impoverished D.C. family.

"You're the best," Lisa said and hugged her. Then the girl turned to Marty. "Take good care of her."

"Believe me, I will."

Chapter 10

November of the same year

As Caitlin and Marty walked along the avenue in the Adams-Morgan area, not far from their houses, they looked up at a soft blue sky with thin, trailing clouds. It was 5:30 P.M. and rapidly getting darker. Crisp fall air heralded the coming winter.

"We're about out of Splenda," Marty said. "Let's stop at the supermarket."

"Why don't you get it?" Caitlin paused. "The market gets crowded. I promised I'd call Dosha around six and I want to be home when I call. Do you mind?"

"Nope. I'm aware of my love-to-talk sister and you when you two get on a phone. I'll be there long before you're finished."

"You're a doll."

"And I keep telling you men aren't dolls."

She smiled at him impishly. "*You* are."

Marty stopped and looked at her, his eyes narrowed. "It seems to me," he said, "we've had this conversation before and often."

Caitlin smiled again. "You're always encouraging me to show my spirit, to stand up for myself. And I say you're a doll."

"And I say you're a little mad, even if you are sweet."

For a moment, Caitlin sighed. "I think I'm going a little crazy if we can't figure out why anyone would steal a painting, then return it. Over two months, and no clue."

"Yeah. Sergeant Draper says they're stumped."

She patted his shoulder. "While you're in there, please pick me up a Chilean honeydew."

"At eight dollars a melon?"

"They're very sweet and incredibly delicious. I'll even share a slice with you."

"Half or I won't buy it."

"Okay, greedy, half, but I eat fast when it's something I like and if I finish my half first . . ."

"We'll talk more about this."

As Marty walked away, Caitlin stood looking at his tall body, broad shoulders, narrow hips. She noted how women openly and shyly looked him over. She and Marty seemed to grow closer by the day. He was teaching her how to look past a persona into a soul. She showed him the delicate art of capturing a blossom's beauty, of delineating its life. Now she looked forward to her talk with Dosha, who constantly encouraged her to open her heart to Marty. "If only I could find a man like my brother, I'd jump the broom in a second."

Caitlin didn't need reminders that Marty was tops and her body warmed when she thought of him. She walked more slowly than she knew and was nearing her house when she felt hot breath on her neck. People were in the street, but most seemed to be hurrying home. She felt strong arms go around her, tried to turn and was held fast. "Going somewhere, Mama?" a hoarse young voice asked.

She put her palms over masculine arms and growled, "Get your hands off me."

"Now, now," he simpered. "Let me look at that pretty face."

He turned her around and she had only a moment to smell the liquor and the sweetish marijuana odor before he tried to kiss her, bending her to his will. She balled up her fist and struck him, then furiously dragged her medium-length length fingernails down his cheeks.

"Now, now, Mama. I must be lighting your fire."

He tripped her and she fell awkwardly, her ankle twisting under her. Knifelike pain shot through her body.

His laugh was softly malevolent. "That's the way I like my women—at my feet."

My God, she thought. There were people out here, but she knew most would think it was a domestic quarrel and wouldn't interfere. The whole thing had happened so swiftly that only then did she think to scream. He was swiftly on her like an animal and her cry enraged him. What did he intend to do? Nothing if she could help it.

He calmed suddenly, snickering. "I hurt you. Now I'm gonna use my tools to help you."

She was struggling valiantly when strong hands snatched her attacker's body up and she heard a string of curses that came from an enraged Marty.

"You picked the wrong woman," Marty snarled and punched him.

He began falling and Marty dragged the youth to his feet, then lifted him off the ground by his coat collar.

"Hey," the youth whimpered, "you don't need to get nasty, Dad. I was only trying to take her for a little long green. Wasn't gonna hurt her. I ain't no savage."

"Shut up!" Marty roared. "And if I ever catch you near her again, I swear I'll make you wish you were dead. Now get the hell away from here!"

The youth limped away slowly, but he paused at a streetlamp and looked back. "Sheesh," he said loudly. "Sure must be some special stuff she lays on you. How was I to know she was your broad?"

"Move!" Marty roared again and this time the limp was gone and the youth sped away.

Marty knelt beside Caitlin, who sat up. She realized then that the youth had pummeled her more than she'd thought.

"Are you okay?" Marty asked tenderly. "Damn it! If he hurt you . . ."

"Marty, don't let it get to you," she told him, touched by his anger and his fierce rescue of her. He still held a killer stance. "I think I twisted my ankle, or something, but I'm sure I'm gonna be okay."

He helped her up and she put her foot down gingerly. Pain shot up her leg and she winced, leaning more heavily on him.

"You're *not* all right." He put his arm around her waist and his touch warmed her. "Stand on your other foot while I pick up your things."

She stood as he had directed and felt better. He picked up the few items that had scattered when her tote had spilled. Her expensive purse hadn't come open. He slung her tote and strap purse over his shoulder and lifted her.

She laughed shakily. "You can't handle all this stuff and me too. I can walk—I think."

"I don't want to risk making a bad situation worse," he said shortly.

He carried her and her head was just above his as they moved along. She bent and kissed the top of his head. "Thank you," she said softly.

Inside her house, only a short distance away from the mugging scene, Marty had Caitlin sit on the sofa as he examined her foot and ankle. His big hands soothed her long legs and she felt cherished. Loved.

"Thank you," she said again. "You're really something in action. You—"

He knelt beside her, studying her gravely. "I what?"

She shook her head quickly. "Nothing." She had been on the verge of saying he turned her on. What the hell was she thinking? she wondered.

"Now plans." He rubbed his hands together, sat back on his heels. "We've got work to do. Take you to the emergency room after I make a police report." He was thoughtful a moment, frowning. "Cait, could this have anything to do with the fool nearly hitting you with his car the first day I was here?"

She drew a deep breath. "I don't think so. That was two months ago. We don't have a clue about the man in the car, but we surely saw *this* one. He was drunk and probably on drugs. Maybe a gang member, maybe not."

"I'm gonna report it to the police, then." He took her hand, kissed her fingertips. They were acting like lovers, she thought.

It was late when they returned from the emergency room and Caitlin was tired. The police had taken the report over the phone and the ER hadn't been too crowded.

"I'm spending the night with you," Marty told her.

"For which I'm grateful. I'd do the same for you." She kept thrilling to the flashback of his defending her. A cavewoman's response to her caveman suitor. She closed her eyes. And make no mistake about it, Marty *was* her suitor.

"You know where everything is by now," she told him. "Are you hungry?"

He rolled his eyes, a slight smile played at his mouth. He was hungry, all right, but no food would satisfy that hunger. "Are you?" he asked.

"I'd like a glass of chocolate milk and—"

"Yes, what else?"

She grinned, teased him. "A small, well-behaved kiss to soothe me."

"I'll do my best to restrain myself. It won't be easy."

He leaned forward and captured her lips with his as she relaxed and leaned into him. They were both magnets. They were filings drawn to those magnets and the kiss ignited from the start. Leapt and blazed. His blood was hot lava as his hands threaded into her soft hair and his fingers kneaded her scalp. He groaned with a nearly desperate need as his tongue feverishly worked the recesses of her sweet, sweet mouth.

And she pressed hard into him, surrendering to his superior physical strength. She no longer asked herself what they were doing. Whatever it was was right. Her tender body ached and her heart and soul cried out for a baby and for love on *this* planet, at *this* time.

"Cait," he said huskily, tearing himself a little away from her. "Are you okay? I don't want to hurt you. I think you need to rest now."

Oh God, she thought, she was dying of need. Was he rejecting her? No, that was Marty, thinking first of *her* needs, *her* welfare.

She touched his face, kissed the corners of his mouth. "You're so sweet," she teased him.

This time he laughed. "Ah, this time I *feel* sweet. I've taken in so much of your sugar, which reminds me, I got to you so quickly because they were out of Splenda."

"Thank God for that," she murmured.

* * *

In bed that night, acutely conscious of Marty in the next bedroom, at first Caitlin tossed and turned before the sleeping pills the doctor had given her took effect. She drifted into a seamless dream of this very room, with its rose and pink and cream decor. She held a burgundy throw pillow in her arms, hugging it, fantasizing Marty was with her. And suddenly in the dream he *was* there. He pulled her up from the bed and held her hard against rippling muscles pressing in on her softness, her breasts flattened against his hard pectorals, tender electrical flashes striking through their loins. She wanted him so badly it was like dying of need. She awakened a little but could not bear to leave the dream. They were like dancers choreographed by a master, their bodies in tune with deepest nature. He entered her and her world turned to golden wonder. A dream, she thought, a *dream of ecstasy*.

And in his bed Marty tossed too. She was just beyond him, his Cait. Sure, he thought, *his* Cait. Only she wasn't his. Last time he'd checked, her life still belonged to Sylvan even if she *had* grown so much closer to him, Marty. He touched his big, engorged shaft and his imagination went wild. He took Cait in his arms, drew her to him, held her tightly, his heart thundering beats. Then he began to cover her with kisses, his tongue patterning his love and flaming desire over her body. He felt he would explode with passion that would pour his seed into her body and together they would make the baby they both wanted so desperately.

His dream was short; it had stopped as he planted his seed into her incredible body. How deep could his love go? And he knew he had the answer to that in Caitlin. Tonight she had wanted his body; her eyes had been glazed with her wanting, but what he wanted was her love and passion, respect and trust all tightly intertwined. She had once told him she'd had all that with

Sylvan. And she didn't expect to find that glory ever again.

Marty frowned. And what would she do if she knew the truth about Sylvan? Would it destroy her? She was the one he had to think of.

Chapter 11

Caitlin came awake early the next morning. Burrowing deeper into the covers, she didn't want to get up, but she was aware of feeling happy.

It was a few minutes before she thought of the mugging and flinched, but that feeling was quickly overcome by sharp memories of Marty's rescuing her. She still felt safe.

She easily managed to get up, anticipating pain that didn't occur. Padding barefoot to her bathroom, she switched on the globe light over the face bowl and studied herself. She surely was a bit banged up.

After washing her face, she dabbed on a very good antibiotic cream, spread on a thick, peach lotion with a heavenly smell on her body, brushed her teeth, and padded back to bed.

Marty knocked and waited until she asked him in. He strode quickly to the bed. "How do you feel?"

"Surprisingly together."

"Great. Smell that coffee I brewed?"

She drew in a deep breath. "Smells wonderful. Marty, how can I thank you?"

He grinned wickedly. "This is no way to talk to a bruised lady, but there may come to be ways."

Caitlin felt ever so slightly uncomfortable, but that was the tip of the iceberg. Deep, complex feelings rippled through her as she felt his meaning. He had never spoken of their making love before. Then she smiled inside. That was a cryptic remark he had just made. Maybe he didn't mean it the way she thought he did. That was what had been in *her* mind. Looking at his wide shoulders and chest in his black shirt and trousers and his white tee showing a bit under his shirt, she imagined his muscular, well-honed body and her glance moved to his narrow hips and the unmistakable bulge in his trousers.

He sat on the edge of the bed as she moved over to give him more space. "How did you sleep, Cait? I looked in on you several times last night. You were dead to the world."

"I can't remember when I've slept like that. I even feel like fixing breakfast, remembering you can't cook."

"No. The doctor said you were to rest all day, so I'm monitoring your movements." He grinned. "I guess you can go to the bathroom. Otherwise, I wait on you. You've told me you only have oatmeal and orange juice in the morning and something heavier between eleven and one. Hell no, I still can't cook, but I've got a Puerto de la Cruz dish down pat. I'm gonna surprise you. Are you sore?"

She raised her eyebrows. "A little, but I feel remarkably well. I'll probably find I'm stiff when you do let me get up. Otherwise, I can't believe how well I feel."

"No bad dreams?"

"None. In fact . . ." Her body flamed as she remembered her long, erotic dream of him and her the past night.

"In fact?"

She shook her head, flexed her shoulders. "Nothing. Did you have dreams of saving me?"

He was more forthcoming as his eyes held hers. "I had dreams, all right, dreams of you and me and all kinds of good things going on." He leaned over and kissed her cheek very lightly. His body, his presence flooded her with desire.

"You can do better than that," she whispered.

"You couldn't take it if I did."

Neither spoke as they gazed at each other, drawn beyond the telling. The rose satin gown she wore had a bodice with many transparent appliqued inserts and the beautiful lustre of her skin shone through. Suddenly his lips captured hers and his tongue explored the delicious warmth and sweetness of her mouth. She kissed him back, probing his mouth as he had probed hers, relentlessly trying to satisfy the hunger that simply could not be satisfied with mere kisses.

This was new territory for them. They had held back, careful to protect a friendship they both treasured. She wondered what would happen now, but she couldn't stop the tidal wave of desire that swept over her. Words she wanted to say to him crowded her brain. This was a primeval feeling as ancient as time itself. She let herself surrender, thinking: *do with me what you will*. And it was strange because she felt free then, more free than she'd ever felt.

He tore his mouth away from hers and sat straight, stroking her. "I don't want to press you. I never want to take advantage of you, and I never will. I'm going to say it even if you don't want to hear me say it: I love you, Cait, with everything that's in me. And I want you so bad it kills me. Maybe I can't wait forever, but I'll wait as long as you let me.

"You want a baby and I want you and only you to bear *my* baby. Maybe my love could be enough for both of us. People have fallen in love long after they married. I'd consider myself the luckiest man in the world if you say you'll marry me."

She couldn't answer, her heart was so full. The thought came unbidden: Sylvan would understand that she found she needed more than her work and the remembered presence of him and Sylvan Junior to make it possible to go on.

"You know I love you as a dearest friend," she said slowly. Her voice got hoarse. "Wanting you so much is new to me, but it makes me feel alive. These feelings have exploded between us. You're whom I would marry if I could marry anyone. God, how I want a baby the same way you want one." She touched his face. "Give me time to think. Just now I'm thinking with my womb."

He grasped her slender hands and squeezed them. "Take all the time you need. I'm going to fix your breakfast, bring it to you, then I'm going to go out for a little while. When I get back, I'm going to cook the only cuisine I can do. Puerto de la Cruz's famous rabbit stew."

He got up and started out, looked back as he reached the door and found her looking steadily at him. He wondered if she knew her eyes were like stars and her tender, loving beauty ravished his heart.

Marty came back in an hour or so with his arms full of roses, lilies, peonies, broadleaf fern, and baby's breath.

"How beautiful!" Caitlin exclaimed. "And so many. You're spoiling me."

"That's just the beginning." He lay the large sheaf of flowers on a table, selected one thornless red rose, took a knife from his pants pocket and cut the stem.

She waited quietly as he put the rose behind her ear. "A kiss for each rose," he teased, but his look was serious. "I'm going to wait, give you time to build up passion."

Time was on his side, she reflected, because desire and passion now stoked her being, set up a clamoring and a craving to know him in every way a woman could know a man.

They spent a lazy morning listening to pop tunes and reading poetry to each other before he went to the kitchen to make his specialty.

"Do you have wild rice and green peas on hand? Plenty of salad makings?" he asked.

"You're in luck. They're all there." And she told him where to find the items he needed. "Does all this go into the dish?"

"Oh no, they're just side dishes. I promise this is gonna hit you where you live."

She smiled as their eyes met and clung again. Everything about this man was hitting her where she lived. Her body yearned for him with a terrible urgency. And she well knew what was going on.

Around eleven-thirty, as she listened to sounds in the kitchen, she drifted to sleep and came awake to him shaking her gently with a damp washcloth in his hand. He sat down as she turned over and ran the cloth over her face. "Ready for something special?"

She laughed delightedly. "I'm ready. Bring it on."

He grinned. "Feeling hungry, are we?"

She nodded. "In more ways than I can tell you." She was glad then that they were old friends because she could feel herself opening to him in thrilling, erotic ways. Sylvan had always thought women should hold back a lot of themselves to tantalize the man they wanted. But she wasn't holding back with Marty. He knew how she wanted him, even if her heart still belonged to Sylvan. Wistfully she wished she could be in love with him the way he seemed to be in love with her.

As the food cooked, Marty cut roses for Caitlin's room and put them in vases. It had been a long time since he'd had a woman, not since Bianca had savaged him. It felt good to love again, even if Caitlin didn't love him and maybe never would.

He stepped out on her screened back porch where an easel stood with a painting begun of a single yellow mum. He shook his head. The unfinished painting was so damn good, with all the perfect lines and perfect composition that was her gift. She had lived completely subsumed by Sylvan's personality, his undeniable genius. And Sylvan had kept her that way as the price for his love. *You had no right to enslave her*, Marty thought bitterly. The time for the love enslavement of women was over, and Sylvan took advantage of her love. Marty drummed his fist on a nearby table and wished for his tobaccoless pipe.

When the food was ready, he sampled it again and set a big wooden tray with fine china, silverware, and crystal. He put a small vase of roses on it. Moving to the beat of a country tune, he felt pleased with himself. He'd decided on the Rocky Road flavor of Ben and Jerry's ice cream and the sinfully rich devil's food cake Caitlin had baked a few days before. That would come later. He prepared his own tray and wheeled them both in to Caitlin on a tea cart.

"Exquisite," she told him. "I wish Ella could see this. She'd love it." Ella was Caitlin's part-time housekeeper.

"How's she doing?"

"Well, a cold always hits her like a ton of bricks. I called and told her what had happened and she wanted to come in anyway. I said you were with me and she calmed down. And oh yes, Dosha called and she was furious about my getting mugged. They're on a field trip to New York. She, ah, liked it that you're staying with me."

He gently mocked her. "I, ah, like it too."

The food was superb, unlike any Caitlin had tasted before. "Exotic rabbit stew," she said. "Such a simple fantasy that name conjures up. Such an intricate taste. You've got to give me this recipe."

He sat by her bedside with a tray fastened over his chair arms. "Whatever I have that you want, you've got it, 24-7."

There it was again, she thought, the feeling of being drawn into another person's very soul. Nature was relentless. Nature saw to it that the race continued. God saw to it that love always abounded somewhere.

"You make a mean salad, too," she said. "What's the dressing? It's good."

"Feta cheese and dried tomatoes. My favorite. I got a big bottle while I was out."

"I'll never again say you can't cook," Caitlin told him.

"Thanks, but I'm a one-dish chef."

"You teach me yours and I'll teach you mine," she said happily.

When the meal had settled, Marty suggested they play Scrabble, a favorite game for both. "Since you can't move about handily, we'll just exercise our minds," he said.

Caitlin smiled widely at the thought of playing Scrabble with Marty. He had a tack-sharp mind, spelled badly, and was always asking her how certain words were spelled. Then to her consternation, he usually built milelong words and won.

"I'm a glutton for punishment, but let's go."

They played in the dining room with bright fall sunlight streaming through the windows, and she was happier than she had been in a very long time. Pausing for a minute in the game, he lifted her hand, kissed it, then trailed kisses up her lower forearm, with its bruises and scratches where she'd fallen. He kissed the deep scratch and his lips lingered as shivers ran the length of her body.

"You would have to be a fantastic lover," she said softly.

She could barely hear him when he whispered, "There's only one way to find out."

His tender glances were turning her on sky high. "I'm a little tired," she murmured. "Do you mind if we stop?"

"I don't mind at all, and if you're tired . . ."

He got up and came around the table. "Raise up a bit."

She did as he asked and he gathered her up in his arms and carried a speechless Caitlin into her bedroom, laid her on the bed. Torpor swept over her and she fumbled with the zipper of her robe. "Help me get it off," she told him.

For a long moment he didn't answer, then his words seemed torn from him. "Cait, be sure this is what you want. I can't bear hurting you. I don't want you to ever be sorry for anything that happens between us."

"Just help me," she begged. "I know what I'm doing and this is what I want." Then came her heart's cry. "Help me put a baby in my womb."

He caught her close, crushed her to him, glorying in her soft, yielding flesh.

His words were fierce, yielding his very soul to her. "I love you, sweetheart," he told her. "I'll always love you. Please don't ever leave me."

She wished fervently she could give him the kind of love he deserved and it made her sad, but she *could* give him the child they both craved. She felt him unzip her robe, remove it, then his paint-roughened hands slipped the nightgown down her body.

"Now you," she told him. "Please stand up."

He did as she asked and she swiftly took off his garments, letting them fall to the floor. "Marty and Michelangelo's *David*," she whispered when he stood naked. "Oh lord, you're one beautiful man."

Marty's voice caught in his throat as he stared in wonder at her voluptuous, rounded body. "You're a little mad, but I love you for it. *You're* the beautiful one, Cait." Her brown breasts were full and slightly pendulous with a large, smooth nipple area. Her waistline sharply indented, and her hips swelled gently into buns that he stroked, then clutched, groaning.

"Please take me now," she whispered, stroking his shaft that was already greatly swollen with desire.

"Not yet, honey," he told her. "I want you to really enjoy this."

He laid her on the bed and switched on the CD player. Lionel Richie's gravelly, compelling "Lady" filled the air. The song so exactly bespoke the way he felt about this woman that he set the machine to keep repeating. Lifting one of her feet, he gently kissed and fondled the toes, then the other foot. He began kissing and licking her well-tended feet and her legs, then began an upward journey over her body.

Blind with savage desire, she felt him at her center, but he didn't linger there. This was like nothing she had ever felt before, not even with Sylvan, and she brushed the thought away. She was glad she had put Shalimar bath oil at strategic pulsing spots over her body. He inhaled deeply, feeling that the fragrance and her presence and the music were all a combination that were driving him crazy with desire without end, with passion, and with a thrilling love that bound it all together.

By the time his lips found hers and a heated dance of desire began, she was crying tears of pure joy.

He asked her gently, "Why are you crying?"

For a moment she didn't answer. "Because I want you so bad. Do you know how much I want you?"

"I'm glad. I know how much I'll always want *you*." He stopped for a minute to stay his rush to pour his seed into her.

He swirled kisses onto her belly, tonguing the deep navel, then moved up to her breasts and slowly, tantalizingly laved and licked one, then the other as she threaded her fingers into his hair and pressed him hard against her. He suckled her breasts then with ravening hunger.

He tried to turn her over as she resisted. "There are things I'm going to do to you," she told him, "but not now. Sweetheart, please don't make me wait any longer for you to be inside me."

She spread her legs and he entered her hotly pulsing secret place with its wondrous network of strong, clutching muscles that welcomed his shaft, took it in, and tenderly gripped him. He was big and he filled her. She raised her legs and put them over his back, felt his hot, swollen shaft throb wildly as he expertly worked her. She moved under him with the grace of an Olympic gymnast.

Then it hit him that they weren't using protection. "Just a minute, baby. I've got to get a condom."

"A condom? But we *want* a baby."

He shook his head. "I'll only be a moment."

She was disappointed, hungry for his seed, but when he got the condom from his pants pocket, she helped him smooth it on, revelling in the beauty of his shaft. When he hesitated a moment, she arched her hips, rolling them as he held himself taut against coming. Then he slid into her avidly clutching body again and felt her womb contract. Lord, he thought, this was like nothing he had ever known. Never before had he felt this wondrous blend of ecstasy and thrills, the beginning of incredible fulfillment. Deep love did this to you, he reflected, and knew he would love this woman forever.

And beneath him, with her legs over his wide shoulders, Caitlin thought this was all the world's glory concentrated in this man. As he paused, she felt him throbbing, then the rhythmic dance began again. He pulled out nearly all the way, then plunged in deeply, gently, swiftly and she felt her body convulse with the music of peak desire. Her inner muscles gripped his shaft and held him prisoner as if she could not bear to let him go.

He felt higher than any mountain as they moved feverishly together, no longer two people, but fused into one, lost in bliss and harmony. This was love in the daylight hours with a bright fall sun shining outside. But there might as well have been twinkling galaxies of stars and a full moon. They could not have felt more wedded to their earth and their universe.

He drew a deep breath and stayed inside her; she held him there. "You're wonderful and I love you so much in so many ways I can't express," he said.

"I think I know and I'm sorry. Oh, I'm not sorry that you love me, but that I can't return the deepest part of your love. I thought we were going to make a baby."

He pulled out gently, stroked her soft pubic hair a moment or two and sighed. "Cait. I think it's pretty clear we both intend to make a baby, but we've got to get married. Why not now? A baby deserves all the care, all the best plans from the beginning."

"I know where you're coming from, but we could have *begun* tonight. Then marriage—if you can live with my not loving you the way you say you love me."

This time, he didn't focus on her last words. "Maybe I worry too much, but condoms sometimes break. Then, too, if something should happen to me, I want to know that you and my child are legally covered in every way. I've wanted a child too long, as you've wanted a child too long not to have it this way. Let's drive over to Elkins, get married tomorrow."

She felt sober and thrilled at once. "You're right. We'll go to Elkins tomorrow."

He caught her and hugged her so tightly she thought for a minute her ribs would break. "I love you," he said again.

"And you know my love for you. It's not just because of the baby that I'm marrying you. This has come about so suddenly. Since you've been here, I find I *need* you. I'm strong, independent, but I . . ."

"You've never *used* the strength and the power you have in full," he said. "You're even more independent than you know. And you're gifted, Cait, really gifted. I'll never let you live in *my* shadow."

His words entranced her, turned her on, and she melted against him. "Superstar lover," she teased him. "There are things I'm going to do to you."

"Promises," he teased back. Then hesitantly, "Did I satisfy you?"

"Yes and yes and yes again."

"There's so much more where that came from."

"Me first." Then she laughed. "I've got scratches and bruises all over. I'm a mess. How much of a turn-on can that be?"

"You turn me on from the inside, sweetheart, as much as from the outside. Your body is still beautiful to me, no matter what."

He kissed her then so savagely, she couldn't breathe for a minute, then he patterned hot kisses down her throat, breasts, belly. He brought her to the edge of the bed and dropped to his knees and put her legs over his shoulders. How sweet she tasted and the bud of her desire was his for the asking as he laved it, loved it, paid it the homage he felt it deserved by virtue of being a part of her.

Above him, she bucked and screamed his name, glory running through every cell of her, pressing his head to her incredibly responsive body. She almost passed out with fervor before he caught her to him again and kissed her thoroughly with all the passion he felt.

They rested for a while and were silent, just being in the moment.

"Thank you," she murmured, getting up.

"Where're you going?"

"You'll see when I get back."

In the bathroom, she found the bottle of Tahitian Monoi oil and brought it back. He asked no questions, merely smiled as she began to spread it over his broad chest, then the length of his body, turning him over, stroking his broad back and narrow hips with the drum-tight buttocks.

"You should do a self-portrait," she said as he lay in a torpid daze. And he thought: Sylvan had done a nude self-portrait. If Caitlin liked his, Marty's, body so much, then he was glad he had a well-kept body.

She began the allover kisses on his body, tonguing, lightly licking his smooth flesh. When she reached his nipples and laved first one, then the other, he shuddered with hot pleasure coursing in his blood. She kissed his shaft as it swelled to maximum size and he groaned. "You're going to give me a heart attack."

"No. I'm giving you heart *health*."

When she had finished, she sat up and impishly asked him the question he had asked her. "Do I satisfy you?"

Then he put her astride him and gloried in her lovely face with its soft, white-toothed smile and softer eyes.

His shaft just wouldn't quit and he was dizzy with joy. She made up for all the times since Bianca when he'd licked his wounds and wanted no woman.

"Marty?"

"Yes, baby."

She smiled. "Nothing. I just wanted to say your name."

"Cait. I feel the same way."

They were a long time then, feeling languorous and full of steadier desire than the maelstrom they'd just been caught in.

They fit perfectly, he thought as he worked her. She probably didn't know it yet, but their spirits fit too. He came almost violently. The next night their lovemaking would herald the beginning of their baby. Focusing on that made him happy.

Trembling with passion and desire, she lightly bit his neck and told him, "Tomorrow we begin and already I feel something inside me I've never felt before. Marty, I think Sylvan would approve of us."

He nodded, but said nothing, thinking that one thing was for certain: He would never betray her the way Sylvan had done.

Chapter 12

"What was your life like in Puerto de La Cruz?"

It was three days after their civil wedding ceremony and Marty raised himself up on one elbow as he and Caitlin lay in their king-sized, indigo-colored bed. He expelled a harsh sigh. "Like nothing I ever want or intend to go through again"

"You and Bianca were in love, and from the videos and photos I've seen, Puerto is a divinely beautiful place."

"*I* was in love. I don't think Bianca ever was. And yes, Puerto's a little bit of heaven." With narrowed eyes, he looked at her closely. "Last night was our wedding night. Why are we talking about Puerto? You responded to me with fabulous abandon and I'm grateful. I feel like I'm on top of life. How do *you* feel?"

She smiled. "About the same. Thank you for bringing me coffee in bed."

"A token payment for what I owe you."

"Then I should be bringing *you* a seven-course meal."

Marty laughed. "Lady, you push all my right buttons."

"Marty?"

"Yes, love."

"Thank you for telling me a little about the organization you're involved with."

Marty was silent for a long while, lying on his back on fat pillows with his arms crossed behind his head. Suddenly he turned and caught her to him. "There're many things I want to tell you about me, Cait, and I will go into detail. The minute I can, I'll tell you everything. I can tell you this. We're one of the finest organizations in the world and the world would be much poorer and in much more danger without us. When I can tell you, you'll be proud."

His eyes on her were tender. "I'll never hurt you if I can possibly help it, and I love you so much sometimes it's hard to take."

"And I love you. I'm truly sorry I can't love you the way I still love Sylvan. I've told you this before since we've been so honest with each other. Bianca is the love of your life; you need to admit it, but we've got good things going with each other. Let's keep it that way."

"Let's keep it the way it is. I find myself loving you more than I ever loved Bianca. I married her to get away from loving you. That love was a dream; this is real. Okay, Sylvan owns a part of you I only wish I had, but I'm satisfied with what I have. I only hope we started our kid from the second time we made love."

She smiled. "That time was so sweet. You bring out all the impulsiveness in me, and you make me a little scared of what I'll do next—with you. Getting completely caught up, making love with you, marrying you . . ."

"All the good stuff."

"Yes. I'm having feelings I never knew before," and she hesitated before she said, "not even with Sylvan."

His heart leapt with hope as he caught her hand, squeezed it.

"I trust you," she said softly. "Maybe I shouldn't, but I do."

A pained shadow crossed his face for only an instant and he caught her to him in a fierce hug. "I'm going to make damned certain I deserve that trust."

The straps on her sheer black lace gown had fallen off her shoulders. He kissed the beautiful brown silken flesh, the smattering of freckles across her breasts, and looked deep into her eyes. "So we're going to Puerto in February on a delayed honeymoon. Let's make it a *prolonged* honeymoon all the way until then. Are you game?"

"Game." Looking at him she frowned involuntarily. Where were all these passionate feelings inside her springing from? She had thought this part of her life was over and had grown used to bland feelings of loss and despair, of happiness in her gallery and her few paintings. She had set her life on a trajectory of fulfilled dreams and blessed memories. And she was far from certain she wanted this new aliveness that gripped her.

With a wicked smile, Marty bent to her throat and began to lick her gently, slowly, tantalizing her so that she clutched his heavy, rippling biceps and drew him closer. Of course he thrilled her, she told herself. They were two intelligent, totally healthy young people with artistic fires burning in their blood. He was wise enough to accept that she didn't love him the way he deserved and he thought he completely loved her when Bianca almost certainly still held him in thrall. As her blood turned hot, his tongue made fancy patterns over her full breasts, then down, licking the tender flesh until she was raw with wanting him.

* * *

Later that day, when Caitlin sat with Dosha at her favorite table at Raymond's Diamond, a Caribbean restaurant several blocks from her gallery, Marty's love patinated her whole body and spirit. She thrummed with what she had known with him the past night, this morning, and since their wedding.

Dosha put her head to one side, drawling, "Well, now, it's for sure you're being touched up around the edges."

Caitlin blushed vividly, her brown skin reddening. She felt a rush of heat in her nether regions—as if she needed reminding. "Well," was all she said, but a grin kept tugging at her mouth.

"You look fabulous today," Dosha said, looking at Caitlin's periwinkle boiled wool jacket and wildflower print skirt. "I'll give you a run for that pintucked blouse."

"Thanks, love. If you like it in cream or tan, my dress store's got another in stock. I'll make you a present. You look great in that pale yellow and I'd say you're keeping secrets. How's Christian?"

Dosha pursed her lips, half closing her eyes. "He calls daily now. You know you'll meet him in Puerto."

"From his photos and videos, he looks like a Latin lover."

Dosha raised her eyebrows and waggled them. "I'll never tell, but my brothers—not just the player who's my twin— wrote the book on loving. Adam had a marriage made in heaven even at that young age. God, how he's suffered . . ." For a moment her eyes filled with tears she brushed away with her fingers. "But Marty's something special. He's always been deeper, more sensitive. It's what makes him such a great artist."

"Marty's a wonderful man, a genius." Caitlin's eyes got dreamy and a vivid smile spread across her face. "He's also a fantastic lover. I'd be satisfied with half of what I get from him."

Dosha made the okay sign as the waiter came and took their order. "I'm going to be the first baby's godmother, right? I'll sue if I'm not."

"Who else? Somebody's got to pay for the kid's Ph.D. Who better than Aunt Dosh?"

"Atta girl," Dosha said, laughing. "Greed is good, some are saying. Have you begun testing for pregnancy?"

"Give me time."

"I'm an anxious aunt-to-be. And Lord, Mom and Dad are climbing the walls with eagerness. Have twins and get it over with. You're a twin like me. It's a great life . . . Oh honey, I'm sorry. You're thinking about your twin, Caleb, aren't you?"

"It's okay," Caitlin assured her, with dry eyes beginning to hurt. "You never get over missing them, Dosh. Losing Sylvan, Caleb, and Sylvan Junior all so close together nearly did me in. I think I would have died or killed myself if it hadn't been for Marty and your family. I owe you all so much."

Dosha looked at her friend and caught her hand, squeezed it. "Paid in full. You're family to us, even if you'd never married old Marty."

The waiter brought their jerk chicken, candied yams, dirty rice with chicken gravy, collard greens, squash and onions, and a huge bowl of garden salad greens and sun-ripened tomato chunks. As they dug in to the delicious food, the owner and manager, Raymond St. Clair, came to them bearing a small plate of golden, buttered cornbread squares.

"From my heart to yours, ladies," he said. "You're both looking gorgeous, as usual. You came at a good time. Things were hectic earlier."

Dosha always flirted with Raymond. "You're one handsome dude. I'll bet you order sticks by the dozen to fight the women off."

Raymond grinned and patted his small middle-aged

paunch. "Well, thank you. No wonder I love you the way I do, and who fights the women off? Not me. Never me.

"What're you offering for dessert?" Caitlin asked, appreciating the banter.

"Peach cobbler made with incredible peaches from Chile and I made it. I want you to take Marty a big serving. I'll bring it out before you leave. I'm assuming the cobbler's what you'll want."

Dosha fluttered her eyelashes at Raymond. "Don't even bother to tell us the other choices. You can pack me a dessert doggy bag."

"Me too," Caitlin added.

"Now that we've taken care of the men, how's school?" Caitlin asked Dosha as Raymond went to greet other customers.

"Couldn't be better. I've got a roomful of students with voices I just can't quite believe. One young woman, Kelly Sears, is a mezzo-soprano who makes chills course through your body. She comes from a poor family, Cait, and I'm helping her. I'm going to pull all the strings to get her on her way. I've introduced her to someone at Juilliard and they're really enthusiastic. I also want to try the New England Conservatory of Music. There's so much I intend to do."

Caitlin smiled. Dosha's face was lit like a star. "Being a banker, Christian is well fixed, and he's from an old, wealthy Spanish family who probably doesn't think I'm good enough for him."

"You're good enough for anybody."

"You're sweet. Christian is coming for a long visit next fall."

"That's good, but I'll have met him by then in Puerto."

"Yes, and I think you'll like him. He's invited me over next summer to meet his family, and I'm trembling."

"Don't. You're beautiful, talented, gifted really, as all you Steeles are. You're fit for a king."

Dosha looked sober. "That's what Christian tells me, but says he also loves me because I have childbearing hips. How's that for male chauvinism?"

"You could do worse. As long as he doesn't keep you *barefoot* and pregnant."

The two women were still laughing as they parted in front of restaurant. "Hey, this was fun," Dosha told her. "Let's do this soon and at the same place."

Glancing at the bag in her hand as she started for the gallery, Caitlin decided to stop by her house. Marty would love the peach cobbler hot.

As she came up the avenue, a man left her house and came slowly down the walk. They met when he was near the bottom of the walk.

"Buenas días, señora." The man tipped his hat, showing black, wavy hair above a sculptured, olive face. She thought him handsome in a dissolute way.

Caitlin spoke and for a moment the man slowed as if he would stop, but she rushed on, let herself in and found Marty in the den, brooding over photographs of her spread out on the sofa.

"Hi, love," he said and got up, came to her and kissed her thoroughly. "Nothing's wrong, is there?"

She shook her head. "You knew Dosha and I had lunch at Raymond's. He made fresh peach cobbler; I thought you'd like some warm."

"I'm drooling. Why don't you take the rest of the day off?"

"I can't." But looking at him in his faded blue jeans and blue painter's smock, with his well-exercised muscles rippling, she wished she could. "Someone's coming over to look at a couple of your paintings. I want to do a show on you, Marty. Will you let me?"

He kissed her then, slowly and deeply. "You bet I'll let you."

That made her happy, but she drew a deep breath. "Who was the man coming down the walk? A salesman?"

It seemed a long while before he spoke in a low voice. "He's Cedric Santiago, from Puerto."

"Oh? A friend?"

"Hell, no. I *hope* he's not an enemy, but he's certainly not a friend."

"Is he a part of your life you can't talk about right now?"

"I'm afraid so. Sweetheart, bear with me. The minute I can get it sorted out, I'll talk with you, tell you what you surely need to know."

Back at the gallery, she was greeted by Rena, who, along with their teacher, shepherded a fairly large group of elementary-school children of every hue known to man. They were multicultural poster kids and Caitlin spoke to them warmly. She asked a lovely little jet-black girl with thick black braids and a little blond boy with bangs how they liked the show.

"I had a great, great, great uncle who was a Black Eagle," the little girl piped up. "I'm proud of him."

"Why, that's wonderful," Caitlin told her. "We have group pictures for distribution. Be sure you pick up one."

The child murmured her thanks and the little blond boy piped up, "I'm gonna be a pilot. My grandpop's a pilot." He made swooping circles with his arms and hands.

"Wonderful." Caitlin patted each child on the back, then said to the boy, "I'm sure you'll be a great pilot. I'd like a seat on your plane."

The boy blushed vividly as a portly, beaming woman

came up to Caitlin and extended her hand. "I'm Mrs. Paulson, teacher for this group, and oh, I must compliment you. You've pulled together one of the best exhibits I've seen. So many of the children already want to come back." She turned and put a finger to her lips, shushing the few who'd become highly ebullient.

The woman's hand in Caitlin's was pudgy, warm, with a friendly grip. "I'm glad you're enjoying it. It's for people like you and these kids. Do come again and again. You're always welcome."

"Mrs. Wright has been so helpful, explaining everything. So much sadness and so much joy. Mrs. Steele, there is a painting in one room of a woman sitting on a log, her head is down and her long black hair is streaming. You cannot see her face, but the lines of her body depict some grief perfectly . . . It moved me. Are there prints?"

Caitlin nodded. "That's my husband, Martin Steele's, painting and there will be prints. Leave me your name and number and I'll notify you."

"Oh, you're kind. I'm a sort of half-baked artist. Watercolors. I read a long article in the *Post* about you and this gallery last year. You do watercolors too."

"Yes. I love working in that medium."

A larger brown girl came up, excused herself, and drew the teacher aside. Other people came in and Caitlin moved on. This show was a rousing success, covered by the *Washington Post*, the *Washington Times*, and the *Washington Informer*. There were crowds every day; the reviews were excellent. She felt the exhibit for Marty's paintings would be her next success.

And for a moment, an old dream gripped her. Sylvan's paintings on exhibit on these walls, beginning a ripple that would spread throughout the United States and Europe. Just under five more years. He had asked her to see that this took place when he would have been thirty-eight.

"Why thirty-eight?" she'd asked him. "You don't want to stay out of sight too long. You need name recognition and you're already getting it in spades."

"I know. Hold me off the scene for a long while, then work with Jayson to bring my name back, if something happens to me. . . ."

He had looked strange then, cut off from her, and she had gone to him. "Are you in some kind of trouble?"

He had kissed her long and ardently. "Does a man in trouble kiss like that? I'm having trouble keeping my hands off you, but I've got to run."

Less than a month later, he was dead, as was her twin, Caleb. Then Sylvan Junior died and the nightmare began, a never-ending nightmare. My God, she thought now. *Three* deaths in less than a year. She was a strong woman, but she could not have made it had it not been for Marty and the Steeles. *Marty.* Her cell phone buzzed.

Nelda, Caitlin's secretary, announced an art appraiser she had known in New York. Caitlin stood as he entered, came around the desk, and hugged him. "Don," she said, "it's always good to see you. Please sit down."

As he seated himself, he shook his head. "I don't know if you'll say that later. I think it'll be more like: kill the messenger."

"What's going on?"

"*Wild Storm at Sea's* a masterful fake."

Catlin's breath almost stopped. "Oh, good Lord. Where in the world is all this leading? If someone is going to copy Sylvan's painting, why? He wasn't an old master, superb as he was."

Don Hylton shrugged. "There are so many possible reasons, I'd hesitate to hazard a guess. Did you file a claim?"

"Yes, of course. They were ready to pay after they investigated. They'd have found the forgery."

"Not necessarily. These days with companies, it's spend a little, get a lot. You know how many arguments art appraisers get into every day over what's fake and what's real. I'm not bragging, but I'm regarded as one of the best art appraisers and I'd bet my shirt on this one."

He drew a deep breath. "Appraising art can be as much a gut feeling as anything. How closely did you study Sylvan's paintings?"

"Not closely enough. I was always so busy with my own studies. Why do you ask?"

"Because if you deal with an art restorer or appraiser, little things like signatures or different details an artist consistently uses can give an art copyist away.

"You see, I remembered Sylvan always using a slight, nearly faded red rose petal somewhere in his paintings. Had you noticed? Did he say?"

She sat straighter. "No. I never noticed and he never said."

"It was *very* subtle, but I noted it early. It was the first thing I looked for in this forgery and it wasn't there. I delved deeper and there were other things." He shook his head. "You'll get my written report."

He began to get up then. "Listen, I've got to rush because I have a plane to catch earlier than I'd intended, but I'm back in D.C. in a couple of weeks. Like to have lunch with me then?"

Don stood, smiling as she accepted his invitation. "How could I forget to congratulate you on your marriage to Marty Steele, one of my favorite artists? Please give him my regards. All three of us ought to have lunch."

"Contact me and it's done."

They hugged again and he left. She called Marty and told him about Don's opinion. He said little about it. "Aren't you shocked?" she asked him. "I certainly am."

He expelled a harsh breath. "Not much shocks me anymore. I'm accustomed to living in Europe and art forgeries happen there all the time. I think the insurance company's P.I. would have caught it. Saying they were ready to pay off may have been a ruse in case you knew something about the forgery. Don't let it get you down, love."

"That painting was Sylvan's all-time favorite—and mine. How could someone copy his gift?"

"You know it happens. I'm sorry."

She shivered a bit. He didn't sound like himself. He sounded distant, not really with her, and she reflected that she once read a contention that a person's voice on the telephone reflected what they really felt.

Then he seemed livelier. "I got something special for dinner from the deli."

"You didn't have to do that. I would have picked something up."

He laughed. "I'm gathering brownie points and when I get enough to cash in, I'm going to demand all you've got to give."

She felt a small tremor go through her body, and she couldn't shake the feeling that he didn't care about Sylvan's painting being a fake, or that he had thoughts he wasn't sharing with her.

Chapter 13

It was the first Sunday in December and the small country church the Steeles belonged to was beautifully decorated with many flickering candles and massive flower arrangements of lilies, birds-of-paradise, and roses flown in from Mexico and South America. This was a more formal ceremony that came after Caitlin and Marty were married by a justice of the peace in Elkins, Maryland.

As maid of honor, Dosha stood by her best friend and sister-in-law, smiling, dreamy eyed. "Maybe you'll do the same for me in the not-too-distant future," she murmured.

Caitlin caught her hand, squeezed it, then her glance locked with Marty's. The look that passed between them sent shivers along her spine because her heart held so many fears and so much hope. She touched her flat belly behind the bouquet of miniature gardenias she held.

In the crowded audience, Rispa Steele wiped a few tears from her eyes. "It's happening, love," she told Mel as he gripped her hand. "This is the wedding we've dreamed of for our firstborn."

Mel could only nod; his heart was too full to speak.

"Dearly beloved," the young minister began, "we are gathered here tonight . . ."

Marty heard the words through a haze. Caitlin's presence filled his heart, took over his brain. She looked so beautiful. Adam was his best man: he and Damien had drawn straws, and they both looked handsome in tailored tuxedos. Ricky, as ringbearer, wore his first tuxedo and couldn't stop grinning as he looked at his new aunt.

But it was Caitlin who stole the show. She was dressed in heavy silk candlelight satin and the old ivory color matched the silk lace overlay of the off-the-shoulder gown that displayed Caitlin's beautiful brown shoulders. A tiara of miniature gardenias sat atop her earth-brown hair that was fashioned into a becoming French twist. She glanced at Marty again, as nervous as if they were just getting married, and his eyes said it all.

They had planned the ceremony with much joy and care. The wedding guests listened intently; then the organ strains of "Oh, Promise Me" eddied around them. Joy filled Marty's loins, his very soul as he thought about this woman who had filled his life with hope where there had been little hope. He was profoundly grateful.

The ceremony was short and a bashful Ricky held out the ring on its ivory satin pillow. Gently Marty removed Caitlin's wedding band for a moment and slid the five-carat, emerald-cut yellow diamond ring set in platinum onto Caitlin's ring finger, then slid the platinum wedding band back in place and touched that hand to his lips.

Caitlin stood thinking, dizzy with unexpected passion, *I am entranced by this man and I never realized it before. I love him as a friend, deeply, and I know this is right because we both want a child. We both deserve a child. And if I never know again the all-encompassing love I knew with Sylvan, then thank you, God, for this.*

She was still dizzy when the minister pronounced them man and wife and Marty kissed her, beginning with a gentle kiss and ending with a kiss that was too long and too passionate for public view. And they both blushed as a wave of sympathetic warmth and merriment swept the wedding guests.

The wedding reception was held at the Steeles' big house and each room in the large downstairs was filled with festivity. Frank and Caroline Steele, and their adult children, Whit, Ashley, and Annice, were all there. Frank was Mel's child with his first wife, and was over twenty years older than his children with Rispa. Frank and his half-siblings loved each other dearly and visited often.

The famous gospel singer, Ashley, came to Caitlin, kissed her warmly. "What an exquisite wedding," she said, as her handsome husband, Derrick, stood by her side, smiling. "And your dress is to die for."

"Yes," Caitlin said. "Marty chose it. He has marvelous taste. But then, he's a Steele; it runs in the family."

Marty threw back his head, laughing. "I exercised that taste when I picked you, love," he told Caitlin.

"I get the best of the bargain," Caitlin complimented back. "Ashley, I hate to ask it because you're our guest, but would you sing 'He's Got the Whole World In His Hands' for us? It's my favorite, as you know, and that's the way I feel tonight."

Ashley looked delighted. "You know I will. Let me round up Damien and some others."

And in just a little while, with Damien on piano, Rispa and Mel with tambourines, and Frank on guitar, they sang the gospel song Caitlin had requested. The rooms of the old stone house rocked with the fervor of the wondrous music they made and you knew why the

Singing Steeles had been famous. Memories flooded Mel of the life he had known with his first wife and Frank, but they were no more precious than the life he'd built with Rispa. After his first wife had left him, doctors had discovered a growth on his larynx and it had proved the end of a highly promising career. Then Frank had married, had children and they had all become the new Singing Steeles, fulfilling Mel's dreams.

Police Captain Jon Ryson and his well-known radio talk show host wife, Francesca, came to them with congratulations and hugged Caitlin. Francesca said to Caitlin, "I'll be calling you about your appearance on our station publicizing the Tuskegee Black Eagles exhibit." Then Francesca shook her head and laughed. "I would kill for that dress. It's gorgeous."

Merry laughter came from behind her as Caitlin turned to face Sherrie Tate, who hugged her. Sherrie's husband, Byron Tate, the highly successful cosmetics manufacturer, and Marty exchanged high fives.

"You're a fabulous ad for my shop," Sherrie told her, "and oh, that dress, that *dress*." She smiled impishly. "If I ever get married again . . ."

Byron drew himself up and growled, "You had damn well better be marrying *me* again." He drew his wife close and kissed her fervently as Marty and Caitlin smiled.

The guests applauded the singers, asked for more, and got another song, "Go Down, Moses." Then Mel stepped forward. "You're enjoying us and we're enjoying you, too, but this is a wedding reception and there's dancing to do. So let's get on with it."

"Yes, let's do just that," Dosha said, sparkling in an ivory silk satin dress and looking as happy as if *she* were the bride. "There's enough food to feed Minden and I love our neighbors who pitched in and gave the caterers a run for their money. You've got all kinds of goody bags to take home." She spoke to a small group of wedding guests.

Violin music caressed them and Damien was in his element as he led four other violinists, a bass fiddle, and a pianist in Borodin's Second String Quartet. Caitlin felt her heart fill as she listened. At a pause in the music, Damien raised his bow in salute to the couple and Caitlin's eyes filled. A pop tune had been taken from that wonderful melody and that song was "This Is My Beloved," an old song that would never be out of date.

There were pop tunes with Frank playing his famous guitar. Marvin Gaye tunes were well represented and Lionel Richie's "Lady" was much requested, with Damien singing in his romantic baritone voice.

The food was sumptuous. The seven-tier wedding cake was an old New Orleans recipe and was filled with big golden currants, sweetmeats, tart granny apple pieces, and sliced cherries, all brandy-soaked and put into rich butter batter. As she and Marty fed each other a slice of cake, he took her index finger in his mouth as she whispered, "Naughty."

He smiled lazily. "In just a little while, there's going to be a whole lot more where that came from."

She blushed hotly and Dosha, who stood nearby and overheard, laughed. "Lovers," she chortled. "They never know when to stop."

"Stop?" Marty murmured. "We've barely started."

There were roast racks of lamb, prime rib roasts, rotisserie golden chickens and Cornish hens, oyster stew, fried oysters constantly brought out and more quickly consumed, huge fresh salad bowls, and fancy-cut fresh vegetables. There was macaroni with sharp cheese, fabulous German and American potato salads, rich black, rye, and wheat breads, and the crisp Parker House and Cloverleaf rolls Rispa had taught so many of her neighbors to make.

Along with the scrumptious wedding cake, the desserts were out of this world. Creamy eggnog and skimmed milk eggnog sat in large silver urns, the spicy aroma delighting the senses. Spiced apple cider. Coffee, tea, and hot chocolate containers lined the long, white damask–covered tables.

"We're gonna need coffee to stay awake," Marty teased Caitlin.

She looked at him slyly. "We don't need coffee."

Her words were more fervent than she had intended and it pleased him greatly. He took her hand. "Are you happy, Cait?" His look was intense and it moved her.

"More than I ever thought I'd be again," she answered softly.

"I know *I* am. I owe you everything."

"We owe each other, and I for one never intend to stop telling you that."

They both turned as a deep voice sounded behind them. "Congratulations and thank you for inviting me."

Marty stiffened. Jayson's eyes on Caitlin were warm and friendly.

"Are you enjoying the festivities?" Caitlin asked.

Jayson smiled. "I'm losing someone precious—you—but I'll survive. I wish you both all the best. Take really good care of her, Steele. She's a rare jewel."

Marty looked at the man who had helped put him on top with sharp deals. He was filled with a sense of triumph. "I know Cait's worth. She's *my* jewel now."

Someone called Marty away and Cait was left alone with Jayson, who looked at her gravely.

"Forgive me for saying this, Cait, but you may have trouble with Bianca. She is a spoiler and Marty was deeply in love with her. I believe he still is. I don't want to see you hurt."

She thought of her own continuing love for Sylvan and said quietly, "I can handle it, Jayson."

"I'm sorry if I spoke out of turn. I just thought . . ."

"It's all right. You were trying to help."

Marty came back and smiled at Caitlin. With narrowed eyes, he looked at Jayson, who looked bothered.

Jayson took Caitlin's hand, bent and kissed it. He stood looking at the couple reflectively. "I'd thought we'd all be going to Puerto de la Cruz for La Carnaval and to exhibit your paintings and Sylvan's. Now someone in Paris has told me about Degas prints I need to see. Unfortunately, they won't be available until that time, so I may have to forego Puerto." Jayson smiled ruefully. "I'm sure I won't be missed."

Caitlin flushed. "I'm sorry to hear that."

Jayson lifted his eyebrows. "Are you? Congratulations again," he said as he moved on.

Caitlin stepped closer to Marty and kissed him at one corner of his mouth, then flicked her tongue across his lips. He squeezed her hand. "You're a provocative woman," he told her.

Caitlin and Marty danced then and she found herself disturbed by thoughts of what Marty had told her at an earlier time. So he had a life away from her, a life that possibly posed some danger. Did Jayson know about Marty's involvement with this secretive group? It was hardly the time, but she suddenly felt she had to say it.

"We need to talk, Marty," she said quietly.

He gave a small snort, smiled, and said gently, "Tonight is our second wedding night, but I guess you'd say the first was a marriage night. Adam is driving us back, so we'll both be rested, giddy with our love. There are so many things I want to do to you . . ." He groaned slightly and she laughed, then sobered.

"All right, it *is* our wedding night, but we need to talk very soon after tonight." The question she asked then had nothing to do with secret organizations. She found her mind flooded with thoughts about Marty and

Bianca. Should she ask him? "Are you still in love with Bianca?"

He shook his head slowly. "I'm in love with *you*. You've got to know that."

"Bianca is one of the most beautiful and exciting women in the world."

"Surely to some."

"And what is she to you?"

He didn't hesitate. "Not even fiftieth fiddle to you. I love you, Cait. No matter what happens. Always know that."

Words, questions crowded her mind, but she brushed them aside. He wanted her, needed her. He was no actor, couldn't pretend so realistically. This was her real, magnificent wedding night and she was going to yield and respond to bring her womb to fruition with the child they both had to have. But a cold wave of anxiety began in her feet and crept up her body.

"What is it, sweetheart?" he asked.

She shook her head. "Nothing," she answered as he took both her hands in his.

"Dance with me again," she told him and they moved onto the floor. She could have wept with frustration. With Sylvan she had *always* felt safe, protected. Would she ever feel that way again?

Chapter 14

At her gallery, Caitlin dug into her blue smock pocket and fished out her cell phone, flipped it open. Marty's sexy voice asked, "How're you fixed for cash? I forgot to stop by the ATM machine."

"I'm cash poor. Look, sweetheart, it's two-thirty now. I need to sign a few papers for my loan on the gallery expansion and they'd like it done today. I'd love your company. Why don't you meet me at the bank and we can both raid our account. You love walking in this area. Or *I* could get cash from the ATM."

"Got ourself a done deal. See you there in a few minutes."

Caitlin crossed her arms. The bank had been held up two days before and she felt spooked at the thought of going there by herself.

The branch bank was very quiet. Marty came up to her and kissed her brow. "You're looking harried, prosperous, like a happy wife."

Before she could answer, the bank manager bustled

up. "I've got your papers ready, Mrs. Costner." Her brown porcelain skin flushed. "Oh, I'm sorry, Mrs. *Steele*."

"It's all right. I haven't been married long."

Caitlin pressed Marty's shoulder and went with the woman. She had already studied the papers carefully, gone over them with her lawyer, and in fifteen minutes had finished signing.

"Are you satisfied?" the bank manager asked.

"Very. I've got great terms."

"We're happy when you're happy, Mrs. Steele, because you're one of our best customers. I was by your gallery last Sunday and I love your Black Eagle exhibit. I wish our world would always respect such formidable talent. We're so imperfect, but things like your exhibit help. It's just great."

"Thank you. I've enjoyed working with it and I've learned so much."

Her back had been to the door and she was surprised when she turned around to see Marty talking with the man he called Cedric Santiago, who was gesticulating wildly. "I tell you, it *has* to be this way," the man hissed as she started over. "Otherwise I will not be responsible for what happens to any of us."

The two men were so caught up that neither saw her quietly approach.

And Marty hissed back before he saw her, "And I will *not* have it go down this way, Cedric, or *I* will not be responsible." Cedric's glance warned him and he stopped abruptly, still frowning. He did not try for ease of manner and remained agitated as he turned to her. "All through, love?"

"Yes," she said. "Good afternoon, Mr. Santiago."

"Ah, the beautiful lady knows my name. And yours is?"

Marty's presence came between Cedric Santiago and Caitlin like a glass shield. "You have no need to know her name although I'm sure you *do* know it since our marriage was mentioned in art news. It was not by oversight that I didn't introduce you to her."

Cedric's eyes nearly closed. "You must be aware that it is my business to know these things. You are Mrs. Steele, Mrs. Martin Edward Steele—Caitlin." He chuckled and looked at Marty triumphantly, then raised his hand in salute. "I leave now, but the three of us will meet again, I would hope on better terms."

Marty stood stock still as Cedric left the bank, a bit of swagger in his walk.

"He is a fool and a hopeless clown," Marty said bittery.

"A fool and a clown you can't talk about."

He looked wretched. "I don't blame you for being bent out of shape, but I have to ask you to trust me. I will never betray you. *Never*. I would die first. You'll understand when I can tell you. And I *will* talk with you a bit when you get home." He smiled. "Unless you want to go back with me now. Our honeymoon is still in effect."

How easily he slid from turmoil and apparent deceit to ecstasy, she thought. She wished she could, and she longed for the clear security of her life with Sylvan.

At home that night, Caitlin found Marty in the kitchen with a Puerto rabbit stew dinner with wild rice ready to serve. "I got some of Mom's cloverleaf rolls out of the freezer. Picked up some of your favorite macaroni salad from the deli and, oh yes, give me a kiss and I'll tell you what wine we'll have."

Caitlin smiled, getting caught up in his banter. "I'll give you a kiss even if you don't tell me."

She came to him, covered his face with small, wet kisses. For the briefest of seconds, she felt a flutter in her abdomen and smiled. Babies didn't move after this short a time. And she made up her mind to test tonight.

The dinner was good and the surprise was the fruity sangria wine she loved. But she was plagued with anxiety brought on by the earlier presence of Cedric Santiago. Was Jayson right about Marty being involved in intrigue and danger? It certainly seemed possible.

Later, sitting on the curved blue sofa in Marty's arms, she was restive. "We're sworn to love, trust, respect each other and our world," she told him. "I need openness, Marty, the way Sylvan and I had it. You know how I will always feel about Sylvan, but we both want a child."

He turned her around to face him and felt sharp, unexpected pain when he thought she would never love him the way she loved her first husband. Still, he had her here in his arms, her ardent kisses on his face—and Sylvan was dead. "Whatever it is you don't understand now, I promise you will later," he said sincerely.

"Very well," she murmured, a bit mollified. She couldn't help thinking of their mingled lives—Marty's, Sylvan and Sylvan Junior's, and hers. Now there was Cedric. What had happened in Marty's life during the past years?

Seeking to soothe her, he asked, "Do you still have dreams of ecstasy?"

Her lips curved in a wide smile. "I'm *living* dreams of ecstasy."

"That goes triple for me."

She slipped out of his arms and went into the bathroom, got the early pregnancy test kit from the medicine cabinet, pulled down her panties, and with bated breath began to urinate on the stick.

In a few minutes, highly excited, she went back into the living room and pulled Marty to his feet, pressing her body hard against his.

"What's this all about?" he asked. "Not that I'm complaining. I'm loving it." He hoped he'd put her mind to rest, at least a little, about Cedric.

She looked at him shyly, thrilling with her news. "In a few months, you won't be able to draw me this close."

His eyes half closed. "I won't be able to draw you . . ." Then it hit him as he whooped and nearly crushed her ribs. "God, you're pregnant. We've done it, love. We've done it!"

He had bought Veuve Clicquot champagne after their first surge of lovemaking. He lifted her and carried her into the kitchen, put her into a chair, and went to the refrigerator.

"You can only have a taste," he said.

"I'll get glasses." She began to get up.

"No, you sit while I wait on you. I'm gonna love every minute of this." His loins felt expanded, powerful as he touched her face, her hair.

The champagne tickled both their noses and they laughed happily. He pulled her up, sat down, and took her onto his lap.

"Hello, little Mama," he teased. "From now on, Papa does your bidding. Honey, welcome to parenthood."

Chapter 15

Caitlin came awake shortly after five the next morning and lay in bed for a moment remembering the past night. *She was going to have a baby*. Joy filled her as she passed her hands over her abdomen. She would go to the gallery early to map out some plans for school visits. Yawning widely, she switched on the soft lights of the lamp on her night table and glanced at Marty's sprawled sleeping figure. She didn't want to wake him, but she just had to touch him gently.

His hand caught hers in a tight grip and she gasped, delighted. "You rascal. You were awake all the time."

"Yeah. Remember the song Sting made famous? 'Every Breath You Take'? From now on, every breath you take, little Mama." He got even more serious then. "You don't have to feel guilty about not loving me the way I love you, Cait. I can handle it for both of us."

She leaned over and kissed him on the lips. "Thank you, but the hell of it is I *do* love you. You're a part of me. I wouldn't have made it without you, Marty, and no way will I ever forget that. It's just that Sylvan was my first. Lord, I was so anxious at seventeen, living in big, old, wild New York City after being brought up on a little Mississippi junior college campus. I was so anxious to give up my hated virginity. I wanted to live to the hilt and my twin . . ."

"Caleb," he said sadly.

"Yes, Caleb. Well, he guarded me like I was a threatened queen, but Sylvan and I managed to get past him and we became lovers . . ." She stopped, remembering, but she was also keenly aware of Marty's body, his presence. Her husband.

"Five years is too long for a vibrant woman like you to be without anyone."

She was quiet for a moment. "I intended it to last forever. I thought I was satisfied until you came back into my life, lit all my fires, made me feel things I've never felt before, not even with Sylvan. Now you've given me your baby, but I'm tearing up sometimes. I don't know whether to bless you or curse you. Sylvan and I made a vow that if anything happened to one of us, the other wouldn't marry again, just raise Sylvan Junior. We felt we had a love that transcended time and death, like Solomon and Sheba."

For a long moment his eyes on her were sad and brooding. "Penny for your thoughts," she finally said.

He breathed deeply. Finally he said huskily, "Like the country song, I don't care who your first love was as long as I'm the last." He stroked her breasts; she was so warm.

"Don't rev up your motor," she said, laughing. "I said I've got to go in early. We got enough last night to last a while."

"Sez who? I just don't seem to get enough of you."

She was thoughtful then. "I surprise myself. I feel hungry, no, *ravenous* for you, all of you. Maybe in time . . ."

"You don't have to push a special love for me. Take your time. I'll always be here for you."

She bent and kissed his belly button, her tongue making swirling patterns around it.

He laughed. "You tell me not to rev my motor, then you do it to me. Is that fair?"

"Oh, I've got the inclination; I just don't have the time. A quick shower, some juice, and a raisin bagel and I'm outta here in a taxi I made arrangements with last night."

"Call Rico back and cancel. I'll pay him double fare. I'll take you in, because I don't want you opening up alone."

"I've done it before."

"Not since you got big with my kid."

Delight filled her at the thought. "Big? I'm not there yet."

"You will be, lady."

"Promises. Why don't you have a bagel and coffee with me?"

"Umm. I'm considering just eating *you* for breakfast. God knows you're tasty enough."

Driving through the streets the six blocks to the gallery, they were quiet. It was seven o'clock and the gallery opened at ten. She could get a lot done before then. Rita usually left at six; then Luther came in. The night-lights of the gallery still suffused the light beige stucco building.

"Your gallery is really quite lovely," Marty said. "We'll come again at this time and I'll take pictures."

"Okay. This place has been a godsend to me." Then she added, "Along with you."

He patted her hand. "Keep pushing all the right buttons and you're going to have a man you can't get rid of."

"It isn't as if I ever *want* to get rid of you. I hope you'll stay with me always."

He drew away a little emotionally from the savage feelings of intense love for her, but he said easily, "Try and drive me away."

He parked in front of the gallery. Going in, the winter air was wonderfully crisp and invigorating. "I'd like to run around the block," she said.

"You've got on flats. Let's do it."

"Don't tempt me. I've got a lot to get through today. I'll come home early and we'll run slowly."

"Ah, I don't think so. I have other things in mind like a dinner sent in from Raymond's."

She looked at him with mock consternation and put a finger to her lips. "Don't tell anyone, but I think I married a sex maniac."

Marty blew a stream of air in her direction. "You're the one who keeps turning me on, waking up hungers I didn't know I had."

He let her navigate the security system with its brass lock and bars that opened only with a special combination and they went in.

"Hey, I'm glad you insisted on coming with me," she said as a chill traversed her body. "I feel spooked for some reason. Let's look around a bit. I hope we never have another break-in."

They went to her office, put their coats in the closet, and opened the blinds. A rosy dawn lay on the horizon.

Marty looked at her sharply. She *was* spooked. Then they both saw the crumpled figure lying face down with a pool of blood coming from beneath the body.

Rita. "My God!" Caitlin gasped.

They both knelt.

"I've had CPR training," Marty said. "Let me handle this.

Caitlin took her cell phone from her purse and dialed 911, then called the nearby stationhouse and asked for Sergeant Draper, who came on the line quickly.

"Yeah."

She told him what they'd found and he swore, said he'd be there immediately, and slammed the phone down.

Probing for a few minutes, Marty found no pulse, no heartbeat. "I think she's dead."

Marty took Caitlin in his arms, wanting to shield her. He had gotten smears of blood on his hands and his tan wool jacket. He heard Caitlin's heart racing and held her tight. Then pushing her into a chair in a nearby niche, he knelt beside her, rubbing her hands.

"I'm all right," she finally said. "Let's go back and be with Rita. Maybe . . ."

"I want to make sure you're all right. I don't think Rita needs us."

With sirens screaming, the ambulance and the police came quickly. The gallery rang with frantic sounds of raised voices and barked orders. Strength flooded Caitlin as she helped and answered questions.

After a brief examination, the assistant medical examiner stood and nodded at the ambulance crew, then spoke to them, his face blandly surveying a scene he saw every day in one or another form or fashion. "We don't need to rush. She isn't going anywhere. I'm really sorry, Jim."

Sergeant Draper stood rigid, his face like a stone mask. A fellow detective, Cliff Anderson, tried to comfort him, but he brushed him off and talked instead to Caitlin. "You heard the medical guy say she's been dead over two hours. I picked her up every morning around six. Sometimes she was late leaving. This morning *I* was late." His voice broke, rasped like metal on glass. "Goddamnit, why couldn't I have been on time?"

The assistant medical examiner shook his head. "I think you would have found her dead. Don't do this to yourself, Jim."

"You just don't know," Sergeant Draper said miserably. "I was going to put a ring on her finger this Sunday. We would have been married during the holidays." Anguish and despair shook him and his lieutenant put his arms around him. "She's still got expensive rings on her fingers, so it wasn't robbery. If the bastard raped her, he's gonna die, and I *will* catch him."

"Don't borrow trouble," Detective Anderson said. "I can take over. Likely it'll be my case. Why don't you go home, pull yourself together?"

"No way. I want to know *everything*. I'm in charge of investigating the earlier break-in here."

"But you're not a homicide detective and I am."

Sergeant Draper turned to Caitlin. "Did she call you last night about anything suspicious?"

"No." Caitlin shook her head. Last night she'd been celebrating her pregnancy, but she'd checked her cell phone for messages and there'd been none.

Sergeant Draper began to pace the floor like a caged tiger, swearing, hot tears burning his eyes. Caitlin went to him, put her arms around him. "Let me help in any way I can," she told him.

"My kids loved her," he said. "They're going to hurt like hell."

"I know," was all Caitlin could say, then more words came to her. "You're a strong man, Jim. Rita used to talk with me about how strong you are, how much she loved you in part because of that strength. She'd want you to hold up, help find her killer."

"Yeah, yeah," he said slowly, a savage look crossing his face. "And when I do . . ."

"Rita was a forgiving person, Jim. She didn't tear herself up with trying to get revenge. Be kind and understanding for *her*; identify with that part of her. It'll help you to heal."

"God," he growled, "I can't even *think* about healing. Maybe I never will."

Quietly she said, "I healed from a hurt like you're feeling. My husband and my little boy died, and my twin. I know you want to die, too, but that's not the answer. It never is."

Caitlin called Rena at eight and she insisted on coming in early. "How're you holding up?" Rena asked.

"I'm as well as I can be under the circumstances."

"Did you call Marty? You shouldn't be coming in so early alone."

"He drove me here."

"Good for him."

She didn't tell Rena about being pregnant; it wasn't the time for celebratory news.

Caitlin went over the short sequence of events with Detective Anderson. There wasn't much to tell. "Jim and I have been friends for a long time," he said. "I don't mind telling you, I'm scared for him now. Anything you can remember will help."

She searched the depths of her mind, told him what she remembered as he nodded. And through it all Marty kept near her, kept being her Rock of Gibraltar. During a lull, he took her hand. "I'd like to see you lie down a while on the sofa in your office."

Caitlin shook her head. "I'll be all right. I'm breathing deeply the way you taught me. Lord, what a nightmare."

Luther had come in around eight and his face went ashen when they told him. He went back to where the two cops stood and stared at the pool of blood a long time. "I'll get that up," he said.

Detective Anderston shook his head. "Not yet. We've got more tests to run."

The chalked outline of Rita's body where she fell was another visual reminder of what had happened.

Finally Detective Anderson said to Caitlin, "You need to check to see if anything is missing."

Caitlin, Marty, Rena, and Lieutenant Anderson walked through the gallery and found everything in place, but a check of the vault proved a different story. It took only a minute to see that Sylvan's second most valuable painting, *Sea Sunset*, had been taken.

Detective Anderson frowned deeply, asked Caitlin, "Did this painting have special significance too?"

She nodded. "Yes. Both this painting and the other one that was stolen."

"I see. I'll need to talk with all your employees and a lot more with you. We need to start right away."

"Yes. we have only a few employees. A cleaning crew comes at six to clean, leaves around ten."

"And Ms. Glass's hours were?"

"New hours. Eight-thirty to six-thirty."

"That runs into a nice chunk of overtime, I'd think."

"Yes. When you find the culprit, I'll go back to high-tech security. We've got so many small galleries in the area and only a few have ever been hit."

Detective Anderson tapped his foot. "The world continues to change and the more it changes, the worse it seems to get—crimewise, that is."

Sergeant Draper joined them, asked brokenly, "Why rush, man? My baby sure isn't in any hurry."

Caitlin touched his shoulder. "I'm so sorry, Jim." It had been so hectic she hadn't gotten as much chance to console him as she wanted.

"Somebody's *not* sorry," he growled, "but the bastard *will* be when I get through with him."

The others who stood there were silent in the face of his terrible grief.

Rena set out to contact the cleaning crew by phone. Then she and Luther went into Rena's office for questioning.

Caitlin stood at the windows of her office thinking how different the clear blue sky looked, how much at odds with the chaos here. She thought she seemed to stand at windows often these past few months. Marty had found her standing at this window, had kissed her later . . .

"Caitlin?"

She turned to face Jayson. "I heard about what happened on my car radio on my way back to New York. I came to offer what help I could."

She nodded. "Thank you. That was kind, but there's nothing really anyone can do, except find the killer."

"Was anything stolen?"

On impulse, she didn't tell him about the missing painting. "No. We were fortunate that way." Why had she lied? she wondered, then decided she didn't want to talk about it with anyone but the police and Marty.

"Does Steele know about this?" Jayson asked.

"Yes. He's getting me coffee."

He shrugged. "Why? You guys make some of the best coffee in the world in this gallery. I certainly intend to have a cup before I leave. That coffee's aromatherapy all by itself."

"I tend to crave raspberry lattes when I'm shaken. Marty knows that. There's a new Starbucks several blocks away."

She didn't have the time or inclination to think about Marty or herself or Jayson. Now the thought of Rita's dead body filled her mind to the breaking point.

Leaning over, she picked up a blue squeeze-me sponge from her desk and squeezed hard.

"You've been hit with lightning," he said gently and touched her shoulder. "The European art scene is ripe with intrigue, especially Spain and Italy." He sighed. "I just wonder . . . I've thought for a long time that Steele is involved in a gang of art thieves. Have you met Cedric Santiago?"

"Why do you ask?"

He shrugged and said cryptically, "No particular reason."

Jayson had left when Marty got back with the raspberry latte. Caitlin got up and went to him.

"You should have worn your overcoat."

"It's heating up fast. Thanks for taking care of me, Little Mama."

That night at home after a dinner at Raymond's that she didn't feel much like eating, Marty suggested they exercise in the fitness room. It had been two hours since they had eaten. The house held a nicely appointed exercise room with an excellent, expensive treadmill, stationary bike, exercise benches, varied weights, a rowing machine, and several other pieces of useful equipment.

They both wore gray sweats, headbands, and special exercise shoes. Caitlin hit the treadmill; Marty did his more strenuous exercises on the machines.

Suddenly, on inspiration, she told Marty, "Honey, let's go outside a bit. I'm nervous and I'm having a hard time working it off. I need a breath of really fresh air. Lord, I keep thinking about Rita and I feel so helpless. Sergeant Draper told me that the thug who attacked me probably belongs to a gang that has a tie-in with whoever is stealing the paintings. The thug's name is Dilly

McKay, Sergeant Draper says. Word gets around on the streets. A group he feels is highly intelligent and well trained is hiring these young guys to do their dirty work, their *enforcing*.

"I'm a target because I'm a witness. I saw two of that crew shoot a man and they know if they ever find the perp, I'll testify."

"Not until after the baby's born and weaned."

She smiled. "That could be a long time. Rispa told me you nursed until you were fourteen months old."

He looked at her breasts, touched them one at a time. "Then and now, lifetime memories of bliss and satisfaction. Mom said she was afraid I'd never stop demanding more."

"The same old Marty," she teased him. "But no, you're very mature, love, and I'm glad about that."

They did not speak of Jayson at all. Marty had promised he would tell her what, if any, part he played in an art group Jayson declared was criminal.

"I'm jittery," she finally said as she got off the treadmill. "Let's go outside and do light calisthenics in the backyard."

"Okay. Are you sure you feel up to it?"

"Yes. It always helps me relax."

They donned heavy sweaters and went out into the brightly lit backyard with its tall, boarded-up and locked fence. Stars spangled the sky and a full moon shone. Rita and Sergeant Draper had had marriage plans for the holidays, Caitlin thought now. His children had come to love her; his ex-wife hated her. Her mind wandered away from painful things. The big elm tree's vein-limbed winter stance was charming against a starlit sky.

"That bare elm tree makes me think of Puerto de la

Cruz and the Drago tree you told me about," she said. "You know, the way the sap is red like blood."

"That fascinates you?"

"Nature's had me hooked all my life.

"You're giving me an idea."

"What?"

"Never mind. You'll find out in time." You'll find out in time."

They stopped and he caught her to him, held her, felt her heart drumming through their heavy sweaters. "Tomorrow," he said, "I'm going to get an appointment for you with Dr. Graham. I've got to know you're all right. Got to help you take care of my seed, help it blossom into the most wondrous kid on earth."

"Oh Lord, a fawning dad waiting to spoil."

"Yeah, I'd guess. You want to bet on twins the way Mama and Dad have?"

"Okay. I say no, not the first time and maybe that'll be it."

"And maybe not. I love kids. So do you."

"We're busy people, Marty. Besides, a famous psychotherapist contends that *one* set of parents only have time to properly raise *one* child."

"I was one of four and we're all happy."

"You all do seem that way much of the time," she murmured, then wondered: *But what about you, Marty, how did you come to choose a woman so different from your loving mother? Was there nothing about her that told you she would wreck you, would destroy your life at least for a while? And you've chosen me, an emotional cripple wed for life to a dead man. Oh, I love you in a special way and you know that, but not the way you want me to.*

"Let's go in, sweetie," Marty said. "It's getting colder and I want to fix us cups of valerian tea for sleep paradise."

As they walked to the house, she thought valerian tea always helped her sleep, but Rita's murder and Marty's secret life struck her to her core and she knew she wouldn't get much sleep that night.

Chapter 16

"I've got an idea. Let's go shopping for maternity clothes for you." Dosha's face was alive with affection for Caitlin as they sat on a big beige leather sofa in Caitlin and Marty's basement family room.

Caitlin raised her eyebrows. "It's a little early for that, isn't it, but the idea does sound interesting."

"Then let's do it. You've got hours before your exam this afternoon and I know you're jittery. This will be a good way to pass the time. Where's Marty?"

"Creating. He's upstairs working on a painting of me. The drawings are fantastic."

"My brother is such a love. I wish he'd dated you first."

Caitlin sighed and looked thoughtful. "We're together now and with the baby coming I'm happier than I ever thought I'd be again."

Dosha leaned over and hugged Caitlin. "And old Marty's living again. He's happy and that makes me and all of us Steeles happy. Look, are you really game for shopping or just pleasing me?"

"Sure I am. Let me tell Marty we're going. I'll keep on the scruffy things I'm wearing."

Dosha looked at Caitlin's close fitting navy knit pants and sweater. "Some scruff. You look fine to me. Gee, I'm glad today's Saturday and I'm off and Rena's handling things and I can spend time with you."

"I'm glad too. Dosha, how well did you get to know Bianca?"

"Well enough. Too well. I don't like calling women names, but she deserves a few of the coarser ones. I had trouble with her in New York. She's always tried to separate Marty from those he knows and loves. On Puerto I think you'll see right away what I mean. She's even more conniving now. Bianca called me before Marty came back to apologize for what she'd done to him. Gossip has it that her old flame didn't marry her and ditched her after the baby came; they're both players who deserve each other. I loathe Bianca. She's an evil woman."

She took Caitlin's hand. "But you've brought love back into my brother's heart. Keep loving him, Cait. It doesn't matter that your marriage isn't perfect. He's happy. You know that."

"So am I." She patted her abdomen. "I can see this baby, hear it gurgling, feel its warm breath on my face. I feel him or her on my breasts. Dosha, tell me I'm not dreaming . . ."

Dosha laughed. "You're not dreaming. Ricky's in hog heaven talking about his first first cousin. He adores you."

"And he's like my own kid." Caitlin glanced at her watch. "It's 9:35. We'll be there when the stores open, and let's tell Marty we're going."

* * *

After the women left, Marty sat in the new studio he and Caitlin had pulled together for him in this house. It lacked the skylight of the other house with its spectacular plays of light, but in some ways this studio was even more satisfactory. Caitlin was here more often than she came to the other house. Her presence soothed him and he sat thinking as he studied his many drawings for the painting he would begin today. It had been several days since Caitlin took the E.P.T. He had leaned on her to see her gynecologist earlier, but Dr. Graham had been out of town for several days. When they came back from the doctor's, he thought now he would begin to paint. He exulted in his prowess and his loins were expanding with fervor.

Had he really wanted to end it all less than a year ago? Now his life was full with Caitlin and the coming child they'd both wanted for so long. He held up the drawing of her beloved form and ran his tongue over his bottom lip. The working title would be the final title: *Madonna Waiting*. He laughed a little then because he felt he needed to do a companion piece—a self-portrait—when this was finished. And he should call that one *Father Waiting*.

He was a man in love the way he fully realized he had never known it before. His marriage to Bianca had brought him highs and excitement, but no comfort. His talent and his love of life made him paint with genius, for which the world richly rewarded him, but he knew now there had been no deep satisfaction. He had been restive, craving something he had not seemed able to get or feel and he'd thought it just a human craving for something else that perhaps didn't exist. Now he knew that bone-deep satisfaction did in fact exist and he now had a lot of it, but he wanted even more. If Cait never came to love him with the wildly romantic love she'd known with Sylvan, what he had with her was good beyond the telling.

He shook his head then as he thought of his old friend Sylvan Costner, and he knew he would carry Sylvan's secret to the grave, because he would die before he'd break Caitlin's heart.

In Dr. Graham's homey office with Caitlin's drawings of infants in various stages of development on one wall, Caitlin and Marty sat across from Dr. Graham, an affable, heavyset, chocolate bar of a man who loved his work. The doctor rubbed his hands together and grinned from ear to ear.

"Pregnant, are we? It's about time."

Caitlin laughed. "We've only been married a very short while.

"It's often happened the first night. I've been waiting. I did the exams and you both are in really good shape, in love. It's people like you who make me crazy about my job. I'll examine you now, Cait." He looked at Marty waggishly. "Try not to break into my examining room with wild impatience, Marty."

Marty laughed easily. "I'll try to keep it together."

Dr. Graham buzzed his nurse, asked her to meet them in the examining room, stood and, with a sweep of his arms, invited Caitlin to come with him.

In a few minutes, with the blue paper gown covering her, Caitlin was grateful for the doctor's expertise. He even had warm instruments, which no other doctor she had known before used, and she shuddered at the thought of that cold, cold steel equipment invading her body. Dr. Graham had been her doctor since she'd moved back to D.C. He was Dosha's and Rispa's doctor too.

With Dr. Graham's nurse standing silently by, at first she was lost in her dreams, then she became aware of an intent, serious look on Dr. Graham's face as he probed. Finishing, he stopped and drew blood, though his nurse usually drew blood.

"Marriage is agreeing with you," he said finally. "You're looking just as you should look inside and I'm pleased."

It wasn't what she expected him to say. Was something wrong?

"George," she said hesitantly, "you don't *look* all that pleased."

He bit his bottom lip and patted her shoulder. "Get dressed and come back out. I need to talk with you and Marty."

"What is it?"

"It's nothing to get upset about, Cait. I just need to talk with you both. Let me help you down."

With fumbling fingers, Caitlin got into her clothes and went back out. Marty caught the subdued expressions on Dr. Graham and Caitlin's faces and tensed.

Marty looked tense. "Well, what's the good news?"

Dr. Graham looked from one to the other. "I want to see you again Monday afternoon. I'll have your bloodwork back and I'll discuss it fully then. I know it's hard, but I won't go further. You're healthy, fine, and I don't want you to worry. I'll have my nurse make an appointment for you."

Outside Caitlin fretted. "What on earth could this be about?" He said I'm healthy. Question is can I survive until Monday?"

Marty drew her close. "You bet you can. I keep thinking there's some minor thing that's going to require care and attention . . ."

As his voice drifted, he squeezed her hand and she

squeezed back. "I'm nervous and I'd like a milkshake so thick I could eat it with a spoon. Banana, I think."

"You've got it. I'll make you one when we get home."

They spent a nervous rest of the weekend and time seemed endless until they were back in Dr. Graham's office. Once they were seated, he didn't mince words.

"Cait isn't pregnant," he said flatly.

Caitlin's voice went hoarse with disappointment. "But I told you over the phone I took the E.P.T and it registered positive. How can that be?"

Dr. Graham signed. "The tests are ninety-eight percent accurate. I'm afraid you fall in the 2 percent that registers wrong. Tell me exactly what you did."

He listened carefully as she described the procedure, then nodded. "You did everything right. That brand is not my favorite and I know a Memphis doctor's patient who had a false pregnancy result. You two are the only failure I know of."

"But I had all the signs—sore breasts, occasional nausea."

Marty took her hand, held it tightly, laced his fingers through hers. "Easy, sweetheart," he told her.

"You *want* to be pregnant so bad," Dr. Graham said slowly. "You both want a baby so badly. The woman in Memphis wanted a baby and she later had three, one at a time, so don't sweat it, you two. Go home and get to work right away. There's no physical reason it can't happen." He smiled gently with half-closed eyes. "Go home and make love like a life depends on it. Call me often and keen me posted on your progress." His smile got even wider, mischievous. "No, I'm not a voyeur, just your very interested and concerned doctor."

Marty got up and helped Caitlin to her feet as the

doctor stood too. "Try to relax, both of you. Tenseness can prevent pregnancy sometimes. Enjoy your life. Revel in it. If I were a betting man, I'd make a wager you two will be pregnant within six months or less."

The doctor shook hands with Marty and embraced Caitlin, patted her back. This simple, heartfelt gesture brought tears to her eyes. Marty took a couple of tissues from the box on the desk and blotted her eyes as he smiled sadly at her, hugged her. "Let's follow the doctor's orders to go home and get started," he told her.

Marty kept Caitlin close to his side as they walked into the parking lot and to his car. He opened the door and helped her in, lightly patting her hip. She was crying again with disappointment and he felt like crying too. But what the hell, he thought, they would begin again with a vengeance.

He leaned over her and kissed the top of her head, her face, her mouth. "Don't cry, baby," he said grimly. "This is just the beginning. I'm disappointed too, but you heard the doctor. There's no physical reason why we can't make a baby."

She rallied a bit with his words. "Let's go home," she said.

"You bet. But first, I'm going to stop by Raymond's and get some of his New England clam chowder. You love it and I want to get some food into you. We were so keyed up, we both ate very little for breakfast."

Raymond also sold flowers from his wife's florist shop and Marty bought two dozen red and white carnations. The spicy odor filled the car and Caitlin smiled as he gave them to her. "Thank you," she said. "You always know what to do to lift my spirits."

He smiled back with a mock leer as he got into the

car and patted her thigh, then squeezed it. "Let's go home and I'll show you some real spirit lifting."

She laughed in spite of herself. "You've got Eveready batteries."

"Only for you, babe. *Only* for you."

At home Caitlin slipped into a transparent black lace gown and took her earth-brown hair down, letting it cascade around her shoulders. She got in the bed on the dusty rose Egyptian cotton sheets and plumped three fat pillows under her head and shoulders. Marty wheeled in the clam chowder, full of juicy clams and diced white potatoes, all in a cream base. He'd set pretty, brown wooden trays with bowls of chowder and oyster crackers. She smacked her lips at the strips of extra sharp cheddar cheese and the small bunch of black grapes. He put the cart just outside the door and came back in.

"Are you trying to seduce me with food, my husband?"

His eyes narrowed and his glance was hot, enthralling. "I intend to seduce you with everything I have, my wife. If you think of anything I've left out, tell me and I'll do that too."

"First on the agenda is relax like the doctor said, but how can I relax when you're looking at me like that?"

"Eat, woman, before I can't stop myself from ravishing you."

He stripped to his black boxer shorts with the big red hearts printed on them. There was an arrow through each heart. He left on his black tee.

"You know," she said, "you shouldn't turn me on like this. You're a fine hunk, Mr. Man. Maybe I'll ravish *you* first."

"That had better be a promise."

The food was delicious, melt-in-your-mouth, and she ate well. He was pleased that she had rallied and it made his food more enjoyable.

"You know," she said, "I tried not to give you those shorts before Valentine's Day, but I kept imagining your great buns in them. Narrow hips, to-die-for buns. You turn me on in ways you would never dream of."

"Ah, but I know very well the ways you turn *me* on. Every which way."

His black eyes were dreamy on her as he chewed his food. His face was flushed and healthy. "Speaking of imagination, mine is going wild. Even the carnations are an aphrodisiac. Hell, everything's like that with me where you're concerned."

"Marty?"

"Yes, love."

She swallowed hard. "You know the special room I have as a shrine to Sylvan and Sylvan Junior? I'm going to move Sylvan's paintings and the memorabilia to that nice room in the basement next week. Having them so prominently displayed isn't fair to you. I'm sorry I didn't think to do this before." She went sober then. "I was focused on getting pregnant—and wondering if getting married was fair to you."

Marty looked at her steadily. "You don't have to do that. I'm comfortable with your shrine. And yes, you did the right thing, marrying me."

She leaned forward and brushed the rough black, flat-grained hair on his temple with her fingers. "I'm going to do it and I insist. You know, love, I'm *feeling* these days, really feeling, in spite of the disappointment today and Rita's death. I still go numb, but I don't stay that way long. It's so good to feel again and I owe that to you."

Then the bowls were empty, the food consumed.

"That was delicious. You're always so thoughtful, kind. How could any woman give you up?"

"As long as *you* don't give me up, no other woman matters."

Did a shadow cross his face? she wondered. A man didn't get over a woman like Bianca in a hurry.

He brought the cart back in, loaded it, and took the dishes out to the kitchen. She lay in bed still tasting the food. Then she shuddered as a sudden wave of sadness swept over her. Disappointment that she wasn't pregnant was a blight on her spirit, but they had time. She thought of Rita, for whom time had run out, and it made her heart hurt. She thought of something else and for a moment suppressed the thought because Marty came back in.

She smiled wanly as he sat on the bed by her side. "There's plenty to be sad about," he said softly, "but you seem even sadder. What's on your mind, sweetheart?"

She drew a deep, ragged breath. Should she tell him this? "Marty, are my memories of Sylvan imprisoning me, keeping me from getting pregnant?"

For a moment, he couldn't speak, her question shook him so. He took her hand. "Don't jump to any quick conclusions, love. Give us time."

Looking at him, her thoughts of Sylvan drifted away and she felt closer than close to the man she'd married. He stroked her face. "Listen, why don't I just hold you and not make love? Wouldn't you like that?"

Even as he talked she relaxed and her blood heated as she looked at his tall, fit body. His eyes on her were mesmerizing. The scent of the carnations he had bought her filled her nostrils as he leaned over, switched on the expensive Bose CD player and Lionel Richie's "Lady" surrounded them. "You're *my* lady," he told her. "And you didn't answer my question."

"You're my man and I don't want you to just hold me."

"I'm glad because that's exactly what I want to be."

Flames were licking at her belly at his tender words, at his beloved face that reflected the love he felt. "I want to whisper something to you," she said.

He leaned closer and her mouth nuzzled his ear. "Please make love to me," she begged him.

"Baby!" He gently pushed her nearer the middle of the bed and got in beside her, his big hands avidly stroking her body, her loosened hair. For long moments he couldn't get his breath as she moaned softly. She was torpid with wanting him and sharp memories of every minute of the times they'd made love gripped her senses.

"My very own Michelangelo's *David*," she murmured.

"And my very own queen of love."

He pulled her gown from her lovely brown silken shoulders and down her body, flinging it to the bottom of the bed and she lay in soft, curved splendor in the lowered light.

"Now let me . . ." she began as she put her hand between his boxer shorts and his smooth, thick skin, slipping the garment down his legs and throwing it atop her gown. He pulled off his tee. She stroked him as he stroked her, stroked his sinewy calves, thighs, then moved to his shaft, fondling it. "How beautiful you are," she whispered.

"No. You're the beautiful one. Cait, we're going to check your daily temps to tell us when you're most likely to conceive. We're going to pray and we're going to make love with a purpose. Tonight, if you decide you want to stop, just tell me and I'll stop."

Unanswering, a wild fervor took her as she bent and flicked her tongue back and forth across his flat breasts and nipples and a delicious shudder ran the length of his body. "Don't *you* stop," he told her. "Don't ever stop."

He gloried in her ministrations; she had never been so abandoned. Her tender hands feverishly roamed his body, stroking, stroking until he could take it no longer. As she pressed her open mouth to his, her tongue explored the hot tissue of his mouth and he turned her onto her back.

"Drive me mad, will you, woman?" he teased her. "Well, I can play that game too." With a wicked mock leer, his fingers massaged her scalp, her face, and throat, and for a few moments his big hands cupped her breasts. His mouth encircled one, then the other breast and suckled them gently at first, then harder as she fiercely held him to her.

He kissed her belly with slow, tantalizing kisses, his tongue bringing ecstasy, sending hot blood coursing through her. He had first kissed her like this in dreams of ecstasy and she had responded as she responded now. His tongue swirled into her belly button and she cried out his name as he swept a line of kisses to her female center, caressing the soft hair, tasting the sweet fluid she exuded. Her frantic moans were music to his ears as he lingered, boldly pleasuring her, then swept on.

His tongue continued the circular motions as he planted kisses down her thighs and her calves, then the soft, tender, well-cared-for feet. She bucked beneath him and grabbed his hair, pulling him back up.

"What is it you want from me?" he teased her mercilessly.

"You know what I want—you inside me, and I want you *now*." She could not remember a time when she'd felt this fire, this intense steam that threatened to explode and drain her.

"Impatient love," he said, laughing. "Don't I give you enough loving?"

"Yes, but tonight I need more, much more. I need all of you, everything you've got to give me."

His oversized shaft had swollen greatly as he spread her legs, overcome with love and lust as he gazed at the intricate female splendor, a part of the source of joy she brought him. He entered her gently, slipping in slowly until he touched her womb and he was in a hurry to be fully inside the haven she offered him.

She clutched his buttocks as she threw her legs over his back and crossed them. He was all the way in, throbbing his passion, his need, his love. And she lay in a daze, her inner walls surrounding him, his love surrounding her. Funny, she thought, how the body responded with raging fever, even when the heart partially held back. But she loved this man with a special love and wanted his child.

He worked her with hot fervor and she moved beneath him rhythmically, tenderly, giving him more of her heart and her soul than she knew. He hooked his arms around her legs and moved them across his shoulders and she gasped hard.

"Did I hurt you?" he asked anxiously.

"A little. But it's exquisite pain. You're pretty big. Did you know I call him 'Buddy'?"

Marty laughed, glad for the diversion because he'd been too near the edge.

"A good name. He's sure been my buddy with you."

"You're so good at this. Does that come from a lot of practice?"

"Not nearly as much as others would have you believe. I *like* women. I've never used one to my advantage."

She had always known he was a man of integrity, as Sylvan had been a man of integrity. She was lucky, and grateful to be that way. Caught up in new torpor, she felt him making circular motions as he licked her breasts, moving up to her throat, her face, then back to her breasts, and she was lost in ecstasy.

Inside her, his mind climbed the tallest mountains with her at his side. In his fantasy, they lay on the Puerto beach as the tide came in and covered them and he took her with a passion that shook them both. But he needed no fantasy. Now reality surpassed all dreams.

"Marty?"

"Yes, love."

"I love you more than you think I do. I'm sorry it's not all thc way."

"It's all right," he assured her. "I'd rather be with you than anybody else on earth."

Even with ecstasy bubbling in her body and her brain, she thought about what Jayson had told her, that Marty would always belong to Bianca. Was it so bad then, so wrong that she was chained to the past and Sylvan?

She chuckled as she lay there, exulting at the feel of his shaft inside her and his tongue making wondrous licking circles on her hotly responsive body.

"Why are you laughing?"

"I'm thinking about what a dentist once told me, that the tongue packs a wallop. It's a powerful tool and Lord, you're sure using it that way. You bring me rapture, and I love what you do to me."

This time, *he* laughed. "Don't tell me that. I'll consider touching you up more often and that'll be *too* often."

Quite fiercely then she said, "I'll give you a baby or I'll die trying."

He stopped moving then and his hands cupped her face. "It takes two of us to make this kid and you *won't* die trying. We'll both *live* trying."

Her next thought brought a chill to her limbs. "I'll

give you a divorce if I don't get pregnant in a reasonable time," she said quietly.

He shook her roughly. "Stop it, Cait. I don't want a divorce if you don't get pregnant. I want *you* and you know that, with or without a baby. We've got Ricky and there'll be other nieces and nephews. The world is full of children desperate for love. Please don't talk about leaving me; I love you too much for that."

"All right, I won't. I just thought it was something you might want."

"Never." His voice went hoarse with feeling and he pressed her even closer to him.

"Let's get on with this passion play," she murmured. "If I told you how you make me feel, how you turn me to delicious wild plum jelly inside, you'd get arrogant."

He shook his head. "No, you constantly show me that I satisfy you, at least in many ways. As for getting arrogant, that would be for a man certain of your love and that's something I've still got to earn—if I can."

Her heart hurt for him then as she told him, "I *do* love you, sweetheart, in a very special way and it gets deeper all the time."

Her words lifted him, soothed and excited him at once. "I'm going to get astride you, work *my* magic," she said.

"You work magic with me with every move you make in every way."

"I'm glad because you do that to me."

He turned over and she lowered herself onto his rigid penis, thrills flashing through her, then moving in steady waves. Her breasts were pebbled, thrusting, begging for his mouth on them and he pulled her forward, his avid mouth covering first one, then the other as he laved them. She fought the orgasm that raced to come; she wasn't nearly ready yet.

"I want you to listen carefully to the next CD," he said. "You like Charley Pride?"

"Oh, Marty, wherever did you find one of his albums? He's been ill and out of circulation, but he's coming back. Imagine a Black guy as a country music legend, and back then when things were so different for us. You bet I like him, *love* him."

In a few minutes, Charley Pride's incredible voice came in on the song he wrote, "You're So Good When You're Bad."

She laughed a bit before he sucked her bottom lip. "You think I'm bad?"

"When you need to be, and you're *really* good when you're bad. Hell, you're good when you're good or bad."

"Thank you, I think. You're good for me all the time. Marty, no matter what the difficulties, we've got something going and I want to keep it."

"You've got it, Babe, the way you've got me ravening inside you. Now old Buddy's cutting up; he likes to spill his seed in you and he's pressuring me."

She bit his ear as he worked her harder, squeezed her buns, stroked her back. "Biting my ear brings me on," he told her. "Are you sure you're ready?"

She nipped him again, then a second time. He gripped her waist, then her buttocks again. "I'll take that as a yes," he said.

Thrills like nothing either had known before swept through them, rocking their bodies gently at first, then harder. He felt her body convulse with orgasms that refused to stop and he heard her tender cries and moans with the awe that always moved him when he was with her. Making love had never been so good, so full of promise, and neither could wait to try it all over again.

Chapter 17

At the gallery the next morning, the atmosphere was subdued, somber. Rena had arrived early, come to Caitlin, hugged her.

"Detective Anderson and Sargeant Draper are already here," Rena said. "They're waiting to talk with you, and I asked them to give you a little while to get settled. You said you were going to see Dr. Graham." She looked at her boss and friend tentatively. "You seem even more down. Is something wrong?"

"I'm not pregnant."

Rena's hand went to her mouth. "Not . . ." she began and hugged Caitlin, who was keenly aware of Rena's swollen abdomen. "Oh Lord, honey, I'm so sorry. But look, you're both young, healthy. You know I didn't get pregnant for four years and oh, how we tried. How's Marty taking this?"

"Like a trouper. Every minute of every day I know how blessed I am to have him as a husband."

"He's a great guy and so good for you. Are you going to be all right? Because you could talk with the policemen, then go back home. This is a body blow and I can handle things."

Caitlin shook her head. "No, I need to be here. Marty's coming by to take me to lunch He's painting my portrait . . ." A few acid tears gathered in her eyes. "D'you know what he's calling that painting? *Madonna Waiting*. He's gonna have to retitle that one."

Rena shook her head. "You know, love, it'd be great if you two were going to Puerto de la Cruz now. Bet you'd get a baby there. Vacations can do that. Look, if there's *anything* I can do, you know you have only to ask."

"You're a love of a woman, Rena. Your baby's fortunate to have you carrying him or her. If you see Luther, tell him I'd like to talk with him for a few minutes. And ask the policemen to give me oh, about twenty minutes and I can, if they wish, give them the rest of the morning. Did the Monet prints come in from Paris?"

"They did and they're gorgeous. We're going to have some grateful customers."

Caitlin stopped by the huge stainless steel coffee urn in the alcove and drew herself a cup of strong black coffee. Jayson was right, she thought as she slowly sipped the brew; their coffee was the best. They also served herbal teas, black and green tea, and cocoa. It was a fairly expensive operation, but people enjoyed it, complimented them, and drank heartily.

In her office, Caitlin opened the blinds, then put her things away. She switched on the classical music radio station and listened to the strains of Mahler's Adagietto from his Fifth Symphony. The intensely beautiful melody soothed her; it was one of Marty's and her favorite recordings. Where to begin her day? She offered up her second short prayer of the day, beginning, "Lord, you know how much we want a baby . . ."

She was sitting quietly, her mind wandering, not letting herself think of Rita, when the knock sounded and at her invitation, two officers came in. Detective Anderson was somber. Jim Draper looked terrible, she thought, as if he hadn't slept in a week. Her heart torn, she got up and went to Sergeant Draper, hugged him. "How much support do you have to help you now?" she asked.

He sighed long and hard. "The case is his baby," he began as he pointed to Detective Anderson. "The captain is letting me help as best I can. As for how I'm holding up, I've got Detective Anderson and a few other good buddies. Cops are the best in the world at times like this. My kids are a great comfort, and we've got good police psychologists and one psychiatrist I swear by. He helped me when I had trouble with my ex who, by the way, may make me do her bodily harm. She called me and laughed when she heard Rita was dead. She doesn't have sense enough to know she could be considered a suspect. She knows a lot of men and one of them could easily be able to break into a place like this."

Caitlin wished she could do more to comfort him. "I'm sorry."

"I know you are. You're a great woman. Rita was like you, caring, affectionate, what I've looked for all my life and finally found. Dear God . . ." His voice broke, but he braced himself as Detective Anderson hugged him.

Jim Draper calmed himself, and they sat down. "Have you had coffee?" she asked the men.

"Too much. We're fine." Sergeant Draper sighed deeply and relaxed as best he could. "Okay. Since this is Detective Anderson's case, I'll let him do the talking."

Detective Anderson nodded. "We've begun to thoroughly check out the premises. It was easy to check your employees since there aren't that many. Jim was able to give us very useful info on Ms. Glass's background, her movements. She liked you, talked to you a lot. Did she give any indication that someone hated her?" He laughed sourly before he added, "Other than Sergeant Draper's ex-wife?"

"Not really. Everybody here was crazy about Rita. Even the kids who came to visit loved her." She suddenly remembered something. "There was a young man, probably not twenty, who came by too often and asked Rena and me about her. He told me he had seen her coming in and leaving and he liked what he saw. I told him she was getting married. That didn't seem to matter to him."

Sergeant Draper growled. "Yeah, she told me about this clown."

"Go on." Detective Anderson shifted in his chair. "Do you think he was stalking her? Think she was afraid of him?" He looked from Caitlin to his fellow cop.

"Ha! Rita wasn't afraid of the devil himself," Jim Draper said. "The dirtbag had been waiting for her a couple of times, but I drove up. She got a minicamera and took photos of him." He got his wallet from his pocket and showed it to Caitlin, who gasped. She recognized this boy.

"Yeah." Sergeant Draper got tense, angry. "The thug in that photo is the guy who mugged you in September. We arrested him on another charge and his well-paid lawyer got a sympathetic judge. He was out before the ink dried on his arrest warrant." He sounded as bitter as gall. "I didn't know you then as well as I do now, although I'd worked with you in community activities. I didn't tell you because I didn't want you running scared, but he threatened to get you and your man if you two testified against him."

Caitlin's head jerked up. "I wouldn't let that stop me from testifying."

"I thank God for citizens like you," Detective Anderson complimented her.

"The thug's name is Dilly McKay," Sergeant Draper continued, "and let me tell you he's got connections all the way to the New York mob. He brags he uses nothing but the purest cocaine. He's been a messenger, a mule for the drug lords. He's an enforcer and he knows characters who could break into your gallery in a heartbeat. He could have killed Rita when she surprised him stealing maybe another painting. Rats like him like pretty, expensive things.

"If he killed her, his ass is mine. New York cops always cooperate with us and we do the same. I don't give a damn what his low-life gangs do to me, I'm gonna eat him alive."

"Simmer down, Jim," Detective Anderson said mildly. "We've got a lot of cops on McKay's tail. We'll get him, but we don't know that he killed Rita."

"I'll break his ribs anyway for what he did to Mrs. Steele," Jim said.

"Thank you for caring," Caitlin told him.

They shared information they'd gotten from the gallery staff.

Finally Detective Anderson asked her, "That painting that was returned, what do you make of that? You told me about it being a fake."

"It's a puzzle," she said. "I've got it under tighter vault control. Rita was keeping special watch."

"I hear it's one of the ones that made your late husband's reputation."

"Yes."

"And your new husband is also a very well-known painter."

"Yes. We began being friends in college. He's in the genius range that Sylvan, my late husband, was in."

"And the employees tell me *you're* really good. I read an article about you in the *Post* and one in the *Informer*."

"Guilty as charged. My late husband stole the show from everyone. My present husband thinks I'm better than I realize. Running this gallery's a full-time job. I don't have much time for painting."

Detective Anderson passed his tongue under his top teeth. This woman was a soft, maternal woman and he loved soft, maternal women. He was glad he had one of his own.

They had talked for over an hour when the two policemen stood. "Well, that about does it for now," Detective Anderson said. "We'll need to talk again though."

"Any time," Caitlin assured him. Then an idea bulb came on in her head. "Jim, how'd you like to have dinner with us soon? Bring the children. In fact, both of you come and bring your families. Just tell me what you like. I'm a fair cook; I've had no complaints."

Jim Draper shook his head. "Lord, I'd love that, but our captain wouldn't approve. He's a stickler for separation of community and us where close socialization is concerned. It warms my heart that you'd invite us and after this is over and I've done what I have to do to whoever did this, I'll talk to our boss and I think he'll ease up."

"I'll talk to him, too, and thank you," Detective Anderson smiled broadly now. "We're gonna lick this thing. The info we've been able to get makes me happy and I expect this to be over soon. Well, old buddy." He clapped Jim Draper on the shoulder and the two men went out.

Caitlin got up and went to the windows again. It was

such a beautiful day. Rita had often said she was greatly affected by the weather. She hadn't seen enough of Rita, who would come in sometimes just to visit because she liked art and museums. She'd bought prints for Jim's young daughter. Caitlin had given her a Lou Stovall silk screen print.

"It's way too expensive for you to give away," Rita had protested.

"Nothing's too expensive to celebrate happiness," she had responded. And Jim Draper had been delighted.

Caitlin grew quiet, thinking that conversation seemed light years ago. Rita had begun a life filled with almost certain happiness. Now her life had been snuffed by some evil hand. Caitlin sighed deeply, pressing the tips of her fingers to a temple.

There was a message from Dosha to call her, but Caitlin wanted to talk with Marty first.

"How's my beautiful wife?" he asked somberly.

"I'm okay," she lied, because she was hurting again.

"I doubt that."

She needed to change the subject. "What're you doing?"

"Working on *Madonna*. You sound down, sweetheart, and trying to deny it."

"You read me all too well."

"I want to take you to some posh place for lunch, or whatever you want. And Cait, I'm going into town tomorrow to pick up the red amaryllis you want to paint."

"Thanks. Right now, I need to come home for an hour or so, pick up something from the deli on the way and lie with you—as the Bible puts it." She was crying then. "I'm greedy for you, Marty. I want to feel you inside me again. Maybe we'll never eat the food I bring, but I . . ."

"Honey, listen," he said sternly, affection heating his voice. "I'm going to come and walk you home, and I'll pick up a few things from the deli on the way over there. I need some sunshine and I need you more than you could ever need me. I'll be there around one."

She made a kissing sound and he made a similar sound and they both kept the line open. "You hang up first," he said.

"No, you. Honey, I can't stay too long because everything's hectic here, but I'll wait for you and I love you."

"I love you more."

His words were a reminder that he told the truth; their love was uneven. But who knew what hers would grow to be? She hung up reluctantly and sat still for a moment, then she dialed Dosha.

"Where are you now?" Caitlin asked.

"You're a lucky woman. I'm on a break and I expected a call from you earlier. I know you two were celebrating last night."

"There's no baby," Caitlin said flatly.

"What d'you mean? You saw Dr. Graham?"

Caitlin explained what the doctor had said and Dosha was vividly sympathetic. "My God, you must be in tatters. Are you at home?"

"I'm at work. I thought that was best for me."

"I'll come to you."

"No don't, sweetie. Marty and I made the best love I've ever known last night. He's picking me up to go home and do more of the same."

"Atta girl, but listen, you don't want to overdo it. Get right back in there, keep track of your temperature. I've heard about different positions that facilitate pregnancy. Different foods that affect the baby's gender; I think it's alkaline for girls, acid for boys. I'm very, very sorry, love, that it didn't happen this time, but you two tigers hang in there and it *will* happen. I just feel it in my bones."

"You're sweet, but my husband is even sweeter."

"Prejudiced. But I can live with it. Don't tell Damien, but I love my oldest brother at least a tad more than I love my twin. And I *will* see you as soon as you get a break from making that baby."

"Marty's the best," Catlin told her and they said good-bye.

Her heart felt a little lighter then. She had a lot to talk with Marty about, but they wouldn't be talking that much about anything this noon hour.

Luther came into her office a little later.

"You wanted to see me, Mrs. Steele?"

She smiled. "I always have to remind you to call me Caitlin, or Cait." She paused. "You look so unhappy. Would you like to talk about it? And I want to ask you something."

He shook his head. "Wouldn't help. I'm still tore up about Rita. I guess we all are, but she was special to me, one of the friendliest women I've ever seen."

"She was special to all of us."

"And Lord, Jim Draper, I hope he don't die from this. I wish there was something I could do for him . . ."

"I wish I could help him too, but right now the only help I think he'd welcome is finding Rita's killer."

"Guess you're right. That what you wanted to talk to me about?"

"No, but I do want you to tell me when things bother you. I like giving and getting aid and comfort."

"I'll remember that." He shifted in his chair, waiting for her to continue.

"I recall you once said you like to travel to pretty places."

"Sure do. You got something in mind?"

Caitlin smiled. "I do. Have you ever heard of a place

called Puerto de la Cruz? It's in the Tenerife segment of the Canary Islands in Spain."

"Can't say I have, but then I haven't heard of that much. I've been around in the States, Mexico, Canada, but not much more than that. Yeah, I been to Cuba, too, a few years back when they started lettin' people go. I like to gamble some."

"Good. Would you like to go to Puerto de la Cruz in Spain's Canary Islands with my husband and me the last week of February? You'd be there for two weeks for a glorious La Carnaval."

It was amazing, she thought, the way his face lit up. "Would I like that?" he breathed. "You bet I would. Now I always go to New Orleans around that time, but heck, I go there every year. It's time I tried something different. Yes, ma'am, I would jump at the chance to go. What would I be doing?"

Caitlin laughed. "Mostly enjoying the festivities. We're carrying a few paintings and I'll need help with handling them. It would be nothing you couldn't easily do. We're showing my late husband's paintings. Marty says the art gallery there is short on help. And there'll be errands to run, little things. You'll have lots of time for fun and games. There are pretty women galore—and they're friendly. Does that catch your fancy?"

He grinned widely. "Does a tomcat love cream? Cait, you have made my whole year. I'm going out and buying me some good-looking threads to net myself some good-looking chicks. Maybe I'll turn into what folks call a *player*." He was almost salivating; he didn't have far to go, she thought.

The conversation was finished and Luther nearly knocked his chair over with excitement as he got up. "Anything you ever need from me, you got," he chortled.

Chapter 18

On Saturday a week later, Caitlin was in Marty's home studio. For the past two nights, he had simply held her as her heart hurt and she knew his hurt no less. It had been an incredibly warm and comforting time. Sylvan hadn't held her like that ever. "You bring out all the passion in me," Marty often said, "and I intend to satisfy that passion."

Now she reflected that passion had many facets. She had badly wanted Sylvan to hold her, stroke her, and it was simply not his style. Surprising how much Marty's doing what she wanted soothed her, the way it was surprising how deep he went into her being so quickly. She was smiling as he came in.

"Breakfast dishes are in the dishwasher. You're looking even more luscious than you did at the breakfast table, and I see you've changed into your modeling garb. Shall we get started?"

He came to her, tipped her head back and kissed her, his tongue tracing her lips with tantalizing slowness. A wet, thrilling kiss.

"If you intend to paint, you'd better stop right there," she warned. "I get horny too, and that's foreplay if I ever felt it."

He shook with teasing laughter. "You can't get horny, love. You don't have a horn."

"Oh, but I *have*." She lightly touched his pants-covered shaft. "I have yours to use as my own. And don't we always say what belongs to one belongs to the other?"

"Woman," he told her. "Let's paint and get lost in ecstasy later."

"I admire your restraint. Wish I had it where you're concerned."

"It's killing me, but my muse is stern this morning and she commands that I paint."

"You always say *I'm* your muse."

"True and she—and you—have a split personality. Wanting to make love. Wanting to paint. Sometimes they're the same thing." He got somber. "You know it's held by some that all art is a fight against death."

"That's true, I think. I know when Sylvan and Caleb died, as well as my baby and my parents, you'll remember how frantically I painted. I didn't want to stop to sleep or eat."

"You painted some of the most wonderful pictures. Where are they now, Cait?"

"Tucked away. I still have them."

"May I see them again? I thought they were incredible."

"Yes, of course. They're in that basement room where I put Sylvan's old paintings and the other artifacts for my shrine. I'll bring them up today or Monday."

"And I'll help you. This is going to be exciting."

"Sylvan had several paintings he did on Puerto de la Cruz, one of the Atlantic Ocean at high tide." She closed her eyes. "Entrancing."

Marty looked extremely interested. "I've been thinking. I want to exhibit several of your paintings in the Puerto Art Museum and several of Sylvan's, not just one each as we'd talked about."

"And what about your own paintings?"

"I'm not forgetting myself. I already have a couple of my paintings exhibited there."

"I don't know. I'll feel overmatched by far with my pictures hanging alongside yours and Sylvan's."

He knelt beside her and took her hand. "Cait, Cait. *When* will you get over this ridiculous modesty? You could be a present-day Georgia O'Keeffe if you chose to be. Okay, maybe you're not as driven to be great as she was, but talent like yours deserves to be seen, known, honored."

She stroked his black, rough-grained hair, touched his ruddy face. "I've got my gallery; that's how I've chosen to live my life. And even more important, I've got *you*. With God's help, we'll have a baby, or we'll adopt one. And then . . ."

"And then?" He wondered why she suddenly looked so stressed.

In a much lower voice she said, "Sylvan didn't exactly discourage me from painting, but he didn't encourage me either. You and Caleb always did. Sylvan always said I had *promise*, that he had all the genius in our family. I loved him, so I internalized his opinions, his beliefs."

He squeezed her hand, said gently, "That's not love, Cait, that's slavery."

He was right and she wondered then why she hadn't realized it before, but she didn't tell him that. Instead she found herself defending Sylvan's beliefs.

"Have you been in your studio today?" he asked.

She shook her head. "Why do you ask?"

"I got you the scarlet amaryllis from the florist. You

said that's what you'd like to paint. Try to paint a little today, will you?"

She felt a rush of happiness, bent forward and kissed the top of his head. "Yes, and thank you. What do you think makes you so sweet?"

"I'm absorbing *your* sugar."

He positioned her on an armless blue plush chair, set up the lights and checked his easel and palette for the brushes and the paint he'd need.

"*Madonna Waiting*," she murmured as she felt a little sadness return. "What'll your new title be?"

"I'll keep that title, like I told you. We always wait for *something*, love. Now I won't show you this until I finish, so no peeking behind my back."

"Okay, but that won't be easy; I'm curious. Will you capture my soul? You know, I kept a couple of paintings you did of me when we were The Four Musketeers. They're incredible. You've always had it, Marty, just like Sylvan."

"You're leaving yourself out again," he said with exasperation, and he stopped, looked at her with concern. "If I do nothing else, I've got to make you see how gifted *you* are. You can run the gallery and paint too. You know I'll always help with any children we have."

His words warmed her, brought her to the bursting-with-anticipation point. "You're filling me with the good things," she told him.

And he chuckled. "Not the way I'm going to fill you later."

Marty sat on his tall chair for long moments, saying nothing, rocking back and forth and from side to side. Caitlin was his muse and she was his helpmeet. She was his *life*.

Sitting there, he pondered the shadings of her beautiful darkest honey skin, with its black-brown, gold, and yellow tints. He needed alizarin crimson for highlights, browns, gray, black, pale yellow colors. Hers was an elusive beauty, seen clearly one moment, obscured as you looked, and he had been fascinated from the beginning way back then. From that same beginning, Sylvan had easily captured her as his prize.

Marty worked with joy and exultation filling him. She was wrapped in cream silk and cerise double chiffon, a long scarf of the same fabric thrown loosely around her head and shoulders, setting up lights and counterlights that would be stunning.

Cait's soul was easy to capture, he thought at first, then frowned. She was so clearly defined, so honest, but there were depths of pain in her that saddened him. She had suffered so many damned losses. He wanted to show those losses in this painting, but he wanted to show more the hope he intended to bring into her life.

He wouldn't paint long because he didn't want to tire her, didn't want her deciding not to do her own painting today after all.

And Caitlin was quiet, wondering, feeling lassitude come over her. The painting would be beautiful because Marty painted it, but she was not at all certain she wanted her pain exhibited to a world that did not know or understand her the way Marty did.

That afternoon Caitlin painted the scarlet amaryllis in her studio. Her breath had caught at the exquisite beauty of the large flower. It was perfect in a way only nature could create and she felt humble in the face of it. With a wry smile she reflected that Sylvan would not have been humble. He would have laughed and said God created nature and she created him, Sylvan, as an equal. That explained his painting, she now thought; he believed in himself as she never could believe in herself. And Marty? Well, Marty seemed to think a lot like her, except that he was extremely confident. But he didn't feel he owned the earth, just that he was in every way a part of it.

She, too, used alizarin crimson for her painting of the gorgeous amaryllis. Black pistils. Yellow center. Long, green, green stems. She had to mix colors for that center—bright yellow and a little brown for subdued effect. No, that center color needed *lifting*, not subduing. After a few false starts, she got it right and the yellow center of the flower blended and contrasted with the wonderful power of alizarin crimson.

She shook her head at the exquisite beauty of the flower she painted. Georgia O'Keeffe, indeed, she thought, a woman she greatly admired and emulated far more than she knew. But she also often thought of Lois Mailou Jones, an African American D.C. artist she adored. The artist, a gifted colorist with her graceful, fluid lines and her moving depictions, often brought her dreams of what she wished she could do with her own work. Was Marty right? Was she so much better than she realized?

Caitlin got up after an hour and a half of steady painting, got a glass of water in the kitchen. As she passed by the door of Marty's studio, she paused and raised her hand to tap on the door, decided not to bother him, and went back to her own studio. Catching sight of herself in a mirror, she smiled. Her mood had lifted. She felt good in the simple gown a dressmaker had fashioned for her. She always felt good when she painted.

An hour more of painting and she flexed her shoulders, stood up and did a deep knee bend, then two more. Going out into the hallway, she met Marty, who told her, "Come into the kitchen. Our phones have been switched off, and Jayson left me a message to call him from my cell phone, said it was very important."

Caitlin felt her body stiffen, felt irritated. "Okay, but he wants to talk with you."

"I'm going to call on the regular line and I want you to listen in."

"It could be private."

"You're privy to everything I've got."

But the thought leapt to Caitlin's mind: *No, not completely, love. You were evasive about Cedric Santiago. You've talked a little about Bianca, but you're holding back something I can't define. I've known you so long, a part of me trusts you in spite of everything. I have to trust you. I was drowning in my own sorrow when you came, and I didn't even realize it. I've clung to you and you've let me. Perhaps because of Bianca, you were drowning too.*

Jayson answered promptly. "I was afraid you wouldn't return my call."

"What's on your mind? I've got a lot to take care of."

"I am going to Puerto after all. Remember I said I wasn't certain I'd be able to."

"How does that affect me?"

"Could you put Cait on the line? Maybe she can persuade you to take advantage of this rare opportunity if I can't."

"Cait's already on the line."

"Smart thinking. Hello, Cait. How are you?"

"I'm fine, thank you." She didn't ask how he was.

Jayson drew a deep breath. "Keith Margolis, art collector par excellence, loves your work, Marty. He saw one at the Prado and he'd like to tie up your best work for a couple of years. You could paint as fast or as slowly as you like. The man is a billionaire in oil. Texas. Mississippi. Newspapers, a movie studio. He's close to several heads of state in North Africa. You couldn't go wrong meeting him and he's the reason I decided to go to Puerto this year. It's the opportunity of a lifetime for you."

"Not interested," Marty said. "He's a close friend of Pedro Allendé, which automatically makes him my enemy."

"Man, you've given it no consideration."

"I don't have to. I know what moves me and what doesn't."

Jayson groaned. "Lord, Cait, can't *you* lean on him?"

Caitlin smiled. "No. Marty's a man who owns and operates his own mind. I wouldn't have it any other way."

"Okay," Jayson said slowly. "Mind telling me *why* you won't take this very large, very sweet and juicy plum?"

"Yeah, quickly and in a word. I know something about Margolis. Like Allendé, he's a spoiler. He doesn't just buy art, he buys the artist. He's a sadistic, hostile, suave bastard and I want no part of him. He ruined a friend of mine."

Jayson thought a moment. "Of course, I think you're wrong. I've dealt with Margolis only a year or so, but I've found him fair and aboveboard and he rewards you. Oh Lord, *how* he rewards you."

Marty tapped the tabletop where he and Caitlin sat. He reached over and took her hand, squeezed it. "You know me well enough to know I like money, but it doesn't rule my life."

"Very well, even if we forget about the money, he could make you famous in about a quarter of the time it will normally take you."

Marty laughed. "I am well on the way to becoming famous, Jayson, or had you forgotten that?"

"Not the way you'd be if you latched onto Margolis. Why don't you consider my proposal for a couple of days, then call me back?"

Marty drew a deep, exasperated breath. "My final answer is no. Will I have to say 'hell no'?"

Jayson was silent. "You're making a mistake. I want Cait to bring several of her paintings, and Cait will be bringing Sylvan's last two paintings. Of course, Cait's work is *very* good, but it isn't in the class with yours and his, but—"

Marty cut in. "That's the most ignorant thing I've ever heard you say. There's nothing Georgia O'Keeffe had that Cait can't match."

Jayson chuckled. "Simmer down, Steele. Like you, I believe in Cait. As for Margolis, I just thought you might like being allied with him. He's one of the wealthiest men in the world. You could benefit from an alliance with him, but I understand if you don't like him. Four divorced wives say he's not lovable. Listen, I've gotta go. I'll call later to talk about Puerto."

They hung up and Marty took both of Caitlin's hands in his big hands, lifted one, and kissed it. "You don't know how much I wish I could tell you everything, love, but it shouldn't be too much longer before I can." He stroked her arm. "Jayson said something that boiled my blood. I'm an art connoisseur, Cait, as well as an artist, and I know talent when I see it. I'm not wrong about your talent and time will prove me right."

His praise warmed her. Marty was inextricably interwoven into the fabric of her very life. Why did he mention now that he wanted to talk with her? She assumed it was about the secret organization. And what about Bianca? You didn't easily forget a woman that beautiful. Could Caitlin take it if he ever betrayed her?

The strains of the melody from Dvorak's Eighth Symphony poured in on the radio and Marty smiled. "Let's start deciding what we'll take to Puerto de la Cruz. I want you to finish the amaryllis painting; I have plans for it."

She looked at him and shook her head. "You really don't care about being rich or famous, do you? You just want to paint."

He didn't hesitate. "What I care about is *you*, my darling, our life together and the baby we'll surely make on Puerto. I just feel it in my bones."

Puerto de la Cruz
Tenerife, Spain
(one of the Canary Islands)

Chapter 19

Late February

"I'm loving this and we're hardly here!"

Caitlin felt the magic of Puerto de la Cruz surround her as she looked at Marty and Luther. "It's such a gorgeous place."

"I keep telling you," Marty said, grinning. "As they say, you ain't seen nothing yet. Let's stop by the museum for a quick look, then on to our villa. I know you're tired."

"Actually, I'm not that tired. I feel exhilarated and I'm thinking . . ."

"Of?"

"I'll tell you later."

Luther had flown in with them and Caitlin didn't think she had ever seen him so enthused and happy. "I just want you to know how grateful I am," he said to Marty and Caitlin. "I'll be at your beck and call 24-7 to show my appreciation."

"Oh, no," Caitlin said quickly. "Normal hours. I want

you to have fun." She frowned as goosebumps peppered her arms in the warm sunlight.

"What is it, honey?" Marty asked.

"I was thinking of Rita," she said slowly. "She and Jim were coming here this summer for their honeymoon and they were to bring his kids."

Marty only nodded and Luther shook his head. "Lordy Lord," he said sadly, "how I miss that girl. I used to go in early sometimes and she often stayed late and we'd talk about just everything. I miss her."

"We all do," Caitlin murmured.

The rental car came then and they piled in, with Marty driving. "We're on our way to the Puerto art museum." He leaned over and patted Caitlin's thigh. "I've been holding back something, what I think will be a pleasant surprise."

The art museum was a lovely sandstone affair with marble floors and spectacular lighting. A tall, dark, olive-skinned man rushed forward to greet them. He and Marty hugged. "Buenas días, my friend," he and Marty said almost at once. Then Marty introduced the man to Caitlin as Pablo Sanchez. He enthusiastically lifted Caitlin's hand and kissed it.

"You have always chosen the fair maidens of Eden," he said. "I am entranced with beauty like yours."

"Why, thank you," Caitlin told him. "But yours is an island of beautiful women. I don't compare."

"Ah yes," Pablo continued, "as you know, Marty and I talk by phone and I have heard much about you, his wife, and the happiness you bring to him. I am certain his paintings now will be inspired beyond his wildest dreams."

Caitlin laughed. "They always were and he is the one who brings *me* happiness."

Pablo turned to Luther then. "I will show you around, help you meet lovely señoritas who will make your stay here memorable. Marty said you are not married."

"That's right."

Luther felt his blood bubble with joy. Not *one* lady; the man had used the plural and Luther was enthralled.

Pablo laughed then, a merry, lustful sound.

"The spirit of La Carnaval is already underway. This week I selected the sardine to be buried."

"The sardine? There should be quite a story behind that," Caitlin said.

"Ah yes," Pablo laughed again. "I will let your husband tell you the story of the sardine."

Marty squeezed Caitlin's arm, smiling as Pablo turned to Luther. "And I will tell *you* the story, which I think you'll appreciate. Now, please come this way with me. I have the paintings you wished me to set up, Marty, and they are beautiful. Luther will help me set up the ones you recently sent. You own and run a gallery, señora, so you know how wonderful it is to display the best talent."

Caitlin felt full of awe as they walked slowly, admiring the many excellent paintings. She had not expected this level of mastery; she found this one of the best small museums she had ever visited. But that would be true, she thought, because Puerto de la Cruz attracted millions of visitors each year and they could be expected to do a thriving business. She walked along, lost in thought and admiration, with Marty catching her hand from time to time.

"Honey," Marty said, "come back to us. Look!"

She looked up and gasped. Her eyes moved from one to the other of three paintings. The first two were her own *Faded Magnolias*, taken from the elder Steeles' home, and her *Scarlet Amaryllis*. Then Sylvan's painting, *Dawn on Chesapeake Bay*, which the Puerto museum owned, and last Marty's fabulous *Sudanese Princess.* The princess he depicted was jet black with burnished skin and elegant features. Long, coiled woolen tresses lay on her shoulders and the life force in that face and body was stunning.

"Oh Marty, that is incredible," she told him, "but then I never wondered that they call you the soul painter. Sylvan showed me the bay painting of the Chesapeake, but your painting . . ."

"And what about yours?"

"I guess it's okay."

"Señora," Pablo said gravely, "your painting draws unusual attention from those who admire nature. I have known individuals to stand for a long time staring at it. The painting captures an ineffable sadness—we might almost say a life sadness—at the loss of freshness of blooms that have been magnificent. I congratulate you. You have a vast audience of admirers here in Puerto and they come, of course, from all over the world. I have intended to ask you, as Marty suggested, that you let me exhibit more of your paintings. My museum and I would be honored. Do me the favor as a fellow art lover."

Caitlin could hardly get her breath as Marty's smile captured her.

"Thank you," she said, blinking back a few tears of intense satisfaction.

"I know I sure like it, the way I've liked other paintings I've seen that you did," Luther said admiringly. "You can paint me a painting any old time."

"And thank you," Caitlin told him.

Paulo Sanchez looked excited. "Yesterday a man offered me a quarter of a million dollars for the princess and said he'd go higher if necessary."

Marty whistled. "Who was he?"

"A gentleman you have certainly heard of, reclusive, the extraordinarily wealthy Pedro Allendé."

Marty stiffened. "No sale. Not ever."

His face looked so cold that Caitlin wondered.

Pablo shook his head, clapped a palm to his forehead as he said quietly, "My friend, I am a *fool*, witless, but forgive me, for the gallery claims my life. I remember now why you must hate him. Others have spoken and I turned a deaf ear. Will you forgive me?"

"There is nothing to forgive. Just convey my message, please. Cait, we should go now. Good luck and much pleasure, Luther."

Marty clapped Pablo on the back. "Worry about nothing. It is La Carnaval time and all is well with the world."

"Unfortunately, there is little time for us to talk, because my gallery is a center of attention." Pablo said then at Marty's nod, "Now, Luther, there are things we must discuss. I will need your help during La Carnaval, but I promise I will not need too much help for you to have a thoroughly good time."

Caitlin had seen many photos of the villa Marty had purchased after Bianca left him to be with her lover, but no photos could do it justice. A big, white stucco edifice built in typical Spanish style, there were sweeping lawns and in front was a very large tree—the Drago tree—that Marty had told her about.

He paused before the tree and took a pocketknife from his pants pocket. "This is what you've wanted to see," he said. Cutting a small piece of bark from the tree let her witness the incredible red sap that ran like blood. Caitlin shook her head. "This is incredible."

"I have something on order that will let you have a part of the Drago tree back in the States."

"And that is?"

"Patience, woman," he said, grinning. "Can you carry my baby for nine months without getting sick with impatience?"

His words shook her; she had not expected them, and she bit her lip. He immediately took her in his arms. "Cait, I'm sorry. I shouldn't have said that."

"It's all right, Marty. I guess I was thinking of what Dosha said about getting pregnant on Puerto. Please God, let it happen."

"Buenas días, señor y señora Steele," cried a couple who came from the house. Marty introduced them to Caitlin as María and Ricardo, the couple who managed and lived in the villa. Middle-aged and beaming, both portly, they looked like brother and sister. "Your luggage arrived and I have unpacked for you. I have also prepared a delicious lunch of your favorite seafood salad," María said. "Oh, your wife is beautiful."

Her husband, Ricardo, nodded. "She is," and smiled at Caitlin, who blushed and thanked them.

"We will be in shortly," Marty told them. "I want to show Cait the swimming pool and our little beach."

The couple went back into the house and Marty walked with Caitlin around the back, where there were many Drago trees, one a granddaddy tree over five hundred years old. This one had many outer roots extending from its trunk; it had sought and found water for a long, long time.

"And now," Marty said. He led her to an area enclosed by evergreens. And behind the evergreens lay a large, oval swimming pool filled with sparkling blue water, surrounded by black sand.

"Oh, I love this! It's like some of the beaches in Tahiti."

"Yes. You're going to find you love everything about

Puerto. And I love it even more now that I have you here."

"Your eyes look dreamy."

"Because I'm dreaming of something I want to happen here at this pool." His voice was low, husky, compelling.

"I can read your mind."

He caught her to him and kissed her long and thoroughly, stroking her back, then kissing her throat. "Does that give you a clue?"

She laughed. "I didn't need a clue. It's the way I also feel."

"Cait, bless you. You're so damn responsive to me. You always let me through and you don't know how grateful I am. I was pushed aside and played with a lot in a past liaison and I never realized until I came back to you how sick I was of the whole charade."

"Umm, I'm grateful to you, too, just for being you."

"I love you," he said gravely.

"And I love you."

But she also remembered the coldness in Marty's manner when Pablo had mentioned the man who wanted to buy his princess painting.

The many Martianez beaches of Puerto are among the most fabulous in the world and Caitlin admired what she saw of them. Planned by the famous painter, César Manrique, they were many, beautifully fashioned, and with La Carnaval season, crowded.

"Well, another day maybe we can enjoy a couple of them," Caitlin suggested to Marty.

"No, this was never my hangout. We'll drive further. We're headed to Playa Martiánez. We've got to come back to Puerto later this year."

"You miss being here."

"I don't miss being anywhere if you're there, but don't you love it too?"

"You bet I do, and anywhere *you* are . . ."

She wondered about his life with Bianca here. Puerto was Bianca's home. Did that have anything to do with his love of the place?

Playa Martiánez was a beautiful beach and many people sunned themselves, but it was not as crowded as the other beaches had been.

"Black sand just fascinates me," Caitlin said softly. They had left their clothes in the car and lolled on the beach with Marty in black swim trunks, his virile tanned body on display.

Caitlin had selected several swimsuits, but the one she wore was a favorite. She took off her white eyelet smock to reveal a cream-colored top and skirt, both fashioned of alternating petals of watermelon pink and cream. The skimpy top and short skirt made Marty whistle lustily and a number of male heads turned.

Sitting on the warm, black sand, she took a big bottle of oil from the beach bag and spread it on Marty's body, going to the flesh between his ribs where he was especially sensitive. Washboard abs. Biceps that wouldn't wait. Pectoral muscles that were to die for, she reflected. As the wild juices flowed through her body, she thought: *There ought to be a law*.

"Watch it, woman," he growled. "I don't believe in public ravishing. Or can a man ravish his own wife?"

Caitlin laughed. "You know damn well he can and you'd better not."

"I'd tell any judge you were asking for it. Okay, love, turn the bottle over to me and I'll do my thing."

Marty's hands massaging the oil into her tender skin were relentless, gentle but firm. Her nipples hardened, pebbled under his amorous stroking, and she murmured, "Women ravish men nowadays."

"Ah, I'm too willing, and anytime you'd care to try . . ."

He was intent when he turned her over and closed his eyes against the flashes of pure fire that heated his blood as he stroked her smooth back and beautifully rounded buttocks.

"Well, fancy meeting you here," a sultry, sexy voice purred above them.

Caitlin turned over and recognized the beautiful international fashion model, Bianca, whose tiny scarlet bikini flattered her every curve.

Marty's voice went ice cold as he looked up and continued massaging Caitlin. "Hello, Bianca, Cedric."

Caitlin pushed her straps back in place as she sat up and looked at Marty's ex-wife, whose photos never did her justice. She was even more beautiful than Caitlin remembered.

"Your marriage is the talk of our group of friends," Bianca began.

"*Your* friends," Marty told her. "Why am I not surprised?"

With apparent amusement, Bianca insolently stared at Caitlin. "That's a nice little swimsuit you're wearing, Caitlin. It's a little prudish for this beach, but then so many of you American women are never very daring."

Caitlin didn't answer the thrust, but looked long and hard at Bianca in her scarlet bikini with her long, black silken hair flowing. Bianca was the great-granddaughter of a World War II brown baby. Her mother had a Spanish husband. Bianca's skin was olive and silken.

The woman was simply gorgeous, Caitlin thought. Marty said she had no soul, but would most men ever need to notice that, faced with her slender, curvy figure? Caitlin was surprised to find that she held her own, and Marty's lustful eyes on her, Caitlin, didn't hurt.

A smiling Cedric just stood there, his eyes half closed. "Hello, Caitlin," he finally said. "I love your swimsuit. You're a shade of tan I'd kill for and you're beautiful. I'm afraid my cousin is a tad jealous."

Bianca was Cedric's cousin? Caitlin thought with a small shock. Marty hadn't told her this. Why? Surely that fact was important.

"Maybe I *am* jealous," Bianca said, "and maybe I find I have reason to be." Her voice changed, got urgent. "Marty, we have to talk. I have news that will both shock and please you."

"To say the least," Cedric murmured.

Bianca turned on him, hissing, "Shut up!" a command that left Cedric unfazed.

"This is our honeymoon," Marty said evenly, and refused to discuss business. "Besides, Bianca, I think you said it all when you left me."

Bianca spread her fingers in apology. "Everyone is a fool at some point; that was my time to play it to the hilt. Please, Marty, I'm begging you. I'll come to your villa if you wish. That way I'll take up even less of your time. You *must* hear my news."

Marty looked down at Caitlin, who sat with her arms around her knees. "Do you mind if we talk with this woman? And I'd prefer it to be at home. What do you say?"

Caitlin nodded. "I think we should, but I don't mind if you see her alone."

"Thank you," Bianca said quickly. "It would be best that I talk with you alone, Marty."

"No," Marty said sharply. "Cait must be there. She's a part of my life now the way you never were."

Bianca looked down. "I deserve that. Could we talk this evening, say around . . ."

"What time will be convenient for you, Cait?" Marty asked.

"Your time is my time. We have dinner at eight."

"Seven, please," Bianca said quietly. "This won't take more than a half hour."

Marty looked at Caitlin again and she nodded. "Seven is fine."

Bianca's face turned rosy with something Caitlin couldn't define. Was there a look of triumph?

Bianca tapped Cedric on the arm. "We will go now, Cousin," she said before she turned to Marty. "I will not disappoint you. You are looking fabulously well, my love. If only I had been wise enough to stay married to you."

As the couple walked away, Bianca didn't fail to strut her stuff, and a few men slavered as she passed, hips undulating, her incredible nearly naked body on a public runway. Would Marty ever give her up completely? Caitlin didn't think so; there had been too much tension between those two at this meeting.

Marty sat back down and resumed massaging Caitlin's long legs. "Caitlin?" he began, and she wondered because he seldom used her full name. He looked troubled as he touched her lips.

Her slender hand rested on his thigh. "Let's enjoy the black sand, my darling," she said gently. "We'll deal with Bianca when she comes this evening."

Later, as they walked through the shopping section of Puerto hand in hand, Marty told Caitlin, "You're being secretive. Where're we going?"

"You'll see. We're almost there. The brochures pointed out choice shops."

In a few minutes they were inside an elegant store that catered to fashionable men. Marty always wanted her help in selecting his clothes. He looked superb in his clothes, but was hardly fashionable.

She helped him select a half dozen pastel shirts and three pairs of summer silk pants and gave the clerk her credit card.

"You're so generous," he told her.

"And you aren't?"

"I can't give you enough."

She flushed when he said it and touched his face. "I have you. That *is* enough."

Ricardo, the caretaker, ushered Bianca into a small sitting room promptly at seven that evening, where Marty and Caitlin waited. A small, dark-haired boy of perhaps two and a half years was with her. She smoothed the boy's hair and he leaned against her leg.

"Enrique," she said. "Say hello to your dad."

Marty's face blanched with shock. "What the hell are you trying to pull?" he demanded. "The boy is Pedro Allendé's son, or so you told me."

"Could we sit down, please?" Bianca said as the boy went toward Marty and Caitlin. The little boy extended his hand and Marty took it, held it, then introduced him to Caitlin, whose heart went out to him. He was so precious, with huge shining, black-olive eyes like Marty's. Who wouldn't want him for a son? She tried not to think of her own body, barren for too long.

In a pale blue sundress, Bianca tried to steal the show, but Marty wouldn't let her. His voice was hoarse, rasping as he told her, "I want to know how you came to the conclusion that the boy is mine?"

Bianca didn't hesitate. "Pedro didn't want to marry me after all, but he was willing to settle a very large sum of money on me and he wished to make Enrique a major heir. He is a man who checks out everything, but he was so pleased that I was pregnant with Enrique that he never questioned his paternity at first. When he did, the DNA showed that *you* are Enrique's father. Remember, love . . ."

"Don't call me that, Bianca."

"Very well, but once you were and I've never forgotten you. When a certain model of notorious virtue accused you of being the father of her child and you furiously dissented, our lawyer had your DNA taken and found you innocent. The woman's child was *not* yours . . ."

"I never touched her in any romantic way," Marty frowned, remembering.

"I know. The lawyer kept the DNA in case another complaint came up, so it was easy to determine that my child is yours." She drew a sharp breath.

The small boy took a package of Wrigley's spearmint gum from his pocket and held it out to Caitlin. It immediately dawned on her that he wanted her to open the package. Children of that age usually clung to their mothers, she thought; this one felt free to explore his territory. And a tightness grew inside her as she saw how much he was like his father.

Caitlin opened the package, pulled two sticks up and handed the package back.

"Thank you," the boy said gravely, then held the pack of gum out again.

"Are you offering me a stick?" she asked him and he nodded. Caitlin took the stick of gum and bent to kiss the velvet cheek. Marty looked at his wife and the child Bianca had said was his. His eyes closed against the onslaught of feelings raging inside him.

Marty looked at Caitlin and caught her hand, massaged it as he spoke. "Caitlin and I must talk about this. You have proof then that Enrique is mine?"

"*Ours*, and I will fight for his rights. You are not a poor man."

"Speak your mind, love," Caitlin said softly. "What do *you* want to do about this? You can't give him up . . ."

"Nor will I allow him to," Bianca said sharply.

Marty's look at Bianca was hard, merciless, but his eyes on his son were tender. "Of course I'll take care of the boy if he *is* my son, but greed is your long suit, Bianca, and I will not let you bleed me dry."

The raven-haired woman wriggled her shoulders, pouted a bit. "You and Caitlin, as I said, are not poor. Raising Enrique as you would want him to be raised will be expensive." She fastened lustful, come-hither eyes on her ex. "Raising him would be easier if we got back together, remarried. God knows, I find I still love you."

"That's out of the question. With Cait, I have the love I've needed all my adult life, and I'll *never* give her up."

Bianca's face went cold then. "She nearly broke us up when Sylvan died, demanding so much of your time. Your family preferred her to me. All right, if you no longer love me—and I think you do—then consider how good it would be for our son to have two parents—living together."

"Stop it, Bianca! That's never going to happen. Did you bring proof with you that Enrique is mine?"

She nodded as the small boy slipped from a sofa onto the floor and played with a yo-yo. Bianca reached into her tote and brought out a sheaf of papers in a folder. Marty and Caitlin read the pages together as Bianca watched them, finally taking her son onto her lap.

Marty finished reading and returned the papers. It was all there. "We will need to talk with my lawyer tomorrow or the next day," Marty said slowly. "Give me your number and I'll call you."

Bianca extracted a card from her purse and gave it to him. "We will go now," she said as she abruptly stood up. "We have taken up so much of your time. You will do the right thing, Marty, as you have always done. It is not in you to be cruel."

"But cruelty certainly lies deep in *your* heart," Marty told her. "We'll call you, either Cait or I."

"Would *you* call, please. I want to make it up to you, what I did to you, betraying you, the possibility of being pregnant by another man. It should never have happened. We were happy, you and I . . ." She sighed. "The American singer, Cher, sings 'If I Could Turn Back Time.' I want to make it up to you in any way I can." She looked at Caitlin then. "And no, I have no pride. Marty and I were once in love and I now find I am still in love with him. He is too stubborn to admit that he still loves me too. What a mess I've made of our lives."

"*Your* life," Marty said evenly. "My life is what I want it to be, what I've always wanted it to be."

With a gentleness that seemed foreign to her, Bianca looked at Caitlin and Marty. "Sometimes we lie to ourselves," she said. "Come, Enrique, we must go."

Caitlin's heart was full as the pair, mother and son, walked to the door. Enrique held out his arms and Cait bent and kissed him again; for a moment, she didn't want to let him go. Marty picked the boy up, held him against his chest, and felt the sting of a few acid tears.

That night as they lay in bed after they made love, Marty propped himself onto one elbow. "Cookie, please tell me what's on your mind."

"That you have a son and I'm glad. You've wanted a son so badly."

"I've wanted a child. A daughter would be just as welcome to me. I know you're hurt, and I've said nothing since Bianca left because I wanted to give you time to sort your feelings."

Caitlin pondered his words a while before she said, "I'm surprised, of course, but I don't think I'm *hurt* about Enrique. I could love him, help raise him, and, given my love for a husband who's dead, which I've always said isn't fair to you, how could I be hurt? If I don't get pregnant we have Enrique. If we decide we want more children, we can adopt."

She hesitated here. "But I *do* think you need to let yourself know how you feel about Bianca. She's beautiful, exciting, fairer skinned, but like the princess you painted."

He leaned over and kissed her slightly open mouth, licked the corners. "And you're even more beautiful, you excite the hell out of me, but you soothe me, too, the way Bianca never could. We're a team, Cait. We'll *always* be a team."

Chapter 20

"Why don't we listen to some more Charley Pride? I put in a couple of his CDs and he always takes my mind off bad things, and Bianca is most often a bad thing."

Marty looked at Caitlin as she lay beside him. She always looked so beautiful and calm after they had made love, as if he had given her some exquisite present she craved. How different his feelings for her were from what he had felt for Bianca. A son. He couldn't get used to it and he worried about Cait and what she really felt.

He shook her lightly. "Hey, you haven't answered me. Mr. Pride or some classical?"

She stretched languidly. "I'm trying to make up my mind. Do I want to rest now or do I want a repeat performance?" She looked at him, a sly smile on her face.

"I know what *I* want," he responded.

He needed closeness to her now the way he never had before.

"Then I guess it's Charley Pride."

He bent and nuzzled her neck. "You're so good when you're bad."

"That's the way I feel about you."

He suddenly thought of something and his eyes narrowed. "I have a present for you. I wasn't going to give it to you until later, but I want to see the pleasure on your face that I think will be there."

"What's the present?"

"You'll see." He got up and started out and she watched his wide-shouldered, slim-tripped figure in all its masculine glory. She didn't need presents, she thought. *He* was her present.

After a few minutes he came back in with a slender package wrapped in dark blue silk and adorned with a sprig of holly, and handed it to her. She undid the exquisite wrappings and found a jeweler's box of dark blue leather.

"What is it?"

"Open the box and see what it is."

Snapping the box open, she blinked at several small diamonds winking at her and stared at a stunning pendant on a heavy herringbone gold chain. It was like nothing she had ever seen before.

"My God, this is beautiful," she said.

"Figure it out. You've been smitten with Drago trees since I showed you videos and photographs of Puerto."

"Now I get it! These are very small parts of the Drago tree. The dark brown bark, the greenish wood and the red sap, all encased in this beautiful oval crystal. How on earth did the jeweler fashion this?"

"It's a mystery that's made him a rich man. He doesn't make many, and he demands a king's ransom for the ones he does. He dries the sap, then forces the powder inside the hollowed crystal."

Caitlin lifted Marty's hand and kissed it. "Thank you," she said simply. "This *and* the Lladro pendant you brought me from New York. Oh Marty, that seems so long ago; we've lived a lifetime since then. Please look forward to more presents from me."

"Hell, you've bought me a new wardrobe and your taste beats mine any day. When I wear these clothes I get the feeling of your arms surrounding me, your body pressed against mine. It's enough, baby, believe me."

"I'm glad. You know something, I'm really looking forward to seeing El Teide tomorrow. I've only seen one other volcano."

"This one's a beauty. We'll need warm sweaters. The air is cool up there, and we'll need a couple of extra cameras. I'm using my old Minolta, none better."

"I'll settle for my digital and my Spectra. And of course, we see the lawyer about Bianca's son tomorrow morning."

"Yeah. That's something I don't like to think about."

Felix Salazar's law offices opened early; Marty and Caitlin were his first clients of the day. A small, dapper man, impeccably attired, Felix's olive face lit up when he saw them come in. His receptionist was late, as usual, he reflected as he greeted them.

He bowed deeply. "It is always so good to see you, señor."

"The feeling is mutual. Let me introduce you to my wife."

Felix took the hand Caitlin extended and kissed her fingers. "She belongs in Puerto," he said, "for it is the rightful home of beauty."

Caitlin blushed at the compliment, thinking they must feed the males of the region honey with their baby formulas.

The lawyer served them Turkish coffee and small scones with strawberry preserves. "My receptionist is late." He sighed. "The girl is always late, but ah, she is beautiful and it is La Carnaval." He threw up his hands, took a small sheaf of papers from Marty. "Now please give me the full details of what you want me to do."

They discussed the case of Bianca's son and her contention that he was Marty's child as Felix Salazar leaned back, then sat forward, making a pyramid with his hands, listening intently. When Marty had finished delineating one aspect, the lawyer leaned back. "Of course, you will be having your own tests run."

"I certainly will."

"I'm sure she'll expect you to. Do you want this child if he proves to be yours?"

Marty glanced at Cait, who spoke up. "I would love to have him, but Bianca would never let him go. She only wants money to raise him."

"Of course she does," the lawyer said. "Such women always do. I know Bianca very well. She has always had her own twisted agendas and to hell with anyone else. I also know her cousin Cedric Santiago very well, as do you, señor. I would warn anyone against those two. I have had trouble with both."

Marty nodded and they talked on. Felix drew Caitlin into the conversation.

Once the legal discussion was finished, Felix said thoughtfully, "I will research this matter thoroughly. The clinic where these tests were run is certainly a reputable one, and I know the doctor. He and Bianca have been friends a long time and it will mark me as a gossip, but I feel mean-spirited toward the woman. Bianca's friends have all too often become her lovers and her lovers pay the price for being so."

A tight smile came to Marty's mouth at that remark, but he didn't comment on it. "We're on our way to El Teide," he said, as a smile warmed his face. He had fond memories of El Teide, one of the world's most famous and beautiful volcanoes.

The lawyer's face lit up. "Oh, you will be entranced," he told Caitlin. "When I was a troubled youth I thought of ending it all and a friend suggested I spend a day at El Teide. I did and I found God there. It is where I go when I seek peace."

"That's a wonderful story," Caitlin said. "Thank you for telling us."

"It is thought that fairies roam El Teide's valleys. They bless lovers and put spells on them to bring them back. I think the two of you need no spells. Go in peace."

Later that morning on the way to El Teide, the magnificent snow-capped inactive volcano, Caitlin and Marty sang tunes from *The Wiz*, then recited poems by Langston Hughes, taking turns. The roads that led to the mountains where the volcano was located were winding, and deep ravines and valleys lined the sides.

"Aren't you taking your life in your hands on the drive up here?" Caitlin shuddered a bit as the volcano loomed ahead.

"Isn't it worth it? And it isn't nearly as dangerous as it seems. A Mercedes-Benz hugs the road, doesn't slide. That's why I swear by them."

"I'm getting hungry."

"So am I. We can stop at one of the picnic grounds ahead and eat. We'd better get out the sweaters. As you can feel, the air up here is far cooler."

A little distance on, Marty parked at a large grassy area with many stone benches and tables. A few other people were there and greeted them cordially. Caitlin unpacked the straw picnic basket and spread a red checkered cloth onto a table, then set out the food.

"Great spread, Cookie. Those devilled eggs are superb. I never met a devilled egg I didn't like, but these are special. What did you put in them?"

"A dressing María made of feta cheese and sun-dried tomatoes."

Marty picked up another half egg and wolfed it down, smacking his lips. "They taste almost as good as *you* taste."

"Make that a double," she said, laughing. "You taste pretty good yourself."

A shiny black Rolls-Royce parked nearby and three men got out and walked over, led by a tall, white-haired man of imposing stature. "Señor Steele," the man said when he reached them, and he made no effort to introduce his companions, who Caitlin thought looked faintly threatening.

Marty looked up with irritation, then stood. "Señor Allendé."

"I am guilty of following you here and I apologize for interrupting your meal, but I wanted to talk a bit with you. Would you introduce me to what I believe is your lovely wife?"

"No, I will not introduce you. There is no need."

"But there is nothing to prevent my simply saying I am Pedro Allendé. I am sorry you are still so furious at what transpired between Bianca and me. It hurt you, I'm sure, but men of the world like us must rise above these things. Your ex-wife is a dangerous woman who entangles men's hearts and ensnares men's minds. Did you not find that so?"

Caitlin watched the byplay with fascination. One of the men with Pedro Allendé kept his hand inside his jacket.

"What is it you want from me, Allendé?"

"The *Nubian Princess* would do very well as a start. I covet that painting, as I'm sure you've been told."

Marty laughed shortly. “I care less than nothing about what you covet.”

Pedro Allendé pursed his lips, sighed. “Jayson Giles came in today. We have talked about deals that would make you even wealthier than you are. With our help, one day you could find yourself wealthy beyond your dreams.”

“I have my share of the world’s goods, and more. I’m satisfied.”

“And I had thought you more sophisticated.”

Caitlin’s mind had stopped at the mention of Jayson’s name; she didn’t look forward to seeing him.

Marty failed to answer Allendé’s last remark and he pressed on. “Then there is Cedric Santiago. Ah, the four of us could be formidable. The art world is fertile ground for talent such as yours and expertise like theirs, all fueled by my money.”

Marty shook his head. “I’m not interested. We have little time here and we wish to enjoy it, so if you’ll excuse us.”

Pedro Allendé looked up at the volcano. “I never see El Teide but I think of Bianca. The last eruption was in the seventeenth century, but one day the volcano will spew lava again.” He looked at Caitlin and his face softened. “I would have liked to meet you, señora. You seem the kind of woman I treasure, but I do not wish your husband to challenge me to a duel. *Vaya con Dios*.”

The men left as abruptly as they had come and Marty sat back down.

“So that is the man Bianca left you for who didn’t marry her after all? She really was a fool to leave you—and she knows it now.”

Marty smiled sourly. “This is La Carnaval season, my love, a time of joy and merriment. I brought you here to make you happy. I hope I can always make you happy and neither Allendé nor Bianca fits any plan I have."

She frowned. "Somehow I'm not pleased that Jayson's here, but the island is large. Maybe we won't run into him too often."

"I'm afraid he'll see that we do."

"Probably."

Caitlin found the food tasted even better in the mountain air. The ham, turkey, and roast beef sandwiches on rye and black bread, spread with creamy mustard and light mayonnaise that their caretaker, María, had made, were delicious. The mixed salad greens with ripe, red tomatoes had an effervescent white wine tang. And Marty had asked Caitlin to make him chocolate chip lace cookies. Now that his lunch was finished, he bit into one.

"When you bake me these, I feel you love me," he said.

"I *do* love you," she said quietly, "never so much as now."

But Marty sat reflecting that there were parts of this woman he loved that he still didn't reach and wondered if he ever would.

Finished, they put the picnic trash into the big wire trash containers and the hamper back into the car. Then they set out on one of the paths that led up to El Teide. Caitlin felt full of awe as they stood looking at this glory.

"I don't wonder that you loved it here in Puerto," she said. "And señor Salazar was right. It's so peaceful here."

"Puerto *is* beautiful, but I came home to you, licking my wounds, and you've healed me."

"Your son will heal you more than I ever could."

"You came first, Cait. I am eternally grateful."

They took photographs with several cameras and

Caitlin was pleased with the Kodak Spectra photos, which were developed immediately.

"We're going to have a huge scrapbook. Now stand over near the Drago tree and look up at El Teide, will you?"

She took several shots and he got the video camera from their knapsack. "Move about," he told her. "Swing those hips as only you can swing them."

"Keep talking, and I'll take off that sweater and your turtleneck and make beefcake photos of you on El Teide."

"You wouldn't be so cruel."

"Oh, wouldn't I? Men can be eye candy too. I'd call the photos *Fine Man, Fine Volcano*."

"I'm flattered."

"You should be."

Allendé and Jayson were forgotten as Marty and Caitlin drank in the sight of the winding roads and ravines below them, with large numbers of people caught up in La Carnaval joy. Looking at them, Caitlin thought they were a cross-section of the world's populations. Black, White, red, brown, yellow—all glorious creations. Two very tall, very blond men passed them, smiled.

"Scandinavians always stand out," she said.

Marty shook his head. "They're *Guanches*, the original settlers of the Canaries."

She repeated the name. "Now I remember reading about them in the literature you ordered for me." She stopped to look at an African couple in beautiful hand-printed cotton robes.

"Buenas días," the woman said and smiled, and then the man smiled too.

"You are Americans," the woman said.

"How did you know?"

Caitlin thought the dark brown–skinned couple so attractive.

"Somehow we always know," the man said. "We are seldom wrong. You have an innocence about you, a belief that the world is good, will always be good."

The couple moved on. "The Moors of North Africa once conquered parts of Italy and Spain," Caitlin said, "and the people show it."

"You're right," Marty nodded. "I love the Spain I've known, but it is the good old USA I found myself longing for."

It was a sentiment she agreed with.

Caitlin and Marty stayed longer than they had intended to stay and drove home in the fresh evening, taking off their sweaters in the much warmer air below.

"I really enjoyed this," Caitlin said as they entered the villa driveway.

"I always enjoy El Teide."

Ricardo came out with a cart and took their cameras and other items from the trunk.

Chapter 21

It had been an exciting week, Caitlin thought as she and Marty traversed another part of Puerto de la Cruz, hand in hand. It was such a gorgeous day. Garbed in a dark blue tee and white trousers, Marty admired the watermelon-colored linen dress with the shoulder cutouts Caitlin wore that showed off her fabulous shoulders and arms. He had long ago found that all women had some spot or spots of beauty. Thus, a perfectly plain woman might have exquisite feet and/or hands.

He shook his head and Caitlin looked at him quizzically. "I was thinking," he said, "that when you see the world with kind eyes, there is so much to admire."

"I've found that to be true. Over there, Marty, in that big area, all those people. Do you know what's going on?"

"I may. I know some of them. They're likely discussing who will be chosen as queens of La Carnaval."

"Then there isn't just one queen?"

"No, and that's one of the ways Puerto's La Carnaval differs from Rio and New Orleans. Let me clue you in:

there are several queens. One is eight or nine or ten years old and there is an old queen, sixty or past that."

"Better not let an American lady hear you calling her old at sixty."

Marty laughed. "Rispa's never minded, but then American women these days are so vibrant and into everything. It's being out of the loop that ages anyone." He continued, "The major queen is eighteen to twenty-five; a donna.

"*And* there is the German queen who is selected in Düsseldorf, Germany and comes here for the La Carnaval. The queens are always full of *joie de vivre.*"

"Full of joy and life," Caitlin mused.

"Yes. Have I told you how beautiful you look? You're *my* queen for all time."

"You've told me several times, but keep saying it. I'm a glutton for your compliments, even if I don't deserve them all."

"You deserve the compliments I give you and more. Let's sit on one of those benches where we hear through the microphones and those big screens tell us what's going on, and I can tell you more about La Carnaval. Your Drago necklace looks beautiful."

"Doesn't it? I'm overdressed I know, but at least my feet are comfortable." She stuck out her feet with the tan, wide-strapped sandals and flexed her ankles as he admired the curve of her legs and ankles. Then she touched the pendant. "I wanted to display this lovely bauble. Go on with my La Carnaval lesson."

"Well," he began, "La Carnaval has gorgeous floats and, like Rio and New Orleans, all manner of favors are thrown from them. Some are directly handed down. On that day the crowd is like a sardine tin." He laughed and his eyes crinkled. "Speaking of sardines, there's a ceremony the night before La Carnaval that is called 'Burying the Sardine.' "

"Pablo mentioned it. Is it called that because it's smelly?"

He laughed again. "Smelly, but then sardines are also delicious and oh, so healthy. A really large papier-mâché fish is fashioned in the shape of a sardine, painted, and adorned with festive flowers and evergreens. It is placed in a wooden coffin painted earth color. Can you guess the meaning of this ceremony?"

"Does it have to do with sex or sexuality?"

"Bingo! Or the lack thereof. The sardine is buried, as I said, the night before Carnival Day, and beginning Carnival night, we are all supposed to be sans sex until Easter."

He smiled broadly. "It is an old tradition and hardly adhered to by the younger people. Foreigners are not expected to be affected. Does that relieve your mind?"

"Relieve *my* mind? Ah Steele, which one of us is the most eager to make love?"

"We're evenly matched, I'd say. And lucky, lucky, lucky."

Marty was silent a moment before he said in a low voice, "Regarding the queens, save for the youngest ones, they all are shapely and beautiful."

"Do they turn you on?"

"Ah, no. I've got mine."

"You lie so adroitly. You're an artist, my love. Looking at and deeply admiring women goes with the territory."

"You're an artist, too. Do *you* look and long for what you look at?"

"Touché. Sometimes I do. I'm a modern woman."

"You'd better not get too modern."

"Threatening me?"

He shook his head. "Not if you keep in line and love just me."

Caitlin and Marty moved on. Back at their car, they discussed where to go next.

"Loro Parque, hands down," he said. "We're not too far away. Let's pick up some snacks."

From a concessionaire's stand they got cheese-flavored popcorn, fresh roasted cashews and peanuts, and mango juice in paper cups. Caitlin's eyes lit up. "A half-smoke! When have I had one of those?"

"I think I'll join you."

"You are Americans," the happy-eyed young vendor said.

"Yes. And you speak very good English."

"I live in Washington, D.C., and have a thriving vending station at the corner of Nineteenth and K Streets, N.W. I come to Puerto for La Carnaval every year. This is my home. I am a student at Howard University, and I arrange my classes to get ten days off."

"We live in D.C.," Marty said.

The young man smiled. "Great! What do you do there?"

"We're both artists," Caitlin said, digging into her straw purse, finding a business card and giving it to him. "I own and run an art gallery. Please come and visit. Bring your friends."

"Ah!" the young vendor said excitedly. "My girlfriend is an artist. I can promise you we *will* visit soon."

They found a park bench and sat down before a high carved fountain. Watching the crystal water sweep up and come back down in sunlit arcs, Caitlin felt happy. Even thinking of Bianca she felt happy as she munched on her half-smoke.

"What are you dreaming of?" Marty asked gently, "because you *are* dreaming."

She didn't hesitate. "I'm dreaming of Enrique and what a precious little boy he is. He looks like you."

A bitter look crossed Marty's face. "Bianca has many 'friends,' some of whom resemble me."

She was surprised at the venom in his voice. "You were in love. Was she always unfaithful?"

"I found out in the end—*always*, from the beginning. She had trysts with Allendé; they never stopped."

She picked up his hand, pressed it. "I'm sorry," she said simply.

"It doesn't matter anymore. I have you and I'm happier than I've ever been."

"God knows I am."

"And I intend to do my part to keep you that way."

Caitlin found huge Loro Parque to be one of the wonder spots of Puerto. She was glad she had worn her walking sandals because she wanted to see as much of the park as she could. And she wanted to come back.

"Oh Lord, this is glorious," she said as she surveyed the part of the park she and Marty first came to. Thousands of budgies—small parrots—and much larger parrots flew free and in aviaries, a colorful paean to nature, bold and unafraid of humans. Hundreds of twittering yellow canaries sang. One green, yellow, and red budgie flew down and sat at their feet, looking up at them.

"Does it want food?" Caitlin asked.

"When you get accustomed to the beauty of this place, you'll notice the signs asking that you feed none of the birds and animals."

A flock of canaries flew off. "Is this why they're called the Canary Islands?"

He shook his head. "I asked the same question early and was told that it's *not* the reason. No one seems to really know how the islands got that name."

The budgie had put its head to one side with eyes that seemed benevolent. I'd swear it's trying to start a conversation," she said.

"Buenas días," Marty said to the bird, who began to hop about at his words. Then the bird squawked something unintelligible, rose, and flew off.

Another sight caught Caitlin's eye and she pointed. "Over there, dolphins leaping in that big pool."

"One of your favorites."

"They're so intelligent and so graceful. I've only seen them up close in Florida."

"You haven't travelled much. Can we change that?"

Caitlin caught Marty's arm, squeezing it affectionately. "As long as you're with me. Sylvan liked to travel alone, although I often wanted to go with him. Living with you has let me know how difficult he could be. I was so in love it didn't matter."

Marty noted that she had used the past tense and he didn't think she was aware of it. She looked at him thoughtfully before she said, "The love I have for you is so different, but it's there and I find it growing. Can you be satisfied with what I can offer you?"

"I *am* satisfied, love. Very satisfied."

"I'm glad."

The dolphins were in fine fettle. Ten or so of them leapt, danced, and flirted in the huge watery enclosure. Marty and Caitlin had taken pictures of the budgies, canaries, and parrots, and they took pictures of the dolphins leaping, being fed, acting friendly.

There were other animals. Marty looked around thoughtfully. "I am told this was once an island inhabited by packs of wild dogs, so many they finally had to be exterminated. In the woods there are still wild rabbits, foxes, squirrels. There are the snowy egrets in the marshes."

"Look at the flamingos," she cried, picking up her camera.

Much later, they had stopped to have a malted milk at a quaint little café with outdoor seating. "I had hoped to find you here," Cedric's voice said as he stood at their table. "May I join you?"

"Do," Marty said, feeling unexpectedly cordial, if not friendly. Cedric sat. "How are you, Cedric?" Both Marty and Caitlin could see that Cedric looked haunted. His face was puffy and he looked as if he hadn't slept well lately.

"Could we order you something?" Caitlin asked.

"No, nothing," he said quickly, "I couldn't swallow it. My throat is constricted with anxiety. Bianca says I am always onstage, an actor. Well, believe me, this is no act."

"What is it, man?" Marty asked.

Cedric was quiet for a few minutes before he put a hand on the table. "I am going to send you a letter, Marty, that will tell the both of you a lot you need to know. And if you're free a few evenings from now, I wish to invite you to my house, where I have a tape to play for you that will interest you greatly . . . The recording is flawed and I had to wrangle a special machine from a carabiniere"—she translated *policeman*—"to understand it. I will tell you the exact day later."

"It all sounds so hush-hush." Marty looked at him closely, noting that Cedric's breathing had shallowed.

"You know where my house is located, Marty; you've been there often with Bianca. There are probably parades you'd like to watch, but please pass them up for that one night."

"We don't go every night," Marty said. "We just select the best ones."

"Then you'll come?"

"Yes. I'd like to know what this is all about."

"Believe me, you'll be glad you did. Look for the letter, which you'll get late today or tonight. God knows I hope I am in time to save you even if I probably can't save myself, and I . . ."

Cedric had clenched his hands and he let them fall into his lap as he looked up frowning, a look of fear and fury on his face. Marty and Caitlin followed his gaze to Pedro Allendé, who came toward their table, his three bullish bodyguards behind him.

"Buenas días, señor and señora Steele," Allendé said pleasantly. "Cedric."

"I have nothing to say to you," Cedric spat.

Allendé looked at Cedric levelly, said, "I have not done the things to you that you believe I've done. In the past we have been friends. Who knows but perhaps . . ." He spread his fingers wide.

They did not ask the tall man to join them; Cedric seemed at some breaking point that possibly had to do with Allendé. For a few minutes Allendé lingered, studying the three people at the table.

The proprietor of the restaurant came over. "Ah, señor Allendé. You do my poor place proud. Please let me offer you a superb table, unless you wish to join your friends."

Cedric muttered under his breath, "A rat has no friends."

Pedro Allendé smiled narrowly. "I wish you a wonderful La Carnaval, señor and señora Steele. And I am no longer sure what to wish you, Cedric. A long and happy life?"

Caitlin thought Cedric would burst with anger as the four men walked off. He sat for a while with them, but he was silent before he glanced at his watch and got up, saying, "I must go. There is someone I have to see."

Walking again, Marty and Caitlin spoke little of Cedric or Allendé, but admired the beauty of Loro Parque.

"The artist, Marquez, is truly gifted," Caitlin finally said.

"He is, and he is a personable, helpful man," Marty

said. "I understand he is away in South America this Carnaval season, but one day I'll introduce you to him."

"Wonderful. I'll look forward to that."

In spite of the orderly throngs of people, Loro Parque seemed peaceful to Caitlin. Not as peaceful as El Teide, but something relaxed inside her with being here.

Later, physically worn out but emotionally stimulated, they took the route home that at first paralleled the Atlantic Ocean. The blue-green-gray waters swirled and eddied with sudden high winds, and the tide had begun to come in. The scene forced her to think of Sylvan and his pursuit of waters to paint, new challenges. He had had so little time to meet *any* challenges and she said a silent prayer for his soul.

It was a long drive home and she was tired, but Caitlin almost hated to see the day end. As the sun set, they lounged on the veranda with tall, cold glasses of raspberry-chocolate coffee in hand, and they spoke of Cedric for the first time since he'd left them at the café.

"Cedric was really a mess today," Marty said. "I wonder what the hell is on his mind."

"Whatever it is," Caitlin said quietly, "it's tearing him to pieces."

The sun began to set then with streaks of flaming red, yellow, and coral, all juxtaposed with a few dark cumulus clouds that meant possible rain.

"I need a photograph of that sunset," Caitlin said, "but my legs have had it for today and they're demanding rest."

Marty began to rise from his chair. "I'll get one for you."

She leaned over and pressed him down. "No, love. I have other shots. I don't want you to leave me just now."

"Okay. I'll massage your legs after we've had a soda bath and I've rubbed French lavender oil all over you."

"And you get the Monoi oil massage from my loving hands."

He was very quiet looking at her. "We will make little or no love for a couple of nights, then Sunday night when there is a full moon, I am having our small black sand beach prepared for us and I plan to drive you out of your mind with joy."

His face was so intense in the twilight as he looked at her that thrills shot through her and she knew that he could and would deliver what he promised.

"Drive me out of my mind, will you? That is a game I've learned to play well, too," she murmured. "And don't you forget it."

Cedric's promised letter came that night after Marty and Caitlin had finished eating dinner. A worried young boy brought it to Ricardo, who came to Marty with him.

"Señor," the boy said. "Señor Santiago says that I am to deliver this directly to you and to no one else. He made me swear to this."

Marty took the letter as Caitlin looked on, then got his billfold and withdrew a few small bills.

"The señor tipped me well . . ." the boy began.

"No doubt," Marty said drily, "but boys always need money. Take this too."

The boy's face flushed with gratitude. "Gracias," he said hoarsely, and again, "Gracias."

After the boy had left, Marty came back to Caitlin's side.

"Aren't you going to open it?" she asked.

"You bet I am."

"I'll get a letter opener."

"I'll use my pocketknife."

With the letter opened, he studied the pages for a

few moments, read them carefully, then handed them to her.

Marty,

This letter is for you, although I know you will show it to Caitlin. As I've said several times, Bianca often accuses me of being melodramatic, histrionic even, but this is real, and I know my life to be in sudden danger.

Bianca's son is not yours, no matter that she claims he is. That will be so easy for you to prove. As to what her reasons are for saying this, I can only guess; it is for you to find out.

Time may well be running out for you as well as me. It is a dangerous game I play, my friend, and no one knows it better than I do, and it is a game you know too much about for your own safety.

You have always been a man of integrity, but you have changed, Marty. No, I don't mean your integrity, but since your breakup with Bianca, you have become bitter and cold. My cousin does that to men.

I know you love your wife, but you should not have brought her here this year. Allendé means to destroy us both—if we let him. And he would end my life at any moment if he knew I have certain tapes to play for you. Allendé never plays, except at love.

And what do the tapes hold? A possible answer to why Bianca told you her son is yours. Actually, he is the son of a former lover, as the tapes will explain.

Marty, I want you to come to my house Sunday night and I will play tapes for you that hold the key to the way Allendé plans to take us out, me anyway. I think he is more than a little afraid of you and your enviable connections.

So, Sunday night at eight, listen well and you will have at least some of the answers you need to know.

Until then—Oh yes, bring Caitlin if you wish.

Cedric

Caitlin drew a very deep breath as she finished reading and laid the letter on the sofa between them. "I wish you had told me," she said. "Will you tell me more now?"

He shook his head, taking her hand. "I'm sorry, my love, but I cannot tell you at this time. But I am told that it won't be too long before I *can* tell you."

She hesitated. "Is it something you're ashamed of?"

He smiled grimly. "God, no. There are things in this life we *must* do, if we are to live with ourselves."

Caitlin leaned back. Revenge? And for what? Did she really know her husband, who had lived away from her for so long?

He kissed her hand. "Will you trust me—please?"

"Do I have any choice? I love you, and yes, I will keep trusting you."

"Cedric says that I have changed, that since Bianca I am bitter and cold. Do you find me like that?"

"No."

"But I *am* bitter and cold to so many like Allendé, and to a certain extent, Cedric. But never to you, Cait. *Never* to you. My love for you is the deepest part of my life."

And hearing him, she knew he spoke the truth, but she thought sadly, he was in trouble and his love for her wasn't likely to save him.

Chapter 22

"Full moon and my arms are full of you."

Saturday had come at last. They had trekked over Puerto de la Cruz that day and Caitlin had been delighted with most of what she saw. Then last night, Cedric's promised letter had come and both felt somber. But even that letter couldn't dim their anticipation of the night Marty had planned. Now they sat on a love seat in their bedroom, teasing each other with light kisses. It was nearly eight P.M.

"I love full moons," she said, "especially since we've been together. My arms are also full of you and so is my heart. Marty, you're such a wonderful man, such a loving partner. I wish us well, but can we . . . ?"

"Can we what, sweetheart?"

She sighed. "I was going to ask if happiness like ours can last, but our lives are far from perfect, beginning with me. At some point I was going to see a therapist about my not being able to let Sylvan go. I've decided I shouldn't live my life like this, but I . . ."

He shook her gently. "You keep starting sentences you don't finish. Go ahead. Say what's on your mind. I think we could both use a marriage counselor to hold the happiness we surely have, even if it's flawed, *especially* if it's flawed."

"I keep wondering if you really know your mind about Bianca. Now with the child on the scene and the fact you've longed to be a father, well, that can't help but create new bonds with you and Bianca. I don't want to lose you, but I'll let you go if that'll make you happy. And I can bear the pain, since pain and I have been bedmates much of my life."

Marty turned her to face him, said fiercely, "I'd never lie to you, Cait. For a long time you've been part of my very soul. On those rare later occasions when I've talked with you in person while Bianca and I were married, those were the times I've lied—to you and myself, my family, friends. I know now that by the end of our third year of marriage, I was no longer in love with Bianca, but she promised me a child and we went on together.

"Then she began to be careless about her affair with Allendé. The tabloids were full of photos of him kissing her on the French Riviera, of her in his arms. She cried and swore to me that those were old photos, and the fact that Allendé is one of the world's richest men and Bianca is the granddaughter of a Spanish brown baby made very good copy."

"And the fact that you're a famous painter didn't hurt."

"Yeah. A private investigator friend of mine took it on himself to chase this down. I didn't ask him to because I didn't want to know. I told myself that I was a sophisticate and in our world there was intrigue and playing around aplenty. But when this P.I. friend laid it out for me, I couldn't take it after all. I confronted Bianca and she admitted the whole thing, but begged my forgiveness and said she'd broken up with Allendé. He wanted to be friends with me, has always wanted to collect my paintings. I said hell no, but Bianca and I stayed together."

Marty brushed a hand across his brow and Caitlin's heart hurt for him. "Cait." He took her hand in his, squeezed it gently. "Tonight is our night under the stars. I've planned it well. When this night is over, tomorrow, after we've rested—because I *will* tire your body and mine tonight—I'll make love to you gently, then tenderly, and then roughly with the out-of-control passion I feel surging in me. Tell me then if you still think I love any woman but you."

"Yes," she whispered hoarsely because her heart was so full she couldn't speak clearly.

They went to the pool area of the house around eight-thirty P.M. and Caitlin gasped at the beautiful scene that had been set that day. Laughing, Marty had forbidden her to go around the pool until she went with him that night, and she had agreed to do as he asked. Now she stood still, surveying the scene with Marty's arms around her.

"Do you like it?"

"Oh Marty, it's like a little paradise."

"And that's what you and I are gonna know tonight, baby."

A light wind stirred the pool waters and the surrounding tiled area had pots of beautiful orchids placed in it. A Bose sound system played romantic tunes with Barbra Streisand's "Evergreen" prominently featured.

But it was the orchid greenhouse that had been transformed into a bower to celebrate romance. There was a small buffet of many quarter-sized sandwiches, fancy crackers, huge green-stemmed strawberries and bing cherries half dipped in dark and light milk chocolate, and a magnum of Veuve Clicquot champagne in an ice bucket.

"This is so beautiful," she said. "What's behind that curtain?"

"Curious woman," he murmured. "Just trust me, will you?"

"With all my heart."

He popped the champagne cork and toasted her. "To our love with its foundation of trust, respect, and integrity. May romance and ardor fill our long lives, and may we always know the blessings we know now!"

"I love your toast."

"Nothing I could say does you justice." He took her arm. "So you want to see the secret behind the rose curtain."

They crossed the floor and he pulled the curtain back to reveal a bed on the floor with rose satin coverings. A single long-stemmed red rose lay on one pillow. The curtain and the bedcovering matched the tiny rose thong bikini he had bought for Caitlin for this night. "You can wear it nowhere else," he'd said. "It's for my eyes only, and I think I'll put it into my painting vault."

"Along with some of your wilder paintings?"

"I've always tried to paint the soul and I feel I *have* captured your soul, Cait, many times. I did that in spades in *Madonna Waiting*."

She didn't say again that she was no longer waiting, stifling the disappointment she always felt. Bianca had accomplished what she, Caitlin, was unable to accomplish. But no sadness could last under this promised happiness and she felt her heart fill with joy again.

"Hungry?" he asked as they went back to the table.

"Not really, although we've eaten little all day. I *would* like a few of the strawberries and cherries, and another glass of champagne. Are you trying to make me drunk to seduce me?"

"I don't need champagne. I'm drunk with loving you, with wanting to be inside you, feeling your fabulous walls pull me in, hold me tightly, and grip me as if they'll never let me go. Don't ever let me go, sweetheart."

"I won't. And don't *you* ever let *me* go."

"Never."

He removed the cream-colored eyelet smock from her shoulders when she had finished eating her fruit. She noticed that he had eaten only two small sandwiches. He stared at her luscious body with his eyes half closed and she looked at his virile, muscular form. Her eyes went wide as if this were her first time seeing him. Then her eyes closed, feeling a riptide of desire sweep over her, take her in its wake.

Gently he unhooked her bikini top and threw it onto a chair. He bent, kissed her belly, and patterned kisses on her body as he slid the bikini bottom down, then threw it on the chair atop her matching bra.

She bent over his back, stroking his hair, his heavily muscled back and shoulders. "You're driving me crazy so early."

"And you're not doing the same to me?"

She laughed throatily as they stood and she slid his black Jockey swim trunks down his lean legs and threw them on top of her swimsuit. He lifted her then, holding his precious burden against him. At the edge of the bed he put her on her feet and pulled her against him so hard she could barely breathe. Then he eased his grip and held her away from him as his eyes swept her body, his gaze riveted to her. She would have looked at him like this, but she was so dizzy with needing him inside her.

They lay on the rose satin-colored air mattress side

by side and he began a sacred journey over her body that made her moan with aching desire. His hot mouth suckled and laved her full breasts, then he moved up and kissed her so hard and so deep it startled her. His fingers on her scalp were gentle as they massaged, but his mouth on hers was savage in its ardor.

"Tell me what you want. *Always* tell me what you want. You know I'll do it for you. There is nothing, Cait, *nothing* I wouldn't give you, do for you. What do you want?"

His tongue was wild on her as he went again to her belly button, laved it for a few seconds, then moved ever downward, stopping at her center to softly kiss her, gently use his tongue to please her so that she bucked above him and pressed his head in to her body that flamed with desire.

In that room with the orchids and the hundreds of roses, the perfume of flowers mingled with the light Tahitian Monoi oil she had placed at strategic places on her body. But there was also the deep pheromone odor—nature's gift to attract a lover. This was the scent of two people in love making love, making life.

"Sweetheart," she cried. "*Now! Please!*"

Rising above her, he did not enter at first, but gently moved his shaft outside before he finally went inside slowly, teasing at first, tantalizing, before he felt her legs close across his back. She was clutching him as he touched her womb and went wilder still.

He thought then that this was paradise on earth. Lord, the times they'd made love—and both were ardent lovers—this surpassed everything they'd known. He was flying, carried on wings of desire no less than love.

She screamed his name with passion and the sweetness of that sound filled his heart and soul.

On edge, he slowed and breathed deeply.

"Think of snow-capped mountains," she said quickly. "Think of El Teide."

"You know what you do to me. I'm always in a hurry to spill my seed in you. I've got an El Teide inside me where you're concerned. Any second now, I'm going to explode."

"Go ahead. We've got the whole night. Fill me again and again. I *want* your seed, my darling." She added wistfully, "And if we're lucky . . ."

He heard the hope in her voice together with her joy at being with him and it thrilled him to his core. This was the woman God and all creation meant for him. She was his and he was hers and they came together with the love-driven lust that promised and delivered happiness beyond imagining.

His sperm-filled loins belonged to her no less than to himself and he craved release inside her with her welcoming womb and body that never denied him. She felt his powerful thrust and he was throbbing inside her as her heart beat wildly. "Marty!" she whimpered, "I love you. I'm always gonna love you."

He licked her lips, then his tongue met hers and they felt a joint ascent to glory and satisfaction. Her body's rhythm thrilled him. Contracting and relaxing. Grip and release. This was an incredible dance that ended the show for the moment. Panting, he shook his head as he asked her, "Will I ever get enough of you?"

They slipped on swimming gear and went to the pool, which was tinted blue-green-gray like the Atlantic Ocean.

"Marty, you didn't do all this by yourself."

"No. There's a couple here in Puerto who run a business called Rendezvous. They set up trysts for people who want something special, memorable. They came out and looked the place over one day when we were gone and this is the result. Like it?"

"I love it. You were so hard tonight, I wondered if you'd ever come down. But then you're always a superb lover. Is it fair for you to be so gifted as a lover *and* a painter?"

Marty grinned, then got somber. "You know I've had my share of heartache too. I'm afraid not everyone considers me a great lover."

"I do. Does that count?"

He drew her to him. "You know damn well it means everything."

They sat on a huge beach towel on the black sand that fascinated her so. Tahiti's black sand had been like this, she thought. But Sylvan had been entranced by the blue and turquoise and aquamarine waters and he had spent more time painting than he had spent with her.

Wrapping his arms around her, Marty leaned her all the way back, picked up a handful of the sand that sparkled like black diamonds in the moonlight. He sprinkled sand across her midsection, then bent and blew most of it off.

"Are you happy?" he asked her. "And are you still upset about Bianca's news?"

She pondered his questions. "Yes, I'm very happy, and I'm taking Bianca in stride."

"Good. I'm doing the same thing."

"Are *you* happy?"

"Sublimely."

She pulled him to lie full length on top of her, his sinewy legs between her soft calves and thighs.

"This night was surely made for love." He looked up at the gorgeous midnight sky and decided that she was even more beautiful.

He had taken her on the sand like this before, and that time lingered in her mouth like honey.

They went and sat at the edge of the pool, dangling their feet in the water. "I think I'll dive," he finally said. "Care to join me? You can go first."

"I'm not sure I like diving, although you're a good teacher. Why don't you go ahead and I'll watch. You're so good at it."

Poised on the diving board, he flexed his muscles, tensed, made the form he sought and dove into the water. She thought he was like a graceful dolphin leaping happily in Loro Parque. "Bravo!" she cried as she slipped into the water and joined him.

Both were powerful swimmers. They raced close together, cutting the warm water with deep strokes. Five times traversing and returning the length of the long oval pool. He stopped for a moment at the end near the orchid greenhouse. Pulling her to him, he splashed her. She splashed back and hugged him.

"Tired?" he asked.

"From this little exertion?"

"We've had plenty more." She felt so good in his arms, her wet body pulsing against him, her heart drumming with excitement. Deep kisses grew from feathery kisses. He had never known her to be so ardent, he thought, loving the new way she clung to him.

"Repeat performance?" he asked.

"In more ways than one." She laughed merrily and her musical voice caressed his ears.

They swam for over an hour before they went back into the greenhouse with the water still dripping from their bodies.

"Let's just let the air dry us off," she said. "I love the feel of your wet body. It excites me so."

"You want it, you've got it.

She picked up a strawberry, then a cherry, and popped

first one then the other into her mouth, craving the sweetness of the chocolate-dipped fruit.

"Aren't you eating more of those than usual?" He looked at her closely.

"I am, but I don't seem to really want anything else. I could eat the whole tray."

He drew her close and stroked her jawline with his thumbs. "Why don't you take another pregnancy test? We'll pick up some tomorrow."

"No. I've taken just one more after we made such passionate love one night at home. It was negative. I won't take another. I'll just wait and trust that I have the symptoms I had with Sylvan Junior—or maybe I never will," she said sadly.

"Believe me, sweetheart, it doesn't matter. I'll always be there for you."

"Thank you. You just don't know how that makes me feel."

He switched on a Lionel Richie album and Richie's haunting "Lady" was a romantic aura in the room. He held out his arms. "Dance with me. We might as well be naked."

"I always feel naked with you, Marty, with all my flaws in full view and your kind eyes on me."

"I think we're both that way. It makes for a far happier life, believe me."

They caressed each other as they moved in the moonlight with the lights turned off. Marty was an excellent dancer and he guided her expertly. She filled his arms with her tender flesh and his life with her loving presence.

Snuggling close, she felt small fires heating in her blood and went even closer. "Sometimes I wish I could meld with you. Right now I *want* fusion. It scares me to feel you so deeply, to be ravenous for everything I get from you."

"Hell, I get scared too, baby. If I should lose you, I'm not sure I could make it."

"If I die you would, because you're strong and I'd want you to go on, be happy. You won't lose me any other way."

"Now how did we get from here to there? We're both going to love each other, live a long, happy, productive and fulfilling life, and have six little ankle biters running around. Okay?"

"Okay. What're you thinking?"

"I'm making love to you in fantasy, which is sweeter than sweet because that's what I'm going to do."

"We have a three-way deal, my darling. You make love to me and I make love to you and we make love to each other. Simply superb."

"And very, very satisfying. Let's start this show all over again."

"You'd think we were very young, the way we want each other."

"Not young, just human—and starved, still starved, like almost dying of thirst in a desert, then finding cool, clear water."

She laughed. "Or champagne. I think I want another glass."

"No. I don't think I'll let you. Pregnant women shouldn't drink too much alcohol. And you could get pregnant at any time, we hope."

She nodded, but it was a dream she didn't want to foster too deeply, only to be disappointed again.

"Have faith," he told her, stroking her temples. "We're just getting started. My buddy's determined to give us what we both want."

She could never help merry laughter when he personalized his shaft.

"I make you laugh," he whispered. "I'll never make you cry."

They danced on, hugged tight together, arms around each other's neck, fondling each other. "What we need is a string of Barry White's music to make love by. I'd knight him if I were a queen."

"You *are* a queen. Mine."

"And you're my king. Marty, I love you so much."

"I keep telling you I love you more. As for Barry, he's up next with his latest CD. A whole lot of him."

With Barry White's silky, sensual voice crooning in the background, Marty lifted her and carried her back to the bed. They slipped out of their swimming gear and he pulled her close again. "Not the bed just now, honey. I want to take you on that big chair."

"You had that brought in just for this night, didn't you?"

"Guilty. I'm replicating home activity."

He sat on the soft velour chair and pulled her down astride him, his mouth going instantly to her smooth, desire-swollen breasts. Laving her nipples, he felt he would burst with joy as he suckled them avidly. Her face above him was a study in passion, in wanting that went to the marrow of her bones. His feeling mirrored hers, and he felt that if he died that moment, the world owed him nothing.

Leaning forward, she licked his nipples and it brought heat surging in him like a wild tide.

"You like that, do you?" she whispered.

"I'm loving it, everything you do drives me crazy. You're so good when you're bad."

"I know what the song means, but what do *you* mean by that?"

"You know mixed-up teenagers have been saying for ages that something is bad when they really mean good. Hell, if I've ever had anything better, it was before my time on this earth."

Sitting astride him, she felt his shaft rise mightily as

thrill after thrill swept her. Her slender fingers caressed the hard flesh that brought her joy and she rose a bit and guided him into her body slowly, easily, rhythmically.

"You drive me out of my mind when you take the initiative. You're like honey inside and honey is one of my favorite foods."

With his shaft throbbing inside her, she was nearly mindless. She bent forward and drew his tongue into her mouth, tenderly caressed it with her own, then licked his lips. His fingers went into her soft natural hair, then massaged her scalp; it was such a small gesture, but it aroused her endlessly.

"I could finish this way, but we haven't used the position that Buddy tells me is a favorite."

"On my knees?"

"On *our* knees."

What was there so special about this night? she wondered. They had known wild, passionate love many times, but this was unusual. Pool-area evergreens sealed them off from everyone. They stood at the top of a gorgeous snow-capped mountain high in the clouds, with the salty air of the Atlantic one-half mile away filling their nostrils. Was it the moon, the stars that spangled the sky with glittering magic, or the midnight blue velvet of the sky? She only knew that she wouldn't swap this moment for any other, and she couldn't remember thinking like this before.

As he slid his greatly swollen shaft into her gripping, welcoming body, he stroked her back, and patterned kisses over her hips and buttocks, then her waist and middle back.

High tides were enveloping both their bodies and a spiritual high tide had taken over, sweeping them onto an emotional black sandy beach unlike most other beaches they had known.

He felt a crescendo of pressure in his blood and pressed himself all the way in, moving with expert ease. He had been born to be this woman's lover, as she had been born to be his. Sylvan and Bianca were forgotten in this new, unbearably sweet surge of life and his hot seed streamed into her womb and fought to stay there.

"Oh hell, you weren't quite ready," he consoled her.

"Don't talk," she gasped, "please just keep moving."

He did as she demanded and soon he felt the beginning of her multiple orgasms that kept him sending his seed until he had given her all he had for the moment. Her womb claimed that seed with hot and greedy hunger that was as precious as anything either had ever known.

Chapter 23

They spent an anxious Sunday, sleeping or talking little, simply waiting until it was time but both savored the night before, filled with passion.

At 7:50 P.M., they neared Cedric's house on a tree-lined street. Large and imposing, thc gray brick structure was over a century old. Marty slowed, took a deep breath. "Well," he said, "here's hoping that we'll get the answers to so many questions."

"Are you scared?" she asked.

"Why would I be scared?"

"The letter warned of danger from Allendé."

"A long-time adversary. I'm not afraid of Allendé."

"Maybe you should be," she said quietly.

Marty braked sharply. "Now what the hell—" he began as they saw the police cars lining the area in front of Cedric's house. Captain Montero came out of the house and down the street, saw Marty's car, and waved at him.

"What *is* it, man?" Marty called before the captain could get to him.

Captain Montero was a policeman Marty knew well.

He came closer to them before he said, "Señor Santiago has been murdered, little more than an hour or so ago."

It took minutes for Marty and Caitlin to absorb the shock, but when they had, Captain Montero asked Marty, "You were coming to visit him?"

"Yes. He sent us a letter inviting us."

"And you have that letter at home or with you?"

"I brought it with me."

"Would you permit me to study it?"

"I would."

He reached into his inner jacket pocket and handed the letter to Captain Montero, who thanked him.

The captain sighed. "I will need to talk with you. The list of people we will question will be long."

Captain Montero questioned Marty early Monday morning, and to Caitlin's surprise, the interview lasted only a short while. Caitlin did some desultory shopping in a square near the courthouse and Marty found her there.

"Well, what did he ask you?"

"A few necessary questions."

"And?" she demanded. "Don't be evasive now. I couldn't stand that."

"I won't be. No suspicion falls on me. The captain knows that. I am not involved in this murder at all, Cait. Stop worrying. We're home free. This doesn't touch me."

And looking at him, Caitlin thought he looked calm, unruffled; but Cedric's letter said he had grown bitter and yes, *cold*. She shuddered a bit. This was foreign soil to her and foreign intrigue, and she longed for the simplicity of home.

Chapter 24

Cedric Santiago's murder was the talk of Puerto's La Carnaval. Gossip in this region was laid-back, interested rather than critical or vicious.

On Ash Wednesday, Caitlin and Marty caught drifts of conversation as they mingled with the ebullient crowd in the Plaza del Charco.

"It is a terrible thing to die during La Carnaval," one woman said. "Such a time of joy. And Cedric was a joyous man."

The woman's male partner demurred. "Ah, Santiago would have found his own death entrancing—not being murdered, no—but to go out the way he lived, in a web of intrigue and danger. I tell you, I knew the man from childhood, and he was different, *fey,* as the English and Americans term it. He would love this."

Caitlin and Marty looked at each other. "How well did *you* know Cedric?" Caitlin asked Marty. "You've never really said."

After a prolonged sigh, Marty looked at her thoughtfully before he spoke. "At first we were good friends.

Cedric had a first-rate mind that he was somehow reluctant to use. Then I gradually found he liked danger for the sake of danger, for the hell of it, and he didn't hesitate to involve others. Bianca warned me about him, but I had to see for myself, and when I did, I pulled away. He continued to hold on to me."

They walked amidst the throngs dressed in western garb, but for the grand day they would be a gypsy baron and his baroness. The crowd was raucous, happy, each person holding a magic of his or her own. The last week of La Carnaval was unusual even by Carnaval standards. Earthly cares were the furthest things from the minds of revelers.

Marty and Caitlin held hands, breathing in the night air under stars without number massed in a dazzling night sky. It was the night of the Funeral of the Sardine.

Marty grinned at Caitlin as the crowd jostled them. "I'm glad we didn't link up with anybody else," he told her. "I want to be alone with you for this. Cedric, Bianca, and I always watched it before . . ." He didn't finish and she looked at him sharply. Was he remembering past times, past loves? Then he did continue. "I've been to carnivals in Rio, New Orleans, and lesser carnivals in other cities. I tell you this is truly special, spectacular in ways even the others in New Orleans and Rio weren't. Maybe it's the African flavor since this is off the northern coast of Africa. I feel something in my bones here at La Carnaval time that I don't feel anywhere else."

She didn't know why she asked it. "Were Bianca and Cedric with you in Rio and New Orleans?"

"Once they were and once they weren't. I only went a few times. I could never bear to be away from here." He laughed then. "So, after this Saturday and the end of La Carnaval, no more lovemaking until Easter. Oh, happy Easter! That rule doesn't apply to foreigners."

"But you're really a native, at least in your heart," she teased him. "So the no-sex rule applies to you, to us."

"I'm upstate New York all the way where this is concerned," he said roguishly. "Puerto is my *second* home. Do you like Puerto?" he asked wistfully.

"I love it. Let's come back to La Carnaval every year."

He paused then and took her in his arms, kissed her long and thoroughly as hot blood surged through them both. "How glorious it all is," he murmured against her mouth.

The sound of music was all around them, fashioned of metal, and covered with papier-mâché in the shape of saxophones, trumpets, and every other popular musical instrument. The famous kazoos held forth lustily, blown by strong lungs with years of practice. This was one of the joys of La Carnaval.

Marty had always laughed at the raunchy songs that gleefully depicted politics and sexuality. These were tossed off with much eyeball rolling and thigh-slapping by the males in the crowd.

"I should have brought paper and pen to write some of these ditties down," Caitlin said when an especially provocative song involving both sex and politics was sung.

"Never mind. I know them all. Someone should put them into a book."

"Maybe *we* will."

"That's a thought."

He put his arms around her, then his hands went to her hips as a rhumba sounded and those hips began to sway as they danced with so many others in the joyous Spanish dance. Her body under his hands was alive, pulsing, thrumming as they danced together.

"*Querida*," he whispered. *Darling.*

She kissed his facc, then ran her tongue under his ear.

He pressed her close. "Keep doing that and I'll take you right here."

She laughed delightedly. "No one would notice. This is a mad, wild scene."

"Best in the world, as long as you're with me."

"I'll always be with you."

"And I'll always be with you."

The music changed then and a provocative, sensuous conga held sway. Long lines snaked around the square, hips writhing, shoulders shaking. That music turned their bloodstreams to pure joy and passion and they and the crowd were dancing, dancing!

The music changed again to the well-loved samba, and again Caitlin and Marty were moving with intricate grace. A woman with one of many elaborate headdresses of fruit and flowers strapped to her graceful head came close and smiled at them. She said only "La Carnaval!" as if that were all that was needed to explain the intense joy that transformed her face. Her partner seemed no less entranced as they moved on.

"You are so beautiful," Marty suddenly told Caitlin.

"*You're* the beautiful one."

He held her away from him. "Our *life* is beautiful, *querida,*" he said gently. "Let's keep it that way."

The costumes around them glittered in the evening lights as a sea of humans sought certain refuge from all that was not love and wonder.

"Imagine," she said. "Suddenly I want ice cream and a half-smoke sandwich and some potato chips."

"Sounds like a pregnant woman's cravings to me," he said somberly. "Do you think . . . ?"

She shook her head. "I don't dare think about it, but you know, love, maybe it *will* happen here."

"I keep praying."

"As I do. Marty, if you really want children . . ."

His finger against her mouth shushed her. "I want *you*, Cait, with or without children. You're the only thing in this world absolutely necessary to me."

The passion in his voice brought tears to her eyes so that she could barely see that the sardine procession was beginning, heralded by the tense anticipation of the throng. "La sardine," someone called and others laughed. "Adiós!"

A family near them dressed as gypsies smiled as Caitlin and Marty snuggled in each other's arms. It was a time of love and lovers. Families dressed in themes, some choosing a different theme each night. La Carnaval was a time to splurge—on material things, on the emotions. Some people spent a year preparing for the next year's La Carnaval.

After a time of jubilation, the giant papier-mâché sardine passed them and they began to move with the throng down to the harbor, where the fantastic procession would end. Then loud cries rent the air as a number of figures dressed in black filed by, weeping and tearing their hair.

"Aren't they kind of counterpoint to all the festivity?" Caitlin asked.

Marty laughed. "They are men dressed as women and women dressed as men—all in mourning black. Can you think of any deeper reason to mourn?"

Caitlin smiled. She noted that the women's faces were daubed in deadly white and they held posies in their hands. Their wailing was truly terrible.

"Let's find you that ice cream and the half-smoke. I know a nearby stand that carries both, but they have trouble keeping the items in supply. Puertos like American food and more of us visit now. Look, we're in luck. Over there."

They pushed through the crowd and stood at the kiosk where a jovial man quickly served them and others. His plump wife worked with happy hands as they heard the wail of the men and women who mourned. The man looked at his wife. "We will make up later for what we will miss," he said, grinning at her as she blushed.

Then, munching on the half-smoke and the ice cream, Caitlin and Marty continued to the harbor, packed in like sardines with the crowd. When they reached it, they watched somber men place the giant sardine on a funeral pyre and light it. Brilliant orange and red flames, tinged with blue, leapt high as a protracted sigh went through the crowd.

"Happy Easter!" some yelled. "Oh hurry that day!"

It really was like the funeral and wake of a loved one, with all the merriment unable to overtake the grief, Caitlin thought as she became aware of small pains in her stomach. She said nothing to Marty, thinking she had eaten too fast; it was bearable.

When the sardine had been incinerated to ashes, the fireworks began and Caitlin narrowed her eyes against all that beauty. Washington, D.C.'s fireworks on the Fourth of July were spectacular by any standards, but this . . .

Burst upon burst of bright colors and pastels lit the air. Round and elongated fire-spangled figures began small and ended impossibly large. All patterns were a go. Caitlin thought she had rarely seen anything so beautiful as this.

Marty held her, nuzzled her neck, and thought that in the bright light she seemed a little wan. "How're you holding up, love?"

"Don't worry about me. I'm okay."

Concern was mirrored on his face. "I'm not sure you are. Maybe we'd better get you home."

"No, really. I want to see this. *Please*."

"Okay, but I do think we'd better head home very soon."

The fireworks lasted a long time and they took photos with mini cameras. "I'll always remember this," she said dreamily.

"We'll be coming back again and again."

"Oh yes," she murmured as a wave of nausea hit her and she swayed against him.

He caught her. "Cait?"

"I'll be all right," she said. "I ate too much, too fast. This has happened to me before."

"Listen," he said urgently. "I know a group of doctors who take turns on duty during La Carnaval. They're open twenty-four hours a day and I know the one on duty now. I'm taking you there."

"Wc were going to stay out all night."

"The hell we are. Hold on and I'll push us through."

Marty fumed as it took longer for them to ram through the crowd than he wanted it to. But they finally reached the nearby doctor's office and went in.

"Marty! I wondered why I haven't seen you. I heard you were here."

Marty and the doctor grinned at each other. "Miguel," Marty said, "I bring my wife, Caitlin, here because she isn't feeling well. And we would have visited you tomorrow anyway."

Miguel Martinez bowed, lifted and kissed Caitlin's hand. "I think you have found at last what you have always deserved," he said to Marty.

He took Caitlin into the small room and had her partially disrobe as Marty waited nervously outside.

"I think it's nothing really," Caitlin told him. "In the

excitement of the sardine funeral, I simply swallowed my food too fast. And I'm not eating greasy foods or sweets anymore."

"You're a very wise woman, and we will see what, if anything, is amiss."

As he pressed and probed her body, his face grew somber, thoughtful. She didn't want to ask him what the trouble was, if he knew. She was not given to negative imagining, but she wondered if some grave thing were wrong with her. Finally, he patted her shoulder and asked her to get dressed, saying he would talk with her and Marty together.

A thrill of fear shot through her. There *was* something wrong. She had always enjoyed good health, but bad hearts ran in her family. Her twin, Caleb, had had a rheumatic heart that he carefully tended. Was she developing the same ailment?

In his office, Dr. Martinez sat across from Marty and Caitlin, his face grave, his eyes kind on them.

"Well, man," Marty asked. "What *is* it?"

"Am I ill?" Caitlin felt her heart flutter. "There *is* something wrong, isn't there?"

The doctor smiled gently. "I'm going to need some blood from you. I'd say there is something very, very *right*. I can get the tests back quickly from my friend's lab. Where will you two be at La Carnaval early tomorrow evening?"

"We'll be near that group of stands where the music is a little softer."

"Good. That's easy to get to from here. I'll meet you there with what news the blood test tells."

"Is my wife pregnant?" Marty demanded, a smile beginning on his face.

"I hazard no guesses ever," the doctor said. Just try to relax as best you can until tomorrow. I will come as early as I can."

Caitlin couldn't suppress the leap of her heart, but she quailed at the possibility of another disappointment.

Marty got up and drew Caitlin to her feet, gently hugging her. "Easy, baby," he whispered.

Next evening they were early at the Plaza del Charco and as they neared the group of stands where they would spend much of the evening, Dr. Martinez met them, grinning.

"So you don't feel too well," he said to Caitlin. "That's because your body is undergoing the oldest change a woman's body can undergo. Yes, you *are* pregnant, my dear. And knowing my friend here, you're *both* pregnant."

Marty got up and drew Caitlin to him, hugged her as if she were breakable porcelain. Tears stood in their eyes as they held on to each other. "Thank God," he whispered. "Thank God."

Only then did exhilaration fill her. Now the crowd seemed rowdier, as if they would share the joy Marty and Caitlin felt.

"So, I will go and join my loved ones," Dr. Martinez said. "When I find them, if they are not too tired, I will bring them by to meet your wife."

Marty stood with his arms around Caitlin, stroking her shoulders.

"Ah, I run into you two at last."

They turned to face a beaming Jayson, and Marty couldn't stop himself from bragging. "Cait's going to have my baby."

They stood under a bright streetlamp and could see Jayson's startled face with its kaleidoscope of emotions crossing it. It was a long moment before he spoke. Then he took Caitlin's hand. "Congratulations, my dear.

It couldn't happen to a better couple." He swallowed hard before he shook Marty's hand.

The three stood for a while discussing this year's Carnaval. Finally Jayson said, "I had planned to see a lot of you two, but many things have come up. I am running into people who want to meet with me and swear it must be now. So I probably will see little of you two until we're back home. I'm sorry about that."

"Don't be," Marty assured him. "Right now we're living in paradise. Don't work too hard, and celebrate. It's the season."

"Yes," Jayson said as his eyes roved Caitlin's form. He thought she had never looked so beautiful. He shrugged. You win some; you lose some. "Adios, amigos," he said easily as he turned and left them.

"Wonder why he's so busy," Caitlin said thoughtfully. "Surely he can take a little time out. He comes to Spain all the time."

"Who can know what's inside Jayson Giles," Marty said. "Right now, I pity anyone who doesn't have what we have."

It was late when they reached home. They were both tired, but Marty insisted on bathing Caitlin and massaging her. "I've gotta take care of my two babies," he said gently, as her heart overflowed with love for him.

Caitlin lay on her back on their big bed, looking up at Marty as he sat on the bed beside her, his long artist's fingers probing her flesh, soothing it. She thought she had never known this level of happiness and she told him this. "With Sylvan and Sylvan Junior I was happy," she said, "but I *expected* happiness like that. This time, I wasn't certain it would ever happen again."

He shook his head. "Somehow I was always certain." He took her hand, kissed it, his tongue licking the soft flesh. "I have plans for us, lady," he told her. "We've been next door to it from the beginning. Now we're moving into paradise, and we're going to stay there, Cait, for the rest of our lives."

Chapter 25

"La Carnaval! La Carnaval!"

Carnaval Day had dawned with gray skies, but little threat of rain. Puerto inhabitants held their collective breath; La Carnaval demanded sunshine. It had not rained on that precious day for twenty years. By nine o'clock, Dios (God) had answered myriad prayers and sunshine poured.

Caught in the throng, Marty and Caitlin jostled and were jostled in the Plaza del Charco. Dressed as a gypsy baron and his baroness, their joyful spirits outdid the wild Carnaval spirit.

Marty touched Caitlin's belly. "I always knew my seed was potent," he teased her.

Caitlin smiled and looked at him shyly. "I would never argue with that. And it feels so good getting planted."

He hugged her. "You are so beautiful in your costume." He touched the exquisite garment of rose silk brocade, shot through with gold. Cut low, the gown displayed her swanlike neck and shoulders. Baby gardenias were woven into her lustrous earth-brown hair, and she glowed with happiness. She was the recipient of many admiring glances.

Marty was dressed in well-tailored black silk broadcloth, as befitted a gypsy baron, with a snow-white shirt and a black cravat around his neck. She thought him incredibly handsome.

Her breath caught in her throat as she told him, "I'm so proud you're my husband and my baby's father. Marty, pinch me."

"I'd rather kiss you." His mouth found hers, and his tongue ravished hers with love and fervor. "We need to be alone and not in a crowd."

As he lifted his head from her mouth, she placed a finger against his lips. "Hush! We've got a lifetime to be alone."

"That's the future. I need you now."

"We'll leave early. Perhaps come back."

"We'll never get back—not this year." He laughed merrily. "I want to tell whoever in the world is in despair to just hang on. Look what happened to me."

"To us, *querido*. To us."

In a little while they had moved away from the Plaza del Charco to another nearby plaza where the Election of the Queens would begin. Caitlin thought she had never seen humans so excited by a coming event. The air grew quieter as the elections began.

Onstage were beautiful young girls, seeming far more innocent than the young girls in American beauty contests. They strutted their stuff and the judges selected a ten-year-old with long brown hair, a peach-bloom complexion, and dreamy eyes.

The crowd cheered the girl, who was dressed in white silk gauze and who looked very much like an angel.

"I'm thinking," Marty said, "that in some future year, *our* daughter, or one of them, will take part in such a

Carnaval day. But I want her inner beauty to matter most, the way yours does." He squeezed her hand.

"Thank you. And if it is a son or sons?"

"Oh, we'll have a daughter. If you bear sons, we'll keep trying until we get a girl."

"Oh, you're interested in working very hard to support us all."

Marty grinned. "I'm interested in having a hell of a lot of pure fun."

Caitlin chuckled. "Did anyone ever tell you you're a sex maniac?"

"It has occurred to me since I've been with you. You bring every cell of me to life. I've never had that before. Thank you, *querida*."

"You're very welcome, and I love you."

"That goes double for me."

They heard a throat clear just behind them, and turned. Captain Montero stood there in full dress uniform. Smiling, he looked at his friend and the friend's new wife. "Your present happiness amazes and pleases me," he said. "My son is so happy for you too."

Marty laughed and clapped the captain's back. "We have cause for rejoicing. We now have *la creatura*. A baby on the way."

Captain Montero's eyes lit up as he hugged them both. "My friends," he said. "You will find this one of the most exciting times of your life."

Marty nodded. "Yes." Then, "It's sad that you have to work on La Carnaval Day."

The captain looked somber for a moment. "I am middle-aged and I have known many glorious Carnavals. My full staff has needed to be on duty for the past several years. Thefts and muggings occur now where they never did before. Then there is Cedric's murder . . ."

Caitlin licked her bottom lip, remembering Cedric. "Any progress there?"

"Little," the captain said flatly. "But I am a determined man and things often happen swiftly in this business. There is one particular lead we are following . . ."

"If there is anything we can do to help, you know we will," Marty told him.

"Thank you. We will need help from everyone and the most from *Dios*."

"Yes, always from God," Marty said.

Captain Montero moved away. A nubile young queen was elected to cheers, stomps, and whistles. *Murga*—street musicians—moved through the throng, lustily singing their quaintly raunchy songs of politics and sex.

Events moved swiftly. One of the high points was the election of the old queen, a sixty-five-year-old woman whose face and body reflected love and care. With silken black hair that belied her age and satin skin that was darker than most of the queens', she was radiant.

"Well, she certainly has *her* act together." Marty whistled his approbation. "That's you at that age."

"I should be so lucky."

The woman onstage was well known to Puerto and they wildly cheered her. Dressed in creamsilk heavy lace, she held a bouquet of white baby orchids and her face was radiant.

"The main queen is going to find her a hard act to follow." Caitlin was filled with admiration for this woman, identified with her because the care reflected on her face reminded her of her own dead mother. Oh, they were of different races, different cultures, but there was the bond of a loving, nurturing nature. She brushed a few tears from her eyes.

Marty drew her close. "Are you crying?"

He looked at her closely with deep sympathy. "I'm going to try to make it up to you—all the heartache you ever knew."

"You already have, love. Who is this woman onstage?"

"She is Cara Santiago, an aunt of Cedric's. Her good deeds are legend. She's a truly lovely woman. I have painted her portrait, and she has a deep soul."

"And you are the painter of souls."

"I hope I am. It's what I aspire to be."

"It's what you certainly are."

The election of the main queen began then. Raven-haired with pale golden skin and a magnificent, slender form, she shone with life and vitality. Finally, the crowd that had been merely raucous went crazy. Like the older woman, she was a favorite in ivory silk chiffon cut in large, intricately layered petals.

Once the elections were done, back at the Plaza del Charco, the parade of floats began. Massive and small floats, each one more beautiful than the last, pulled along the packed human corridors with float occupants flinging trinkets, candy, flowers. Often those on the floats simply handed an object to someone in the crowd and this was regarded as a special favor.

Caitlin took a really good look around her then. It was so different here at the Puerto Carnaval. Old, ragged cars were part and parcel of the celebration. There were those dressed in beggar's clothes as well as fantastic finery. One group was dressed as a sheikh and his harem, and the gems they wore flashed like real gems. Caitlin asked Marty about this. He nodded. "They well might be. There are people here of incredible wealth and they don't mind flaunting it."

Motorcycles garlanded with flowers and old, ragged shoes sputtered among the crowd and riders mingled, barely able to stay balanced. The growl of the cycles was drowned in the noise of the crowd.

South American music and dances predominated. It

could well have been Carnival in Rio, but most thought it far better. There was something even more earthy here, closer to truth. In this world there was richness and there was poverty and La Carnaval reflected this.

One queen resplendent on her float followed the next, with many floats of every description in between. There were bands, the kazoos were out in full force, the entertainers worked the crowd. It was a splendid cacophony that would be remembered and treasured all year.

"You look pensive," Caitlin said.

"I was thinking again of Cedric."

"And I was thinking of Rita," she sighed. "I talked with Jim and forgot to tell you. He said they're beginning to feel the thug who mugged me, or rather his gang, may be behind her murder. Rita was known to be fearless. They may have been trying to rob her and the museum. Jim thinks they were after our safe, and like he's said before, that they're connected to a powerful drug gang or the Mafia. And we still don't know why someone would steal a painting, then return a forgery."

"Buenas días!"

A grinning Luther stood before them with a scantily clad young woman in tow who couldn't have been more than twenty.

"Luther," Caitlin greeted him. "Where've you been hiding?"

Luther's grin split his face. "Doesn't this tell you where? Every spare minute, she and me've been making it. Haven't we, babe?" He didn't give her name and didn't introduce her.

The young woman's grin was as wide as Luther's. Caitlin looked from one to the other. It wasn't kosher, she thought, but she was going to say it anyway. "Isn't she a little young, Luther?" Her voice was almost sad.

"We like each other," Luther said defiantly, looking closely at the girl, who nodded. "Don't we, babe?"

"And her parents approve?" Caitlin just wanted to be sure.

"Hell," Luther scoffed, "they're gonna use me as their ticket to get to the States and I'm willing. I always did like young meat."

The young woman gave sultry glances to Marty. She wasn't beautiful by any means, but there was something about her that was highly attractive. She could, and probably would at some future time, do better than Luther.

"Well, lady," Luther said, still grinning at Caitlin, "I sure thank you for bringing me over. It's been a blast, and I'm setting out to see this blast continues. Listen, we gotta get going. We're meeting her parents to do this Carnaval." He did a wild jig and Caitlin realized he was nearly drunk. Until then, she had focused mainly on his companion.

As they left, the woman's demeanor grew softer and she told them, looking closely at Marty, "*Vaya con Dios*."

A young blade who resembled the late movie star Tyrone Power suddenly stood before them. "La Carnaval!" he greeted them, but his eyes were on Caitlin. He swayed a little and they smelled the wine on his breath.

"You are lovely, even for Puerto," he said as if Marty didn't exist.

Marty's glance was harsh. "She *is* lovely," he told the man. "And she is my wife, which means she is mine."

The man seemed taken aback. "Sorry, señor," he muttered. "My eyes were on her and I did not notice you. Dios, but she is radiant!"

Marty put his arms around Caitlin. "And as I said, she is mine. Where is your wife or your woman?"

The man threw up his hands in despair. "She is gone, señor, a year ago, and as you can see, I am very, very lonely. I am sorry."

The man moved away, and as he turned, Caitlin thought she saw tears in his eyes and her heart went out to him.

"I wanted to ask him questions," Caitlin said. "Where did his wife go? Are there children? Oh Marty . . ."

He looked at her, lifted her chin with his finger. "You've got a big heart, Cait. That's one of the reasons I love you so. Give your old man a kiss?"

She laughed. "We're always hugging and kissing, and we keep touching each other."

"We haven't been married very long."

She shrugged. "I think we'll be this way forever."

"Mel and Rispa are still like that. God, they're fierce for each other."

"I know. My parents were very affectionate, but Mel and Rispa, ah, they've got something special going."

"And we haven't?"

"You know damn well we have. Don't ever leave me, Marty, I mean not through death or *anything*. Just take care. Don't speed, don't drink too much." She leaned into him. "You stay with me, you hear!"

His heart thundered with passionate desire to just pick her up and run home with her. Lie with her in his arms, to be deep inside her. He knew she was hurting with her memories of Sylvan and Sylvan Junior and it tormented him.

"I will always be here to shield you," he said tenderly, "from any pain you'll ever feel. I hate what happened to you with Sylvan and your son."

The din of the crowd was nearly deafening, but they

could hear each other as they spoke above the noise, intent on hearing what the other was saying.

"It's all right so much of the time now," she said. "You're with me, and I can't tell you how much you help."

Chapter 26

La Carnaval Day's procession of queens was long and lusty, and was one of the most entrancing scenes of the Carnaval season. The crowd mirrored the vivid enthusiasm of the earlier crowd at the election of the queens. But this time, the roar of approbation for the main Carnaval queen could be heard for miles.

Pressed in with others, the float slowed as it went by Marty and Caitlin, and the queen smiled directly at Marty, bent down and handed him two objects. She was oblivious to Caitlin, although Marty had an arm around her waist.

And as the float pulled on, the queen looked back with eyes that seemed haunted to Caitlin.

"She is truly stunning, but so are they all," Caitlin said. "Who is she?"

"Isabella Santiago," he said shortly.

Something in his voice made her look at him closely. "A relative of Cedric's again?"

"Yes. She's his first cousin. Cedric and she are the children of brothers."

Very slowly she asked, "Do you know this woman well?"

"I know her well," he said flatly, then, "Look over there." He pointed to their left, where a woman with a huge birdcage carrying three papier-mâché doves balanced the whole affair on her sturdy head and shoulders.

With some exasperation, Caitlin told Marty, "You're being evasive, sweetheart, and you almost never are. Were you in love with Isabella Santiago?"

He expelled a harsh breath. "Hardly. I had been so badly hurt by Bianca that I didn't think *any* woman could help me heal." His smile was direct, disarming. "But that was before I saw you again."

She blushed. "Did you date the queen?"

"She was kind to me, and Lord, I needed that. We went out a few times. Her parents knew me, liked me. We saw each other for several months."

"Did you . . ." She hesitated, uncertain of how to ask the question.

He shook his head, smiling crookedly. "Did I sleep with her? No. We never had that type of relationship."

"But she was interested in you, I'm sure."

"How can you be so sure?"

She laughed merrily. "Because you are to women what catnip is to cats. They can't resist you."

"Maybe this will hurt you a little, but if you hadn't wanted a child so much, you'd have resisted me. Wouldn't you?"

Her mood suddenly went somber. "I'm not so sure about that. My feelings for you are so deep, Marty. They go to the core of me. Maybe we don't have what Sylvan and I had, but we have something that satisfies me beyond what I had ever hoped for or expected to have again. I'm sorry if that isn't enough for you."

"It *is* enough for me," he assured her, then added to

himself, *for now*. He didn't know what made him think there would come to be even deeper feelings from her, but he did.

Caitlin grinned impishly. "So you could have had a queen and you chose me; I'm flattered."

"I know what I want and I go for it."

Another hush of anticipation had fallen over the crowd and a murmur swept them. The German queen's float was about to roll through and it soon came into sight. The float was made entirely of thousands of white catalya orchids and even the wealthiest revelers gasped at what it must have cost. Intricately draped in dazzling white silk jersey, the German queen was a butter blonde with alabaster skin and blue, blue eyes.

"She's lovely, and she looks more like a Scandinavian. Focus on that bone structure, honey," Caitlin said.

"Yeah, I *am* focusing. The cheekbones alone are worth the view."

"Not to mention the skin. Oh, the wrinkles that skin is going to develop, and early."

"It's delicate skin all right. They say in Puerto about a woman's looks, 'Glow at sunrise, weep at sunset.' But I've seen looks last—when they begin inside."

"You really believe in that."

"It's God's truth."

The German queen was gracious as she handed down and threw trinkets, small goldfoil-wrapped wedges of various German cheeses wrapped in thick cellophane, Belgian chocolates wrapped in silver foil, and small chocolate bottles filled with expensive cognac also wrapped in thick cellophane. Revelers greedily reached for the miniature bottles, eagerly tore off the wrappers, and devoured the contents. The queen was the daughter of a German industrialist and it had been rumored that her float could be counted on to hand out unique and wonderful gifts.

As Caitlin admired the float, the German queen's eyes linked with hers and she handed down a trinket that Caitlin accepted, to find herself staring at a beautiful unwrapped Austrian crystal pendant.

"But isn't this expensive?" she asked Marty.

"You're damn right it is. That's platinum and crystal. It was said she'd do this. Maria saved several of the Puerto papers for me telling what this year's festival would be like. The article said it would be one of the most lavish German floats ever witnessed."

"And I'm one of the chief recipients. Hmmm."

"Let me put it on you." He took the pendant and fastened it around her neck, bent and kissed her throat.

As the floats passed on, people Marty knew began to come to them, asking why he hadn't chosen their company for La Carnaval. He grinned and told them that as a newlywed, he needed to be alone with his bride. They laughed and slapped him on the back, kissed her cheek, and congratulated them both fervently.

Marty and Caitlin ate around one o'clock. They selected a meal put together from the booths that lined the outer square, each blaring loud music. Every booth had electronic equipment playing a different tune. She wanted another half-smoke and more vanilla ice cream, and he chose the same.

"At least," he said, "we know now what causes your cravings."

She wrinkled her nose at him. "I see you're eating half-smokes and ice cream too. You know what the doctor said: Some men get pregnant along with their wives."

"In Creole Louisiana, they call it *couvade*."

They pushed through the crowd and found benches outside the square where a man lay sprawled on one, fast asleep. "It's like the homeless situation in the U.S.," Caitlin said. "Does Puerto have homeless?"

Marty shook his head. "Not the way we have it, but there are growing numbers of poor people. And with the euro going up, people who formerly didn't have to worry about money are beginning to worry."

"Well, hello," a voice said behind them as they started to sit down. "It's nice to know someone else gets tired."

Behind them stood Pablo Sanchez, Puerto's art gallery owner, and by him a petite woman and two small children who were like whirling dervishes. Pablo introduced his group to Marty and Caitlin and said, "I surely thought I'd see more of you while you're here. People are flooding me with inquiries about paintings from both of you. I wish you'd reconsider selling."

Marty shook his head. "That painting is too precious to me, and of course, my wife's painting belongs to my family."

"Then you both absolutely *must* send me paintings I can deliver to interested parties. Allendé is determined to own paintings from both Steeles."

"My husband is the artist," Caitlin murmured and Marty shook her, saying to Pablo, "Never believe that."

"I don't believe it because I've seen *Fading Magnolias* and it has fast become one of my favorites. It reminds me so much of Georgia O'Keeffe."

"I keep telling her," Marty said.

"You're both too kind," Caitlin murmured, paying close attention to the energetic children.

"Please see me before you leave," Pablo told Marty. "Which is?"

"In a couple of days, and we will do that."

Then the woman was off to manage the two whirling dervishes and the group moved on. Caitlin and Marty settled on the park bench and watched the gallery owner and his family walk away.

Caitlin looked at Marty shyly. "You really do like my paintings, don't you? Thank you."

"Why do you thank me? Goya, Bearden, Lois Maillou Jones never thanked anyone for appreciating their talents. They were and are geniuses, and well aware of it."

"I'm not a genius. Sylvan never praised me the way you do. He was the artist and I was to be the gallery owner. I enjoy running an art gallery. You know that, but living with you has made me want to paint more too. *Can* I have it all?"

Marty looked at her fiercely. "You're damn right you can, baby. In fact, I'm going to see that you do just that."

She leaned around and kissed him, and he found her mouth that was sweet with the ice cream she had just eaten delicious. So his tongue probed it for a few minutes and they looked up to find a couple of teenagers staring down at them from a short distance away.

"When we get middle-aged, I want us to be just like them," the girl said. Then, embarrassed when Marty and Caitlin looked up, the couple waved and strolled on.

"La Carnaval!" Marty said, laughing. He lifted the pendant from her breast, saying, "It's beautiful. The Germans sure know how to manage a Carnaval float."

Caitlin smiled suddenly. "Enjoying all this makes me think of calmer places like Firenze, Italy." She flashed him a shy smile, "and . . ."

Marty chuckled. "And Michelangelo's *David*?"

"Yes. Let's stop there on the way home. Firenze is so charming. All that gorgeous art restores my spirit."

"Mine, too. Yes, let's do it."

For the rest of the afternoon they danced with the crowd and sang with the *Murga,* since Marty knew the racy songs and had taught her a few. Finally Caitlin said to him, "See here, I don't see any other women singing with them. I'm the only one."

Marty kissed her cheek. "You're American, honey, which gives you rights. If you weren't pregnant, I'd get you some of the sangria you love and you'd know it doesn't matter."

An old *músico* had listened to their conversation. "Ah," he assured her, "you're an honorary entertainer. The new women own the world these days."

Caitlin looked at him obliquely. "I keep telling myself."

Then, more South American dances, more pushing through the crowd and resting on park benches before they walked to a small park filled with budgies, the small parrots so common to Puerto.

Caitlin found the pint-sized birds with their quizzical expressions darling. "I'd like to take a couple of budgies home with us, but customs won't allow it."

"When we get home, I'll buy you as many as you'd like."

"I'll hold you to that. Look at the canaries."

"A regular bird show."

The small birds sang lustily, perched on tree limbs. Their bright yellow color enhanced their surroundings, and they hopped about from limb to limb. The canaries were long tamed by the presence of benign humans and had no fear.

"We're so comfortable together, you and I," Caitlin said suddenly. "I've rarely felt this degree of comfort with anyone. Ah, Marty, you're so good for me."

Marty thought now that he was happier than he had ever been. He had Caitlin and now this dream of a baby and that was enough.

Looking at her, he drawled, "Well, I'm comfortable

with *you*. We can practically read each other's minds. We've known each othcr a very long time, *querida*."

They went back to the Plaza del Charco and found that the festivities had gotten even rowdier, wilder. Wigs had slipped and the air shimmered with nearly explosive merriment. Another La Carnaval Day would close at midnight. Another Carnaval season was ending.

"Tired?" he asked her.

"A little, but I'm going to tough it out. We'll just keep going to rest. How much did you rest on other Carnaval Days?"

"Very little. Bianca had amazing energy, but let's not talk about Bianca."

She couldn't help teasing him, "Or Isabella."

"Or Isabella," he echoed.

This time they saw Captain Montero push through to them and Marty spoke as he reached where they stood. "El Capitan, you look bothered."

Captain Montero nodded, his handsome face somber. "I *am* bothered, Marty. We have just arrested Bianca for the murder of Cedric. She requests that you come to her. Those are her words. And she said, 'He will still come if I need him and I need him now.' "

In the din, the captain was silent as he waited for Marty's answer. Then he said, "I would like to have you come with me so I can take you to her. This is a volatile situation, Marty. There is a major art theft ring taking root all over Europe and beginning to be established in the United States. There are many ramifications I intended to talk with you about, but Cedric's murder hasn't left me with enough time to do so. I would like to talk with you by phone once you are home. Will you be going directly there?"

Caitlin looked at Marty, saw the tenseness in his body. "No, we go to Italy. Cait wants to see Michelangelo's *David* again." He paused and looked at her fondly. "Another craving. And I intend to satisfy all her cravings."

The captain laughed heartily. "How much you two remind me of the early years of my own marriage to *el amor de mi vida*."

Marty smiled and told Caitlin, "Translated roughly, the love of his life."

The captain and Marty talked of love, and love was very much in Caitlin's thoughts.

The captain rubbed his nose with a forefinger. "Of course, Bianca protests that she didn't do it, but Cedric was, and Bianca is, tied up in much intrigue. They always have been, and where there is intrigue, there is danger. And I don't have to tell you about Cedric and danger."

Marty looked at Caitlin, who remembered what he had told her about Cedric.

Someone came up and demanded, "Is it true? My brother says you have arrested Bianca Santiago? He saw you take her in in handcuffs. This is La Carnaval, El Capitan. Couldn't you have waited until tomorrow?"

The captain fixed the man with a steely eye. "No, I could not have. Tomorrow the señora could be far away. Go back to your merrymaking and leave policing to us."

The man shuffled off, grumbling. "I must get back," the captain said. "There is much to be done. I would go home early if I were you. A group that Bianca runs with may try to foment trouble to kidnap her, although we have her in secure lockup. We are too busy to deal with more trouble."

"I think you should go to talk with her," Caitlin said to Marty.

Marty nodded. "Let's do it, then."

* * *

That night's sky was truly splendid as Marty and Caitlin looked up from the madly swaying throng. "We'll do as he suggests," Marty told her. "After that, I'm taking you home."

"Yes. I think that's best." She wondered how he was feeling about the news regarding Bianca. He looked okay—quiet, thoughtful, but okay. She slipped her arm under his. "What're you thinking?"

"That Bianca could be in big trouble, that I can't decide whether she could kill someone. And I'm thinking about what I've been thinking about all day—you and me and what's going to happen on a big bed in a certain bedroom. Love and lust and passion without end. La Carnaval will be over tonight for this year, but you and I will know its passion until it comes around next year."

Puerto's new jail and court was state of the art. Built to deal with growing trouble during the Carnaval season, its bright shininess belied the grim business it was largely heir to.

Bianca was housed in the bowels of the building and she came to her cell door as Captain Montero escorted Marty and Caitlin to her. She stretched her arms against the bars and pressed her body toward them, ignoring Caitlin and Captain Montero. She looked only at Marty with hot, impassioned eyes.

"Tell them, *querido*, that I could not *do* this thing. I loved Cedric, even if we did quarrel bitterly at times." Then her voice softened. "I thought you would come alone. We have much to talk about, but I knew you'd come to me."

Bianca looked arrogant when she said that, and Caitlin saw with hurt and anger that in spite of being disheveled and out of place in her beaten gold and white queen's costume, she was beautiful and knew well her power over men. And, Caitlin amended, *over this man*.

Caitlin was surprised that Marty answered Bianca in a cool, dispassionate voice. "I came because my wife thought I should."

"I know I hurt you, but I am the only one you'll ever love. I was so wrong and I . . ."

"Why did you lie to me about the boy?" Marty demanded. "Why did you say I'm the father? Didn't you kill Cedric because he called your lie?"

"No. No. No." Bianca wrung her hands. "It is a small thing. You are a brilliant man as well as artist. I needed—*need* money, *querido*, badly."

"Don't call me *querido*. It was a lie even when you said it in the past. It's a lie now."

"It was never a lie. *Never*. I have never loved any man as I love you. But we are all given at least one chance to be stupid. We were raised with the grand name of Santiago, but almost no money. You were wealthy, but it is your art you care about, and those you love, not money. Allendé has fabled wealth and I am ashamed to say I loved his world. I think I said Enrique is your son because I wanted him to be."

Marty shook his head. "Always the liar. You left me when you knew you were pregnant because you knew the boy is Allendé's son."

"He *could* have been ours. You could love him. You know you could." Here she turned scathing eyes on Caitlin. "She will never bear you a son. She has borne no children since she lost her son because of her negligence."

Caitlin's heart squeezed dry as Marty thundered, "Don't say any more about this subject, Bianca! You see nothing clearly here, as you never have seen anything clearly." He put his arm around Caitlin's shoulder. "Cait is pregnant. My real *querida* is pregnant with a child I can be sure is mine."

Bianca seemed to shrivel before their eyes. She still

looked beautiful, but empty. "The money," she said hollowly. "I really need the money to get out of here, for lawyers. So much. If you could find it in your heart . . . I have a small inheritance from a wealthy aunt that is available next year when I am thirty-five. I will pay you back. For God's sake, forgive me. Help me."

Captain Montero stood with narrowed eyes, thinking that this one was quite the actress. She would be worth her weight in diamonds to an art theft ring.

Marty looked at Caitlin and her heart blossomed with the wealth of love and respect she saw there. Perhaps he couldn't help loving Bianca, but he was trying.

"Should we?" he asked Caitlin.

"How much?" Caitlin demanded of Bianca, who quickly named a sum that was less than they had expected, and Bianca saw them nod at each other in a gesture of intimacy that cut her.

"Oh, thank God!" Bianca began to cry, ruining her makeup.

"There is sufficient evidence to hold her, so she will only need money for a lawyer at this time," Captain Montero told them.

Bianca looked at Marty with sorrowful eyes. "I would give anything to be back in the United States," she said softly.

Marty looked at her coolly. "Even in the U.S. you would be in deep trouble. I will not see you again, Bianca. We leave Puerto Monday. Tonight I will ask my lawyer to transfer funds to you on that day so you can get yourself a lawyer." He paused before he said, "And Bianca, you have Caitlin to thank for this. I'm not sure I would have done it."

"You would have, *quer*—"

Marty's eyes warned her not to use the word regarding him and she quietly backed down.

The eyes Bianca turned on Caitlin were tormented. "Thank you. I can be quite the bitch and I know it. I have not had an easy life. Cedric never had an easy life. The Santiagos of Puerto are and were a difficult family."

As they walked down the corridor, a young policeman stopped Captain Montero, who excused himself as the man said, "El capitan," then spoke in rapid Spanish.

Captain Montero smiled and nodded as the man finished speaking and left. He turned to Marty and Caitlin. "I was not sure the translation of the tape could be made in time for you to read before you leave Puerto, but my staff is proficient and the tape is done.

"The translation may give you answers to why Bianca lied. Also perhaps to why Cedric met his untimely end." He paused a long moment. "It is late. Perhaps you wish to come back tomorrow although it is Sunday; I will be here. Tonight I know you had planned to leave the festivities early."

Captain Montero spoke to Caitlin. "If you are tired . . ."

She shook her head and looked at Marty. "I want to know what's on the tape as soon as possible."

"That takes care of it, then," Marty said. "We'll stay and read the translation."

The captain seated them in his big, comfortable office, took two copies from a stack of papers, and handed a packet to each.

Cait found her breath coming faster as she read a note on top of the pages written in Cedric's elegant script.

Marty,

I am putting the tape back in my safe because unwelcome visitors may come before you do.

I said I was not sure what Bianca intends to

do, nor Allendé, but I have new information that I am including.

This is not a long tape and you will wonder why I didn't simply tell you, but I intend to give this tape to El Capitan and he can do whatever is necessary.

Cedric

Marty and Caitlin moved on to the tape translation.

Marty,

I have wished to see your face after you read this translation, but I may be dead when you arrive. Captain Montero has the combination to my safe and he is aware of the danger I am in. I have taken precautions to get a new safe and I do not think whoever reaches me will have time to get inside.

I will tell you what you most want to know immediately. Bianca's reason for claiming that the boy is yours is that she and Allendé are once more a team and were when she contacted you.

It is Allendé's belief—and of course, Bianca has always followed his lead—that if they could prove that Enrique is your child, it would give Bianca continuing access to you. She and Allendé have many nefarious schemes planned.

Bianca has long known of your desire for a son, or a child. If she could make you believe you are the boy's father, some of your wealth would accrue to her for his care. She often laughed and told me when you were married, that you are a lovable pussycat who is easily persuaded to do her bidding.

An art theft and copyist scheme run by a ring of the multi-talented, few of whom I know, is op-

erating in Spain, Italy, and the United Kingdom. Russia is to be cultivated later. Ah, the art treasures that country has.

Bianca intends to trade added time with the boy for favors she will ask from you. As you know, Allendé has long coveted your Nubian Princess *painting. He would literally kill for that painting. We all believe it to be a masterpiece. And you handle it so carelessly, knowing that there are many others in your psyche.*

So Enrique is to be the key to you. Bianca and Allendé are heartless. Please do not underestimate them.

Bianca has the papers to "prove" that Enrique is your child because she has been the lover of the doctor who owns and runs the clinic in Madrid where Enrique was delivered. He has falsely declared that your DNA runs in Enrique's blood, and it is a lie.

When I began my investigation, I contacted the man I had heard was Enrique's father and talked with him. He readily admitted his paternity and went with me to a laboratory where they took his DNA. I "borrowed" Enrique one day and took him to that lab. It is this man's blood that runs in Enrique's veins, not yours.

We have so much more to talk about, you and I, but I suppose it will have to wait until I visit Washington in March. There are other schemes that are fast unfolding, other people involved that I will tell you about as soon as I know—if my luck holds out. You need to know these things.

You were furious when you found after you got here that your wife may be in some danger, but you have guarded her well and our leader has sworn that he will leave no stone unturned to pro-

tect her. You know he will do whatever is necessary to ensure her safety.

Ah, my friend, I speak of visiting you in March. Who knows, but perhaps our last visit was my last visit with you. The die is cast. After the next few years, the fast-growing art theft and forgery ring that Allendé heads will make him one of the richest men in the world.

Be careful and be happy. Your wife seems to me to be the prize you have always sought. Hold her close.

Your friend,
Cedric

A big, looping signature spread a quarter of the way across the page.

Sighing, Marty looked at Caitlin, then at Captain Montero when they had finished reading.

"You may keep the copies, of course," Captain Montero told them. "Does this give you the answers you seek?"

Marty nodded. "Yes, and thank you."

"You know my help is always available to you. Allendé is a formidable man, and with his many lawyers behind him, we may never be able to bring him to justice. His is a powerful group, but a lawless one. We are powerful too, and we are good at what we do. Go in peace, my friends, and keep in constant touch."

Then he addressed Marty. "It seems to me that my son, Christian, is smitten with your beauteous sister, Dosha. Who knows, but perhaps you and I will find our families, and you and I, far closer."

Caitlin was conscious of their splendid costumes as Captain Montero led them back through the polished hallways. The captain asked Marty, "You will go home early tonight?"

"Yes." Marty offered his hand and the captain shook it, then kissed Caitlin lightly on the cheek.

"Hold on to her," he told Marty, "for nothing is so precious as a woman you love and respect and trust who returns those blessings. If Bianca's fate concerns you, we will be talking of other matters and I will keep you both well informed. *Vaya con Dios, amigo.*"

The two men hugged and Caitlin and Marty went down the wide front steps and back over to the Plaza del Charco, where the revelers still moved in wild and joyous abandon. The music and the singing seemed to Caitlin to be louder than ever and she couldn't help smiling as Marty squeezed her hand, then tucked her arm under his.

Chapter 27

Florence (Firenze), Italy

Two days later, as Caitlin and Marty stood in the Galleria dell'Accademia in Florence gazing at Michelangelo's incredibly moving statue of the biblical David, both felt an artist's surge of pure joy and passion.

Tears came to Caitlin's eyes. "This is my third time seeing it," she said, "and I could see it daily and never grow tired."

Marty nodded. "Remember the first time when we were students at Pratt? You and Sylvan and I and Cresswell, who we didn't know very well and who just wanted to tag along. Lord, we were young, giddy, and we had fun. I wanted you even then, Cait, but you couldn't see anyone but Sylvan."

"I know," she said. "I love you now."

"Michelangelo's *David*," she commented softly. "How anyone can look at this and not believe in God, I'll never know. Donatello and a couple of other artists have depicted David *after* he killed Goliath. Michelangelo chose to show him as he *considered* it, which is genius in itself. Look at those muscles that make you feel you're witnessing flesh itself. A young David, long before he was king. A young man hellbent on saving his city and his people."

"We could use a few Davids now," Marty commented.

The back side of the statue was beautifully rendered, with its tight buttocks and long-waisted, muscular back, but it was the front of the boy that caught you, held you in thrall, Marty thought.

"The man had *soul*," Caitlin murmured, "the way you've got it."

"Ha, I don't have even a fraction of what he's got."

She smiled, looked at him closely. "You have and you know it, as others know it. Why else do we call you the painter of souls?"

"Kindness. People can be kind the way you are."

"You're so easy to be kind to. You're so beautiful. Like David."

"David was a boy. A very young man."

"With old thoughts and passions and aims. He was ageless the way you are. And I know damn well you're even more beautiful."

Marty laughed as a young woman nearby kept looking at them approvingly.

"Keep it up," he told her, "and you've got a willing slave on your hands for life."

"Why not? You've got one."

They stayed in the museum a very long while, absorbing each detail of the statue anew, feeling new bonds in the wake of this magnificence. They looked at other works of Michelangelo, some unfinished, which only added to their magic, but this statue was like no other in Caitlin's eyes.

Outside, they briefly went through parts of the lovely city that was the center of art and culture for the country. In front of the old city hall and perched on a hill, copies of *David* stood in lesser splendor. The sun was bright, yet soft, and a glow seemed to patinate the city.

"Hungry?"

She shook her head. "No. The sculpture . . ." she paused and grinned slyly, "and *you*, fill me."

"I'd like to do an even better job of that, but I think you need to eat something. You only had a bagel and cream cheese for breakfast, and a small glass of orange and cranberry juice. I'm gonna take care of you, Cait, in every way."

"You already do."

"Not the way you take care of me. You're even more maternal than my mother, and that's saying a lot. I'll tell you something about your maternalism."

"What about it?"

"Later. Just a little later."

"Very well, you secretive man. Sweetheart, let's go back to Fiesole and have lunch sent out to our terrace."

"Hey, that's a splendid idea. I've had enough of crowds. I just want to be alone with my wife. But first, I want to buy something for you."

"You've bought me so much already."

"And you haven't done the same for me?"

"I love giving you things, including myself."

Marty laughed. "Anytime you want me or anything I have, you've got it."

They found a nearby shop near the new city hall and went in. The lovely, silver-haired proprietor greeted them. "You're Americans," she said, smiling. "The best kind."

Marty took the woman aside and explained what he wanted. There were only two more customers. She had Marty and Caitlin sit in deep plush chairs before elegant goldleaf-trimmed mirrors. They waited until she came back, beaming, carrying a sheer off-the-shoulder caftan of unearthly pastel beauty. Pale shades of pink, rose, and coral made a soft rainbow. Marty nodded. "Do you like it?"

Caitlin held the silky, cloudsoft fabric. "I love it."

"You are *bella*," the woman said. *Beautiful*. "Please come and try it on."

The garment fit over its own slip and it caressed Caitlin's skin as she went back out to Marty, who whistled softly. He gave the woman a credit card.

"Wrap it up."

She thanked them and said, "You are here for a long visit, one hopes."

"No. We will leave day after tomorrow."

"Ah, that is a shame. You make such desirable guests. You must visit often."

"We will be back," Caitlin assured her, "as long as the statue of David remains here."

The woman laughed. "Ah yes, that is to say, forever."

On their private terrace at Fiesole Villa in the hills above Florence, Caitlin wore the shimmering caftan and held hands with Marty across a heavy, wide, glass-topped table. A waiter served them fresh poached salmon, asparagus, new potatoes in sour cream with sprinkles of chives, and garden salad with celery, onions, and excellent cherry tomatoes.

"You read my mind. I keep craving seafood."

"You have to tell me, love," he said gently. "Unfortunately, I can't read your mind."

She looked at him and the glance caught fire, striking electricity between them and setting up a chemistry they both knew all too well.

"I'm afraid you can read my mind right now," she said laughing.

He nodded. "I'm reading it and loving every second."

Later, stretched out on the big firm bed with its expensive, specially constructed mattress that the villa was famous for, Caitlin and Marty stroked each other slowly, languidly, delighting in giving themselves to each other with desire that went to the marrow of their bones. Her lips were slightly swollen with that desire as his fingertips traced them.

She stroked his face and teased his collarbone with her tongue. Then she turned him over and stroked his back in long, tender movements. Turning his head, she kissed the corners of his mouth, again teasing him with her tongue.

"I love it when you do this to me," he said. "Nuzzling the way a mother does her babe. Your maternalism turns me on, Cait. God, it turns me *on*."

"Is that what you were going to tell me?"

"Yes."

"I figured that out for myself. You mother me, too, and, like you, I get turned on."

"I want to turn you on in every way a man can turn a woman on."

"You will. We'll turn each other on. We've gone so far so fast."

"Not really. We go way back, and I know now I've loved you for a very long time."

His hotly seeking mouth found her breasts and laved them, gently suckling, then harder, first one, then the other, tenderly. He guarded himself from suckling too hard, but his kisses on her stomach and belly were gentler, with his tongue patterning nibbling bites. Moving to her navel indention, he pressed his head in to her and made circular licking swirls around her belly button as she wriggled her hips. He eased then with loving precision to her belly and the flesh over her womb that held his child, then to the tender bud of her womanhood. His tongue flicked wickedly until she wildly clutched the cream silk sheets and cried out his name.

Her very dark honey face and body aroused him to nearly go mad with wanting her. Her beautiful face reflected her love, lust and passion for him.

The room swam in shimmering waves around them and her pheromone bath oil permeated both their senses. She was dizzy with joy as he moved down her thighs, past her calves, and to her feet, where he tongued her instep with bold, sweeping strokes.

"You're driving me crazy," she murmured, as she smoothed his crisp and curly black hair, then threaded her fingers into it and gripped it tightly as he came back to her center and consumed her avidly again. She was his canvas and he painted ancient pictures on and in her body and rejoiced with his talent for what he did, as she pressed his head to her body.

The room was pale rose with rose sheer curtains. They had a honeymoon suite and nothing had been left undone to ensure their pleasure.

"Wouldn't music make this even better?" she asked.

"You *are* music, sweetheart, but I put several CDs on." He leaned over and switched on the CD player. Barry White's moans of ecstasy and exhortations to love surrounded them. "Satisfied?" he asked, grinning.

"More than. Barry really sets my juices flowing."

"We'll see if *I* can do even better." His long fingers stroked her private flesh and with one finger he probed. "Peach syrup in there and I've got to get inside."

He arched above and entered her and she lay passive for a few minutes, feeling thrill after thrill flash through her brain and spirit no less than her body. "Cait, Cait," he whispered, as his big shaft slid in smoothly and deeply until it touched her womb. "You have an exquisite way of giving yourself to me. I go into your heart and your soul no less than your body, and I feel your love around and in me like a blessing. I'm so glad you let me into your life."

She heard his tender words through a haze of desire and longing. Lovemaking like this had begun their baby. His seed grew in her womb, and this time she vowed it would last.

She sat astride him then, bent forward, her full breasts swinging and the wings of her hair half in his face. She felt the massive strength of his body surge up to her as his big hands squeezed her buttocks again and again.

He pulled her down harder onto his shaft. Lovingly, expertly, he worked with insistent passion and joy in what they did.

"Please don't ever leave me," she murmured, and he remembered she had said this before.

"I'll never leave you. Don't you know that by now?"

"I think I know."

"And don't *you* ever leave *me*."

"I won't. We're bonded for life."

"You better believe it."

Then he was on top again, his big shaft like a throbbing heart inside her, jerking and twisting as he fought to slow himself.

"Don't hold back," she told him. "This is too good to last. *I* surely can't last."

She pressed his buttocks hard as he pulled her legs over his shoulders and worked her with desire and passion that went beyond anything they had known. After a siege of wildly ecstatic moments, she felt herself begin the convulsive movements that shook her and shook her in wondrous multiple orgasms.

"Hey!" he said softly. "You're really coming even more

than usual. Woman, you're driving me insane with desire and passion."

She laughed shakily, too dazed by her feelings to say much. "I never had all this vivid feeling before you."

Marty felt his heart leap when she said it, certain that they were getting even closer. She moved her hips in a hard grind beneath him, and his loins and body shuddered with volcanic violence and spilled his seed into her waiting, willing body. Then they lay spent and still.

Chapter 28

Back in D.C.

"Oh, I'm so glad you're back!"

Rena hugged Caitlin fervently and laughed. "My belly's out to here and you'll be in the same boat in a very little while. Let's hug while we can." She gave Caitlin another hug, then looked at the package Caitlin had given her, asking, "What wonderful thing have you gotten for me now?"

"Open it and see."

The gallery was not yet active and the two women enjoyed the minutes of quiet camaraderie. Rena undid the ivory linen wrap with the fake cherry and green leaves fastening it and whooped with delight at a beautiful gold Wittnauer watch.

"It's gorgeous!" She threw her arms around Caitlin again. "How did you know just what to get me?"

Caitlin looked at her and said waggishly, "Oh, a hint dropped here and there. Puerto has the world's best selection of gifts and the best bargains, but then I don't look for bargains for you, my best friend after Marty."

"You bet this was no bargain. I love it! Consider yourself hugged for a very long time. You're radiant, sweetie. That baby has made you Mrs. America, and I'd guess the trip didn't hurt. Todd and I are going to Puerto for La Carnaval one season soon."

"Do. You'll love it."

Rena bit her bottom lip. "I hate to bring up bad news, but Jim wants to see you as soon as possible. It's about Rita. He's helping Lt. Anderson all he can."

"A breakthrough?"

"I think so. The poor guy's ragged and I find myself missing Rita like crazy. If they nail the perp, I hope they hang him. She had everything to live for, and her life was just getting good where things had been rotten for her for many moons."

"I'm with you there. Rita was quite a woman. We'll all do everything we can to help Jim and Lt. Anderson."

Rena nodded. "My husband's coming in later to bring us seafood pasta for lunch. He makes a mean one."

"Oh great, I've been craving seafood for a few days now."

Rena rolled her eyes. "Those damned cravings. Night before last I wanted strawberries covered with powdered sugar in the middle of the night. Lord, I felt I'd die if I didn't get them. Todd got up and went over to Georgetown. Luckily he knows a guy who has a restaurant and they get out-of-season fruit from Chile. He came back with the berries and the powdered sugar, and li'l old mama me ate them like there was no tomorrow."

Caitlin laughed. "Your body probably needs something in the strawberries."

Rena licked her lips. "I still remember the taste. Listen, Luther's told me about some young chick he picked up over in Puerto."

"Yeah. A nice-looking woman and way too young for Luther."

Rena shrugged. "Who's to say, love. Todd's quite a few years older than I am."

"You're both very mature and I don't think this woman has had a chance to be."

"Well, he's surely excited."

"Tell me about it."

Sgt. Jim Draper came in a half hour later. As they sat side by side in two tub chairs in her office, Caitlin couldn't help reflecting that he looked ten years older. Raw grief sat on his features like a vulture.

"I hope you had a good time," he said. "You look like you did. How's Marty?"

"Couldn't be better. Yes, we had a great time. And I'm pregnant, Jim."

"Hey, congratulations!" Tears stood in his eyes as he thought that in another year, he would surely have gotten Rita pregnant.

She leaned over and pressed his hand. "Jim, you know how sorry we all are, and we want to do everything we can to help you."

"I know," he said hollowly. "You've told me before, and you do help just by being kind the way you can't help being. Hold that baby close to your heart, Cait. It's one of the magical things that will happen in your life." His voice broke then. "And it's something Rita never had a chance to know."

She got up and hugged his shoulders for a few moments. He slumped for a brief while, then straightened. "It helps that I think Detective Anderson's team's got her killer."

"Oh really." She felt excitement course through her, as an expression of severe distaste crossed his face.

"Yeah. Remember the creep who mugged you last year?"

"Dilly McKay?"

"That's the—" he thought better of what he'd been going to say. "You're a lady so I won't use that word. We've got a skintight tail on this bastard and it's succeeding beyond our wildest dreams. We're not there yet, but we're sure getting there. We expect to be able to haul his ass in before too long." He seemed to look far into the distance. "Rita baby, *nobody* gets away with what was done to you, not while *I'm* breathing."

"I'm glad, Jim," Caitlin said simply, "but not as glad as I'll be when you haul him in."

"And by God, we'll make it stick. We're gonna see that no scummy defense lawyer gets him off. We thought he and his gang had ties to the Cali cartel, but he's Mafia connected and that's even worse, if possible. Wish me luck, Cait, because we're going to need all the luck we can get. Detective Anderson will be talking with you shortly."

She bent over and kissed his cheek. "You know I do. Come to dinner, Jim. I've invited you before. Just tell me when."

He shook his head. "You don't know how much I appreciate your invitation, but remember, our captain doesn't think it's wise to have too close social bonds within the community. Right now I'm working and sleeping and eating little. I take time out for my kids, but I'll beg my captain and I'll be there one day and help you cook like crazy."

He left then and she watched him cross the room, with his wide shoulders slightly slumped and his head held like a bull that was slamming into an enemy.

She leaned back in her chair, thinking with sadness of Jim and Rita, and of Cedric. A slight shudder took her as her buzzer sounded.

"Are you free to take a call from Mr. Sanchez—Pablo?" Nelda asked.

"Yes. Put him through." And in a few seconds, Pablo's warm voice came through. Immediately he asked, "When will you and Marty send me new paintings?"

Caitlin laughed. "Paintings take time, you know. And I paint much more slowly than my husband. On top of that, I've got a gallery to run. Have you talked with Marty?"

"Not yet. You hold the key to his heart, and he would relent for at least one painting if you asked him to. Allendé is driving me insane. He truly admires the paintings you exhibited here in my gallery. Do me this favor and I will grant you anything in my power to do."

"Umm, tempting, but no, I'm pretty sure neither of us will sell to Allendé. He's not a nice man and I'm fond of nice people. They make the world turn more smoothly."

Pablo laughed. "I like the way you put that. And you're right, Señor Allendé is not a nice man, but he *is* a rich man who has long bent the world to his shape." He paused. "I will convey your regrets and he will continue to haunt me, and I suspect later, both of you."

"I can deal with him and I have no regrets about not selling our paintings to him. I don't think Marty has any regrets either. Neither of us could ever find anyone we'd rather turn down."

Pablo chuckled. "Come back to Puerto soon. You don't have to wait until La Carnaval. And we will be coming to D.C. this November. I hope to see you then."

"Of course you'll see us then. We'll have you over for a lavish dinner and show you all the sights, although you've been here before."

"Ah, *gracias, señora*. I have seen your gorgeous city and you are not beautiful for nothing."

After Caitlin hung up the phone, only a few moments passed before Luther stuck his head in the door. "Can I take up a few minutes of your time?"

"Certainly. What can I help you with? Please sit down."

He shook his head. "Guess I'm too excited to sit. I just wanted to tell you Dulcé and me're getting hitched in June. She wanted it sooner, but I'm getting someone to tutor her in English and I want her to have a fabulous wedding. She deserves the best."

Caitlin nodded. "I think you're being wise to delay your wedding and I like the way you're thinking. How do your children feel about this?"

He shrugged. "They don't care. Whatever makes me happy; they know I like young women. Dulcé's the best."

So Dulcé was her name, Caitlin thought. Before this conversation, he had never said. "How old is Dulcé?"

"Twenty in April. And I'm fifty. Big difference, but I'm young at heart and Dulcé tells me she's led a hard life and she's old. Well, I thought you'd want'a know. You're always so good to us here at the gallery. You're way young'rn me, but it's like finding my own mama again."

He gave her a wide smile and left, closing the door softly behind him.

It was after one when Marty called. "I was busy painting and I started missing you. Come home early so I can make wild, passionate love to you. We were both so tired, we missed last night."

"One little night without. Can't you take it? Once the baby gets here, I suspect we'll both be without many nights."

"Oh? Tell the little rascal—he or she—Papa plans to keep his presence known. I was here first. I can smell your delicious perfume, feel your soft flesh now under my stroking hands and my hungry mouth is on your breasts . . ."

"Marty, stop! I'm going to kill you! I'm at work and you're burning me up."

He laughed merrily. "Burn, baby, burn! Do it for me. I'll let you go and I love you so very, very much. When we're really old, we'll look back on this with remembered rapture."

And Caitlin retorted, "Knowing you, honey, you're going to be sowing your oats in my body as long as we're married, if we live to be over a hundred."

"Thank God I've got a beloved wife who understands me well."

Caitlin and Rena had had the late pasta lunch that Caitlin found delicious. Todd had come late and joined them, but left shortly after. Now her secretary's smooth, young voice came over the intercom. "His Majesty, Herr Giles, would like to be bowed in," she said.

Caitlin couldn't help laughing. "He's a snob, but he's harmless," she said.

"Well, I'm from the common classes and I don't like snobs. I finished Howard, but I sometimes speak Black English, and it's plain he detests my style."

"He isn't worth getting bent out of shape for. Show him in and make yourself a cup of hyssop tea."

"What a lovely idea. That'll settle my retching stomach."

After a few minutes, Jayson opened the door and paused on the threshold for a long time as Caitlin looked at him. He was particularly elegant today in charcoal gray silk broadcloth with a pale blue shirt and a color-coordinated tie.

"Are you coming in?" she finally asked, thinking he looked strange.

"Give me a moment. I'm looking at you, my love,

and I find you breathtakingly beautiful. You ought to wear that pale coral more often. It's you."

"Thank you. You look pretty spiffy yourself. You didn't call; why are you here? Come in and have a seat."

"I apologize if you're very busy, but I won't stay long. Cait, your news about the baby floored me, but I'm getting used to it."

Her head went to one side. "It's what happens to married people, and some who aren't married."

He smiled ruefully. "You're quite a woman and you'll always be first with me, but I want you to be happy. I'd love being the baby's godfather."

"Oh Jayson, that's so sweet of you, but one of Marty's brothers, Damien, spoke for that honor almost from the beginning."

"I understand. Just be happy. That's all I want for you."

"Thank you."

She wished for someone for Jayson, but the thought made her smile inside. Jayson had a world of women at his command. He didn't need her help.

"How long will you be in town?" she asked.

"For at least two weeks. A woman I know is opening an art gallery in Minden that specializes in all-African art. I mean, most of the African countries are represented. I've bought a house in the country out from Minden, so I'll only be fifty miles away from you when I'm down this way."

"And Marty."

He half closed his eyes and smiled. "Yes, Steele."

He came to her, bent, and kissed her cheek. "You're glowing," he said wistfully. "You look happy."

As he had promised, he didn't stay long. After he left, she edited a new flyer advertising their Black Eagle exhibit. And she thought about Jayson. She was sorry he was in love with her, but he'd been a really good sport about her marriage.

The afternoon groups were surprisingly full and so interested in the Tuskegee exhibit. She had to notify an on-call docent to come over and help, and she and Rena were elated. The Tuskegee Black Eagles exhibit was soaring.

Chapter 29

"Surprise!"

Coming home a little later than she'd intended to, Caitlin opened her front door to be met by a grinning bevy of siblings—Dosha, Marty, Adam—and there was also Adam's pride and joy, Ricky.

Happy tears came to Caitlin's eyes as she came in and Ricky hugged her tightly. "Hey, you look beautiful, Aunt Cait," he told her. He had begun calling her aunt when he heard about her pregnancy.

"Thanks, sweetie. You look pretty beautiful yourself." She patted his face as he blushed. Caitlin glanced around at the beaming faces, her heart lifting even beyond its now omnipresent joy. "To what do I owe this surprise?"

"Well, it isn't every day you bring the Steele family another heir. And just because we love you. Isn't that enough?" Dosha said.

"It sure is."

Adam shook his head. "Pregnancy surely becomes you, Cait. You're positively glowing."

"Hey, she's a good-looking woman," Ricky said.

Adam laughed and smoothed his son's crisp hair. "And you're a delightfully fresh young turk."

"Your husband knew about this." Dosha stood close to Caitlin. "In fact, he was the one who tipped us off that you were having seafood cravings. Mom hopped right on it and planned this little seafood celebration. Use your freezer and you won't need to look for seafood or cook it for a long time."

"Mom and Dad'll be in any minute," Adam said. "They've both practically floated ever since they got the news about the baby."

"They're not the only ones," Marty said, grinning. "I've landed and stayed on cloud nine myself. Or maybe cloud twenty."

"Oh, this is so wonderful," Caitlin told them. "Let me change and I'll be right with you. And may I borrow my husband for just a few minutes?"

"Take all the time you need with him," Dosha drawled, grinning.

In their bedroom, Caitlin began to change into cream silk jersey lounging pajamas with a leopard-print sash as Marty's eyes lovingly roamed her body.

She turned to him. "You promised me a good time tonight, but this surpasses even that."

"Nothing surpasses *that*." Putting a thumb under her cheekbone, he rubbed it back and forth, then felt her stomach as she melted.

"And you knew all the time. Later for you."

"I knew and I know how much you like surprises. Which reminds me: don't forget the gifts for the folks."

"They're in the hall closet. Why don't you get them out?"

"Okay. Hurry and get dressed. You've been gone all day and I'm used to having you around since Puerto. When the folks leave tonight, our ball begins. I insisted you rest last night because I knew what was coming up, but tonight . . ."

They heard the door chimes and Marty went out to check, but Dosha and Ricky had answered the door. A florist's van was parked at the curb with a late delivery and Rispa and Mel stood on the porch bearing three big boxes.

"Hurry up and let us in so I can put these boxes down and hug the breath out of you," Rispa said, laughing.

"And I'm coming in on that." Mel looked even happier than his wife.

The florist's delivery man came onto the porch carrying a big and beautiful bird-of-paradise plant.

"How gorgeous. Thank you,and let me tip you," Caitlin said.

"No, ma'am." The older delivery man shook his head. "Everything's been taken care of."

"Was it enough? Are you satisfied?"

"Shoot, ma'am, I'm more than satisfied."

Inside, they looked at the card from Damien. It read: *Welcome to baby city. It's a part of my plans, too, and I'm making connections*.

Marty shrugged. "Cryptic note, like my brother. If it's true, it's about time."

"Well, dear," Rispa said as she looked at him, " 'A child once burned always fears fire,' as you've heard. And no, I'm not talking about you because you found Cait and I was always sure you'd be all right, even if you didn't believe me." She frowned. "But Damien is different. He takes things so hard."

"You're right, Mom," Dosha chimed in. "Sometimes it seems that my twin's got a woman's tenderness and I've got a man's toughness. Fortunately, we know now that both genders need both qualities in spades."

Marty had given out carefully selected presents for everybody. Quickly unwrapping them, the family raved over the gifts. Damien's was tucked away in the credenza drawer.

Dosha came to stand by Caitlin. "I'll bet you spent hours on your feet getting these together. You're going to have to take care of yourself now."

"I don't. I'm not that pregnant yet."

Dosha grinned. "Just a little bit, huh? I'm appointing myself your guardian angel."

"I'll like that."

In the kitchen Ricky helped the women spread the food and cook more as Marty, Mel, and Adam gathered around the grand piano that his mother had given Mel. Mel in turn had passed the gift on to Marty.

"Ooh, this is wonderful stuff." Caitlin kept lightly sampling Rispa's prize seafood salad made of crab meat, lobster, shrimp, pasta shells, Miracle Whip, and her own special recipe for mayonnaise. Most of the people she knew used either Miracle Whip or mayonnaise. Dosha and she used both.

"And *I* made the crab cakes," Ricky piped up. "I'm getting to be good at this. Maybe I'll be a chef. A first-class chef."

Caitlin smiled at him. "Ricky, love, you're gonna make a first-class whatever you choose to be."

"Thank you," the boy said gravely as Rispa stood thinking he looked so much like his late mother, it had to break her son's heart when he looked at him.

Rispa heated half Australian butter and half extra virgin olive oil in two big iron skillets, let the mixture get hot, and dropped big oysters into them. One batch was dipped in cornmeal and seasoning, the other in breadcrumbs and seasoning. And she watched both skillets with a careful eye as they sizzled.

Caitlin shredded lettuce, sliced sweet Vidalia onions,

cucumbers, green peppers, and mushrooms for the garden salad, then added chopped celery and red cabbage. She placed the whole lot in the huge crystal salad bowl and got down a large container of parmesan cheese for those who wanted it.

French bread and homemade cloverleaf rolls that were Dosha's specialty were put on linen cloths; she split the rolls, buttered and wrapped them. With the oysters done and blotted, Rispa took big cartons that she'd stored when she came in from the refrigerator.

"We made eggnog with Splenda because we know you're partial to it—both the nog and the Splenda. I've found it a great sugar substitute, as you have. We're all going to see that your baby is the best possible kid."

With the bread finished, Dosha sprinkled string-cut white and sweet potatoes with oil and put them into the oven to fry. Then she opened two very large bags, got big platters, and piled high her famous chocolate chip and chocolate lace cookies and the only slightly less famous oatmeal cookies, stuffed with big juicy raisins, walnuts, and shredded coconut.

Caitlin shook her head. "Kings and queens don't have it any better, and I doubt if they have it as good."

The door chimes sounded again and Caitlin swung the door open between the kitchen and the dining room to see who it was. The men had gone to the door to greet Frank and Caroline Steele; their daughter, the famous gospel diva, Ashley; and her husband, Derrick. Behind them was their son Whit Steele, another gospel notable; and his wife, Minden police lieutenant Dani. Mel switched on gospel music on the CD player and the women came in from the kitchen for a moment to greet and fervently hug the newcomers, then rushed back.

Tears came to Mel's eyes as he held most of his two sets of children gathered here. In spite of his heartbreak when Frank's mother had deserted him for another, he felt himself to be a lucky man. He'd found Rispa and she had been his answer to any pain he'd ever known.

Caitlin went into the food pantry to get brombeer jelly the German wife of a close friend of hers had given her. She heard Marty open the door softly and come in, felt him nuzzle her neck. She turned, smiling. "Why can't we keep our hands off each other? Oh well—"

She turned, leaned into him and slid her tongue lazily back and forth under his ear, wriggling slightly against him.

"Okay," he said hoarsely, "keep it up, you little minx, and you're going to make me take you right here and right now."

Caitlin smiled. "I don't think your family would approve, under these circumstances."

"I don't know. We could latch the door." His face grew somber. "Dad always told me to wait until I was able to treasure it when a woman gave me her body. He always said, 'Son, sex is God's gift to man and woman when they choose a proper person, place, and time.' Lord knows you're the proper person . . ."

She laughed merrily. "That's such a beautiful sentiment, but love, this isn't the proper place or time."

He smiled with half-closed eyes. "Maybe not, but a little on the sly never hurt a married couple so much in love they can't wait. Bet they'd understand."

Caitlin's stomach shook with laughter and she felt her heart soaring. She was carrying a child for this man and the joy she knew was all out of proportion to anything she'd known before, even with her first child that she'd lost. A sliver of sadness came to lodge in her heart then, but she felt it, let it pass.

"Hey," Adam called, knocking on the door. "Are you two *growing* the blackberries for that brombeer jelly?"

"It's safe to come in," Caitlin said, leaning back and opening the door. Adam looked from one of them to the other.

"You two remind me so much of Marta and me." And they thought, but neither was sure, that he murmured, "God, why did it have to end?"

The Steeles took a long time to eat the delicious food, slowly savoring the truly memorable fare. After they had finished and rested, Mel turned to them as they sat and sprawled about the living room.

"You ladies are all looking fabulous tonight," Mel complimented them as both Whit and Derrick agreed.

"I hope I get a wife as good as my aunts and grandmother," Ricky said.

His father laughed. "You're a chip off two blocks, Dad and me."

"You gonna sing for us, Ashley, Whit?" Mel asked.

"I could," Ashley answered.

"And so could I." Whit came in. "Sound off on who'd like to hear what."

They settled on the first song with Ashley singing, Mel playing the piano, and Whit, Marty, and Adam picking up guitars. As he strummed before the singing began, the group reflected that Marty was good. And Adam laughed, "As a guitar player, I'm a damned good cop." But he played anyway.

The song they'd chosen was "He's Got the Whole World In His Hands," and Ashley's superb mezzo-soprano led as her husband looked at her, enraptured. He never tired of his woman or her songs.

Rispa thought the same thing as her husband played

and sang backup. And Whit's wife, Danielle, met his eyes with deep love and understanding.

Waves of gospel melody surrounded them as they began to sing the first verse:

He's got the whole world
In His hands—
The whole world in His hands

He's got the little bitty baby
In His hands
The little bitty baby
In His hands.
He's got the whole world
In His hands.

At the end of that verse, Caitlin and Marty felt the start of tears. A family steeped in God's and human love blessed their baby and their love. They both felt their hearts fill to bursting.

The group paused then, discussed the beauty of gospel music and its soothing, uplifting presence in the Black and in the general American communities.

Ricky's breaking voice came into the group. "I've got the world's best, most loving family. That's what I'm gonna have when I grow up. Dad, you should've brought Raven."

"She was busy tonight, son. Better luck next time."

The family didn't pry, but they all looked interested. Adam explained, "Raven's a woman I've just met. She's a TV investigative reporter for WMRY, and she's winding up a big case. You'll all meet her soon."

"Hey, Raven's neat." Ricky looked excited. "I like her and she likes me. She's got a little girl who's neat too, and usually I can't stand still for girls. They're silly sometimes."

Adam lifted his eyebrows. "From the mouth of a connoisseur of women." He grinned affectionately at his son.

Whit sang his signature song then, "Go Down, Moses," and you knew, as you knew with Ashley, why he was one of the most adored of the great gospel singers. Both voices were pure gold, rich with feeling and compassion, with love and hope.

Go down, Moses, way down in Egypt land
Tell old Pharoah to let my people go!

Mel's deep bass added its luster to the group and he was Papa Music, who had fathered and raised two sets of children who were all any man could hope for. And he had a wife sent straight from God's bosom.

It was very late when the Steeles left; they all felt reluctant to part.

"This has been quite a night, quite a celebration," Rispa finally said. "We have a new unborn child in our midst and we greet him or her with gladness and songs of praise, gospel music that will live forever. Now we've got to leave these two lovebirds alone because I know how I felt when my children were newly nestled in my womb."

In so short a time, they had all gone, after clearing up and storing the large amount of leftover food.

After she undressed, Caitlin did a few stretching exercises and took a lukewarm shower. Marty had taken one earlier. "You know," she said, "I should be tired because I had a hard day, but I'm not. It was such a great thing to do and I feel rested, soothed."

Marty was already in bed with his bare muscular torso and tanned skin. She smiled at him, thinking that his workouts in their home gym certainly paid huge dividends. Her eyes on him held hunger, and she remembered Florence and Michelangelo's *David*, as her glance caressed him.

She pulled on a lowcut, gauzy cream nightgown and got in bed, rolled over to him. He held her close for a few minutes. "I'm going to let you rest again tonight, fight my impulses. I'm gonna take good care of you and the bambino."

"Latinos have a name for a baby: *la creatura*. And you'll note it's always feminine because no one knows or knew at one time what gender the baby will be."

"Doesn't matter to me, as long as it's yours and mine. Thank me now for my forbearance, for holding myself down and off you."

She looked at him with a wicked smile. "Oh no, buster, you give me what you promised on the phone, upsetting my equilibrium, or I'm going to start screaming."

Chapter 30

"Pilates for life!" Caitlin told Marty the following Saturday morning, as they did the famous exercises on special floor mats. Her trainer had put together special, milder exercises in the system.

"And healthy limbs," he added.

"I'm so glad this came along in my time. It's done wonders for me."

He smiled at her. "And you turned *me* on to it."

In their exercise room, Marty did the sets for forty-five minutes three times weekly; Caitlin did far milder exercises the same number of times. Friends told them they looked younger, fitter, and more exuberant. Then, friends climbed on the bandwagon. They had an excellent treadmill, too, a rowing machine, and other machines and varied-sized weights.

"Not that we need exercise after last night." Marty closed his eyes for a moment. "We should rest all day."

She blushed under his loving look and continued her Pilates movements.

"Oh I—" she began when the telephone rang.

"They'll leave a message," he said.

"It may be Dosha. She's doing a bit of research for me."

She took the call in their bedroom, and a voice she didn't recognize came on. "Mrs. Steele?"

"Yes, this is Caitlin Steele."

"My name is Donna Wilkins. You probably don't remember me since I only met you once, but I was a very good friend of your late husband, Sylvan. As you know, he rented space at my art gallery here in New York City, the only artist I've ever allowed to do this."

The woman's voice was warm, cultured and Caitlin responded, "Yes, I remember that and I remember you. I met you at a party in honor of Sylvan that took place in SoHo."

"Right. You have a very good memory. There were so *many* parties for Sylvan. What a loss."

"Yes."

"Well, I'm calling because Sylvan left many papers in his desk drawers. When he died, I was away in the Far East and couldn't get back. My assistant packed what he left into large envelopes, put them in a closet and forgot to tell me. After so long a time—five years—we're preparing to move to a more spacious place on the Upper West Side and I've shipped you what he left. I didn't examine anything because I thought you'd like to do that. This is Saturday and I sent the package off yesterday by FedEx Priority Overnight, Saturday delivery. You should get it this morning.

"I would have called earlier, but everything's been so hectic. I just didn't want you to be caught by surprise."

"Thank you so much." She couldn't help wondering what the packages would contain. But Donna was saying something else. "I read in one of the art newsletters that you had married Marty Steele. He's such a love of a guy. Congratulations."

"Thank you; he is that."

"Please give him my regards. We dated a couple of times. I caught fire, but he certainly didn't. Ah, life. Please, either of you, call me any time you wish to."

"We will. I'll give Marty your message, and congratulations on your gallery's move to a larger place."

"I'm forgetting. You run an art gallery and I've read in the newsletters about it too, that it's fabulous and very much a part of the African American community. A gallery to be proud of. Let's visit when either one of us is in town."

"Yes, I—*we'd* like that. And thank you for sending that material of Sylvan's along."

Caitlin and Marty were having a late breakfast when the package arrived; three large, not particularly heavy boxes. She and Marty quickly opened them and spread the contents on the dining room table. In the second package there was a stack of five thick letters secured with a woman's wide, ruffled rose-colored garter.

"What the hell?" Caitlin frowned.

Marty licked dry lips, dreading what would follow. "Why don't you take those aside and go to another room to be alone, read them."

"Why?" she demanded.

"Just do as I ask you, Cait," he said gently and she picked up the packet of letters and went to their bedroom, sat on the bed, unfastened the now somewhat faded garter, and after she had noted the postmark date, opened and read the letter that was on top. It was written on heavy, rose-colored stationery.

My darling, Sylvan—my one and only forever and always love,

Caitlin felt her breath grow shorter. The letter was dated one week before the accident that had killed him on that bitter night in December as she had waited for him to come home.

You say you know now what I have known all the time, that we are fated. We married as mere youth, at nineteen for me and seventeen for you. We may not have been really old enough, but we were wise enough to know our own hearts.

Your parents had great faith in your talent and hated me for interfering with their plans for you, but we married anyway and I helped nurture you as they had. My parents didn't care about me. They had always left me to my own devices. And I ran wild. You knew that and loved me anyway.

Sylvan, I betrayed you because I know now, I felt I didn't deserve your love, anyone's love. And you were so hurt. I still could kill myself for what I did to you. You married on the rebound, but you admitted you never loved this woman the way you still love me and always will.

Now we see each other every second week and we're happy again. And we have made glorious love once more for more than a year. You couldn't trust me once. Can I trust you now to get the divorce you say you'll get? I hope so. I hope you really have forgiven me.

I've been faithful since I betrayed you that one time. We're in each other's bloodstream, my darling, no greater love. You were right when you said that even if Caitlin does have a baby, you will tell her because you're so tired of living a lie. You said you care about this woman and she loves you devotedly, but I am your true love, always have been, always will be.

Oh my love, my darling, until I see you again.

Your Lolla

With dry, painful eyes and a nearly closed throat, Caitlin refolded and put the letter back into its envelope and quickly leafed through the others. Dare she read them? The first one had been the last one written and was the most important. She slowed her glance on one outpouring of love, then moved on until she had scanned the five letters. Then, with a heavy heart, she picked up the letters and the garter and went back out to Marty.

He sat at the dining table sorting Sylvan's last papers and he got up as she came in, went to her and reached for her, but she sidestepped him, thrust the letters at him, the most damning one on top.

"Read this one first," she said dully.

He held the other letters as he read the first and he sat, shaking his head from time to time. He stopped reading every so often to look at her with concern, wanting to hold her against the storm that had to be raging in her breast. She noted that with all his compassion, there was no surprise mirrored on his face.

With her heart breaking, she accused him. "You *knew*, didn't you? Why haven't you told me since we've been married? Why did you let me make a fool of myself with my undying love for Sylvan that shut you out from so large a part of my life?"

He got up, came to her side and knelt by her chair.

She let him take her in his arms as he laid the letters on the table and held her, feeling the slow, pained beats of her aching heart. And very gently he told her, "There are no fools in love, sweetheart. And you would have hated me if I had told you."

After a little while she quieted. "Tell me about them, about this Lolla that he was going to leave me for. Was he *really* going to leave me, Marty?"

He nodded. "Yes, but you have to understand that Sylvan and Lolla grew up together. They had always been together; her letter says it all. They married, but Sylvan wanted to finish Pratt and be a major success before they lived together. He was younger than she, remember, and obsessed with his art. She was alone, young, wanted children he couldn't see having right away. He was deeply involved in his life, but she was lonely and she took up with a clown who had no future and very little present. He gossiped about her, bragged to the town that he was sleeping with another man's wife, and Sylvan found out."

Caitlin swallowed hard as she put the pieces together. And it came to her after Marty had said it. "She was the flame to his moth," Marty said. "He cried like a baby when he found out she was cheating. He asked me, 'What am I going to do? Lolla's me and I'm her. You know damn well life will never be any good for me without her, but she's weak, faithless. Maybe she's going to cheat on me again.'

"We both got roaring drunk that night and Sylvan stayed drunk for three days and nights. You sobered him up, took care of him and gradually he turned to you, much to my hurt. I was saving you until a time when I had more to offer, and before I could tell you what was in my heart, you and Sylvan eloped to Vegas." He stopped for a long time. "And I met and married Bianca, a family friend of Jayson's. Sylvan didn't care anymore and neither did I."

She felt guilty. "But you fell in love with Bianca later."

"Yes, but my first passion was you, as Lolla was Sylvan's."

"Was he coming back from meeting her when he died?"

"He was. I'm sorry."

She felt his quiet strength as he sat with her in his arms and she had to tell him. "Thank you again for being so kind when he died. You two were brought up together in the same small upstate New York town. You were like brothers, so it hurt you the way it hurt me when Sylvan *and* my twin, Caleb, died. Now I have you, Marty. I have your love and I'm grateful."

"It isn't enough, is it? With the baby, with all we have, I can't fill your heart the way he did. He's *your* flame as Lolla was his."

"Oh God," she moaned and she said it without knowing she would. "I have to go somewhere else to be alone, love, to think and feel this through. I'm sorry."

"Don't be. We'll go somewhere with a separate room for you and I'll be there only when you need me. Why don't we go somewhere beautiful, restful. Costa Rica?"

She shook her head. "Thank you for being so thoughtful, but I want to go nearby, out from Minden. Just five miles from Rispa and Mel, there's a bed and breakfast, The Haven. They're noted for nurturing. Couples breaking up—one or the other—go there. I understand their place is beautiful. Sweetheart, please don't be hurt that I don't want you to go with me. This way is best, believe me."

Maybe it was hopeless, but he had to try. "We need to be together now. You're hurting and I can help you heal. I *know* how you love him, Cait, and I think you always will."

It crushed her to hear him say it because it was true and it set up powerful waves of fear that nauseated her. Was this netherworld of hopeless love never going to end?

"Was I living a lie with you?" she asked him. "On my part, certainly not yours."

He answered immediately with grave passion. "What we have together is no lie. It's truth the way few people have ever lived it. Let me see you, Cait. Please. Together, we can work this through."

Marty felt his heart constrict with love and sympathy for her and a sharp ache of anxiety that he could lose her, that he *had* lost her. Old loves died hard, if they *ever* died.

Marty continued, "I'll make a reservation. It's March, and they won't be full."

She shook her head. "No, love. I'll call ahead. I want to drive up, clear my mind on the way."

"Cait, I'm not sure you're in any condition to drive."

"I've got to do this. I'll be all right.

Every instinct said he had to let her go. He hugged her. "I'll pack for you. You'll call?"

"The minute I get there and every day. I won't be staying long. I'll call Rena from there, and Dosha. Please call your parents, and Adam and Damien. Oh my darling, I thank you so much."

When she was packed and ready to go, they stood at the door that led to the garage and he began to kiss her gently, but the kiss turned savage and she answered him in kind. Flames of desire swept both of them and she moaned softly from remembered passion. But passion was not necessarily love, she thought, and Marty had said it best a few minutes ago. "I think you always will"—love Sylvan, that is.

Holding her, Marty said fiercely, "You're carrying my child, *our* child. I've got to come by to check on you at least once to see that you're okay, because, Cait, you're *my* flame."

She nodded, her eyes wet with tears, and he sadly let her go, but he went with her and helped her into the car, then walked to the edge of their driveway and stood until she backed out, drove down the street, turned the corner, and was out of sight.

Chapter 31

At The Haven, bed-and-breakfast extraordinaire, Caitlin stood at the window in her comfortable bedroom looking out at a large grove of poplar trees swaying in the wind in the back of the estate. It was such a beautiful place, planted with massive evergreens and flowers of the season. In the meadow beyond the house a few black-and-white Holstein cows grazed and four sleek horses trotted.

She had unpacked the moment she got in, needing something to do with her hands, something to occupy her mind. She told herself she couldn't stand at the window forever. Slowly walking over to the cherrywood triple dresser, she looked down at the three pendants she'd brought with her. She picked up the Lladro first, noting the brilliant display of changing light. Marty had brought her this pendant from New York. She held it for a long time before she pressed it to her lips. Next was the Drago tree pendant, fashioned of bark, woodchips, and red sap, and so beautifully encased in fine crystal. The Drago tree was one of the oldest trees in the world and Marty had said, "This is the way my love for you will last—forever." She pressed that pendant to her heart and held it, then laid it back on the dresser.

With a faint smile, she held the Austrian crystal and platinum pendant that the German queen had handed to her from that fabulous float in Puerto. And she laughed through the pain in her body. "Pregnant in Puerto," Marty had whispered after the doctor had told them. It was almost as if the German queen had known she was carrying Marty's child. He had said her joy caught fire and radiated, that she and the German queen were on a similar wavelength of extreme happiness and recognized each other.

Pregnant in Puerto. Shc held to that as a talisman. Why in hell couldn't she love Marty thc way she'd loved Sylvan? Sylvan, who'd lied to her, been planning to divorce her and marry Lolla, his consuming love. Or had he lied to Lolla too? She didn't think so. She believed Marty, who'd said Lolla was a flame to Sylvan's moth. Marty was so incredibly sweet, had been so good for and to her for so long. Why couldn't it be different? Yes, she loved him, but she was enslaved to her memories of Sylvan.

A knock on the door brought her out of her pained reminiscences. Mrs. Fast, one of the owners, stood there, her middle-aged, brown and tender face concerned.

"I don't want to disturb you, Mrs. Steele—"

"Please call me Caitlin or Cait."

Lila Fast had had her share of misfortunes and heartbreak and she ached with compassion for the pain reflected on this woman's face, wanting to hold her as she'd held her own children when they were growing up.

The woman smiled. "All right, then. I'm Lila. My husband is Kenneth. Well, I couldn't help noticing how distraught you were when you came in, but I wanted to give you a chance to pull yourself together." She paused a moment. "I bring trays to those who'd like them—snack trays, breakfast, lunch, or dinner. I have plenty of help. Of course, you're free to come downstairs and raid a special fridge. We want you to feel at home and anything we can do to that end, we'll gladly do."

Caitlin smiled. "That's very kind of you. No wonder you're so widely loved. What is it people who know about you say: 'Go to the The Haven and heal your hurt.' "

Lila smiled. " 'If ye but believe.' We have some truly wonderful turkey pot pie that'll be ready in an hour or so. We have veggies, and our salads are something to write home about. I'd be happy to fix you a sandwich, and we have the makings of most anything you'd want . . ."

Caitlin stood reflecting. She and Marty had had a late breakfast, a *happy* breakfast, before the FedEx package arrived with Sylvan's letters. But that had been hours ago and she felt twinges of hunger.

"You know," Caitlin said, "the pot pie sounds delicious. I'd like that and any one of your garden salads."

"Great, and I don't mean to be intrusive, but you're pregnant, aren't you?"

Caitlin's face lit up. "Yes."

"It's plain you're upset about something, but you've got what I call the 'pregnant glow.' I find it unmistakable, and I'm happy for you."

"Thank you."

"One more thing. I was at your wedding to Marty. He went to school in New York as a teenager and I didn't see much of him anymore, but I always thought all the Steeles are just the best people going. And I think it's plain you fit in well with them."

For a moment Caitlin pondered her memory. "I knew I remembered you from somewhere. Oh Lord, I was in such a joyous daze . . ."

"No wonder. Now, if you need anything at all, give

me a call. Day or night. My two numbers are pasted on your telephone. And I'll be back with your food . . . Oh, what d' you want to drink and what for dessert?"

"The dessert requires no thought. Vanilla ice cream and any old cookie. Do you happen to have the no-sugar-added kind?"

"You bet we do and we've got plenty of vanilla and great sugarless as well as sugar cookies. We make it all ourselves with Splenda, the new sugar substitute."

"Very good. And I'll take nettle tea with lemon juice, if you've got it."

"We have, and if I didn't, we go into Minden to get things for guests all day. We really do aim to please. Now, rest if you can and I'll see you in a very little while. If you change your mind and want to come down at any time, do join us. We'll be happy to have you."

Going down the steps near Caitlin's bedroom, Lila shook her head. She didn't think Cait would be coming down tonight, and it greatly bothered her that she seemed so terribly undone.

Caitlin closed the door and leaned against it for a few minutes. She'd left the packet of letters on the dresser when she'd unpacked and she'd forced herself not to look at them. Now she was drawn to go back and slip another letter from its rose-garter binding and open it. She walked over and sat on the bed. Half blind, her eyes swept over the pages until she came to the paragraph about what Lolla and Sylvan intended to name their first child—Peter for his father and Anthony for Lolla's father. Why did it hurt so badly that Sylvan hadn't permitted her to name *her* son after Sylvan's father? And she knew that some part of her had intuited even then that Sylvan had a life apart from her. She had explained to him how much she'd wanted her child to bear her beloved dead father's name, his father's name and Caleb's, but he had been unyielding. She'd told herself that he wanted a junior to perpetuate himself, but she hadn't really believed that, even then.

"I will not flagellate myself," she said softly. "Whatever is true is true." And she kept wondering what Marty was doing now. She picked up her cell phone from the night table and started to dial him, then decided she'd do it later, after she'd had more time to think.

She took a shower, letting the lukewarm water sluice over her, breathing in the fragrance of the pheromone shower drops she added. And again she wondered what Marty was doing.

By the time Lila brought her dinner tray, Caitlin had changed to the beautiful multi-rose shaded caftan Marty had bought her in Florence. She wore it over a heavier silk slip, so it wasn't revealing the way it had been with him.

"How lovely you look," Lila exclaimed. "Feeling better?"

"A little. My husband bought this caftan for me on a recent trip."

Lila's eyes lit up. She loved hearing romantic stories.

"Hmmm, he's got taste and he loves you very much."

Caitlin blushed.

The food was delicious and she ate most of it, thinking she'd never tasted pot pie this good, and she'd never have known the ice cream was sugarless and fat free, it was so yummy.

That night in the big queen-sized bed, Caitlin slept in the cream-colored silk gauze nightgown she'd worn in Florence. Marty had played with the empire lines and the ties before he'd slowly slipped it from her shoulders and begun to kiss her.

Drifting off to sleep, she moaned as she began immediately a dream of ecstasy the way she'd dreamed it when Marty had first come back to D.C. and she had hungered for his body, but only to give her a child. Her heart had clung to its undying love for Sylvan. But it had been Marty who'd encouraged her, made her believe for the first time in her life that she could run her gallery, paint pictures he found entrancing, valuable, be his wife and a mother to his child. Her heart soared at the thought of it all.

She slid further into the dream and his hands, his mouth, his love covered her, entered her, set her very soul on honeyed fire. Her own moans brought her sharply awake. Dreams of ecstasy had brought them together into a relationship she had never truly understood. She groped for the phone on the night table and called his number.

"Cait?"

"It's me, sweetheart. What're you doing? You sound so wide awake. Can't you sleep?"

"And you sound sleepy and I'm delighted that you could sleep. I'm so glad you called."

She wasn't sure of the meaning of what she said. "I've been asleep since you came to D.C., asleep since we got married. I have to ask for more time, but I'm not asleep any longer."

"This sounds promising."

"It is. Please give me a little more time to think this through. You know I love you. I wouldn't have married you if I didn't love you. I know we both wanted a child, but you always said it was so much more. I want to leave Sylvan in the dust of my life the way I should have left my memories of him years back. He never encouraged me to live the way you have. It was always about him, *never* about me, or us. He was lord of the manor and I was the little match girl. I want to come to you whole, my darling. *Querido*. You deserve that, and more."

"Take all the time you need. I'll back off a bit, not inundate you with my calls or my love until you can work it through. But I *do* need to see you. I'd come up for a few hours, then drive back."

"If I can let you go. Marty, please come day after tomorrow. This is working itself out fast or *I'm* working it out. Thank you with all my heart. I'll have something ultra-important to say to you very soon."

"Maybe you've already said it, Cait."

"Not the way I'm going to say it when I see you. I want to tell you between fevered kisses and hugs that crack your ribs. My gorgeous husband, inside and out. Buns of steel and a heart and soul of diamonds and every other precious stone."

"I love you, baby, and I think I'm gonna explode before I can get to you."

"Me too."

When their conversation had ended, she reluctantly hung up, put the phone back on the night table, and snuggled under the covers. Then she got up, excited, and padded over to the window, opened the blinds, drew them up, and stood looking out onto the moon-drenched, night-shadowed farm. A cow lowed and a night bird sang. Quiet as the scene was, it reminded her of their time in Puerto. *Pregnant in Puerto*.

So she loved Marty as deeply as he loved her and she carried his child. She gently touched her swelling belly. Soon would come ultrasounds, sacred movements; now there was love and lovemaking beyond belief. She had been living an illusion and she thought about the letters that had hurt her so, then blessed her with revelation, set her free. Sylvan and even her dead son were her past and she could forgive herself for not being able to properly tend her son. Marty, too, had been her past with his tender care and concern, even when he was married to Bianca, who hadn't wanted Marty to be her friend.

And Marty was her glorious present. She hugged herself and walked across the floor. In bed she slipped beneath the covers and soon slept deeply and well.

The next morning, she got up early, bathed, dressed in a navy cashmere turtleneck sweater and slacks, and went down to the big, stainless steel kitchen. Rummaging in the special refrigerator, she found dry cereal, milk, and strawberries. She was munching happily at a long table in the kitchen when Lila walked in, her hands clasped in front of her.

"Love the Lord, don't you look pretty this morning—and happy. How about a hug?"

She walked over, bent down, and hugged Caitlin's shoulders, then chuckled. "Dry cereal, even with strawberries? Shucks, we're having sourdough pancakes and blueberry syrup, so don't eat too much."

"I surely look forward to that. What time? I'm going to walk in the woods for a bit."

"Well, we eat later and at a far more leisurely pace during the week. This weekend, we'll be eating nearly in shifts. Around nine today, I think. Other guests will do what you're doing and go exploring, reflecting. This is home. Be sure you dress warmly enough because it turned colder last night."

Caitlin thought she had never seen the world so beautiful or felt it as more sublime. Five years of anguish had been lifted from her shoulders and she repeated yet again what she had begun saying the night before: "Thank you, God."

There was a very large man-made catfish pond at the bottom of a grass-covered hill, and she sat on a log and watched the fish cavort. A lazy turtle ambled along, then gracefully slid into the water. And a canary sang his heart out.

She lost sight of time as she sat there until she shook herself, and looking at her watch, saw that it was nearly eight-thirty. Time to start back to the house and breakfast. She stood up and pulled her navy loden cloth coat closer. No matter the weather, this coat kept her warm. And she smiled softly. The coat was like Marty's and her love for each other.

"Cait!" Jayson's voice came from behind her as he strode to where she stood.

"What is it?" she asked him, seeing the shock on his face as he came to her.

"Marty's been hurt. He's in Minden Hospital. Do you have your cell phone with you?"

"No. I left it in my room. Let's stop for it now."

"No, let's don't stop. You're upset, and we've got to move fast. He wants you there, and he's been so badly hurt. God Cait, I'm afraid for him. Every second counts."

Chapter 32

In Jayson's car, as they drove along the highway that led to Minden and the hospital there, Caitlin found she could hardly get her breath. Her heart raced with anxiety. "Tell me what happened," she demanded. "How did *you* come to be with him when he was hurt?"

"Yes, you're surprised and so was I. Marty called and—"

"No, first tell me *how* he was hurt."

"Of course. We were in my car going to have an early breakfast at a place near Baltimore. Some fool crowded us and I lost control. Marty was thrown out of the car and his leg was cut on a broken glass bottle by the roadside. It was a very deep gash, so he lost a lot of blood, but he was coherent all the way to the hospital." He reached over and pressed her hand. "He's going to be okay. I wasn't hurt."

"I'm glad it was no worse than it was. You said he called you?"

"Yes. I called him the other day when you weren't around and asked him to go with me. I told him about a woman, my protégée, who's opening the art gallery in Baltimore. She's keenly interested in his work.

"Look, I know you plan to promote him heavily come fall, but this would be in addition to, not in competition with, you. He was interested, said he was rethinking his strained relationship with me because he wanted a great future for you and the baby. He's going to see that you have a great life, Cait, and I'm happy for you all."

"How did you know how to find me?" she asked.

"Pure dumb luck. Someone overheard Rena and your secretary talking about you and they mentioned this place."

"And that someone was?"

"I won't say just now, but the information helped me find you and take you to Marty."

Visions of Marty bleeding at the side of the road haunted her and she could pay little attention to what Jayson said, but some of it seeped through.

Suddenly she noticed a change in direction. "We're off the Baltimore-Washington Parkway."

"Yes. I'm going to stop by my place here to get a series of miniatures Marty did on Puerto years ago. It's fortunate I bought here, as well as kept my New York condo. I've still got them and they're part of the exhibit my friend wants to do in a couple of months. Sick as Marty was, he asked me to bring them to him right away. He wants to make a decision on which ones to exhibit." He turned to her, smiled wryly. "He's a man on a mission for his family now, and he's in a hurry."

"Okay, but please let's get going. I want to be with him."

Jayson pulled up to a stunning graybrick Tudor-style home set far back on well-manicured grounds. He buzzed them through an electronic gate in the black, wrought-iron fence. Under the brick-columned portico, he turned to her. "I'm hurrying, but I need you to come in for a few minutes and help me select which paintings. You can best judge since you're an artist."

"Oh Lord," she began, "any one of Marty's paintings will be superb. I wish you hadn't stopped."

"He *begged* me not to stay in the hospital with him, but to come here and get the paintings, then come with you. Cait, please, he's suffering . . ."

"All right." She got out of her side of the vehicle and they raced to the door, where he opened it and they walked in.

"The paintings are in this room." He indicated a door to their right. "We'll get them and immediately be on our way."

As he opened the door, she heard a strange, low groaning sound and nearly fainted to see Marty gagged and bound to a big straight chair. Her eyes went wide with shock and horror as her beloved looked at her, fury clouding his countenance.

"What in hell . . . ?" came her strangled cry as she lunged forward to help him, free him, but Jayson held her back as his strong arms went around her waist and arms, holding her, hugging her. She swung one foot back and kicked him in his leg.

"Little bitch!" he shouted with a triumphant look at Marty who struggled in spite of his bonds. Someone else came into the room, closed the door.

"Tie her up, Luther," Jayson ordered.

Caitlin's eyes went wide again. Luther? Was he a part of this scheme that was so new to her she couldn't begin to fathom it? It had to be Luther who had overheard the conversation about her between Rena and Nelda.

Luther came to them and kept his eyes averted as he

got thin ropes and big dust rags from a closet, started cutting them with his pocket knife, then ripped enough pieces free.

Deftly, he tied her hands behind her back as Jayson squatted and wrapped his arms around her legs, stroking them as he did so. She tried to kick him in the face, but he laughed and caught one leg, running his hand up and down it.

"Kick me now and you fall right onto me," Jayson said. "I will make love to you right here on the floor. It would serve Steele right for taking you away from me."

"I was never yours to take away. How could you do this?"

Jayson laughed nastily. "You've got to know I love you and I'm never going to give you up, Cait. What's mine is mine always. Every once in a while someone kills and the reason they give is: 'If I can't have you, nobody can have you.' It's taken me a while to get to that point, but I'm there. You're lucky. You get a chance to make up your mind; it's me or the cold, cold grave, because I *am* going to kill you, you know, if I can't have you.

"And Steele here, well, we have a *double* score to settle. Did you know Steele is with Interpol? I'll bet he's never told you that. I'm connected to the Mafia, a well-kept secret he's working hard to publicize. He's planning to call my hand, let the world know that Allendé and I are masterminding a major art forgery and theft ring. Luther, here, forges top artists like Steele over there . . ." He gloated as he shot Marty a vicious glance. "And the late Sylvan Costner—yes, and yourself. There are so many others. As for me, Cait, I need money to maintain a lifestyle I love almost as much as I love you. I'll never let Steele and Interpol take that away."

Marty started violently as if he would throw himself over the side of his chair. "Go ahead," Jayson roared.

"Knock yourself over and see if I don't damn well let you stay where you fall."

Coolly Luther came forward and gagged her.

Caitlin tried to rail and couldn't speak. "Don't *do* this," she said in her throat.

Marty sat still, seething. He could take what Jayson did to him, but he could have killed Jayson for manhandling Cait. Jayson's feeling Caitlin's precious body with his miserable hands brought up rage that nearly undid him. He prayed that he'd get a chance to tell Cait about his work with Interpol. Since Puerto, he'd known he *had* to tell her and his captain kept saying "Soon." Now it was too late.

With Caitlin seated on a chair near Marty, gagged and bound to the chair the way he was, Jayson stood up straight, a beatific smile on his face. He said to Luther, "I have the appointment in town with Allendé I told you about and you know I have to keep it."

Pulling a small handgun from a shoulder holster, he waved it in front of first Caitlin, then Marty. "Thank you for not making me use this. Surprise is an element I've always been able to count on." He shoved the gun back into the holster and laughed again, sang, "Everything's coming up roses!"

"Think you can handle these two until I get back, Luther? Allendé may be with me. He likes a good show and while he loves his paintings, he hates Steele. It's going to be great, making a fortune from Steele's paintings once he's dead. He *has* been mightily prolific. Old Luther here is going to see that he's far more prolific *after* he's gone."

Marty and Cait both stared at Luther. Caitlin felt sad that she'd trusted him. How did he fit into this?

It almost seemed that Jayson was reading both their minds. "Whets your appetite, does it, when I say that? Well, I won't keep you wondering. Luther here is our artist in residence, a man who can copy even Michelangelo. I tell you no lie. Luther's talent has always astonished me, but Luther, you see, has little confidence in himself. He does not believe he deserves the world the way *I* feel I deserve the world and intend to have it."

Jayson licked his lips and his eyes got colder. "Men like Luther need men like me and Allendé to guide them, get them their share, right, Luther?"

Luther nodded, smiling like a complimented child.

"He's done well working with us and he's getting his share of the world's goods that he never could have gotten without us. Right, Luther?"

Luther scratched his face. "I'd guess."

"You'd *guess* . . ."

"Well, yes. You're right."

"You're damn right I'm right. Maybe Luther wouldn't die for us, but he'd take a prison rap for us at any time because he knows he'd come out filthy rich."

Here Luther's eyes went wide and he frowned. "Well, I sure hope it don't come to *that* . . ."

Jayson walked over, slapped Luther on the back. "Just testing the waters, my friend. The best of us sometimes get prison time these days. It's not likely to happen, but—"

He shrugged and his glance was half sly, half provocative. "Well, chatter time is over. Show me your gun, Luther, just to let me know you have it."

Luther opened his leather jacket and drew a magnum .357 gun from a holster and showed it to Jayson, who slapped him on the back again. Jayson nodded and said, "If it happens that you have to take them out, don't hesitate. Steele intends to end our ballgame. It's all right if we end his first. And since Caitlin loves him so much, perhaps she will *want* to die with him, and the child dies also."

Marty felt rage unlike any he had ever known and his brain cleared, became crafty. He and Cait weren't going down without one hell of a fight. Glancing at Cait, he caressed her with his eyes and she returned his look of love.

Caitlin felt a momentary calmness she couldn't believe, and it had to do with Luther. She thought she knew him far better than Marty did, thought she knew he couldn't do this dastardly thing.

How much time did they have before Jayson returned—perhaps, he'd said, with Allendé? They both knew now that Jayson Giles *would* kill them both, now knew he was quite mad.

After Jayson left, Luther sat backward on a straight chair and looked them over carefully. Finally he said, "It never was my idea, you know, this thing Jayson's doing to you. You've both treated me right, respected me, and hell, the only thing Jayson respects is money, a world of it. Jayson's greedy with a capital G.

"I wish it could've been different, you know. I guess I like money like Jayson and Allendé—way too much. 'Course Allendé was born with it. Jayson got it early, he tells me." He shook his head. "Too bad you was gonna spill your guts to the spy outfit you work for, Marty. You and Cait're too nice to die, at least by my hand. Hell, by *anybody*'s hand, especially Jayson's." He shook his head. "I'm an art forger, one of the best, and I'm a thief, but I'm nobody's killer."

For a long while Luther was silent before he got up and began to pace, going deep into his mind, pondering. Thinking had never been his long suit, he preferred to *act*. But this present deal called for some serious thinking, he reflected.

Again Caitlin and Marty sought each other's eyes and again their glances held. Eyes could convey so much and this was all they could do at this moment.

Marty tested his bonds and felt them tight. Caitlin did the same.

Luther saw what they did and chuckled. "I tie a mean knot, he said. He stopped and drew a deep breath. "You won't be getting free anytime soon—*unless I want you to.*"

What did he mean by that statement? they both wondered, but hope sprang high.

With his hands clasped behind his back, Luther went to the window and peered out for long moments. Finally, he came back close to them.

"You remember Dilly McKay?" Luther asked Marty and Caitlin.

Both nodded as Luther gave a short, bitter laugh.

"Jayson's in on most of what they do—from drugs to mugging. He mostly uses them for scut work and he pays them well. Jayson's got a team of New York lawyers the devil would envy. Jayson gave orders Dilly wasn't to hurt you too bad."

Caitlin thought sourly: *Thanks for nothing*.

Luther continued, "The hell of it is he loves you, Caitlin, as much as he *can* love. He wants you real bad and Brother Jayson's had a lifetime of getting what he wants. I watch his eyes when he talks about you since you married Marty. They're a killer's eyes."

Luther stopped in front of them. "Well, I'm gonna get somethin' to eat. I'll bring you two something, take off your gags, feed you. I fixed fried pork chops and onion rings, grits and eggs. Drop biscuits. Whet your appetite?"

Caitlin wondered if her appetite would ever be whetted again.

Luther left and in a few minutes came back with his food and theirs on a tea cart. They were surprised to have him loosen their gags and slip them down, freeing them to eat food from the platter. Luther gave Caitlin a few bites, then Marty. Neither could eat much, but they drank the grapefruit juice he poured from a pitcher, two whole glasses of it. He didn't rush them and when they had finished, he sat down at a table and ate his own food, belching loudly when he'd finished.

"Oh, 'scuz me," he told them. "I embarrass myself sometimes. Dulcé don't like for me to belch. Haven't done it for a while. My mama always said a *scared* person belches."

Finishing, he took the tea cart back to the kitchen. Marty said low, "I love you, sweetheart, and our baby. I'll *always* love you. Just hold on."

Her eyes filled with tears as she told him, "You know how I love you. At least we'll be together and we'll fight this."

"You're damn right we will. We didn't put all that passion into making a baby to lose it and ourselves . . ."

Luther came back shortly, came to them and looked at them as he frowned. "Maybe I'm a fool, but I want to talk to you both." He paced the floor again as he talked.

"I never killed nobody. Never intended to, and I'm thinking—hard. My mama didn't raise killers. She always said it's as easy to love as to hate. She wouldn't like this one damn bit." He licked dry lips and seemed to look into the distance.

He walked over to them. "I'm gonna loosen your hands enough for you to free yourselves if we get to follow my plan. In a little bit, I'll cut your leg bonds. If Allendé comes back with Jayson, even drunk they'll put up a stiff fight. Jayson's got a Glock he keeps in his car. Pray he don't bring it in."

Caitlin thought it felt so good when the circulation fully came back into her hands and arms and she breathed deeply while Luther talked to them as he loosened Marty's bonds.

Luther left the room for only a few minutes, then said as he came back in, "You talk now about being gifted, and I can, like I said, *copy* Michelangelo even, do collages like Bearden and paint Paris scenes like Lois Maillou Jones, but they're and you're *originals*—" He paused and his breath came faster. "Something in me keeps me *copying* what other painters *conceive*. Damn it!" His fists struck his forehead. "You know how easy it is for a master copyist like me to copy art. Got myself the best opaque projector made, great cameras for great photographs of what I want to copy, blow it up, and work from that. And the fun begins." His body seemed to shake with loving what he did. "Well," he grinned crookedly at them, a little shamefaced at his outburst. "This is what I plan . . ."

But Luther's plan was too late because they heard Jayson open the front door and slam it as he came into the living room singing a ribald La Carnaval song and chuckling to himself. He let himself into the room where the others were and they saw he held the gun Luther had warned them about.

He swore a blue streak when he saw that the gags had been slipped down on Marty and Caitlin, but he swayed slightly and that gave them hope. It was plain he had been drinking heavily. "So you choose to sleep with these two," he muttered to Luther. "Get over there with them. Maybe you'd like to die with them."

Chapter 33

"So this is how we're going to die," Caitlin muttered to herself, but her mind couldn't conceive of never bearing her child, never loving Marty again or responding to his tender love.

And Marty's spirit valiantly fought the thought of dying. He sat remembering everything Luther had said to them. One bit of luck was on their side. Jayson was drunk.

"Sit down," Jayson barked to Luther. "Oh, this is going to be good. Three rats dispensed with. Three big, deadly Glock bullets."

With bated breath, Marty and Caitlin saw Luther begin to rush Jayson, but Jayson was steadier on his feet than he seemed. He shot into the air and a part of the chandelier dangled from the ceiling. Luther jumped back, his eyes glittering, but he sat down.

Jayson waved his gun. "Mr. Interpol," he taunted, glaring at Marty. "And Caitlin, who betrayed me."

Caitlin wondered how best to answer him, but his attention turned to Luther. "You're such a damn coward, can't stand a little blood. I thought you'd never stop puking when I shot Rita. I had no choice; she guessed I was the one who stole the paintings and she confronted me with it. I stop anybody who gets in my way. And you were even worse when I killed Cedric. Well, Cedric was blackmailing me, trying to take my place with Allendé. He had a master plan for exposing me alone and he was blackmailing me not to do it. And you won't send me to prison, Marty, because I'm sending you and Caitlin and your damn unborn brat to hell." His eyes were bloodshot when he turned to Luther. "You damn near caused me to get caught when you were crying like a woman and couldn't drive in Puerto after I'd taken him out."

Jayson's face was a study in evil as he pushed the gun near Luther's face. "Now I want no puking and no crying from you when I kill these two. Do you hear me?"

"I'm not going to *let* you kill them," Luther said calmly.

Jayson exploded, "What? Do you want me to kill you first?"

She shouldn't have spoken, but Caitlin felt she had to say it. "Jayson, be reasonable. You're wrong all the way. You don't kill people because they don't do what you want them to do. Both Rita and Cedric would have caused you to do jail time, taking your freedom for a while. You took their *lives*. And I was *never* yours to betray you. Marty and I belong together. I know now we've always belonged together."

Marty leaned forward in response to her words and Jayson yelled, "Shut up!" Bitter laughter escaped him before he said, "I've tried to get over you and it just doesn't happen. I've said you shouldn't have married Steele. Now, I'm going to make you pay the price. Good-bye, my love. You should have let me prove how good *my* love can be."

His voice was harsh, blazing with the rage of hopelessness. Caitlin was silent then. Shaken by his own fury, his attention on Caitlin and Marty, Jayson didn't see Luther get up and begin to tackle him. Both men went down, tangling on the floor. Both were fit, but Jayson had the edge of being younger.

For a moment Luther gripped Jayson's arm with the Glock and was wrenching it away when Jayson kneed him in the groin and he buckled just enough for Jayson to get control of the gun again. They were silent, intent on what they did, grunting and breathing hard.

Once a Boy Scout, Marty knew how to deal with knots, and in a very few minutes he had loosened his ankle bonds and was on his feet. He saw Caitlin struggling and vehemently shook his head, "No." She had to protect the baby.

Luther breathed heavily, aching in his groin and Jayson shot Luther as Luther pushed Jayson's arm up, deflecting the bullet to his shoulder. A second shot brought blood spurting from a severed artery in Luther's chest as he fell sideways.

Racing to the men, Marty kicked the gun from Jayson's hand and picked it up. As Marty stood, Jayson got up and lunged for him, but Marty sidestepped him and held on to the gun, savagely protecting his beloved.

"You *will* die!" Jayson raged as Marty aimed at him, thinking: *So it has come to this*. He prepared to pull the trigger when police sirens sounded outside and in seconds police burst through the doors.

Marty knew one of the policemen, who had worked with his brother, Adam; he explained what was going on. A policeman immediately called for an ambulance, and using rough force on Jayson, a policewoman handcuffed him and led him out.

Going to Caitlin, Marty fell on his knees, took her in his arms. In a moment, he would undo her ankle bonds, but just now he had to hold her, kiss her fervently.

"*Querida*," he murmured again and again, "My darling love." And the policemen stood back, gave him time to hold her, touch her belly with his child growing in it. They were in awe of this tender show of what so much of life was really all about.

Epilogue

September again and how different from last year, Caitlin thought as she surveyed the Labor Day scene in Mom and Dad Steele's backyard. Marty stood by her side, holding a week-old twin in each arm. The two blended Steele families were here today. Rena and her family had come early and her husband helped with the barbecue as Rena briefly chatted with Marty and Caitlin, holding her own baby girl.

"I can just feel a really good day coming on," Rena said, "and I plan to enjoy, enjoy. Even the twins look like they know what's going on."

Marty laughed. "They just came aboard. All the world's a show to them."

The famous gospel singer Whit, Marty's half brother, came with his wife, Danielle, and their little boy came to Caitlin and Marty's side.

"Well, hello you two, and Malinda and Caleb Myles, our newest Steeles." The couple very lightly chucked the babies under the chin as the twins yawned and stretched. Caitlin bent and hugged Whit and Danielle's little boy.

Marty smiled. "My wife gets her wish at last, to have one kid named for both her father *and* her brother. Now we don't have to rush to have another baby so we can have one named for both parents."

Caitlin looked at him pertly. "We weren't going to rush anyway."

Ricky came and picked up Whit and Danielle's little boy, held him, then touched the twins' cheeks. "Boy," he said, "they're something. And I'm a first cousin." Then with all the aplomb of a debonair man, he looked at Caitlin. "I'm gonna be a built-in baby-sitter for you two." He put on a droll face. "Hey, mama, you're looking good for a woman who's just had a baby."

Marty laughed. "You say you're thirty, circling back to fourteen?"

Ricky shrugged and smiled. "Well, twenty anyway."

It was warm and sunny at eleven A.M. The huge backyard was gaily decorated with balloons and red, white, and blue crepe paper streamers. Long, white linen–covered tables groaned under food of every delicious description and taste, and the odor of spring chickens frying in washpots of hot olive oil was a throwback to Mel's youth. The pit barbecue grills with pork ribs and chickens held aloft on wire frames were a throwback too. Mel wiped his eyes as he hugged Rispa. The Singing Steeles were all here: Frank, Caroline, and their children, Ashley, Whit, and Annice. And his children by Rispa were Marty; their twins, Dosha and Damien; and Adam.

So, Mel thought, he had successfully blended two wonderful families long before it became common. They couldn't be closer.

Jim Draper shepherded his prepubescent son and two daughters. His face was still shadowed in grief for his beloved Rita, but he smiled more now. His captain had relented and permitted this visit.

"Great spread you're having today and these are great kids." He licked his lips. "It's at gatherings like this that I miss her so. Rita *loved* people . . ."

"And she loved you and your kids," Caitlin said softly, feeling her eyes dampen.

A gaily laughing Dosha brought her new friend from Puerto, Christian Montero, to pat the twins. She hugged Caitlin fervently and introduced him.

"Well, at last we meet," Caitlin told him. "I missed you at La Carnaval."

"Yeah, Chris," Marty said. "We had a great time."

"And next year will be even better because Dosha and I will both be there." He was a handsome man, Caitlin thought, and the couple were very much in love, but there was some trouble in paradise, Dosha had confided. Both had strong personalities and were passionate people with a continent between them. Which continent would they choose to live on? Or would this separate them for good?

The whole family was slowly drifting over, mesmerized by the twins, but family members also circulated among their many invited friends. At two o'clock the gospel-song get-together would begin and afterward there would be dancing, but just then, simple camaraderie held sway. A gentle breeze swept over them.

Marty glanced at his watch as he looked at Caitlin, his heart in his eyes. "Are you getting tired?"

"No way. You're the one who should be tired, holding the twins all morning."

"It's a labor of intense love. My wife bore them for me. Wonderful woman. I'll introduce you two sometime."

Caitlin nearly closed her eyes as she laughed at his teasing. "If you've got another wife, you're gonna have me to answer to, and she's losing you to me. Hey! *I* could take those little rascals for a while."

"Nope. They're too precious to give up."

They walked over then to where Adam stood with the tall, low-key beauty, Raven McCloud, a well-known D.C. television investigative reporter. She was a poised, highly attractive woman with creamy tan skin. Adam introduced them.

Acknowledging the introduction, Raven looked at the twins with eyes of love. "They're so beautiful," she said. "This takes me back to having my own kid, Merla." But she bit her bottom lip and fell silent.

Caitlin noted that Adam looked at Raven with love and concern and squeezed her hand as an ebullient Ricky came up. "Hey! Hey! The gang's all here. You look neat, Raven."

So this was the woman Adam was so plainly falling for, Caitlin thought, and her heart went out to both Adam and Dosha, who deserved so much happiness. And where was Damien? As if summoned, Damien came out the back door in his swimming trunks with a T-shirt covering his broad, well-muscled chest. He stood silently staring down at the twins before he hugged Caitlin fiercely.

"You two did it," he told them. "And I'm an uncle again."

"The question is: When will you be a *father*. And *if?*"

The flash of pain in Damien's eyes made Caitlin say softly to her husband, "Don't tease him, love."

"Sorry," Marty told his brother.

"It's okay." Damien smiled crookedly. "I'm working on it, but the best-laid plans of mice and men oft go astray. You know the old saying."

"Yeah," Marty said. "Just hang in there, bro. Things didn't work out for me for the longest time, as you know. Now look at me—at *us*." He looked at Caitlin. "I want to hug her, but my arms are full."

Damien grinned and suddenly felt better. "Let me take them and you can hug away."

Marty shifted his babies to his brother's arms and hugged Caitlin passionately as a nearby group clapped. And coming out from his fond embrace, Caitlin thought it was such a gorgeous day. Looking up, she saw cerulean skies with fat, white clouds and not a hint of rain. She felt buoyed by the events going on around her, as if she would never be tired again.

It helped that Dilly McKay and two of his crew members now languished in prison with life terms for killing a rival crew member. She hunched her shoulders, shuddering with the memory of a car with tinted windows that had tried to run her down. And even worse was the memory of Dilly's hot, evil breath on her face and body that night as he tried to do God knows what to her.

With the babies in his arms, Marty winked at her and she smiled. Not that much time had passed, but it all seemed like ages ago.

Damien had moved away and Caitlin stood alone, deciding which group she would join next.

She couldn't help thinking of Bianca, who had languished in the Puerto prison for over a year. She was free now. Would she and Allendé ever get together again? He was spending a fortune fighting charges that he and Jayson had run a lucrative art theft and forgery ring. Caitlin shook her head. Allendé and Bianca deserved each other.

Suddenly Caitlin saw Luther and Dulcé coming to the group as he grinned from ear to ear, looking fondly at his beloved Dulcé.

Caitlin smiled as they peeked at the twins. "You're looking happy, prosperous," she said.

"And *alive*," he said drily, "thanks to you and your mister."

Dulcé nodded. "Those are wonderful babies over there. I didn't kiss them because I know we shouldn't at that age, but I can hardly keep my hands off them. One day—"

She touched the hem of one twin's soft, white gown as Luther explained, "We decided we wouldn't get married right away. She's so young and she wants to be a lawyer, we'll wait a year or so until she gets everything underway."

"Ah," Dulcé said sadly, "I've led a hard life and I'm old, but Luther is young—at heart, in every way. I'm just kind of scared that he'll stop loving me if we wait."

"Baby, no way," Luther protested and hugged Dulcé's shoulders.

"I think you're both fortunate to have each other. Let love reign supreme!" Caitlin said gaily.

"Lady, I love you for that," Luther said, "but then I always have. I'm painting *originals* now. No more copies and some say they're good. Well, we'll see."

His saying it brought Jayson to mind and Caitlin didn't want to think about Jayson. He had killed Rita and Cedric. Had tried to kill her, Marty, Luther, the arresting cops, anyone who stood in his perverted way. Jayson had been sentenced to life in prison without parole and a higher court had turned down his appeal. The evidence against him was rock solid.

Caitlin shuddered a bit. Even now, thoughts of Jayson caused her flesh to crawl. But she had only to become lost in Marty's loving glances and everything was the way she wanted it to be. She closed her eyes and Jayson faded from mind, replaced by her fine, loving husband and adorable twins.

That night, still at Mel and Rispa's with the festivities winding down and people dancing to romantic music from the CD player and amplifiers, Marty and Caitlin sat on the veranda by their bedroom. They watched the monitor from the twins' room, ready to attend to them in an instant.

"I think I'll go in," Caitlin told him. "I'm just not comfortable away from them.

"Hell, I'm not either. They're so great. They're in my arms even when they're not."

"Hey! What about me? I need your arms too."

Marty stood up and drew her up and to him, thrilling at the outlines of her luscious, soft, childbearing body and the depth of her wonderful spirit, and she thrilled to his strong, muscular body and his deep tenderness.

Marty released her, then squeezed her shoulders, said huskily, "It's plain I'm never going to get tired of loving you, kissing you, holding you, making love to you."

"That's only fair," she murmured. "It's the way I feel about you. I wanted more time, sweetheart, when I didn't know I had finished grieving Sylvan and never loved him the way I love you. Now, God has blessed us with Caleb Myles and Malinda. We have more than our share of paradise on earth."

"Yeah," he said softly, thrilling again, "and we're going to keep it that way for the rest of our lives."

Dear Readers,

I am absolutely delighted to get your many letters of support for my romance novels. Please keep writing and I *will* answer.

Don't forget to check out my quarterly "Romance Newsletter" and the interesting and rewarding contests that are connected to my published titles. I think you'll always like the lovely prizes.

All my books are dear to me, but *Dreams of Ecstasy* is especially so because it deals with a couple's deep desire to make and raise beloved children and that is so necessary in our world today.

I always enjoy your letters and feel I'm chatting with a friend. You may reach me at the following addresses:

Francine Craft
P.O. Box 44204
Washington, D.C. 20026 or

francinecraft@yahoo.com or

my Web site is: www.francinecraft.com

ABOUT THE AUTHOR

Francine Craft is the pen name of a Washington, D.C.–based writer who has enjoyed writing for many years. A native Mississippian, she has lived in New Orleans and found it one of the most fascinating places imaginable.

A veteran of many interesting jobs, Francine has been a research assistant for a large psychiatric organization, an elementary school teacher, a business school instructor, and a federal government legal secretary.

She is constantly on the best-selling list for Amazon.com's multicultural romance writers and receives rave reviews from reviewers and readers. She is a member of Romance Writers of America.

Francine's hobbies are prodigious reading, photography, and songwriting. She deeply enjoys time spent with friends.